Arms of *Love*

Arms of Love

Carmen Marcoux

ONE WAY PUBLISHING HOUSE
Saskatoon, Saskatchewan

Arms of Love

One Way Publishing House

©2002 by Carmen Marcoux
First Printing 2002 *** Second Printing 2004
Third Printing 2005 *** Fourth Printing 2007

Published in Canada; Printed in the United States of America
ISBN: 978-0-9732075-0-7
Cover art & design: Shawna Kunz
Cover photo: Mary Couture   Cover painting: Gay Couture
Printing: R.R. Donnelly, Menasha, WI

All Scripture quotations are taken from
The Catholic Edition of the Revised Standard Version of the Bible,
copyright © 1965, 1966 by the Division of Christian Education
of the National Council of the Churches of Christ
in the United States of America.
Used by permission. All rights reserved.

Excerpt from *Catechism of the Catholic Church,*
Copyright © Concacan Inc., 1999.
All rights reserved. Used with permission.

The setting of this novel is Saskatoon, Saskatchewan. While Saskatoon is a
city located on the prairies in western Canada, with the South Saskatchewan
River flowing through it and the Meewasin Valley Trail developed along the
river's banks, the specific locations of the city and the characters described
within this novel are purely fictitious. Any similarities to real events or persons, either living or deceased, are entirely coincidental.

Library and Archives Canada Cataloguing in Publication
Marcoux, Carmen, 1966-
Arms of love / Carmen Marcoux.

ISBN-13: 978-0-9732075-0-7
ISBN-10: 0-9732075-0-7

I. Title.

PS8576.A6422A75 2002 C813'.6 C2002-911371-7

ONE WAY PUBLISHING HOUSE
Site 500 Box 17 R.R. #5
Saskatoon, Saskatchewan, S7K 3J8
1-800-705-7396
Website: www.courtshipnow.com

I dedicate this book to the glory of Jesus Christ.

To my husband and best friend, Jim,
our children,
Hannah, Rebekah, Mikaelah, Jacinta, and Matthew,
(who inspired and supported me during the time of writing)
Gemma, Benjamin, and Jacob
(who were born after Arms of Love first came to print)

. . . thank you for reflecting to me
the love of Jesus in my life each day.

꿍꿍

"Take delight in the Lord,
and he will give you the desires of your heart."
Psalm 37:4

"For I know the plans I have for you, says the Lord,
plans for welfare and not for evil,
to give you a future and a hope."
Jeremiah 29:11

"Let no one despise your youth,
but set the believers an example
in speech and conduct, in love, in faith, in purity."
1 Timothy 4: 12

"Blessed are the pure in heart,
for they shall see God."
Matthew 5:8

꿍꿍

Foreword

In the Book of Genesis, sacred Scripture teaches us, "God created man in his own image, in the image of God he created him; male and female he created them." (Gen. 1:27) The Bible also teaches us "they become one flesh". (Gen. 2:24)

Pope John Paul II, in our own day, offers us new—both theological and anthropological—insights into the nuptial meaning of the body. Our Pope is treating "one flesh" to a deeper analysis.

When I took up and read the novel *Arms of Love*, by Carmen Marcoux, I was both thrilled and entertained by the wholesome story that unfolded before me. It presented me with well-developed human and family situations that were delightful. The novel gave me a deeper insight into the loves of those who choose to follow the Christian way of marriage. It presents the reader with a contrast: it provides you with a family—father, mother, and children—who choose to live the life of love, as opposed to individuals who choose to follow the secular way of selfishness. The former leads to deep joy and contentment; the latter, to frustration, discouragement, and despair.

May I be so bold as to present to you "a must read"! Be entertained, be inspired, be edified, and be renewed in hope for marriage and family life in our own day!

Father Alex MacLellan
Havre Boucher, NS
April 2004

Preface

It is my hope that those who read this book will be inspired to a greater love for Jesus Christ and an earnest desire to live according to the truths of our faith. My intention is to promote the message of chastity and provide an example of Christian courtship being lived out. There are many ways in which honourable Christian courtship can be put into practice. This story merely uses one model.

For some families, the model presented in this book could not work because of the structure of the family or the location of the children in relation to their parents. Still, what is important to keep in mind is that courtship is a wonderful way for young people, discerning and preparing for marriage, to live out the virtue of chastity.

Christian courtship involves a framework for practising chastity as it places the relationship of a young couple back into the context of the family. It allows parents to play a vital role in providing valuable wisdom and guidance while fostering a lifelong relationship of trust and respect between the two generations. There are guidelines which encourage self-discipline, responsibility, and accountability. It promotes maturity and lays a beautiful foundation for marriage.

The *Catechism of the Catholic Church*, in section 1632, quoting from the Pastoral Constitution, *Gaudium et Spes*, exhorts the value of courtship and the importance of the family within the preparation for marriage.

> *It is imperative to give suitable and timely instruction to young people, above all in the heart of their own families, about the dignity of married love, its role and its exercise, so that, having learned the value of chastity, they will be able at a suitable age to engage in honourable courtship and enter upon a marriage of their own.*

I believe that Christian families should discuss a model of courtship that will work for them and then raise their children with this understanding. Hopefully this book will open the doors to such discussions in the homes of those who read it.

Secular society bombards us with images of impure and sinful relationships. Young people have many examples of relationships that go completely against Christian values. We need to promote models which will help them to grow in virtue and in holiness.

Being Catholic, I write from my perspective. I love the Church and fully embrace her teachings and am very grateful for the rich heritage of traditions and teachings that the Church preserves for us.

I hope that my Christian brothers and sisters of other denominations, reading this work, will come to see the Catholic Church in a new light. Not being distracted by the differences which exist among us, may we come to an appreciation of all that we share in common.

The message of Christian courtship is one that, I believe, when put into practice, can transform our society. Marriages that blossom out of this practice will be strong and will be equipped with the graces to stand the test of time. Families that grow out of these relationships will be a beacon of light in our world: the light of Truth, which is Jesus Christ.

It is to His glory that I dedicate this work!

Carmen Marcoux
December 2002

Prologue

The constant bleep from the life support equipment echoed in Caroline's ears as the twelve-year-old girl sat, leaning over her father's bedside. Her head was pressed into her crossed arms, her eyes were closed. With rosary clutched in her hand, she prayed that God would not take her daddy. The car accident had already claimed her mother's life two days earlier. Her father was holding on, but in a coma. How Caroline longed to hear once more the tender, lilting voice of this man.

Her sisters, Mary and Sharon, played quietly in the corner of the room. They were young and maybe they did not completely understand how this accident was robbing them of their lives, their happy home, their childhood. But Caroline understood. She was the eldest. "Just hang in there, Daddy. Please don't leave us alone. . . . I need you so much."

There was a shifting, a movement. "Daddy, I'm here!" The young girl sat up and took hold of her father's hand, carefully avoiding the tubes that were connecting him to life.

Thomas Mahoney's eyes flickered open, not widely, for the light was too bright. A smile lifted from the corners of his mouth. It was a feeble attempt, but Caroline saw it.

"Carrie," only her daddy ever called her that, "darling . . ." The dying man's voice was weak, but there was a certain determination to say what he had to say. "I . . ."

"Oh, Daddy," Caroline cut him off, the weight of emotion carrying her relief that he had recognized her.

"Listen, Carrie, I want you . . . do something for me . . . I . . . I don't have a lot to leave you, but . . ." He paused and breathed laboriously.

"No, Daddy, you're not leaving me!" Caroline cried out, through sobs.

"Carrie, be brave now, darling—listen to me—hold fast to your faith. It is all I have . . . to leave you."

"Daddy, no!"

By this time Caroline's sisters had come to the bedside.

"Daddy's awake," six-year-old Sharon exclaimed.

"Oh, my babies." The broken man perked up at the sound of his little girls' voices.

"We've been waiting for you to wake up," eight-year-old Mary told him. Her voice quavered for she sensed he was leaving them—this time for good.

"Listen, my darlings," the man went on with purpose. "You keep your faith . . . and someday we will all be together again, in heaven."

Caroline cried out, "You can't leave us, Daddy! Mom has already gone. We'll be all alone!"

"You won't be alone, Carrie. We will be praying for you . . . I promise." The devoted father's heart was breaking, knowing the pain that his children would suffer. But he trusted in God, even as he faced his death. It was a trusting that comes from knowing that the time has come. "God has His reasons for everything. . . . It'll be all right."

"No, Daddy." Caroline refused to allow him to give in to death.

"My beautiful daughters, be brave. . . . Your mother and I will be praying for you." Thomas Mahoney's eyes were wide open now and his countenance revealed a certain joy that was positively illuminating.

Mary leaned over and kissed her daddy's face. "Good-bye daddy. I love you," she said through her tears.

The man no longer spoke. Though his spirit had not yet left him, he was no longer able to respond.

"Daddy, I love you." Sharon threw herself across his stomach and hugged her father, tears flowing freely.

Caroline could not bring herself to say good-bye. It was too bitter a word. She held on to her father's hand firmly, until at last he drew a final breath and his grip on her hand released. She looked down at the lifeless hand in her own and laid it down on the bed beside her father's empty body.

Caroline wanted to draw courage from the faith of her father. She wanted to honour him by being obedient to his request. But the fragile heart of this twelve-year-old girl laboured under the heavy burden that she would now have to carry.

Following the interment of her parents, Caroline stood at the graveside, looking down at the two caskets below, partially covered with earth. As she forced the tears to cease, something died that day inside the tender child's heart. It would be years before she would be able to cry again. Until that time, the keys to the treasure which had been her only inheritance from her parents would remain locked away in her broken heart.

✞   ✞   ✞

Faith is a torch that has been passed on from one generation to the next, as the light of Christ has spread to all the corners of the earth. In the course of a family's history that torch can be extinguished for a time. But the Lord, in His abundant love and mercy, always finds a way to bring the light of faith back into the path of those who walk in darkness.

Until that day, the torch waits to be lit again with the fire of Jesus' love. . . .

Chapter 1

As Joanie Collins stepped into the stately old office building, she knew that she was now crossing over an important threshold in life. This was it: the crowning moment of all her training. Closing her eyes, she took a deep breath—she really wanted this job.

The young journalist could not believe she was finally at this stage. This was the interview that would determine whether or not she would get the job; having been at the top of her class in college had certainly paid off. Still, that awareness was not enough to quell her fears.

Was she ready for this moment? Four years of Journalism, piggy-backed onto twelve years of home-schooling, hardly seemed adequate preparation as she stood in the entrance, her hand still clutching the door handle behind her. Her thoughts darted through her mind as if she were trapped in time, not at all searching for another moment.

It was time to pray. Joanie shook off the ambiguity and regained her focus. *Oh, Lord, I'm sorry for trapping myself in fear. You brought me here, I know. I want to be here. . . . Right!*

Reforming her resolve, like a soldier turning back to the battle, she gathered up her confidence and marched into a new era in her life.

✝   ✝   ✝

CNB Television Station served the province of Saskatchewan and was connected to a larger national network. Joanie was familiar with the environment that she was entering. She had been here just a week ago for her major interview, at which time she had to pitch three story ideas and defend them to three big-wigs from the station. She had also come here a number of times with her class on training sessions.

Her summer jobs at the local cable station as a rookie community reporter had been great experiences. It was the six-month internship, though, that had put the real shine on her polish. Though it had been out of town in a smaller station, Joanie had done exceptionally well and her references showed it. Research-reporting had become second nature to her by now. So why be nervous?

Gradually, a sense of purpose was replacing her fears. She would face this moment with confidence. This job would open the door to a whole new adventure in her life, launching her into a career. If she got this job . . .

what a sense of independence and accomplishment that would be. If not, there would be other opportunities for her. One way or the other, it was all terribly exciting.

She sat in the reception area, waiting to meet Mr. Lemay. Her appointment was scheduled for one-thirty, and it was now quarter past. At last she found herself sitting across a large oak desk from the man in his bright, sunny office. She waited as he reviewed her resume and portfolio. Mr. Lemay was the Station Manager, the man with the power to hire her or not. She had met him at her first interview.

Joanie was nervous inside, but to the onlooker, she was completely composed.

"This is an impressive resume, Joanie. You did well in Journalism as I see from your transcript and references."

Mr. Lemay appeared to be an amiable man, somewhere in his late fifties. His round features and friendly expression gave Joanie the impression of a big teddy bear, which helped her to feel comfortable in his presence.

"Thank you, sir," she replied.

"I was really impressed by the samples of your work that you included. You have a nice style. It's young. It's fresh. It's uncomplicated. And yet your writing has depth all the same. I like that in a reporter," he commented, with one eye still perusing the resume in his hand. "I was very pleased with your interview last week. I thought you presented yourself exceptionally well. You have confidence. And your demo tape was a good example of your work."

"I'm glad to hear that, sir." Joanie was fumbling even if she was not showing it. She wanted to respond. She just wished he would ask her something.

"Tell me, why are you interested in the job at this station?"

Finally . . . a question she could answer.

"This is my home town, sir. I love Saskatoon. I know the city; I know the issues that are relevant here. I believe I could dig up stories of real interest for the local area. And on a more personal note, I have a number of commitments holding me here for the time being. I'm still completing some musical studies, and I also sing in a band. It would be much less complicated right now to be living here in town."

"Uh-huh. Your references were very enthusiastic about your abilities and your character." He looked up at Joanie, perceptively taking in everything he could about her.

Her dark brown hair was pulled up at the back and hung down loosely in curls. Though she wore little make-up and dressed quite simply in a skirt and a short-sleeved sweater, she carried herself proudly and confidently.

There was a meekness about her as well. He could see why her references had spoken highly of her. In his two meetings with her, he had been duly impressed. Her dark eyes sparkled with energy as she met his gaze.

After a moment he said, "I want you to know I expect a lot of my workers. But I think you'll find me to be a fair employer."

"Yes, of course, Mr. Lemay." Joanie hardly knew what to say. "Then," she hesitated over the presumption, "I have the job, sir?"

The hearty laugh set Joanie's heart at ease. "You certainly do." His jolly demeanour broke through his determined business manner. This man was exactly what Joanie had prayed for.

Joanie turned her head to the sound of a knock. The partially opened office door swung wide, and there stood a tall woman with a bright smile, beaming down at her. "Hello, Joanie, I'm sorry I was held up."

Mr. Lemay interjected, "Joanie, I'm sure you remember Shelly Lesichyn from your first interview."

"Yes, of course I do. Hello again, Mrs. Lesichyn." Joanie hesitated over the title, but she had noticed a wedding ring and hoped the woman would not be offended. Shelly was about the same age as Joanie's mother, and Joanie was uncomfortable with presuming to be on a first name basis.

"Please, call me Shelly," the kindly woman said. "I'd catch too much flack around here if anyone heard you call me Mrs. . . . We're rather informal that way."

"Fine, Shelly," Joanie returned.

Mr. Lemay smiled and went on, "Shelly is our Senior Producer. She'll be heading the morning conferences with the journalist team and normally will be the one vetting your assignments before they air."

"I'll also be doing your orientation with you," Shelly added. "If you'd like, I'll show you around the station now."

"That would be great," Joanie acknowledged. She turned to thank Mr. Lemay again. He informed her that a contract would be ready for her to sign by the time she and Shelly were done. She could stop on her way out at his receptionist's desk and do that. Joanie got up to follow Shelly, who was already heading out the office door.

✞   ✞   ✞

Joanie loved the atmosphere of a television station. The hustle and bustle was not unlike that of growing up in a home-schooling family with eight children. She had learned to work through distractions, or she would not have survived. The big difference was—it was much quieter here.

The main office area for the journalists was a plain, wide-open room on the second floor of the station. The small cubicle that had been assigned to Joanie was away from the only two windows that brought in natural light. That was something of a disappointment, but she knew from past experience that she would be spending much of her time out of the office on assignments. That was part of what made her job exciting: each day would be a new job, a new experience, and she would be on the go.

The editorial rooms and voice recording rooms were tucked away at the back of the station. There was nothing unfamiliar in these rooms, filled with computerized equipment. Joanie remembered how intimidated she had been by all the equipment when she first began training.

Shelly took some time to explain the general filing system, assuring Joanie that she would be available to help her locate the research files as she needed them.

Shelly was a delightful woman. Tall and thin, she carried her height proudly. Her hair was short and stylish and her smile, friendly. Joanie enjoyed the way Shelly would put on her glasses to read something and then immediately take them off, using them to point to things as she carried them around in her hand. She was a thorough woman. Joanie could tell by the manner in which Shelly was instructing her that this woman had very high standards.

The third floor was the production area of the studio. Commercials and local programming were produced here, as well as the local news broadcasts. The main floor of the station, behind the reception area, was for radio broadcasting. Beyond that was the staff lounge. The station had almost fifty employees all together. It would take Joanie a while to feel completely at home here.

As she walked around with Shelly, Joanie was grateful to notice that the workers dressed casually. Joanie did not have an expansive wardrobe and what she did have was extended by sharing with her sisters and mother. She figured she could manage comfortably with what few clothes she owned for now, until she could afford more with her first paycheque.

A paycheque. The idea that Joanie had the job still seemed unreal.

✞ ✞ ✞

Brandon Vaughn stood at his office door on the third floor, watching intently as Shelly Lesichyn walked about with a very attractive young woman. The twenty-six-year-old commercial producer was aware that the station was going to be hiring a new research-reporter. Brandon wondered if this hot little number with Shelly was going to be that reporter. He motioned across the large room for Paul Petros, a camera technician, to come over.

Paul, thirty-three years old and a very talented cameraman, rather astutely followed Brandon's line of vision as he approached the young producer. "Something caught your attention there, Brandon?" he inquired, perceptively.

"Who's the new set of legs?" Brandon asked, not taking his eyes off Joanie, whose back was now to him.

"I don't know, Brandon," Paul stated, "but I'm sure it won't take you long to find out." Paul laughed and shook his head at the handsome young man before him.

Brandon looked at Paul and returned the laugh. "No, I don't suppose it will," he agreed.

"Brandon," Paul asked with real curiosity, "when you look over there . . . is all you see just a nice set of legs?"

"What else should I see?" Brandon returned, in a rather cavalier manner.

"Well, what I see is a sweet young girl who would do well to stay away from a guy like you, buddy!" Paul asserted, patting Brandon on the shoulder in a friendly way.

Brandon laughed, "You have to see her that way, Paul. You're married."

Paul nudged Brandon and motioned his head toward Joanie. "You see that medal around her neck?"

"Uh-hum," Brandon acknowledged it as he observed Joanie daintily playing with the golden medal between her fingers as she spoke with Shelly.

"I'll bet you that girl's a Catholic," Paul suggested.

"So what if she is? I've dated Catholics before," Brandon replied, shrugging off Paul's comment. "That's never made a difference."

Paul crossed his arms over his chest and looked squarely at Brandon. "Yeah? Maybe not, but some people wear their religion more than others, Brandon. I'll bet you that girl's the genuine article." Paul nodded to himself, satisfied with his assessment of the pretty young woman.

"Well, if she were," Brandon responded to his co-worker's assertion, "that would just make the chase all the more interesting."

"What if she's married?" Paul asked.

"No ring," Brandon pointed out. "But if she were, I'd stay back. Even I have my standards, Paul."

"You know, Brandon," Paul asked, with real curiosity, "haven't you ever thought of giving up your womanizing ways and settling down with just one good woman?"

"Nah," Brandon returned, "that's not my style."

"Well, look at me," Paul continued, offering advice to his younger colleague. "I'm a happily married man. I don't have to worry about who my next partner will be."

Brandon shifted his bright blue eyes curiously at Paul. "I never worry about that."

"No, I don't suppose you do," Paul chuckled, shaking his head in amusement.

"And I've seen you, Paul, dragging yourself in here in the mornings, after being up all night with those kids of yours," Brandon continued to make his point. "Don't try to convince me that your life is free of worries."

"It's not worry-free at all, Brandon," Paul admitted, "but I wouldn't trade what I've got with my wife and kids for anything in the world."

Brandon looked at his friend and nodded. "More power to you, *Dad*. As for me . . . *that's* a title I don't ever intend to wear."

By this time Joanie and Shelly had left the production area as they continued their tour of the station. Paul returned to his work and Brandon went back into his office and sat at his desk. Running his fingers through his sandy-brown hair, he reflected on Paul's friendly advice. *That marriage business is okay for guys like Paul. But not for me!*

Carefree and happy, Brandon Vaughn was not at all interested in messing with a good thing. He had youth and good looks in his favour. He had a great job, great friends, and he answered to no one for anything. Now why would a guy want anything more, or less, out of life than that?

Chapter 2

Six o'clock was no real challenge for Joanie—she was a morning person. However, the nervousness of the new job was holding her in a grip which was manifested in the covers being clung tightly around her small frame. She was fighting an interior battle against the temptation to stay in the security of her warm bed. Finally though, taking charge over her fears, she ordered herself, *That's it, girl! Get up!*

Rolling out, with blankets dragging around her, she fell, kneeling beside her bed. With her forehead held up by clutched fists and elbows driven deeply into the mattress, Joanie made her morning offering. This was her heroic moment when she offered up her day to the Lord and drew strength from the grace of overcoming the first battle of many for that day.

Joanie stood, stretched out the night, and breathed in the new day. Attracted by the chirping of birds, she stepped over to the window. She drew back the lacy curtain that had been gently moving in the soft morning breeze. The sun had risen nearly an hour earlier. The wispy clouds of the western sky that she was facing from her second storey window stood out boldly against the bright blue backdrop. It was going to be another gorgeous day.

She watched a papa robin, perched on the telephone line in the alley. He was announcing the day to the world as he guarded his mate, nesting in the branches of a nearby apple tree. Joanie glanced down at the apple tree in their yard. The thick growth of leaves now obscured her view of the friendly robins' home, which her family had watched being built so attentively by the parent birds earlier that spring.

The house was still quiet with only the far-off sound of the shower in her parents' bathroom. Joanie assumed it to be her father getting ready for work.

Without making a sound, she walked over to her chair where she had carefully laid out her clothes the night before. Picking them up, she continued out of the room so as not to wake her sisters. Joanie pulled the heavy wooden door slowly behind her, carefully manipulating the old fashioned doorknob, hoping not to make a sound when she released it. There was a slight click that made Joanie pause as it latched.

After years of experience, Joanie knew exactly where to step in the hallway to avoid the spots that creaked in the old wooden floor. This was her time alone in the morning; she was not about to wake up any of the little kids. She closed two other bedroom doors before heading to the bathroom to get herself ready for the day.

✚   ✚   ✚

Joanie carried herself as confidently as she could, as she walked up the old brick steps to the station's main doors. The Canadian Network Broadcasting sign, hanging proudly above the entrance, reminded Joanie that she was entering today as an employee. She held her head high and clung onto the purse strap over her left shoulder, making every effort to appear comfortable in this new world where she now belonged.

The reception area was filled with beautiful plants, and a lovely fountain burbled in the corner. At the centre, a large oak counter formed a semicircle in which two women were busily establishing themselves for the workday. Joanie smiled to greet them as she entered.

There were many people coming into the station now, and the open staircase that extended past the large front windows of the building was full and busy. Joanie headed up to the third floor, hoping that the other workers around her could not sense how small and nervous she felt.

Why the newsroom looked entirely different to Joanie today was indeed a mystery to her. It was as though she had never been there before. In that moment, she was certain she had forgotten everything Shelly had shown her the day before.

Jesus, help me!

The short prayer was quickly answered, for just then Shelly came from her office and greeted Joanie. Somehow just the sight of this gracious woman set Joanie at ease. From her warm smile to her gentle manner, Shelly was a real gem.

"How are you doing today?" Shelly asked, sensing Joanie's apprehensions.

"I have to confess, I'm sort of nervous," Joanie answered, hugging her black soft-covered briefcase.

"You'll do just fine, Joanie. Take some time to set up at your workstation. Our morning conference is at nine, so you have over half an hour to get prepared. Call me if you need help with anything. My line is four-twenty-six." Shelly smiled and gave Joanie a pat of encouragement on the shoulder.

The six-foot-wide workstation, which would be her new home, had enough room for an L-shaped desk on which sat a computer, radio scanner, telephone, and stacking tray for assignments. Joanie sat back comfortably in the cushioned, swivel chair and began to investigate her workspace.

There were two drawers in the desk: one contained general office supplies, the other was empty. Joanie put her purse and briefcase in the empty one.

The two side walls of the cubicle were blue, with a calendar hanging on the right side and a whiteboard on the other. In spite of the plainness of Joanie's new little home, there was a cozy and safe feeling here; it was her very own space.

A few of the other workers came over to meet her. They offered to help Joanie find things that she needed and encouraged her not to hesitate to ask. This was a friendly work environment, consistent with Joanie's experience of television stations. She was feeling better all the time.

Before settling into her work, Joanie decided to make a quick job of home decorating. From her purse she produced a prayer book. She took out two small pictures: one of the Sacred Heart of Jesus and the other of the Immaculate Heart of Mary. Taping them to the wall beside the calendar, she smiled and nodded. They were not obvious to anyone passing by, but she could look up at them often. They served to remind her to make each moment of the day one of prayer and offering to the Lord.

The young research-reporter started up her computer and set to work, checking out the e-mails and faxes. She scanned the radio stations quickly and made some brief notes to take in with her to the morning conference.

The conference went very well. Shelly introduced Joanie around to the other reporters, some of whom she had already met in the newsroom. Her day file was set up; Shelly gave Joanie the go-ahead on a story she had pitched. A senior citizen in one of the city's nursing residences was turning one hundred and ten years old that day. It was a delightful prospect for Joanie to go and meet with this woman.

Joanie returned to her workstation and set up a meeting for that afternoon with Mrs. Jones and the director of St. John's Nursing Home. She prepared her preliminary write-up and contacted a few of Mrs. Jones' relatives to join them at the interview. This woman had outlived all of her children, and her grandchildren were now senior citizens.

Towards the end of the morning, Shelly brought around Paul Petros. He was the cameraman with whom Joanie would be going out on location that afternoon. A nice looking, friendly man, of average height and build, she figured him to be in his mid-thirties. He had a very dark complexion with short, straight, jet black hair and eyes so dark Joanie could have sworn they were black as well. Married with two small children, he was in awe learning about Joanie's large family.

"How can your parents afford it?" he asked, genuinely interested in the young reporter's background.

"Money's tight at times," Joanie admitted, "but we've never lacked for anything. And I wouldn't trade having grown up in a large family for anything."

You are the genuine article, aren't you? he thought, remembering his conversation with Brandon from the day before. Responding to Joanie's comments, Paul asserted, "Well, my wife says we're done having kids. I figure it's up to her, since she's the one having them."

Joanie smiled. She knew how counter-cultural it was to have a large family. She was grateful that her parents had been willing to go against the tide: her siblings were the greatest treasure in the world to her.

Paul was knowledgeable and very helpful. He spent some time talking to Joanie about the station. As a new reporter, she looked forward to going out on assignments with such an experienced partner. Paul left for lunch, and Joanie turned back to her work. She was glad to have been occupied all morning.

By ten after twelve there was a knock on the side of her cubicle. "Joanie, take a break. Come have lunch." Shelly looked down at the rookie through gentle eyes, with a smile that said she understood how hard it was to be new on the scene.

Joanie pulled herself away from her work and walked with Shelly to the lunchroom on the main floor.

✟   ✟   ✟

The lounge was bright and cheerful, a refreshing change from her dark corner in the newsroom. There was a large lunch table in the middle of the room, with cozy chairs and couches around the edges. The abundant potted plants around the spacious open lounge were evidence of someone's attentive care.

There was a kitchen area with lovely oak cupboards along one wall and wallpaper wainscotting around the other three. Joanie appreciated the homey atmosphere that the lounge afforded. No doubt the renovations had happened during the boom in the early eighties. Money was far too tight in broadcasting for that kind of extravagance now.

It was a noisy room at the moment, with people sitting around, talking and laughing over their lunches. Joanie was impressed with what a pleasant group of people they seemed to be. Before too long, someone approached Shelly. The Senior Producer excused herself, taking her leave of the new employee.

As she stood by herself, surrounded by strangers, Joanie suddenly felt very isolated. Determined to get her footing in this new terrain, she looked around the room, calling to mind the names of the workers whom she had already met. The person who caught her attention the most was Taylor, a sound technician. He was lying on the same couch he had occupied yesterday, and she was amused, wondering if he had ever left.

Spying an empty chair by a window, with a beautiful dragon palm extending over it, Joanie went and sat down. Taking a brief moment to say grace, the young rookie hoped that, as she made the sign of the cross, she would not attract attention to herself. Her awkwardness became apparent when she looked up and realized a young man had been watching. He winked at her boldly then, laughing to himself, he turned around to get a coffee. Joanie shrank back inside, acutely aware of her conspicuousness.

She nervously fixed her eyes on his tall frame, as he had his back turned to her. His broad shoulders and trim build gave the impression of a very athletic man. He was dressed in casual slacks and his shirt sleeves were rolled up part way, showing off his strong, tanned arms. His sandy-brown hair was styled perfectly, which only served to increase Joanie's sense of intimidation. It was, though, his striking blue eyes that stood out in her mind. Joanie suffered a panicked moment, waiting for some remark to be directed at her. But after getting his coffee, he continued out of the lounge and never looked back.

Joanie's sigh of relief was so audible that Tessa, sitting on the other side of the dragon palm, looked over. Joanie smiled back and reintroduced herself.

"Don't worry, Joanie," said Tessa, "I was nervous, too, when I began. But that was five years ago and I not only survived, but I really love it here. You'll see. And," she gestured, with her sandwich held in both hands, "don't pay any attention to Brandon. He's a commercial producer here at the station and a good one at that. But he thinks he's God's gift to women, and he's nervier than a fox in a henhouse. If you can get past that, he's almost bearable. He's just amusing himself, trying to size up a praying girl."

Joanie was speechless. Tessa had seen everything! "I . . ." Joanie fumbled for words.

"I pray, too." Tessa smiled. "I'm just not Catholic." She made a friendly gesture, indicating the sign of the cross, by lifting her right hand to her forehead. "It's cool with me!"

Joanie instantly liked Tessa. She had a warm and friendly smile and a calm and gentle voice. She held her head slightly to the side as she spoke, causing her shoulder-length hair to hang down loosely from the right side of her head. Her hair was smooth and shiny, with light-blond highlights that shimmered above the darker-blond undertones. Her blue-grey eyes looked directly at Joanie, giving her undivided attention to their conversation.

Although Tessa was for sure several years older than she, Joanie suspected that the two of them would forge a very good friendship.

They visited, eagerly learning more about each other. Tessa Farrow was a receptionist at the front office of the station. She was engaged to get married that fall and was a very committed Evangelical Christian. The young reporter and the receptionist discovered, as they shared about their faith, that they had very much in common. Lunch hour slipped by in no time.

Back at her workstation after lunch, Joanie said a quick prayer as she glanced up at Jesus' and Mary's gentle faces. She was grateful for having found a friend in Tessa. All at once her brief encounter with Brandon flashed through her mind and, reluctantly, she thanked God for the opportunity to practise the virtue of humility. It was a challenge to force herself not to think about those piercing blue eyes as she gathered up her stuff to meet Paul down at the station van and head out on her first assignment.

Chapter 3

At the end of that first work day, Joanie stepped down off the bus a block from her house. She could see the old two-storey across the street, and she smiled at the sight of it. The Collins family lived in one of those picturesque areas of town, developed in the 1920's, with lovely old homes and spacious yards. The elm trees that gracefully lined the sidewalks hung over the street, giving the impression of walking through a tunnel. It was a charming feeling, strolling up the street. Joanie enjoyed the shade offered by the trees, protecting her from the heat of the late afternoon sun on this delightful June day.

As Joanie came up the walk, Zack, Aaron, and Jessie came running out to meet her. They were the three youngest of her siblings. The novelty of Joanie's new job had stirred them to a vigilant watch that afternoon, waiting for Joanie's return from work. It would eventually wear off, but for now Joanie lapped up the special attention they lavished upon her. The children clamoured at Joanie's arms and legs, according to their heights, as she walked up to the house.

Zack, who had just turned eight, was an energetic ball of fire, from his tussled head of auburn hair to his dirty, little barefoot toes. Aaron, a brown-eyed, blond sweetheart, was five years old and had a much more subdued nature than did Zack. Still, he often found himself drawn into mischief with his older partner in crime.

Jessie was Joanie's little doll. She was three-and-a-half years old and attached herself to Joanie, her second mother, with real devotion. Her shiny auburn hair was usually pulled up into stylish little hairdos. She changed her clothes many times a day, modelling her pretty dresses as she sought the praise and attention of those around her. Her hazel eyes took in everything in her busy environment, and she always seemed to sparkle with childish delight.

Seeing Jessie's failing attempts to get past her brothers, Joanie swooped down to pick her up over the boys' heads. Jessie's gratitude was expressed in a bear hug as she clasped her arms around her big sister's neck.

Joanie knew that she would not have a moment to herself until all the excitement wore off. Her mother stood back, smiling . . . patiently waiting her turn to greet her eldest daughter.

Judy Collins was a woman of average build, with dark hair and eyes like Joanie's. She wore her hair shoulder length in a simple, layered style that framed her gentle face. Dressed in blue jeans and a T-shirt, she was drying her hands as she leaned against the dark wooden door frame to the kitchen, taking in the whole scene.

Finally, Joanie made her way over and gave her mother a hug, somewhat comparable to the hug Jessie had bestowed upon her.

"Thank you, Mom," she whispered.

"For what?" her mother wondered, without breaking the hug.

"For everything. You're the best, Mom!"

If it had not been for such moments, Joanie's mom would never have survived the challenges of raising a large family. She cherished each moment of grace and stored them up for those overwhelming times that inevitably would come.

"Well, thanks! How about lending a hand with supper? I'd enjoy the opportunity to hear all about your day at work." Judy never missed a beat. She swiftly returned to her many busy tasks and handed Joanie a paring knife, motioning for her daughter to wash up before she began.

Joanie appreciated these times with her mom. In a large family, working alongside each other had as much meaning as playtime. And chores were so much easier when you were not alone. The fatigue and stresses of the work day washed away as Joanie submerged herself into her family life.

"Joanie!" The largeness of the voice and the intensity of the tone, coming from behind Joanie's back, gave her a start, causing her to drop the knife with the potato she had been peeling. She whirled around to greet her father. A large man, over six feet tall, he was in his late-forties and, although heavy-set, he still carried himself in a way that showed he had once been quite athletic.

Joanie hugged her father, while at the same time reproaching him for scaring the wits out of her. Judy lectured him with a "you should know better than to startle someone with a knife" speech. They all laughed, and John joined in the conversation.

Joanie had a tremendous affection for her father. She knew the many sacrifices that this hero in her life had made to support a large family on a single income. John Collins was a teacher by profession but a handyman by night. He supplemented the family income by taking on every repair job that would have been an extra expense.

When they had moved into the old house where they now lived, Joanie was ten. She remembered very well the countless hours he had spent alone, slaving away at renovations before they could move in. It was this dedication that she admired in her father. John was a family man, a just and fair father, and he took seriously his responsibility as spiritual head of the home.

John treated Joanie with affection and respect, and modelled what she wanted in a husband for herself. They often went out alone together on "dates", and her father would explain to her, "This is how I want you to be treated by a man. Don't ever settle for anything less." When it came to dealing with men, Joanie demonstrated a confidence that came from having the security of a father who loved her.

While she was naturally interested in men, her parents had not allowed their children to date before eighteen. Joanie was now twenty-two. After going out on a few dates during her first two years of university, Joanie stopped bothering altogether with the dating thing. Dependency on attention from men was not a driving factor in her life.

Joanie had goals and dreams, but above all she possessed a strong moral fibre that helped her to stay on course. She realized that until she was ready in her life for a long-term commitment there was no point in distracting herself with unnecessary relationships. Now that she had finished school and was working she could consider the possibility, but so far she had not met any man that had inspired her to want a serious relationship.

She knew she would marry someday, certain of that being her vocation, but she was in no particular hurry to find someone. For now, Daddy fit the bill quite nicely. Though she was the eldest of eight children, with five daughters in the home, Joanie still delighted in being Daddy's little girl.

That evening, the family gathered around to watch the local news together before supper. There was tremendous anticipation as they waited for Joanie's report. Finally it came on, and Joanie was suddenly catapulted to the status of a real celebrity in their home. Her younger siblings were amazed over the fact that Joanie was actually on real television—not just on video. They had not seen any of the clips from her internship on a real news broadcast.

This had been a good piece. Joanie had truly enjoyed meeting Mrs. Jones: an amazing woman whose goal was to live long enough to be able to set foot into three centuries in her lifetime. She had four years until the turn of the millennium and, although her eyesight was beginning to fail, she was still able to walk and had all her faculties about her. Joanie's news piece reflected how personally inspired she had been by this beautiful woman. Her skill as a reporter served to move her audience to be equally inspired.

✙   ✙   ✙

When Brandon got in that night from his beach volleyball game, he checked his messages: only one, from his mother, Caroline. Brandon had grown up an only child, raised alone by his mother after his parents had divorced. He was very close to his mom who now lived in Calgary. For years it had just been him and her, with no other family and very few relatives, as she had been orphaned as a child. Turning on the television, he decided to return her call after the news.

Sitting with a can of beer, he watched with great curiosity. At last, there it was: the news clip he had been waiting to see. As the piece finished he read the bottom of the screen and muttered to himself, repeating after the young reporter: "Joanie Collins." He put the name to memory.

"Pretty face, great legs!" he mused out loud, "I'll have to make a point of stopping by the staff lounge more often."

✞   ✞   ✞

Paul Petros sat at the edge of Joanie's cubicle, discussing the details of a shoot that afternoon. They had hit it off very well, and Joanie was grateful that she would be working again with Paul.

From over Paul's shoulder, Joanie caught sight of Brandon as he walked across the newsroom toward them. She became obviously distracted, and Paul turned around to see Brandon approaching.

"I was told I'd find you here, Paul," Brandon said, casually taking his place, leaning on Joanie's cubicle.

Joanie remained seated in her swivel chair, desperately trying to appear calm, despite Brandon's intrusion.

"What can I do for you, Brandon?" Paul responded in his friendly manner, knowing exactly why Brandon was there.

"I need to go over a commercial shoot with you. Can we meet this afternoon?"

"Yeah, sure. Joanie and I'll be back by two-thirty." Paul paused, looking between Brandon and Joanie, who had firmly fixed their eyes upon each other. Against his better judgment, he decided to make the introduction. "Have you two met?"

Brandon smiled, not taking his eyes from Joanie's. "Only once . . . in the staff lounge, yesterday."

Joanie was awkward in Brandon's presence. She foolishly worried over how she looked and then chastised herself for even caring whether or not she was making a good impression on him. *What do I care what this guy thinks?*

Brandon continued in his smooth way, "But we've never been introduced." He lifted his eyebrows and flashed his eyes at Joanie.

Paul watched with amusement, not oblivious to the effect Brandon was having on Joanie. "Brandon Vaughn, this is—"

"Joanie Collins," Brandon cut him off. "CNB's newest reporter. I saw your clip last night on the news. . . . Very quaint. Sweet old lady, wasn't she?"

"Yes, she was . . . Mr. Vaughn," Joanie replied, guardedly.

Joanie could feel the blood rushing to her cheeks. She resented the way Brandon was amusing himself at her expense with his patronizing tone. More than that, though, she hated the way she was allowing him to shake her confidence. She straightened her shoulders and elegantly crossed her legs, trying to re-establish her presence in this situation.

Brandon cast down his eyes at Joanie's shapely leg. He smiled and looked back up at her. She was proud and spirited; he could tell by the way she held herself up against his teasing.

Paul began laughing, and he put his hand on Joanie's shoulder. "Back off, Brandon! Take it easy on our rookie, here. She's a nice kid." He deliberately emphasized the word *nice,* and he threw Brandon a look that clearly said, *Back off!*

Turning to Joanie, Paul offered, "Don't let this guy ruffle your feathers, Joanie. If he gives you any trouble, you come and see me."

With a feigned air of innocence—lifting his hands up to defend himself—Brandon acknowledged Paul's look and stated, "I'll behave." Returning to his professional manner, he asked, "You'll come up and meet me in my office at three, then?"

"You bet," Paul replied, getting up to leave as well. Turning back to Joanie with a reassuring look, he added, "I'll meet you at the van in about twenty minutes, okay, Joanie?"

"Thanks, Paul," she replied, sincerely. The intensity of her frustration toward Brandon had subsided. She sat back in her chair and watched the two men walk out together.

☦   ☦   ☦

As Paul left the newsroom with Brandon, he warned him, "I'm telling you, Brandon, that girl's too good for you!"

"What's that supposed to mean?" Brandon laughed off the assertion.

"Look, Brandon, I like you as much as anybody. You're a great guy and lots of fun to work with. But I'd hate to see a sweet girl like that be spoiled by a guy like you!" Paul's face was serious.

Brandon returned his look with a reassuring smile and nodded. "Well, don't worry, buddy. I'm not about to spoil anybody. I'm just checking out—"

"New territory," Paul jumped in. "I know you, Brandon. I just don't want to see Joanie get hurt. I like her—a lot!"

Brandon chuckled as he turned to go up the stairs, parting from Paul. "I'm not in the business of hurting sweet girls, Paul. Relax!"

Paul shook his head with amusement. "I'll see you at three, Brandon."

✣   ✣   ✣

Once the two men were out of sight, Joanie turned in her swivel chair to face her pictures of Jesus and Mary. *Did You place Brandon in my life just so I could work on the virtue of humility? If so, perhaps You could send someone else who doesn't have such distractingly blue eyes and rugged good looks. I'm really having a hard time trying to refocus here.*

Brandon Vaughn. She brought the handsome producer's name to mind. The name struck Joanie as suiting this man: clean cut, stylish, and boldly full of confidence.

Any time soon, Lord, You can take him off my mind so I can get back to work!

✣   ✣   ✣

Joanie wondered if Paul would mention Brandon when they were out together, but he did not. She was grateful for that, as she kept pushing Brandon's image away from invading her thoughts so that she could carry on without distraction.

The news piece was on a sit-in at one of the high schools. Students were protesting a school policy that was imposing a stricter dress code. Joanie found the students highly amusing and wondered if she had ever been as full of herself as these kids were. Although not sympathetic to the protesters' cause, Joanie managed to pull off some interesting interview clips. She was sure to include some with students who supported the school policy. Why give all the limelight only to those who were craving it?

Coming home from the shoot, Paul commented, "I'm impressed with your work, Joanie. You're a natural in front of that camera." He could not get over how casual and informal she was as they drove around. She was fun, and she even laughed at Paul's jokes, which not everybody did. *Obviously, she has a sophisticated sense of humour, like me,* he thought to himself. Yet once that camera was rolling, she was the model of professionalism.

"I don't know about being a natural," Joanie replied. "But years of training in musical performance have helped me."

"What kind of training?" Paul asked.

"Mostly singing," she replied.

"Well, it's paid off," he reaffirmed. "You're good at what you do, kiddo!"

"Thanks, Paul. I can't tell you how grateful I am to be working with someone like you," she returned with real sincerity.

The assignment finished up well that day. Shelly was happy with Joanie's report. She, too, agreed that perhaps these students were vying a bit too much for the spotlight. She liked the way Joanie had put it all together—getting both sides of the story.

The young reporter felt satisfied with herself as she stepped onto the bus at the end of the day. The ride home was a welcome time of retreat for Joanie. She leisurely gazed out the window, taking in the activity of the city around her.

Saskatoon was just an average-sized city, located in the middle of nowhere out on the open prairies of western Canada. This was Joanie's home. She loved it. Nothing terribly exciting ever happened here, but that was part of what made it such a wonderful place to have grown up. It was large enough to have everything a city needed, but small enough to still be friendly.

Her favourite part of the bus ride, to and from work, was crossing the bridge. The trees were just now in full foliage with their greenery showcasing the picturesque riverbank. The clear, blue water of the river reflected the bright sky above. The rowers were out at this time of day, their paddles moving rhythmically in unison as they pushed on against the current of the water.

Once past the river Joanie closed her eyes, leaned her head against the window and took a moment to rest quietly for the last six blocks of the bus ride home.

Joanie's mind drifted back to her meeting with Brandon that day. She smiled, in spite of herself, wondering about this mysterious man. Why would a good-looking guy like that bother with a girl like her? He was obviously just having fun tormenting her. She could hold her own against him, though. Resolving to keep up her guard, she vowed to be better prepared to deal with him next time.

Chapter 4

The week slipped by in no time as Joanie was caught up in the fast-paced momentum of research-reporting. She loved the excitement of her new job. Shelly had been pleased with Joanie's work, and Joanie was feeling very much at home in the station environment. As she bid farewell to her co-workers and headed out to the bus stop Friday after work, her heart was full of gratitude. What a blessing this job had turned out to be. Life was amazingly good, and she was on top of the world.

Her thoughts gradually turned to the events of the upcoming weekend. She would be singing at a wedding Saturday afternoon and at a concert that same night at a neighbouring Evangelical church. Sundays were always spent in a relaxed atmosphere with family and friends. There would not be much time for her, though.

Joanie was the lead singer in a Christian praise and worship group called *New Spring*. The group had formed four years back with some cousins, friends, and two of her sisters. All of the members were really committed to the goal of evangelizing through music, and they had worked hard to keep the band going despite the busy schedules of school and work. Sometimes they wondered how long the group would hold together, but they left that in the Lord's hands. He had blessed their ministry from the start and, for the time being, they were committed to gigs all summer.

They performed at one or two concerts a month in the local area, and the second Friday of each month they led a praise and worship night at Joanie's church. They had sung at over twenty weddings over the past three years and were booked almost solid for the summer "wedding season" ahead.

It was a passion of Joanie's to sing. She always dreamed that she might someday record Christian music. The trick was going to be in finding a way to fit her two loves, music and journalism, together. So far she had managed well. Teaching music had supplemented the cost of her education, greatly reducing her student loans. Now journalism would become the means to support her real dream of singing, as long as she could keep up with the busy pace of both in her life.

✟ ✟ ✟

The weekend had flown past, and Joanie was not quite sure she was ready for Monday morning. But it came . . . as inevitably it would. As she leaned against the window of the bus, Joanie mentally prepared herself for the morning conference. She had a few leads from the weekend. All at once, the thrill of a new assignment took over. She loved how her work presented for her each day a new problem that she would have to solve. The set deadline fed Joanie's energy and enthusiasm all day long, until she got her job done.

She closed her eyes, and a smile crept up from the corners of her mouth as the names and faces of fellow employees flashed through her mind. Suddenly, Joanie cringed at the memory of Brandon leaning against her cubicle, smiling down at her. She opened her eyes and looked around on the bus, feeling obvious and exposed.

There had been only two encounters with Brandon last week, but both times he had made a very strong impression. It amazed her that just the thought of him could completely unnerve her. No man had ever had that effect on her before. She was grateful that he did not come by often, but reminded herself of her resolve to be on her guard around him.

Resolutely shaking off the uncomfortable feeling that the thought of Brandon had evoked, Joanie focussed to regain her confidence. By now she could see the old CNB building rising up to greet her over the horizon. She smiled at the sight of it. *Thank you, Jesus, for giving me such a great place to work!*

"See you tomorrow, Joanie!" the bus driver called after her as she stepped down. In only six days of bus riding, her charming and sweet nature had captivated this grandfatherly man. His friendly greetings were a real boost to her morale. She marvelled at how even the simplest pleasantries can mean so much. She waved and smiled back at him, then turned to meet the challenges of the new day.

Seeing Tessa at the front desk was a tremendous plus for Joanie, and she thanked the Lord for this dear woman. She stopped, and they had a quick visit before Joanie headed up to the second floor.

The swivel chair of her cozy little home offered Joanie the comfort of an old friend. She eagerly started up her computer and began her preparations for the morning conference.

✝   ✝   ✝

Lunch hour was a welcome break. Joanie had been looking forward to catching up with Tessa after the weekend. Nestled into their corner of the lounge by the window, Joanie interrogated Tessa about the receptionist's wedding plans for September. What twenty-two-year-old girl could resist that topic? They were leaning over to look at a bridal magazine together, when their conversation was interrupted.

As she looked down at the pair of oxfords before her, Joanie just knew that the cool, low voice above her belonged to Brandon. She could not easily forget his voice, nor her resolution to be on guard. It was a quick prayer to St. Joan of Arc, her patron saint, that Joanie made before looking up. In that instant she drew the courage to meet this man face to face—without being intimidated.

"Hello," Joanie smiled politely, managing to put on an air of confidence. The long curls of her upswept hair fell gracefully over her shoulder, as she tilted her head sideways, taking him in.

Neither girl had registered what Brandon had said when he had approached, since they had been so absorbed in their own discussion.

"I should have guessed two religious girls like you would have hit it off so well," he casually remarked.

"Brandon," Tessa smiled, with a tone of annoyance, "is there something we can do for you?"

"Hey, I'm just being friendly here. Is there any law against that? You know, kiddo," he turned to look Joanie squarely on, "whatever Tessa has said about me is probably true, but don't let that stop you from getting to know me yourself." He was calm, collected, and dangerously inviting, from the gleam in his eyes to the curious way he lifted the left corner of his mouth as he spoke.

Suddenly, Joanie realized that Brandon was evoking a whole new set of emotions within her. She had been around boys her whole life. Some of her closest friends were boys. During her brief stint at dating in university she had gone out with some really great guys, and the not-so-great guys who had tried to ask her out—she had simply disregarded. But none of them had ever had the ability to shake Joanie's confidence the way Brandon did.

Brandon was not the kind of guy to whom Joanie would have normally felt any kind of attraction. True, he was astoundingly handsome. But Joanie had always prided herself in looking deeper than the surface. She would gladly have gone out with a man who had genuine character, regardless of his looks.

So why was she experiencing these feelings with Brandon? She struggled to retain her confidence. He might be shaking it, but she was holding on with determination. After their encounter last week, she was not about to allow Brandon to realize what an effect he had on her.

She daintily reached up to the golden miraculous medal that hung around her neck and wove it through her slender fingers.

The medal caught Brandon's eye, and he smiled.

"I'll be in here most days for lunch. Feel free to join us," she replied, effortlessly.

Joanie's manner was so cordial, and her head was held in such a noble fashion, Brandon became aware that he was unsure of how to proceed. He had not shaken her one bit. She was proud and confident. This situation was definitely presenting itself as a new and real challenge to a guy who loved nothing more than that.

"See you 'round," he said with a wink and nod, in a gesture that indicated the respect of a rival. He would be back once he had worked out a new strategy—she was sure of that.

Brandon strode away, making casual conversation with other workers around the room. He had a commanding presence about him. Joanie found it a challenge not to be distracted to glance at him out of the corner of her eye, as she and Tessa continued to look at the magazine. There was something about his smile that was hard to resist.

He approached Taylor, who was lying comfortably on the couch, and playfully kicked him on the leg. Taylor impressed Joanie as a character who probably had spent too much of his twenty-some years of life partying. He groaned and opened his eyes, and the two men had a friendly exchange.

Joanie's eyes followed Brandon as he left the lounge. Not once had he looked back at her.

Chapter 5

The beautiful oak table, centred in the open dining room of the Collins home, was an impressive piece of furniture, stretching out a full nine feet. It had taken John and Judy several years to save up for it, in order to seat comfortably their large family. They placed a high value on gathering together for eating. Suppertime was normally the best meal of the day, for it was that one time when all the family was pretty much guaranteed to be there.

Presently, twelve-year-old Isaac was enthusiastically sharing about a science experiment he had done that day involving ants, water, and electrical currents. He was terribly creative and busy all the time. Joanie had a special fondness for this dark-haired, dark-eyed Einstein.

But as she sat there listening to the family conversations tonight, Joanie was distracted and even irritable with her younger siblings. Her shortness did not go unnoticed by her mother.

Joanie was aware that, above all, her frustration came from not quite knowing how to talk about the situation of Brandon with her mother. She had always been able to discuss anything with her mom. This was different. Brandon had stirred very new feelings in Joanie, and she was not sure how to open up about them just yet.

Joanie's thoughts were interrupted by a kafuffle that had stirred up around the table. Zack was tormenting Jessie by repeating everything she was saying.

Joanie snapped at the eight-year-old boy. "Stop it already, Zack! Leave her alone."

Jessie, having crawled up onto Joanie's knee, was by now crying very dramatic tears.

"You know, what is it about boys that they think they need to torment girls by teasing? Who teaches that to you? Is it just some sort of male insecurity thing? Make the girl feel smaller than you—and you'll feel like some big man!" Joanie's tone was sharp and openly mocking.

Zack stared at his big sister in amazement. "All right! I'm sorry, Jessie. You don't have to get so carried away, Joanie."

"Whoa! Where'd that come from, Joanie? Get a grip there," admonished her father, with a look of confusion.

Joanie stopped, suddenly aware that the chatter around the table had ceased. She looked around at the sea of eyes that had come to rest upon her during her little tirade. Turning to Zack, she apologized for getting so carried away.

Maggie, who was two years younger than Joanie, caught her older sister's eye with a look that said she knew something was up. Maggie was Joanie's dearest companion and friend. They shared everything, but Joanie was not prepared to share about Brandon with her just yet, either. She was afraid that she might somehow give Maggie the wrong impression about her feelings for Brandon.

What were her feelings for Brandon, anyway? Clearly, Joanie needed to sort this all out if she was going to "get a grip" on dealing with this mysterious man who had suddenly appeared in her life.

"I'm going to Mass and adoration tonight," Joanie announced, as she got up and began to clear the table. "Anyone care to join me?"

"Why don't you go early, so you can get to Confession, too?" piped up Zack.

Joanie laughed along with the rest of her family. Kids can be very perceptive at times. Mussing up his hair as she walked by, she replied, "That's not a bad idea, Zack!"

✟   ✟   ✟

Amie and Katie, the next two sisters in the family, joined up with Maggie and Joanie to do the dishes. When they were done, the four of them headed off to the church together.

Twenty-year-old Maggie was slightly shorter than Joanie. Her colouring was lighter, having blue-green eyes and light brown hair that shone with lovely natural red highlights. Maggie wore it shoulder length, straight cut, and often had it up in a ponytail. Although she was a very pretty girl, she was not the least bit preoccupied with her appearance. She had always been a tomboy who was more interested in swinging a bat than putting on make-up.

Amie was an eighteen-year-old beauty. No longer wearing braces, and just having outgrown the battle with acne, she had suddenly become a young lady, carrying herself with real confidence. She was as tall as Joanie and resembled Joanie in her slender build, her straight narrow nose, her distinctive jaw line, and her dazzling round eyes. But her colouring was completely different. Amie's long curly hair was sandy-blond, and she had clear blue eyes that sparkled whenever she spoke. Her whole face lit up each time she smiled. She was a real people person.

Katie was a fifteen-year-old romantic. She was at a stage in life where she would spend hours dreamily distracted in her own little world. Her older sisters had never really gone through that. Katie paid special attention to her looks. She had beautiful thick, dark, shoulder-length hair, layered stylishly around her dainty face. Her bright blue eyes shone out in stunning contrast to her darker, spotless complexion. She was very concerned about her image both physically and socially, and always sought to please others with her fun-loving and outgoing personality.

These four sisters had always shared a bedroom and, with that, a special bond. They enjoyed their time together and over the years there had been plenty of that. Except for Katie, who was still too young, they were all members of *New Spring*. They fought like sisters sometimes do, but they made up swiftly and sincerely and were generally the best of pals.

✜ ✜ ✜

St. James was one of the smallest parishes in the city. Built in 1927, the brick church was rather plain from the outside. It was shaped like a cross, with pews extending the length of the base and out the two arms. An addition had been made in the seventies, offering a spacious foyer and ample office area just off the main entrance, and the basement had been renovated to allow for community functions.

The sanctuary was at the top of the cross-shaped structure with the Tabernacle off to the right side, behind the altar. Prominently located, the ornately decorated Tabernacle drew one's attention immediately to the Sacrificial Presence of Christ in the church.

A beautiful crucifix had been donated to the parish years back. The life-size wooden carving of the corpus of Jesus was absolutely breathtaking. Statues of the Blessed Mother and St. Joseph were located on either side of the altar.

High above each of the four wings of the church were stained glass windows, each one depicting a different scene of the life of Jesus. There was the nativity above the back, south entry. On the east and west wings were depictions of the Baptism of the Lord and the Transfiguration. Behind the altar, on the north wing, was Jesus at the Last Supper, elevating the bread and cup.

Other than these lovely windows, there was nothing terribly impressive about the structure or decor of this humble little church. But the Real Presence of Jesus Christ in the Holy Eucharist transforms the plainest of structures . . . and there was no mistaking that this was holy ground.

As Joanie entered the church with her sisters for Mass, the love and fellowship of this small community—which was the outflow of their Eucharistic devotion—made it feel like home for her. She smiled and nodded a friendly greeting to some of the parishioners who had looked up when the girls walked in. The four sisters genuflected and knelt to pray silently before Mass began.

After Mass the Blessed Sacrament was left in exposition at the front of the church. The ornate, gold monstrance remained on the altar, surrounded by candles, welcoming all to come spend some time in quiet with Jesus. Their time in adoration was truly precious to all four girls.

Tonight Joanie was carrying with her a particular burden of the heart that she wished to leave behind with the Lord. She wanted to be freed of the distraction that Brandon had become to her through their few encounters. She prayed for a peace that would allow her to deal with him with the grace and respect befitting a young Christian woman.

It was hard for her not to be taken in by his forward ways. Joanie petitioned the Lord to armour her with the virtues she needed to be strong in Brandon's presence. She asked Jesus to help her keep His love at the centre of her heart, with her eyes focussed on Him.

When the four sisters left the church and headed out for slurpees, Joanie knew that the Lord, in His faithfulness, had answered her prayer. She felt strengthened in Jesus' love.

Her manner had changed so dramatically by the time they returned home that her mom caught Joanie by the arm, smiled at her, and said, "Isn't it wonderful to know Jesus in the Blessed Sacrament?"

Joanie smiled back. Her mother was so perceptive. No more needed to be said for now.

Chapter 6

The rest of the work week passed by uneventfully. Joanie had comfortably settled into the routines of her new life. The job was going well, and Shelly had complimented Joanie several times on the reports that she had been turning out daily.

It was Thursday of the following week before Brandon made an appearance in the staff lounge at lunch time. Since that night at adoration, Joanie knew she would have much more confidence in dealing with Brandon. This, though, would be her first opportunity to exercise that confidence. As Brandon approached, Joanie braced herself with a quick prayer.

"Won't you join us, Brandon?" she asked, without so much as looking at him while she poured herself a coffee. She went to sit at the lunch table with Tessa.

Tessa grabbed Joanie's arm at the elbow. Once they were out of earshot she reprimanded Joanie. "Why do you encourage him? Listen, Joanie, he's no good!" Her tone was steady and somewhat severe, like that of an older sister looking out for the younger one. Joanie knew it well.

"Relax, Tessa, the Lord ate with sinners all the time." Joanie smiled with such gentle strength that Tessa could not help but back down.

Brandon chuckled to himself as he poured a coffee, imagining the exchange between these two women as they walked away. He liked the spunkiness that Joanie possessed and found it amusing that she had avoided eye contact with him. She was unlike any girl he had ever before pursued—resistant to his advances.

"Ladies." Brandon nodded to them both as he took a spot across the table. His eyes met Joanie's, and this time she returned his look with complete sincerity.

"Tell me about your work, Brandon. You must be awfully busy, since I rarely have the pleasure of seeing you here." Her hand turned gracefully as she indicated the staff lounge.

"I'm touched that you've missed me," he returned, placing his hand to his heart, feigning flattery. In spite of his little act, he was distracted by Joanie's hand as she moved it back to pick up her cup. It occurred to him that not only did her voice carry a certain musical quality, but so did her movements.

"Yes, well, you've been so friendly each time we've met that I certainly have looked forward to getting to know you better." That was no word of a lie. Mostly, though, Joanie was simply determined to keep the conversation on level ground. She returned to the question. "So, do tell me about your work. You're a commercial producer, I understand."

Brandon smiled, conceding the silent battle. He decided to follow her lead for now as he began to explain his position at the station. "Well, let's see. I meet with prospective clients, figure out what they're looking for in their advertising and then . . . I put it all together. Voilà!" He lifted his hands in a gesture that indicated the ease with which things were done.

Joanie completed his arrogant assertion, her voice filled with exaggerated amazement. "And a commercial just appears—out of thin air!" The smile on her face as she imitated his little hand motion was completely amusing to Brandon. Her bright eyes sparkled back at his. For the first time they were looking at each other with a genuine sense of enjoying each other's company.

"Something like that," he nodded.

"Really, Brandon," she entreated him to go on, "what do you do, apart from waving your magic wand?"

There was something so irresistible about her eyes. As she leaned against her forearms on the table, he could sense that she was genuinely interested, and he found himself giving in to her, again. "Okay. Let's say you were my client." Wanting to put her back on the spot, he put forth the question, "What are you advertising?"

Joanie looked over at Tessa to bring her into the conversation. Tessa smiled back at her friend, amused with Joanie's persistence. "What are we advertising, Tessa?"

Tessa glanced up at Brandon and back to Joanie. "How about chastity?"

"Perfect," Joanie agreed. "Okay, Mr. Commercial Producer, what would you do with that?" Joanie threw the idea back at Brandon. She was proud that Tessa had been so bold.

"Chastity?" Brandon threw out the word, his eyebrows raised in amusement. "Do you suppose anybody advertising a concept like that would have the budget to pay for a television commercial?"

"We're loaded," Tessa asserted. "Just do your job!" She waved him on with her hand.

He chuckled at the two girls before him. "Fair enough," he went on. "First, I'd create a storyboard for your commercial and then present it to you."

"Well, go ahead," Joanie prompted him. "We're waiting." She looked over at Tessa, who nodded back to Brandon.

"Generally my clients give me more time to form an idea," he put forth as a disclaimer, "but I'll just give you a real sketchy impression here." He looked away momentarily, thoughtfully considering the topic. "Fine." He was ready.

Leaning back in his chair, he proceeded. "Picture a beautiful young woman in different scenes with men approaching her. She rejects them every time. And at the end you see this same woman, now an old spinster, knitting in a parlour. Lonely . . . pensive . . . wishing she hadn't been such a prude when she was young and beautiful and had the chance, 'cause now she realizes the parade has passed her by." His expression was completely controlled as he waited for a response.

Joanie and Tessa both burst out laughing at the same time and shook their heads in amazement.

"Wow!" Joanie exclaimed. "If I didn't think you were kidding, I'd hit you!"

Brandon's eyes flashed playfully at the young woman before him. He shrugged his shoulders innocently. "You asked for it, honey! But please," he put his hands up before him, "no violence."

Joanie turned to Tessa, who was still laughing. Tessa responded, "Well, Joanie, I guess you can't advertise something of which you have absolutely no concept!"

"You got that right, sister!" Brandon replied, quite candidly.

Joanie resumed a professional manner, still wanting to find out about Brandon's work. "Okay, Mr. Producer, we accept—love the idea! It gives such a clear image of the subject. Now what?"

Brandon smiled at her. "You don't give up, do you?"

"Not often," Joanie admitted.

"Well, from there I'd hire the actors and produce the commercial. There's editing and mixing, the usual stuff. It's not much different from your news clips, except . . . I get to be creative with the little extras, like the music." His manner changed and he leaned forward with enthusiasm as he continued. "That's my favourite part. You know music really makes or breaks a commercial. It carries it . . . it grabs a person's attention, makes them remember it. It basically sells the product, even after the commercial's over."

Brandon had become quite open and reflective. Joanie looked at him with her head tilted slightly and smiled. "I agree," she stated plainly. The façade was down. Brandon's arrogant ways seemed to have disappeared. In fact, he really impressed her with his sensitivity to the nature of his work. There really was more to this guy than what had first met the eye.

All at once Brandon found himself caught up in Joanie's eyes with his guard down. He resumed his typical manner so abruptly that Joanie started. "Yeah, well," he continued, "then I take it back to my client and get approval on the product, and it airs. That's pretty much it." He glanced down at his watch, uncomfortably. "I'm late here. Nice visiting with you ladies—I'll catch you 'round." He nodded his head to them and rushed off, without a chance for reply.

Joanie and Tessa exchanged a look as much as to say: *What just happened here?* They laughed and gave each other a high-five.

"I owe you an apology, Joanie," Tessa confessed, shaking her head in disbelief. "Here I call myself a Christian, yet I never saw anything good in that guy, other than his looks. But I think there just might be some depth to his personality after all . . . even if he has no concept of chastity."

Joanie smiled and just kept shaking her head in disbelief. "To be honest, Tessa, I hadn't seen anything there either. But I think you might just be right!"

✠   ✠   ✠

That night at the supper table, Joanie found herself talking for the first time about Brandon. She was keenly interested in his field of work. And now she could talk about him without the embarrassment and confusion she had first experienced upon making his acquaintance.

Joanie's mother's and father's eyes caught each other several times over the course of that meal. John was telling Judy that he was not going to sit by and watch his little girl get carried off by the first good-looking, smooth-talking commercial producer she met.

Her mother's eyes returned his look with a confidence that said: *We've raised a bright and beautiful girl, who stands rock-solid on the foundation we laid for her. Relax!*

After twenty-three years of marriage, they could read each others' minds as easily as they spoke. Joanie, caught up in her excitement, missed the entire conversation.

✠   ✠   ✠

Over the next few weeks at work, Joanie and Tessa actually came to look forward to Brandon's occasional drop-in visits in the staff lounge. There was something easy about the relationship they were forging, and Joanie was grateful for Tessa's presence. It helped to keep her on track and grounded. And it certainly seemed to help Brandon behave. Tessa, at twenty-eight, was only two years his senior, but still she held a certain amount of clout over him.

Their conversations generally centred on his work, since Joanie was endlessly questioning him about new projects. Brandon always managed, though, to work in mention of Joanie's news reports. He would tease her that it was the only thing he looked forward to seeing on the news each night.

She humbly received his praise. It was an effort not to allow him to work his charm over her. Brandon found the humility of her responses curiously alluring. She was not easily overcome by flattery.

It did not take long before Brandon was expressing further interest in Joanie. She shared with him the basic details: she was Catholic, from a large family, and had been home-schooled. But she was guarded at allowing him to probe too deeply. Concerned with the effect he had upon her, Joanie was determined to establish a certain emotional distance with this man. As her resistance to his inquiries fortified, Brandon became all the more intrigued.

✟   ✟   ✟

One Friday afternoon, in early July, Brandon showed up unexpectedly at coffee break. Joanie had only ever seen him there at lunch hours, and she suddenly found herself caught off-guard. He strolled over to the coffee machine where she was standing and gave Joanie a look that set off an alarm inside of her. Tessa was not there, and Joanie felt an instant wave of panic grab her.

His physical stature was impressive, and she felt weak and small with him so close up. Never before had she realized how distracting a man's cologne could be, but it was. She fumbled a quick, *Help Lord*, as she faced her adversary.

"Why, hello, Brandon, what brings you here? I never see you at coffee time. I was—" she was desperately searching for words to gain control of the situation when he cut her off.

"What are you up to this weekend?" His manner was that of a skilled hunter. He was cool and collected as he closed in on his prey.

Pray! Joanie reproached herself. She threw her heart before the mercy of heaven in a wordless plea for divine assistance.

Brandon fixed her firmly in his gaze. She felt like a deer caught in the headlights. "Um . . . uh," her fumbling only served to boost his confidence.

"Tonight, for example?" Even his body language was closing in on her. He casually reached his arm between Joanie and the coffee maker to refill his cup, cornering her by the counter.

"I'm busy—always," she replied, grasping at the most confident smile she could muster up. As she moved to slip past him, his hand reached over and caught her arm. Her heart pounded in her throat. Surely if she opened her mouth, it would come leaping out. She looked down at his strong hand holding, what now seemed to be, her really wimpy arm. *Hold fast girl*, she prayed intently.

"So what keeps you so busy, Church-Girl?"

The sudden, condescending reference to her faith snapped Joanie out of her panicked state of mind. Like a soldier who had been knocked off her steed in battle, she swiftly regained her mount and looked Brandon squarely in the eye. He had given her the out. *Thank you, Lord.*

She answered him plainly: "Church." She pulled her arm free, walked over to the lunch table, and sat, composed with confidence. Her elbows were planted firmly on the table, and she watched over her coffee cup as he approached, unrelenting.

"You know," he continued in a most alluring tone of voice, "there's more to life than church, and I'd be happy to show it to you." His eyes were so blue and his look was so enticing—with the left side of his mouth lifted in a half-smile—that Joanie could see why he was irresistible to girls and how he had acquired the reputation that he had.

Her resolve was firm, though, and she would not be overcome. Smiling in a nonchalant way she replied, "Thank you, no." Simplicity does have its merit.

Before he had a chance to go on, Joanie confidently took the lead. She reached over, picked up a pen that was lying on the lunch table, and took hold of Brandon's right hand with her left. Leaning across the table, she wrote out the name and address of her church and looked up at him, saying, "You're always welcome to join us. Seven-thirty tonight. Who knows, maybe I can show you more to life than you thought I could."

With that she stood up and carried herself out of the room with the grace of a ballerina leaving the stage.

He shook his head, closed his eyes, and chuckled to himself. She had done it again. Glancing down at the writing on his hand, he thought, *Somehow that girl always manages to get the upper hand on me! That does demand respect.*

The thought had no sooner escaped his mind when a haunting feeling came over him that he just might be headed for danger with this girl. *I'd do better to read the writing on the wall,* he told himself, not taking his eyes from his hand.

But the thrill of the hunt took over his moment of sobriety. He caught up his hand as though catching a set of keys and headed back up to the sound room where he had been working.

Back at her cubicle, Joanie breathed deeply, her eyes fixed on the picture of Jesus. *I'm not sure what I've gotten us into, Lord, but we're in on it together. . . . Deal? Deal!*

Chapter 7

"I can't decide," Joanie muttered to herself. "Which outfit do you like better?" she asked Maggie, who was lying on her bed reading a book. Joanie held out two outfits. One was a light summer dress; the other was a set of overall shorts.

"What does it matter, Joanie? You know, you'd think something important was going to happen tonight, by all your fussing here." Maggie knew there was something up, but she also could tell Joanie was not about to disclose any secrets either. That was fine with Maggie; she just wanted to let Joanie know that she had noticed.

"Why do I even bother asking you?" Joanie retorted, covering up her awkwardness with a personal attack. "You've got about as much fashion sense as a . . . as a porcupine."

"Nice simile, Joanie," Maggie returned in a patronizing tone. "Look, you can pick on me all you want, but I've been ready to go for half an hour, and you're still standing there in a bath towel," Maggie pointed out, as she glanced up from her book. "If you were more like me, you'd have a lot less worries. I don't fuss over my looks for anyone. Take me or leave me; I am who I am!"

"Who said I was fussing over my looks for anybody. I just . . . I take pride in my personal appearance. That doesn't make me shallow, you know." Joanie felt foolish inside. If Maggie only knew for whom she was fussing, Maggie would probably have a fit. Joanie knew full well that Brandon was not worth the fuss—no matter how blue his eyes were. He was a complete heathen who was only interested in her for—well, likely for all the wrong reasons. Maggie was right. Why fuss? *I don't need to impress him. . . . It would be wonderful, though, if You made an impression on Brandon tonight, Lord.*

Joanie looked over at Maggie, who had turned back to her book. She resented the fact that Maggie could read *her* like a book. On the other hand, it was that very intimacy that had made Maggie the cherished friend that she was to Joanie.

Finally, Joanie settled on her light blue dress. It was straight cut and knee length with spaghetti straps, under which she wore a light T-shirt. She fixed her make-up and swept up her hair, leaving loose curls to fall. A few times, she glanced through the mirror back at Maggie to see if her sister was paying attention to her ongoing fussiness. Maggie kept her nose to the book.

When Joanie was almost done, Amie came into the room all ready to go. "What are we waiting for? We should have left five minutes ago!"

Maggie set down her book, got up off the bed, and looked over at Joanie. "We're coming, Amie."

Amie left the room. Maggie walked up to Joanie and glanced in the mirror at her older sister. "You look good, Joanie. I'm sure whoever he is, he'll be impressed!"

Joanie did not have a chance to reply; Maggie had already walked out of the room. Joanie shook off her pride with a little laugh and ran down the hall to catch up to Maggie on the stairs. She looped her arm through Maggie's and said softly, "I'm sorry I snapped at you. Please don't say anything to anybody. I'll explain it all later tonight, okay?"

Maggie nodded, and the two girls headed out to the car where Amie was anxiously waiting to go.

✟   ✟   ✟

St. James Church had begun a music ministry program three years earlier that involved a monthly concert at which *New Spring* often did the opening and closing sets. Overall, the level of talent that these concerts showcased, from youth to adults, was quite remarkable. It was an awesome way to get young people involved in praise and worship and to develop their talents for the Lord. The popularity of *Praise Event*, as it was called, was evidenced by the numbers showing up each month.

The various performers arrived early enough to help with set-up in the basement. With everything in place, the performers were now gathering for prayer, as was their routine. Joanie was just as anxious at the church as she had been at home. No one seemed to be able to get her attention.

"Joanie, get with the program, already. What's with you tonight?" her cousin, Leah, anxiously called over to her. A year younger than Joanie, Leah had always been a close friend. She was a violinist who brought beautiful texture and colour to the music of *New Spring*. She stood eye to eye with Joanie, and shaking her cousin's arms, she continued, "We're on in twenty minutes. Don't you want to pray with the group before the concert begins?"

"Yeah, of course I do," Joanie returned, slowly recovering from her daze.

"Okay, girl, what's on your mind?" This time Leah's tone was firm and demanding. "We can't pull off a concert with your head in the clouds. What's up?"

"Nothing, really." Joanie searched for an explanation but decided against it. "Let's pray." This time her response was full of resolve and

Leah's apprehensions eased. They walked into a side room to join the others.

Joanie was particularly focussed during prayer time, and it did not take long for the anxiety to leave her. Rising from where they had been praying, Joanie thanked Jesus for fortifying her. She had a strong suspicion that tonight was just the beginning of a whole spiritual battle with evil, and she did not mean with Brandon, personally. Joanie was certain that there were very few, if any, prayer warriors in his life going to battle for his soul. She knew it was important for her to be sincere and focussed on Jesus.

Please, Lord, help me set foolish sentiments and emotions aside. Help me to care for Your son, Brandon, as You would have me care for him, my brother.

Leaving the other musicians, Joanie slipped upstairs to the foyer of the church and made her way through the crowd of people coming in for the concert. Several friends tried to get her attention, but she motioned her haste and moved on.

As Joanie got to the front doors of the church, she paused, breathed deeply and opened the door.

Lord, if it's Your will for Brandon to be here, help me to do my part.

Her eyes raced across the church steps and up and down the street. No sign of him. She closed the door and took up a conversation with a friend coming in.

✟   ✟   ✟

Brandon clasped his car keys in his right hand. He was dressed for a typical night on the town: blue jeans and jean jacket and, as always, not a hair out of place. He had no hesitations as he drove off in his Nissan Pathfinder. He headed straight to the address written on his hand.

He was looking forward to tonight. Brandon was attracted to Joanie—she was a good-looking girl. But there was more to it than her looks. He searched his mind to decide what it was about her that had made the conquest of this girl such an obsession for him. Maybe it was the way that she carried herself so gracefully, or the way that she spoke with such confidence, or the way that her eyes dazzled him when she smiled. Maybe it was the fact that she was so resistant to his charms.

He had never faced this kind of a challenge before. Brandon was a ladies' man who had never failed to get a girl on whom he had set his sights. But there was something different about Joanie than about all those other girls and—even more disconcerting—there was something new stirring in him that he had never before experienced.

He glanced down at his hand again and suddenly the name *St. James* jumped out at him. He had read it several times on his hand since his memorable meeting with Joanie that afternoon. Yet all of a sudden the memory of his father, whose name was James, flashed through his mind and stuck like an arrow in his chest.

His father had left Brandon and his mother when Brandon was only eight. Brandon had tried so hard to earn the affection of his dad, and the pain of rejection was one that did not sit easily with him. He now hated his father.

The silver-grey Pathfinder turned the last corner and, as Brandon saw St. James Church at the end of the street, he felt an anger well up inside him that he had forgotten existed.

He had a choice now. What would it be? He was fighting against emotions that were beginning to surface unexpectedly. Was it really worth it to him to go through with this? She was, after all, just a girl. He could head over to *Shooters* and meet up with Mark and the gang and pick up any girl there that he wanted. Instead, he was going to a church on a Friday night? It did not make sense to him at all.

Still, he told himself, as he pulled up to the church, *It's not just any girl. It's Joanie. And she just might be worth it!*

He parked down the street from the church, got out of his vehicle, and walked up to the front doors. There were other people coming in at the same time and he began to experience a certain uneasiness. He held the door open for a group of young girls who smiled shyly and thanked him.

Taking a deep breath, he stepped across the threshold of the church which was an occasion to mark in his mind. The last church he had entered was some fifteen years before, at his grandmother's funeral. Up until now, there had been no reason to go back. Now, there was a girl. . . .

"Joanie!" he exclaimed.

Her presence so interrupted his thoughts that he appeared shocked to see her. "Weren't you expecting to meet me here?" Joanie asked, bewildered.

"Yes—no—I just was thinking about something else." Never before had he found himself stammering for words in front of a girl.

Joanie found it cute to see this awkward side of him. It did not last long, though, for he quickly regained his bold confidence.

His entire demeanour changed. He threw back his shoulders, raked his fingers through his hair, and winked down at Joanie. "So what are we here for, Church-Girl?"

The tone of condescension that he had used at work that day was replaced now with playful affection. It was not lost upon Joanie, and she returned his wink with a smile that lit up the entire church entry.

Brandon was inclined to believe that he would follow this girl anywhere. That was not a familiar feeling. He felt childish in her presence, like a school boy with a crush on his first-grade teacher. *But she never had Joanie's smile—or her legs,* he reminded himself, looking over the elegant figure before him.

Joanie could feel Brandon's eyes on her, and her discomfort became obvious. She struggled to recall his question, then regaining her focus, she replied, "There's a concert. I've got seats for us near the front. Come on," she urged him along to the auditorium in the basement, making their way through the people who were standing around visiting.

"What's the rush? Must be a real hot concert," he mused, sarcasm mingled with his usual confidence.

"Well, that's for you to decide when it's over," Joanie threw back over her shoulder.

He followed Joanie into a row of chairs and sat down. They were not seated for long when she jumped up and said, "If you'll excuse me, I have something I need to do. But I'll be back in a bit."

"Hey, what gives? What kind of date is this?" He caught her arm.

"It isn't a date, Brandon. If it were, you would've had to call and ask my father's permission. And I would've had to tell him to tell you—no!" she returned, in a matter-of-fact tone.

"No?" Brandon was visibly taken aback. "Why not?"

"'Cause you're a perfect heathen, Brandon." She winked back at him and left.

"Well, at least I'm perfect at something," he called after her. She waved over her shoulder without looking back and was soon out of sight.

Great, Brandon sighed. *What the hell am I doing here? Church-Boy!* he mocked himself as he crossed his arms and debated leaving or waiting for Joanie to return. *Permission?* He laughed. *What century is this girl outta anyway?*

Joanie rushed off to join up with *New Spring.* She knew Brandon would have a hard time swallowing the concept of asking her father's permission for taking her on a date, but that was how it was done in their family. The fact was, Joanie really appreciated it. It was sort of the litmus test for suitors. The decent guys had no problem with the concept, even if it did make them nervous. The jerks never bothered, and Joanie was just as glad not to have had to deal with them.

She wondered if Brandon would ever have the nerve, or interest, to go through with that for her. She scolded herself: this was not the time to be thinking about that. She needed to stay focussed on Jesus tonight.

At the front of the auditorium, the MC cleared his throat in the microphone. *Oh, great,* Brandon thought, *some teenage Jesus-freak is going to lead us in prayer no doubt. Where the hell is Joanie, and what am I doing here?* His disgust was visibly set in the furrow of his brow.

"Well, folks, if you'll quickly take your seats, we're about ready to begin. . . ."

The young boy's voice faded from Brandon's ears. His attention was now focussed on what was happening on the stage behind the MC.

That's Joanie up there! Maybe this evening would not turn out to be such a write-off after all. On the other hand, he was still stuck sitting by himself in a church basement, which made him feel awkward enough. Was it worth sticking around? He could slip out now, before Joanie noticed. Still, he was curious to see what she had to show up there. He decided it was probably worth the wait. He could always walk out later if it got too dull.

As the band took their places, he kept his eyes on Joanie who had not once looked his direction. He smiled. That was her style: avoid and conquer. Every time they were together, she avoided his advances and took control of the conversations. In a month's time, he had not figured out how to unlock the mystery of this girl. Maybe tonight would give him some clues.

Distracted in thought, he ignored the commentaries that were being made up front. The music began and all at once a voice, with incredible strength and beauty, caught him by surprise. It was Joanie.

Brandon was completely captivated by the beauty of this girl. He watched in awe as she poured out her heart in song. No woman had ever had an effect on him like Joanie had. She was young, attractive, intelligent, and talented . . . and she was quickly working her way into his heart—a place where no girl had ever before been. That scared him, and he considered heeding the danger sign and getting out of there. But everything about her drew him in, like the rushing waters of a river. He felt himself losing the battle against the undertows of the current, and he really did not have the will to fight back.

Her voice floated through the auditorium as though it had wings. Her hands moved gently before her and then pulled close to her heart. It was clear to see the deep convictions of her soul. Never before had his eyes beheld such dignity and grace in a woman. He sat mesmerized . . . by the girl, by the song, by the moment.

One song flowed into the next. People all around clapped. They joined in singing. They prayed out loud, and they raised their hands. He was a stranger in a very strange land. He felt so awkward that he would have left, but he just couldn't. He remained there, motionless.

When Joanie's band stepped down, she looked over at Brandon for the first time. Brandon's gaze did not move from her. She approached him with his eyes fixed upon her, as though he were looking right through her. It made her feel uneasy, as she sat again beside him.

"Is everything all right, Brandon?" Joanie queried.

There was no response from Brandon. She reached out and placed her hand gently on his right forearm. When he felt the warmth of her hand on his arm, he was drawn out of his deep thought. Bringing to mind her question, he responded in that alluring manner which so characterized him, "Yeah, sure."

As Joanie took her hand away from his arm, Brandon reached out with his left hand and grabbed it back. He held on to it firmly. She did not dare pull it away. The gaze in which he held her was so starkly penetrating that she could scarcely breathe.

Oh, Jesus, help me here. I'm completely inadequate to deal with this man. Joanie realized that she was feeling something inside herself that she had never before experienced with a man: fear. Not fear of him, but fear of losing herself in his eyes. She could not look away. She did not dare move or speak. *Please, Jesus, make the next move for me!* Her prayer was desperate and full.

A smile began to surface on Brandon's face as he looked down at her delicate, soft hand in his, and he chuckled softly. "I guess I should have asked your *pa's* permission for that?"

Joanie's laugh was light, yet full of relief. "Well, there won't be a next time until you do!" she assured him, trying to pull back her hand. He held on firmly.

When he looked back up to meet her eyes, he feared he was on the edge with this girl. He struggled within himself to regain control of the situation. "Well, in that case, I'd better make the most of it."

Resuming his confident posture, he rearranged her left hand into his right hand and turned back toward the concert. He did not look back down at her, afraid of being disarmed again by that curious mixture of confidence and sweetness that she possessed.

I'm going to enjoy this moment, he told himself, feeling somewhat confident of a victory. He knew he had the advantage here. She would never make a scene in this setting, and he was discreet enough in how he was holding her hand so as not to make it obvious to others. This was a silent war between them, and he had won this battle.

Joanie was at an absolute loss for words. She felt her small hand lost in the largeness of his. The strength of his grip was very compelling. She was not sure how to get out of this fix or—for that matter—if she really wanted to get out of it. That worried her the most!

What if her sisters saw her? She was surrounded here by friends and family. She really did not want to make a scene and draw attention to herself with Brandon.

She closed her eyes. The feeling of his hand over hers and the warmth of his arm against her arm, as they sat shoulder to shoulder, was such a new and wonderful experience. She was now the stranger in a strange and wonderful land. Boys had held her hand before, but none of them had ever made her feel like this. She really did not want this moment to end, but her conviction compelled her to do something.

Pray! Yes. Jesus, please help me out here. I'm suddenly down a path I hadn't intended to take, and I need Your direction to get me back on track.

Brandon leaned down to Joanie's ear and whispered, with striking tone, "I'll get even with you yet, Church-Girl!"

Her eyes widened, and she looked up at him, shocked and confused by his words. "What do you mean? Why?"

"You always get your way. You control every conversation we have, and you work your sweet charm over me . . . but not this time. It's my turn to sit in the driver's seat. So squirm all you want, Joanie, but I'm not letting go 'til the fat lady sings!" He winked at her and squeezed her hand just to inform her that he was in control here and not about to relinquish it to her.

Her mouth must have been hanging open, speechless and somewhat in shock. He smiled as he reached up with his left hand and gently touched her chin.

Joanie fixed her jaw firmly then made a stifled noise under her breath. "Well, there is no fat lady here, buddy! This isn't the opera, you know!" Her tone was frustrated. She turned her head in disgust with herself for having given Brandon the satisfaction of seeing her annoyance.

He just chuckled and held on, savouring his victory, satisfied in his smooth recovery, and totally captivated by how much it could mean to him simply to hold hands with a girl. He closed his eyes as though he were taking in the music, but his ears were tuned in to Joanie's breathing.

At first her breaths were heavy and punctuated, but she gradually calmed down and settled in, resigning herself to her fate. She could have kicked herself for having been trapped like this. Yet somehow she was grateful that she could not have seen it coming.

Oh, Jesus, don't let me fail You in my heart. I prayed to You to give me an out and instead You've hardened his heart! Show me what I'm supposed to do now.

Gradually, Joanie's mind drifted away from the situation with Brandon as she joined in singing the song being performed by a high school group. It was one of her favourites. She closed her eyes and focussed her heart on the praise and worship.

As her sweet voice drifted up to his ear, Brandon looked down and once again recognized the same conviction that he had seen in her when she had sung on the stage. There was no showiness to this girl. She simply could not help herself. She was so much in love . . . with Jesus.

The thought lingered in his mind, leaving him to feel like a defeated warrior. How could he be such a fool? He marvelled at her sweet innocence, and he realized there was so much more to her than he could ever begin to fathom.

The song ended and Brandon inclined himself toward Joanie and said, "If you want me to let go of your hand, I will." His tone was sincere.

Joanie looked up into his eyes—they were so blue. There was something about him that, against all her better judgment, drew her in to his charm. Beyond all the arrogant façades, he was sincere and gentle.

Focus, Joanie! Pull yourself together, girl! She smiled sweetly at Brandon and replied, "Yes, please."

"Fine," he said, letting go of her hand with a little squeeze. "But I'm not convinced that you really wanted me to."

He found the way that she bit down on her bottom lip shyly, to be absolutely entreating. *You are such a sweet girl.*

"Well, thank you, anyway," is all she could come up with in response. He was right, and she could not see any advantage in trying to argue with the truth.

Reclining his posture, Brandon crossed his arms over his chest and smiled. . . . He, too, knew that he had been right.

Joanie was about to stand up and join in with the on-going praise, when Brandon addressed her. "You have an incredible voice, and you're absolutely beautiful when you sing."

Still bashful with his attentiveness, Joanie replied, "Thank you."

"You're blushing," he pressed on.

"Well, I wasn't expecting you to say that," she defended herself.

"No," he agreed, glancing around the large room, "that was not the praise for which you were singing. Even a heathen like I am could tell that much."

Joanie laughed. *Oh, Jesus, just touch his heart somehow tonight.*

Brandon looked back at the young woman beside him. Changing his tone he confessed, "You know you really are a mystery to me."

"How so?" she inquired.

"Well, look at you. You're a journalist. I mean, that's such a worldly profession for such an unworldly girl. I don't get it." He sat there, slowly shaking his head, keeping her fixed in his gaze.

"I may be detached from worldliness, but I'm not completely naïve to what's going on around me, Brandon. And I think my detachment allows me to report news far more accurately than those who buy into the secular culture. Anyway, I'm convinced that the news media needs strong Christians to be an influence. And I promise you—I am completely uncompromising when it comes to my morals!"

"Oh, I think I've come to realize that about you!" he returned, rather emphatically. Her point had not been lost on him.

Joanie laughed.

"But don't you find it difficult? Surely you find yourself placed in anti-Christian situations at times. How do you deal with it?" he asked.

"One of the first assignments I did during my internship was at a rock concert in the town where I was stationed, with some start-up band playing. It was awful. There was everything in that music: sex, drugs, and rock-and-roll! I mean it was explicit. And the kids who had come out to the concert were young."

"I guess they weren't there to advertise chastity, eh?" he teased her, thinking back on the first time they had sat and talked together at work. He was so amused by how proudly she carried her religion.

"No. If they were, they did an even worse job at advertising it than you did," she pointedly returned his teasing.

He laughed at her assertion. "So how'd you deal with it?" His manner revealed that he was genuinely interested in what she had to say.

"Actually, my report focussed on the need for parents to educate themselves about what their children are listening to and to train their children to be critical thinkers, not just to go with the flow."

"And," he prompted her on.

"The station got lots of positive calls on that news report. Parents were grateful to have found out what that band was all about. It was a really good experience in the end. And it felt good to have been a positive influence in the community." Joanie smiled, in her sweet way.

"I'm surprised that that many people would really care what their children were listening to," he remarked.

"People care," she asserted. "There are a lot of strong Christians out there. It's secular society that would have us think that morals are a thing of the past. And unfortunately, journalism seems to strongly propagate that view. That's why we need good journalists who are committed to their faith!"

"Like you," he confirmed, duly impressed with her fortitude.

"Well . . . I like to think so," she concurred, smiling rather humbly.

Brandon shook his head, thoughtfully. "More power to you, Church-Girl!"

Joanie laughed and watched as Brandon turned his gaze again to look around the auditorium. People were still singing, some sitting, but most of them standing. The look of praise on people's faces was completely foreign to this man who had avoided church his entire life.

When he looked back to Joanie, she said, "This must seem terribly weird to you."

"You have no idea!" he responded, honestly.

"You know, you don't have to stay, if you don't want to." Joanie regretted having said it, the moment it came out of her mouth.

"Do you wish you hadn't brought me here?" he asked, pointedly.

"No! I'm glad you came," she answered, emphatically. "Do you wish you hadn't come?" Her voice betrayed a certain nervousness.

"No . . . I'm glad I came," he assured her, sitting up tall again. "But if you wanted to leave now, we could go out for a drink or something."

"I can't," she replied, softly.

"Oh, right," he nodded with amusement, "I forgot about that 'permission thing' from Pa."

"Well, yeah," she laughed, knowing he was mocking her, "that . . . and the fact that I still have two songs to sing. My band always closes these concerts."

"Oh, well . . . then I have something worth waiting for." He winked down at her.

Joanie looked up at him severely. "Stop toying with me, Brandon!" Her voice was firm, but not at all threatening.

"What! What did I do?" he asked, defensively.

"You—with your winks and your charm and your flattery—do you think I'm so easily undone, sir? Well, I'm not! So, just remember that!"

Joanie sat, with her arms crossed and her eyes flashing at him.

He met her eyes straight on, not at all backing down. "I bet you're a real feisty woman. Aren't you?" he teased her, in his low, husky voice. "I can just see it in those fiery eyes of yours."

Joanie did not favour his comment with a response. She stood up and joined back in with the singing. She glanced back down at Brandon, and when their eyes met, they both began to laugh. He stood up beside her, but he did not sing.

Brandon watched Joanie out of the corner of his eye. After awhile she became absorbed in the music. She was so beautiful. Yet as he reflected on her more and more, he felt a strange stirring within him. It was an uncomfortable feeling. He could not explain it. He certainly did not understand it. But it left him feeling awkward and hollow inside. He began to feel as though his skin was the only thing holding him together.

Was this the effect Joanie had upon him? Yet talking with her had been so comfortable and easy. Turned back to the concert now, Brandon was beginning to wish he had left. All he could think about was his vehicle parked down the street and how much he wanted to be in it, driving away. He made up his mind to leave as soon as the concert was over.

Joanie excused herself from Brandon to go and finish the last set. There were only two songs, both of them very upbeat. As she sang, Joanie's face was alive, and her eyes seemed to have fire burning in them.

Where does that come from? Brandon wondered in amazement. *That girl has such passion for Jesus.* The thought seemed to stir up that awful churning feeling in the pit of his stomach . . . again. He was ready to leave. He had seen enough—maybe too much. Somehow he sensed he would have a hard time shaking off this experience. It had sunk down way too deep for comfort.

He looked around and recognized on the faces of people all over the auditorium the same love and joy that so characterized Joanie to him. The realization was dawning on him. This was not a "Joanie thing". . . this was a "Jesus thing".

I just don't get it. He stood there like a boy lost in the woods. For the life of him he could not understand why all the fuss over Jesus. What rational, intelligent person would get caught up in this kind of hype? He was grateful for the simplicity of his own life, and he could not wait to get out of there and shake off the uneasiness that he was experiencing.

Joanie met up with Brandon after the concert as he was walking out from his row. He forced a smile and a calm demeanour, not about to allow her to see how easily he had been undone tonight.

"I'm gonna get going," he commented, motioning his head toward the staircase.

"Oh," disappointment was apparent in her voice, "I was hoping to introduce you to the band. We always gather after these concerts for . . .

visiting." She was just about to say, *for juice and cookies.* She grimaced inside, imagining how well that would have been received by Brandon.

"No, thanks," he replied, quite anxiously. "I've got some friends I'm meeting up with at the bar."

Joanie nodded and raised her eyebrows bashfully. "I hope you don't regret having come, Brandon. It was really nice having you here tonight."

She was melting him, like only Joanie could do. He leaned forward to meet her eye to eye. "No regrets," he smiled sincerely. "Thanks for the invitation."

She nodded and smiled back up at him.

"I'll be seeing you around, Church-Girl." He winked down at her, in typical Brandon fashion, and left.

✝   ✝   ✝

As Brandon walked out into the night he felt that inner turmoil grab hold of him with far more force than he could stand. He was grateful to be getting into his vehicle and driving away. He could not bring himself to go out to the bar. The emotions that were stirring within him made him far too uneasy to want to be around anybody. He headed home.

He could not help but bring Joanie's face to mind. Though everything about her drew him in, he found that he was inexplicably overwhelmed by her sweetness and innocence. There was a line—and Brandon was not willing to cross it. The conquest was over and he conceded defeat. Joanie had won his respect.

Chapter 8

Brandon stepped into his condo and threw his keys on the floor by the door. Kicking off his shoes, he walked through the living room and dining area to the small kitchen, opened the fridge and got himself a beer. Home was a welcome refuge after the concert. He was boss—king of the castle—and in control here. Twisting off the beer cap, he looked around the tidy living area.

It was a spacious room that gave evidence all around to Brandon's impeccable taste, from the set of black leather furniture to the marble-surrounded fireplace. Two well-cared-for ivies spread their long tendrils across the ornately carved oak mantle. Directly across from the fireplace sat a reclining rocker, beside which stood an oak end table. On it was an assortment of remote controls for the elaborate entertainment centre which stood to the left of the fireplace.

Brandon walked over to his chair and picked up the remote for the television. He flicked around from channel to channel disinterestedly; however, even that futile activity was better than thinking about Joanie and the concert.

There was an unrest inside of him for which he could not account. Why was he so disturbed? It made no sense to him at all. It had just been a concert, and Joanie was just a girl. So why the emptiness? What was this deep longing that was now stirring within?

After a few restless hours wasted in front of the television, Brandon went to bed. Sleep came surprisingly quickly to him that night. He was exhausted, spent from all the emotions of the evening. Brandon was not the emotional type and he vowed that he would never put himself through anything like that again. No girl was worth that, not even Joanie.

☦   ☦   ☦

By two-thirty in the morning he awoke and Joanie's name seemed to be haunting his every thought. He could not shut her out of his mind. Each time he closed his eyes he saw her sweet face. He heard her voice as though it were floating through his apartment. He felt her soft hand as though it were still resting in his. . . . And he braced himself for one of the most miserable nights of his life.

After an hour and a half of tossing and turning, he called out in desperation, "God, what do you want from me?" The words seemed to bounce off the walls back at him, as he realized, *That was a prayer.*

He had used God's name many times in his life, but never before had it been to pray.

"She's got me praying—I can't believe it," he said out loud.

Then Brandon articulated a series of profanities, as though he could scare off whatever it was that had possessed him to pray in the first place. He heaved a sigh and buried his face in his hands. Sitting at the edge of his bed, Brandon did something that he had not done since his father had walked out on him eighteen years earlier. He wept. Bitterly, he wept!

✝   ✝   ✝

Joanie stood awkwardly in the auditorium of the church after Brandon had left. She was aware that her sisters and friends would be asking her about the handsome stranger with whom she had been sitting. She searched her mind for an explanation of Brandon. It would have helped had she had a better grasp herself of her own feelings. The only thing to which she could compare it was the experience of just having stepped off a ten-ticket ride at the fair. It had been thrilling and fun, but it left her a little dizzy all the same. Still, she knew that she would get right back on it if she could. Her lack of good judgment regarding Brandon was a constant worry to her.

It did not take long before Maggie, Amie, and Leah approached her.

"Who was that man, Joanie?" Leah asked, her eyes still fixed on the door through which Brandon had gone.

Joanie looked up and smiled at the three of them. "Um," she rubbed her forehead with her hand and brought it down to hold on to her miraculous medal, her other arm crossed against her body. "Well, that was Brandon Vaughn."

"*That*—was Brandon Vaughn?" Amie almost yelled it out, her hand pointing toward the staircase. Scolding Joanie, she continued, "In all the times you've talked about him at home, you never once mentioned he looked like that!"

"Yeah? Well, it slipped my mind," Joanie offered as a rather weak defence.

"You're kidding, right?" Amie responded in disbelief.

Maggie looked at Joanie, her eyebrows lifted upward and she began to laugh. To her credit, she did not call Joanie a liar. *So that's the mystery man for whom you fuss? That man has not slipped your mind in the past four weeks, girl, least of all tonight . . . and you know it!*

Joanie squirmed awkwardly, reading Maggie's thoughts as she knew Maggie was reading hers. Their eyes met. She knew Maggie would not make a big deal about it. That was just the thing about Maggie: she was such a noble girl.

"Would someone please just tell me *who* Brandon Vaughn is? I've obviously missed out on something good here," Leah piped in. Her curiosity over the handsome stranger was getting the most of her.

"He's just a commercial producer from the station I've been . . ." *What have I been? How do I explain Brandon?* Joanie smiled shyly over her hesitation. "I've talked to him a number of times at work, and I've mentioned him at home a few times, that's all. He's . . ."

"What was he doing here tonight?" Amie pressed the point.

"I invited him at work today," Joanie explained. "I didn't think he would ever come, so I never mentioned it before the concert."

"But that's why you were so distracted," Leah commented.

"Wouldn't you have been?" Amie asked Leah. They both laughed, then looked back at Joanie.

Joanie rolled her eyes and started to laugh.

"Look, Joanie," Leah went on, "we're not stupid here. What's really going on between you two?"

"Nothing," Joanie grasped for an explanation. "I don't know. Look, he's just some guy who won't leave me alone at work. So I figured I'd give him a good dose of religion to scare him away—which I'm sure it has."

"Why would you want him to leave you alone?" Amie asked, pointedly. Again, she and Leah began to laugh.

"Come on guys, back off. I'm not sure what to make of this whole thing." Joanie rubbed her temples and looked back up at the three girls before her.

"You like him, don't you?" Leah pursued.

Joanie looked at Maggie, knowing Maggie would see through anything Joanie said. "Yes, I like him. Of course, I like him. I'm not blind, you know. But there's more to being interested in a man than his looks. I'm . . . I'm just trying to keep my cool with him. And trust me, it isn't easy."

With the open honesty of Joanie's voice, her three companions backed off.

"Come on," Maggie jumped in to the rescue. Gesturing for the group of them to join with the others, she said, "Let's go get something to eat."

Juice and cookies, perhaps? Joanie mocked herself. She was so relieved that she had not said that in front of Brandon—as he headed out to the bar!

To Joanie's relief her three companions did not bring up Brandon again that night. When others commented on the handsome stranger, Joanie just explained that he was a guy from work who was interested in hearing the music. She actually managed to be quite comfortable with that explanation.

✞   ✞   ✞

As the three girls drove home that night, Joanie asked her sisters not to talk about Brandon at home. She wanted to be the one to bring up the situation first with their mom. Maggie and Amie agreed, sensing that Joanie was really struggling over this guy. Amie found it all to be terribly exciting: a secret romance. Joanie scolded her, saying there was nothing romantic going on between her and Brandon. Amie backed off, hurt by the sharpness of her sister's tone.

When they were going to bed that night, Joanie found Amie alone for a moment and apologized for her rudeness. Amie forgave her and, as they hugged, Joanie thanked her for keeping her confidence.

As the young reporter crawled into bed she began to search out her own feelings. It had been quite a night.

What had she been thinking, bringing Brandon to the concert? Did she truly think she could bring Jesus into his life? She recalled the look on Brandon's face when she had come back to sit with him. Maybe Jesus had really touched Brandon tonight. Or was she just kidding herself because she was attracted to him? She *was* attracted to him; there was no doubt about that.

But was it possible that Brandon could really be interested in her? This guy probably had more girls flocking around him than Joanie could begin to imagine. She must seem so plain and backward to him, obviously not the kind of girl he would bother to date. How could she have let her heart get so caught up with this guy? Still, he had been the one making advances toward her at work. He had decided—on his own—to come out tonight. He was the one who had taken her hand and would not let go.

Her mind drifted back to the concert and the feeling of his hand on hers. She admonished herself for her indiscretion; yet, she would have done it all again, in a heartbeat. She lay in bed, slowly running the fingers of her right hand over her left hand, not wanting to forget the thrill of Brandon's touch.

Spending time with him had been so much fun. In spite of her defensiveness, she had grown to like the way he teased her. She liked the way he looked at her with those piercing blue eyes. She liked all the attention. . . .

Oh, here I go again. Jesus, why do I have such a frail heart? Why do I let it get away on me so easily? Please help me to sort this all out—properly!

Chapter 9

Two-thirty in the morning found Joanie still awake and confused over the events of, not only the evening, but the past four weeks of her life. Joanie could not remember exactly how she ended up there, but she found herself kneeling down by her mother's bedside, softly shaking her mother awake.

"Who's there?" Joanie's mom was no stranger to the night shift, what with eight children and all. In fact, she could slip in and out of bed many times through the night without ever waking her husband. As Judy recognized Joanie's form in the darkness, she motioned for Joanie to meet her in the hall.

Together they slipped down the wide staircase and went into the large living room that opened up at the bottom of the stairs. The soft moonlight streamed in through the large bay window at the front of the house, filling the room with an undisturbed tranquillity. Quietly, they got themselves cozy with a blanket that was on the couch.

Up until now Judy had not pressed Joanie for any information on what had been bothering her. She knew it had something to do with work. Her motherly intuition told her that the commercial producer, of whom Joanie had occasionally spoken, was probably at the centre of it. She had seen a look in Joanie's eyes when she spoke of Brandon that Judy had never before seen on her daughter.

This man had sparked Joanie's interest. It was different than those teenage crushes she had gone through. Judy had wondered when Joanie would finally open up about the situation. She trusted Joanie, and she knew her daughter well. Joanie would come around when she was ready. It did not surprise her mother in the least that it would be the middle of the night when Joanie finally sought out her counsel.

"I'm sorry for waking you up, Mom," Joanie began. Without intending it, tears began welling up in Joanie's eyes, and her voice quavered to a halt.

"It's okay, darling, just have a good cry and then we'll talk." Judy held her daughter in her arms. Minutes passed and finally, equipped with several tissues, Joanie was ready to begin.

She told her mom every detail of her relationship with Brandon. Judy sat and listened attentively, nodding and smiling as Joanie recounted one event after another.

"I'm so confused, Mom. I've never felt this way before, and I hate it! It feels like I have no control over my emotions anymore." Anxiety rang through the young girl's voice.

"Joanie," her mother's tender voice broke through, "you are a young woman now—a beautiful young woman! It was just a matter of time before one of the young men in your life finally caught your attention. I might have preferred it to have been one of the nice boys that you know from church or that you've met through Campus Evangelization. But you never gave those guys any real consideration . . . which is fine. . . . So what is it about Brandon that has got you feeling this way?"

Joanie looked at her mother, shaking her head. "I don't know. He's everything I would have avoided in a man. He's arrogant and conceited. He's got a terrible reputation with women. I mean, why should I even care if I ever see him again? But I do."

"Is he handsome?" Judy asked, rather candidly.

"Mom!" Joanie responded, defensively.

"Is he?" Her mother persisted.

Joanie laughed. "Oh, Mom, he's the most handsome man I've ever seen." Joanie's eyes got a faraway look as she brought Brandon's face to mind. "His eyes are *so* blue. They seem to look right through me."

Judy smiled, knowingly. "And does he have any good qualities, aside from his looks?"

"He's so talented, Mom, at his job. He's amazing. Everyone at the station thinks so," Joanie explained. "And he really seems to be sincere. There's a gentleness about him, once you get past all the teasing."

"Teasing? That has a familiar ring to it," Judy remarked.

"Yeah, well, I guess I shouldn't have taken it out on Zack that night," Joanie reflected, rather meekly.

"I figured there was something behind that little eruption of yours," Judy laughed. "And what about this reputation Brandon has?" she asked, rather soberly.

"All I know is that he's been around, Mom . . . and I know for certain he doesn't practise chastity." Joanie chuckled to herself at the inside joke. But her amusement turned to disgust when she considered the real implication of that statement. "See, this is the thing, Mom. Why don't I just walk away from this situation? He's not my type—and I promise you—I'm not his type!"

Judy laughed. "I'm glad to hear that! Look, Joanie," she went on, compassionately, "you are a dedicated, loving Christian woman. I know your heart. You'd give anything to draw a person closer to Jesus. I've seen this in you for years. Why do you think your music affects people so strongly? It's an inner conviction that you just can't fake, girl! And now you've met a young man whom you'd like to bring to Jesus. But you're confused and worried that your desire to evangelize has somehow been compromised by the attraction you feel toward him."

Joanie nodded.

Her mother went on, "Joanie, who is your heart's desire?"

"Jesus!"

"Of course He is. That hasn't changed. And if you keep Jesus where He belongs, at the centre of your heart and mind, your faith in Him will be justified. He is a loving, faithful God. He cannot turn His heart from you. And He has not turned His heart from Brandon. Just remember, He wants Brandon to know Him, even more than you want Brandon to know Him!

"God brought you and Brandon into each other's lives for a reason. Let God reveal to you what His will is for this relationship. Take time. Pray. And keep all things in their proper order—with Christ at the centre of your life. You won't fail if you do that."

"But, Mom, I feel like I already have failed," Joanie stated.

"Believe me, child, I failed many more times than you have by the time I was your age. I grew up with the dating game. Trial and error dating! I suffered so many broken hearts because I never knew the safety that comes from taking refuge in Jesus' Sacred Heart. I was much older than you before the Lord broke through my dullness and set me on fire with His love. You children have had that fire all along. I am so confident in your virtues, and I have no fear sending you out into the world, dear girl."

"But I keep letting my heart get carried away with Brandon. It's so hard to fight these feelings," Joanie confessed.

"Life isn't easy, Joanie. And relationships can be very challenging. But remember, it was God who designed that attraction between a man and a woman in the first place. He understands it. Ask for His help. I don't know if Brandon is going to become a significant factor in your life or not. You may find in a few weeks from now that you have no interest in him at all."

Joanie acknowledged her mother's words.

Then taking Joanie's hand into her own, Judy asserted, "Listen carefully, Joanie. Do not allow yourself to give over your heart to any man who does not know, love, and serve the Lord with all his heart. You were raised up for this, Joanie. And your heart will never find peace with a man that you are waiting to convert.

"Brandon may or may not be the man for you. Just keep praying to Jesus that God will use you, in any way that He chooses, to be an instrument of His peace in Brandon's life. But—until Brandon's heart is united to our Lord's—you will know for certain that he is not for you. So guard your own heart and do not give it away! You've been bought and paid for at a very dear price—with the Precious Blood of Jesus. You belong to Him. And He will never forsake you. Right?" She mussed Joanie's hair in a playful fashion.

Joanie smiled at her mother through her tear-filled eyes. "Right! Thanks, Mom. I do feel better about everything. I shouldn't have waited so long to come and talk to you," Joanie confessed.

"God's timing is always right," her mother assured her.

"Would you pray with me for Brandon, Mom?" Joanie asked, humbly.

"Of course I will."

Together they prayed for the Lord to touch Brandon's heart and to bring him to Jesus. As they said "Amen" together, Joanie's arms found their way around her mother's neck and she held on, like the child she was in her mother's arms.

✟   ✟   ✟

Joanie's mother had instructed the other children to let Joanie sleep in that morning, since it had been a rough night for her. With a dreaminess that was still hanging over her, Joanie sighed deeply and her eyes flickered opened. Seeing 10:28 on her alarm clock radio, she panicked and shot straight up. All at once it hit her—this was Saturday morning and she was not late for work.

She melted back down into her sheets and nestled herself under the covers. She would never get back to sleep now, but the sensation of her body snuggled up in the smooth sheets was so enticing that she could not resist the temptation to laze in bed. She rarely got the chance to sleep in. This morning it felt particularly good to have this space all to herself and time to think over the events of last evening.

She smiled and sighed, recalling every moment like it were happening all over again. She could still feel Brandon's hand on hers and see his mouth take that curious upturned shape it would get when he knew he had the upper hand. She could smell his cologne. *Wow, does that man ever smell good!* she marvelled to herself.

She knew she was deeply attracted to Brandon in a way that she had never before experienced with any other man. She had known her share of teenage crushes on several guys at church and university, but this was different. Brandon had something about him that was dangerously alluring to Joanie. She worried about that, fearful that she might cave in and compromise her principles. She was committed to their family's model for courtship, and she was certain Brandon would never understand that, at least... not unless he became a Christian. That would change everything. But until then, she would have to hold her heart.

She remembered her talk with her mom through the night. Joanie knew full well that no matter how intrigued she was by Brandon's charms, he might never be for her. She gathered up her resolve and sliding to the bedside for her morning offering, she offered the day to the Lord and prayed for the virtues of fortitude and prudence.

And dear, sweet Jesus, please help me to keep You at the centre of my heart. Help me to love Brandon only as You would have me love him, and to seek out his friendship sincerely. And don't let anyone ever take my heart away from You!

Her conversation with Jesus would have gone on had it not been interrupted by the door crashing open. Zack came racing in with Aaron and Jessie close on his heels. "Joanie, get up! You're supposed to take us to Uncle Jack's and Auntie Karen's today. Hurry! We waited as long as we could!"

Together they bombarded her with the excitement of looking forward to playing with their cousins for the day. The boys pulled on Joanie's arms and legs. Jessie just snuggled up to Joanie, who was still kneeling, and wrapped her arms around her neck to give her a hug.

Finally, Jessie had a chance to talk and, looking Joanie straight in the eyes, she said, "I alweady packed my packpack, and I even have my," she cupped her little hands around Joanie's ear and whispered, "my swimming snowsuit." Joanie laughed to herself that they had never been able to get Jessie to just say "swimsuit".

"What a big girl you are, Jessie," responded Joanie in exaggerated tone. "I guess I'd better hurry." Turning to the boys who had begun a pillow fight in her room, with obvious authority she said, "If you guys don't get out of here, I'll leave you behind and just take Jessie. Now get lost!"

She chased them out, still holding onto Jessie as she closed the door behind them. It was shaping up for a busy day, but Joanie was relieved to have plenty of distractions which, in a family of ten people, were not likely to be in short supply.

Chapter 10

Saturday night was a welcome diversion for Brandon. He was meeting his best friend Mark and Mark's girlfriend, Justine, at *Shooters*. All of their friends hung out there, and Brandon figured he could find someone to help take his mind off Joanie.

He walked into the bar. It was smoky; the music was loud; and the band that was playing tonight was lousy. The room was large, with tables of boisterous people creating a maze through which to walk. Brandon headed to the usual corner where he found Mark, Justine, and a few other friends sitting around talking.

Mark Jacobs was slightly shorter than Brandon, somewhat thinner in build, but very athletic all the same. He was quite a handsome fellow, with his wavy brown hair, green eyes, and a smile that told the world he never intended to stop being a boy. Justine Foster sat beside him, demurely playing with her drink and visiting with a girlfriend.

Justine was blond, blue-eyed, and incontestably beautiful. Her features were perfectly balanced on her delicate face, with cheekbones that drew one's attention immediately to her exquisite, almond-shaped eyes. She could have been a model, but had never pursued such a career. Instead, she worked as a nurse's aide in a care home for the elderly.

Brandon caught the arm of a waitress passing by and politely ordered a lager on tap. She smiled at him and winked. She liked Brandon; he was a regular at the bar and no stranger to many of the workers there. Brandon pulled up between Justine and Ashley, the girl with whom she had been visiting.

"Now, Justine, you've got Mark to keep you company there. Make some room and give a guy a chance here," Brandon said, as he stole his arm around Ashley.

Ashley Wilson was an attractive young woman. She had luxuriously curly, blond hair that shimmered in the low overhead lights of the dimly-lit bar. Her smile was coy and alluring, and she snuggled up to Brandon in a very familiar way.

"Well, stranger, I haven't had the pleasure of an evening with you in awhile," she cooed lightly under his chin.

"Well, then we're due to catch up," Brandon replied, in his most enticing way.

"Hey, I object," spoke out Lyle who had been telling jokes with Mark on the other side of the table. "Why does this guy get to come in here and steal away the girls like that?"

He had directed his question to Ashley who blew him a kiss from across the table, then snuggled up to Brandon all the more.

Lyle turned to Brandon and in good humour continued, "You don't even give the rest of us decent guys a chance, Brandon. Come on, Ashley, Brandon's too foot-loose and fancy-free. Why not take up with someone who'll be around tomorrow?"

Lyle was pleasant looking, fair-haired and clumsily cute. His character was genuinely nice and everyone liked having him around. But next to a ladies' man like Brandon, Lyle did not stand a chance. Girls just lined up and took their turns with Brandon, knowing he would never commit to any serious relationship. It never seemed to bother them, as if somehow his irresistible charm made up for his lack of integrity.

The evening was spent in amusing conversation and coarse laughs, as Mark entertained them all with his never-ending supply of dirty jokes. Finally, as people started to head out, Ashley whispered to Brandon that her roommate was out of town for the weekend and they could go back to her place. Brandon said good-night to Mark and Justine, who were going home to their apartment, and continued on with Ashley. He walked her to her car and told her he would follow her back to her place.

✢   ✢   ✢

As Brandon drove, there was a bad feeling working its way up inside of him. He kept trying to push it back down, refusing to let his mind be distracted from his present pursuit. He turned up the stereo, rolled down his window, and drove on.

Ashley waited by her car to walk in with Brandon. She took him by the hand, and he followed behind, eyeing her shapely form in the shadowy light of the night.

Once they had entered through the front door of the duplex where Ashley lived, Brandon grabbed her arm and pulled her back up to him for a kiss. She laughed at his anxiousness and complied. Pulling on his belt loops, she began to lead him down the hallway to her bedroom.

In spite of his best efforts to keep his mind focussed, Brandon was still fighting an interior battle, and the alluring young woman soon sensed his detachment. She pulled herself back slightly from his embrace and, enticing him with her eyes, she taunted, "What's the problem, Big Boy? It's not like you have to get permission, you know."

With that Brandon reached out and caught both of Ashley's hands in his own and stopped her from going any further.

She was startled. "What are you doing, Brandon?"

He just stood there—dumbfounded. With her off-handed comment, Ashley had unlatched the floodgate that had been holding Joanie back from Brandon's mind. Now Joanie's name, her face, her voice, her smile, her touch was invading his entire being.

He felt dirty and low being here with Ashley. He was not sure why, but he had the unaccountable feeling that he was cheating on Joanie. As absurd as that was to him, he just could not go on.

"I'm sorry, Ashley, but I can't tonight. It wouldn't be fair to you or . . . to anyone," he awkwardly tried to explain, as he stood back from the rejected girl.

Ashley made a motion to approach Brandon, but he put up his hand in a way that told her to stay back. He apologized again for everything, turned and walked out, closing the door behind him as he went.

✠   ✠   ✠

Brandon had never walked out on a woman before. This was all so strange to him; he could not begin to search for an explanation. All he knew was that Joanie was at the heart of it. That was it: the heart. No girl had ever found her way into Brandon's heart before. The emotions were completely overwhelming to him.

He got into his vehicle, drove in the clutch with deliberate force, revved up the engine, and drove off. He headed to the outskirts of town, off the west side of the city, got onto the divided highway, and drove. He drove for over ten minutes before he ever began to wonder where he was going. It made no difference to him; he needed to clear his mind. So with radio blaring and windows rolled down, he blazed a trail into the night.

When the police lights began to flash, Brandon looked down at the speedometer and realized that he was doing one hundred thirty-five kilometres an hour. He braced himself for the officer and hoped against hope that he was not over the legal limit.

The officer asked for license and registration, and Brandon complied respectfully. He just kept thinking to himself, while the officer was off checking things out in the cruiser, *This is what I get for allowing a girl into my heart. I should have stayed away from her the minute I saw her praying.* He sat there, shaking his head in disgust with himself.

The officer finally returned and, flashing his light toward Brandon, he asked with a light but animated Irish accent, "You're a friend of Joanie Collins, aren't you now?"

Brandon was so taken aback that he hardly knew what to answer. "Yes, sir. Uh, why do you ask?"

"It's just I was sure I had seen you before. It was at the *Praise Event* last night at St. James. You were sitting with Joanie. We go to the same church, you know. My youngest daughter was singing at the concert, so I went along. I sat just a few rows back from you. The name is Douglas O'Neill. I've known Joanie's family since I first arrived from Ireland sixteen years back. Lovely girl, isn't she?" His manner was friendly and sincere. Brandon could not believe his ears.

Brandon looked at the officer, guessing him to be in his mid-fifties. "Yes, sir, she certainly is a lovely girl. I'm aware of that."

The officer laughed jovially and added, "I bet you are, Brandon. You know I'm going to let you off here tonight with just a warnin'. Any friend o' Joanie's is a friend o' mine. But let me offer you a bit of advice. You'd do well to slow down. Flyin' through life at that speed, you're bound to get yourself into real trouble!" He handed Brandon's papers back to him and looked him squarely in the eyes and said, thickening his accent, "You be sure to be thankin' Joanie for savin' ya here tonight!"

"Yes, sir," Brandon nodded, respectfully. He thanked the officer for the break and wished him a good-night.

As Brandon rolled up his window, he began to laugh. He could not help himself from speaking out loud, "Okay, Joanie, I'm impressed with you or your God or something. I'm not sure who to be thankin'," he imitated Officer O'Neill's accent, "but thanks for savin' me here tonight!"

He headed home and to bed.

Chapter 11

Joanie was not quite sure what to expect Monday morning, but she braced herself over and over in prayer as she rode the bus to work. Each step seemed to be a prayer for Brandon and a prayer for her to be able to guard her own heart. She waited and watched anxiously for the handsome commercial producer at each coffee and lunch break, but there was no sign of him. There was nothing unusual in that, since he did not make it to the staff lounge everyday anyway. Still, her disappointment getting on the bus that afternoon was heavy.

Pray, she urged herself on.

Staying focussed on her work was not difficult at all. Preparing for morning conferences, making a day file, booking appointments, going out on shoots, viewing, writing, shot listing, editing, laying down voice tracks . . . the job demanded her to be mentally sharp all the time. She worked hard each day until the assignment was done.

Her favourite part was going out on location. There was never a dull moment with Paul, and it seemed he was the camera technician with whom she usually went. They had great conversations as they drove around together. Joanie appreciated his humour and his skill as a cameraman.

One afternoon, as they were driving back to the station following a shoot, Paul made an unusual remark. "I don't know what's happened to our friend, Brandon Vaughn, but something's sure gotten under his skin lately."

"What do you mean?" Joanie asked, not sure if she should betray her personal interest, yet her burning curiosity would not allow her to hold back from inquiring.

Paul glanced over at the young journalist. She had taken the bait. He had a strong inclination that he knew exactly what, or rather who, had gotten under Brandon's skin. "Well," he began, "he's been pretty grouchy these past few days. He's impatient with everyone. I've never seen Brandon chew anyone out, before today—that was a first."

"What do you suppose is his problem?" Joanie asked, hesitantly.

"There's something on his mind. Brandon's not the kind of guy to let his personal life interfere with work, but . . . I'd say he's got some problems in love-land." Paul laughed.

"Oh . . ." Joanie's voice faded, and her manner became detached. She looked out the window as Paul drove. She had absolutely no interest in Brandon's love life!

"Yeah, I'd say Brandon has come up against his match. If my intuition is right, I would guess he's met someone who's made him think twice about his life. I don't know—I could be completely wrong here, too—but I think

Brandon Vaughn might just have a heart under all that macho façade!"
Paul did not look over at Joanie.

Joanie did not make any further inquiries. She was far too confused in
her own mind to make any sense out of what Paul had been saying. Still,
something in her heart stirred her to a sense of hope. *Maybe, just maybe,
that somebody who's got Brandon thinking twice, is Jesus.*

✛   ✛   ✛

With Paul's new information, it was even harder for Joanie to get
Brandon off her mind. Still, she had her job to do, and she was not prepared
to compromise it over a man—no matter how blue his eyes were. Her reports
were airing just about every day. Her younger siblings were thrilled each
time they saw Joanie on television. Her sense of accomplishment at work
was greatly boosted by the enthusiastic support of the other journalists.
Sure, they were just making a big deal about it because she was the new
kid on the scene. But all the attention felt good, just the same.

By the end of the second week, Joanie was convinced that Brandon was
avoiding her, but she was beginning to take comfort in the thought that
perhaps this was God's answer to her prayers. Maybe this was how He
was guarding her tender and oh-so-green heart.

Paul had never mentioned Brandon again to her. Maybe Paul had
been all wrong in his assumptions. She could not place too much value
on his comments. Still, she wanted to believe something had happened
to Brandon. She wanted to believe God was working on his heart. She
just had to keep handing the situation over in prayer, each time her heart
pulled her that way.

To the onlooker, nothing seemed unusual about Joanie. She carried on with
her cheerful and sociable ways. Work was really exciting. Joanie loved all the
challenges that each assignment presented. The routines of the newsroom,
both in work and in socializing, had become second nature to Joanie. And
both Shelly and Mr. Lemay had expressed real satisfaction with her work.

So detached had her emotions become regarding Brandon that on the
Friday of the third week when she ran into him on the staircase, Joanie
was caught completely by surprise.

"Brandon," she blurted out, "what are you doing here?"

"I've got a meeting with Mr. Lemay, and his office is on the fourth floor,"
Brandon pointed up and proceeded on course.

"Wait, Brandon, please," Joanie begged in a hushed voice, not to attract attention to them as other workers passed by on the stairs. "I'd like to talk to you."

He stopped in his tracks. As he turned to face Joanie, the look in his eyes was so vacant of emotion it caused her to shudder. He stepped back down until he stood just above her on the stairs. His voice was hushed and bore a tone of severity.

"Look, Joanie, there's nothing to talk about. I thought you would have gotten that message by now. I'm not interested. I'm back to where I was when this whole thing began. And you—you are just another pretty face to pass by on the stairs. That's it—the end of the story. Move on to the next chapter, little girl." And with that, he turned and went on his way.

The tone of his voice sent a chill through Joanie. She had been prepared to deal with his usual coolness, but this was cold! Reclaiming her dignity, feeling as though it had been stripped from her, she turned to go back down the stairs, still stunned by the verbal assault.

Pray, she told herself. *This is not about you, 'little-girl',* his cold tone echoed in her mind, *this is about Brandon—and a battle for his soul.*

✟   ✟   ✟

When Joanie arrived home that afternoon she went straight out to the workshop in their garage in search of her father. She was relieved to find him alone, at work on a project. This was a rare find, indeed, for often there was at least one of her siblings out there working alongside him.

As she entered the tidy shop she paused and reached out her hand to touch the picture of St. Joseph that hung on the wall by the door. It was an old print that her mother had from childhood. Tattered and torn, Judy could not bring herself to part with it. The image was very compelling of St. Joseph, leaning to the side with his elbow on the table. He was instructing the young Jesus who was working with a tool and a piece of wood. Judy had framed it and placed it in the workshop—an appropriate place—with a prayer to St. Joseph the Carpenter for the protection of all who would enter there.

Joanie stood back for awhile and watched her father at work. She was intrigued by his skill and creativity, but what fascinated Joanie most was that her father always knew what tool was needed for each job. "Any job is easier when you're using the right tool," he would tell his children.

Maybe that was why Joanie had come to him for advice on Brandon. She just had no idea what tool she needed to deal with this situation.

Without looking up from his work, her father addressed her, "What's up, Sweet Pea?" He had called her this since she was a baby.

Joanie described her conversation with Paul a few weeks earlier and then her encounter with Brandon that day. What could possibly be at the root of such coldness? She was at a loss to know how to react.

"It seems to me as though that young man got more than he ever bargained for when he went out to the concert that night," her father commented, as though he were announcing the weather forecast for the day.

"Could you explain what you mean, Dad?" Joanie just wanted something a little more tangible than that.

"Can't you see, honey?" He looked up from his work, his hands never pausing. "I'm convinced something happened to Brandon there that night. He met God. But everything changes in your life when that happens. You don't see anything the same as you did before.

"I suspect that boy's done a lot of living, the kind that blinds you to truth. So now where does he go? He's lost control because, the truth is, he never really was in control. That was an illusion. He can't turn back, and he's afraid to move on. See, Satan fills us with the lie that if we give ourselves over to God, we'll be trapped in misery. Yet the truth is—and you know it—living according to God's laws sets you free. Fear can never hold you in its grip again.

"But until a man has tasted the freedom of living as a child of God, he'll clasp on to the lies and the fears. It seems to me that right now Brandon is trapped somewhere between fear and faith. It's a good sign, Sweet Pea; it means that something's happening. And it's much bigger than you can imagine."

He stopped his work and stretched out his arms to release the tightness in his back, gesturing for Joanie to come for a hug. As he wrapped his big arms around her, he continued with a new thought, "I have to say that, in rejecting you, Brandon has demonstrated real character—something impressive to me."

Joanie pulled back her head and looked up at her father as if to say, *Are you insane?*

"Think about it, Sweet Pea. Brandon knows he's not worthy of you—and he's not!" John tapped the end of her nose with his finger. "You deserve better than him, and he sees that. It shows integrity. Now just hear me out," he interrupted the beginning signs of her protest. "I'm not saying he'd never be good enough. In fact, it may just be that Brandon will turn out to be a very fine Christian man someday. And who knows? Maybe the Lord will bring the two of you together. If that happens, I'm sure I'd give you both my blessing.

"But for now, I suspect that Brandon is just waking up to his own sinfulness. And what road to conversion does not begin there? If we never recognized our own weaknesses and sinful tendencies, what need would we have for a saviour?"

He paused and silence filled the space around them—like a punctuation mark to his assertion. After a moment he squeezed her gently and turned back to his work. He lifted his hand, gesturing a motion toward heaven. Without looking back up at her he added, "Remember, Sweet Pea, Father knows best!"

Joanie knew he was referring to their Heavenly Father, and as she closed the garage door behind her, she prayed: *Dear Father in heaven, I commend Brandon to You, in all his struggles. I know You love him and desire this son to come home.*

Then, as a matter of closure, she added, *St. Joseph, protect Brandon and guide him as you once did the child Jesus.*

At that, courage surged up within Joanie and she headed into the house to act upon an inspiration before she lost her nerve.

☦   ☦   ☦

Meeting up with Joanie that afternoon at work was something on which Brandon had not counted. In fact, he had been avoiding it for three weeks. How could he have been so clumsy?

He thought back to a conversation he had had with Paul two weeks earlier in his office. Brandon had been in a terrible mood that day. Paul, wise to Brandon, made some inquiries. "So what's on your mind, Brandon?"

"Nothing I care to discuss," Brandon brushed off his friendly coworker.

"No problem. I've just noticed that you've been awfully testy lately," Paul observed.

Brandon grunted a response and turned in his chair to face his computer.

Paul went on. "It's sure nice to see how well Joanie's been doing with her news reports, isn't it?"

Abruptly turning in his chair to face Paul, Brandon shot a look of confused annoyance at his colleague. "Now why would you mention her? What the hell would I care what she's been up to?" Brandon snapped at Paul, consumed so much in his own frustration that he was not aware of how defensive he was being.

"Need I remind you that *you* were the one who had been interested in her in the first place?" Paul was pushing, but he was not quite sure how far he could go with this. "Have you lost interest so quickly?"

"You were right," Brandon returned, fidgeting with a pen, not looking up at Paul. Paul stood back comfortably with his arms crossed, leaning against a wall.

"Right about what?" Paul asked.

"She's too religious for me. Who needs that headache?" Brandon eased back into his chair and put his elbows on the armrests. "You know, I can't get over how some people can put some unseen, make-believe, fairy-tale figure, like God, at the centre of their lives. It just boggles my mind. Why not live in the real world? Why give your heart and soul over for an idea?" Aware that he had suddenly become rather introspective, he shook his head and looked up at Paul with a more casual demeanour. "It's too bad. What a waste of a great set of legs!" This time he laughed, and Paul laughed with him.

"Probably for the best there, buddy," Paul said. "You wouldn't want to get yourself caught up with any girl who would make you think twice about that hedonistic lifestyle you cling to so dearly!"

Brandon chuckled with Paul, but he was not entirely sure that Paul was not laughing at him. He had a strong feeling that Paul was reading his mind far more clearly than he was himself! Paul left the office, but his statement haunted Brandon for a long time.

✟   ✟   ✟

Brandon's thoughts returned to that afternoon and the meeting with Mr. Lemay. In all honesty, Brandon knew that he was lucky to still have a job. He could not account to Mr. Lemay for the careless mistakes which had been showing up in his work. All he could offer was a firm resolve to make sure they did not happen anymore. It was such a blow to Brandon's pride. He was a perfectionist and had always demonstrated excellence on the job.

It was bad enough that Brandon's social life had screeched to a halt since *that* night, but to let this situation now worm its way into his work was just the final blow.

Joanie had caught the brunt of that. Brandon felt bad now, but he figured he should leave well enough alone. She was better off seeing him for the jerk that he really was and moving on with her life. Maybe hurting her, he convinced himself, was the best thing for her.

She'll get over a guy like me, no problem. The question is—will I get over a girl like her?

✝   ✝   ✝

Brandon cringed upon entering his apartment that evening. He had never been a slob. He liked his world neat and orderly; yet since that night, his whole life had become a shambles. What he saw before his eyes, in terms of mess, was nothing compared to the hurricane that had swept through the inside of him.

He slammed down his keys and glared at the answering machine with eight messages. "Why do they bother? Every Friday night it's the same thing. Can't they take a hint? I'm not interested. Go party with someone who cares! I couldn't stand to be around anyone having a good time."

The annoyance in his voice was directed at the answering machine, which mutely flashed back at him: 8 . . . 8 . . . 8 . . . 8 . . .

"Agh!" He shook his hand over it, before absent-mindedly turning on *play* as he walked off to the kitchen. He came back into the room with a beer in hand and sucked back on the bottle, deep and hard.

As he heard the voices on the machine, one by one he skipped on to the next message. There was Ashley, Mark, Lyle, Mark again, Tracey, Mark again, and—"Joanie!" Her name flew out past his lips.

His heart skipped a beat and he backed up the machine. It was the last voice he had ever expected to hear, and yet he knew it without a doubt. Falling back into his armchair, he listened, then hit repeat, and listened again. Three times he repeated this process before he finally turned off the whole machine.

That feeling—which had become all-too-familiar to him—now returned in full force. It was churning in his gut like an insatiable hunger, a deep longing.

Yet Joanie's voice had been so clear and calm, not the slightest hint of anger or hurt could he detect: "Brandon, it's Joanie. . . . I just want to say that it seems to me you might be needing a friend right about now. And without being pushy, I want you to know that I . . . I really want to be your friend. And I'm here, if you want to talk. . . . I'll be around all evening. So if you get this message, you can reach me at eight two eight, ninety-one nineteen. I . . . I hope you call."

Brandon picked up his handset and as he scrolled through the call display he saw her number: 828-9119. "Nine-One-One?" his voice trailed off in disbelief. "This girl's got a 'Nine-One-One' number? I don't believe it! No, I do believe it—Joanie's 'Nine-One-One Rescue the Lost Sinner Emergency Line'!"

As he muttered on, his fingers proceeded to dial the number before his eyes. Before he was aware of what he had done, he heard a man's voice on the other end: "Hello. . . . Hello?"

"Hello, sir," Brandon panicked for words—this was Joanie's father. "I was wondering . . . could I please speak with Joanie Collins?"

There was a brief hesitation on the other end. Brandon wanted to hang up. "Yes, you may. Just a moment, please."

Brandon could hear the muffled sound of Joanie's father calling her. As Brandon waited for her to pick up the line, it occurred to him: *I just asked her father's permission to speak with her. I can't believe it—she wins every time!*

His amazement was interrupted by the sound of her sweet voice in his ear. "Hello. . . . Hello . . . Brandon? Is that you?"

He was speechless. What would he say? He didn't even know why he had called. "Uh, yeah, Joanie . . . listen, I'm sorry for earlier—"

"Brandon, forget it," she cut him off. "I'm just so grateful you called. Will you meet me for coffee?"

"Sure. When?" He would have said anything to get off the phone.

"Tonight at seven-thirty, at *Doug's Donuts* on Main. I'll meet you there."

"Don't I need to get your father's permission here?"

His tone was hard to interpret, but Joanie suspected he was sincere in asking. "No, I'll smudge it over with him this time, Brandon." She deliberately emphasized *this* and gave a little giggle. "Seven-thirty at *Doug's*—I'll be there."

Her tone was emphatic. The kind of tone that made Brandon certain he would be there, too.

Chapter 12

Without hesitation, Joanie, Maggie, and Amie, began to clear the dining room table and tackle the job of kitchen duty following supper. The large island and counter of the remodelled kitchen were cluttered with the evidence of meal preparation and the many dishes used to feed a regiment of their size.

Judy approached Joanie, took the dishrag from her hand, and said, "Go! Isaac can do this job."

"But I don't have to be there for another hour and a half," Joanie informed her mother.

"Not there. Go spend some time in prayer before you meet with him. What warrior enters the battlefield without armour? The church is on the way. You can take the keys and stop in to visit the Blessed Sacrament for awhile before you head over to *Doug's Donuts*." Her mother smiled and motioned her head toward the door. "Go, sweetheart. You'll be glad you did."

"But be home by eleven-thirty." Her father's voice came up over his newspaper, across the room.

"Daddy!" Joanie's voice carried a certain indignation to it.

Her father looked over his paper, squarely into Joanie's eyes. "I love you, and I trust you. But you will be back here by eleven-thirty because I do love you, and I do not know this man!"

Joanie knew better than to argue. She really had not even considered that she would be that late. If past experience indicated anything, Brandon would be walking out on her long before that. She might be twenty-two years old, but she was still living under her parents' roof. And she loved them for giving her guidelines. She would honour them with her obedience. She headed upstairs to get ready to go.

Joanie debated changing her clothes, but decided to stay in her blue jeans and red T-shirt. She brushed out her hair, leaving it down, fixed her make-up, and put on some earrings.

Katie was across the room watching Joanie as she fussed in front of the large dresser mirror.

"Is he really as handsome as Amie says?" Katie asked, dreamily.

"Yes, but that's not why I'm going out to meet him, Katie, so don't go filling your head with all sorts of romantic notions. He needs a friend, and more importantly, he needs Jesus! Why don't you say a prayer for him?"

She had been speaking to Katie through the reflection in the mirror. Turning to look directly at her younger sister, she smiled, and added humbly, "And you can say a prayer for me, too—because he is incredibly handsome, and I don't want to let that distract me from what's really important here."

She walked across the large bedroom to Katie who was lying on her bed. Joanie affectionately mussed up the thick, dark hair of her younger sister and thanked her in advance.

Katie got up off the bed and, straightening her hair, she followed her older sister down the stairs. Joanie entered the dining room and kissed her father who was still sitting reading the paper. "Bye, Daddy. I'll see you *before* eleven-thirty," she assured him.

He smiled, looked up, and wished her well as he kissed her on the cheek.

Her mother followed her to the door, as did her three youngest siblings. Joanie knew the good-bye rituals well and lovingly said good-night and gave hugs and kisses to all.

As she left, her mother's eyes told her that she would be praying for Joanie and Brandon. Joanie took comfort and courage in that.

✝   ✝   ✝

Brandon drove around for quite a long time. He needed space to think, and he found his apartment way too depressing. He was a rack of nerves. He really had no idea why he was going. He kept wondering to himself if Joanie really thought that he had no friends. But since he had shut everyone out of his life for the past three weeks, maybe she was right.

He futilely tried to sort out what had become of his life. He just could not put it all together. All he knew was that this emptiness and longing within him had become so much a part of who he was now, he was willing to do anything to try to free himself from it.

The thought that kept haunting him was the same which had so disarmed him the night of the concert. *Joanie really is in love with Him. I can't even imagine what that must be like. . . . Jesus.* The name was foreign and uncomfortable in his mind because he had never used it before, except to swear.

How could anybody love someone they've never seen? Yet as Brandon fixed his mind on the memory of Joanie, singing song after song to Jesus, he knew she was not making it up. It was real. She was in love with a real person, and her every movement and expression gave testimony to how real He was to her.

But I just can't see how. How do you get from being here to there? The leap seemed to be impossible. Brandon just could not wrap his mind around it. *It isn't rational. It . . . it's crazy!*

An anger unexpectedly began to well up in Brandon. It gripped his mind, and he in turn gripped the steering wheel until his knuckles turned white.

"I hate her for it. She's making me absolutely crazy! How could I have let anyone get under my skin like this?" He spoke out loud, clenching his teeth, the disdain and anger strangling his voice in his throat. He could not form his thoughts beyond this point. His anger was too consuming.

As he drove on for a few blocks, he noticed his speedometer and slowed down. The thought of Officer O'Neill and his accented advice brought a flicker of amusement to Brandon's mind. His anger quickly began to subside.

He laughed and turned his car toward the doughnut shop. "I guess I still owe Joanie a debt of gratitude," he mused aloud.

It was precisely seven-thirty when he pulled into the parking lot at *Doug's Donuts*. He could not decide. *Do I go in? Do I leave?*

Though his anger had cooled, his composure had been weakened by the inner turmoil. He hated being vulnerable. It was new territory for Brandon, although it certainly was becoming familiar enough for him when he was around Joanie. What was it about her that turned him into some weak-kneed, fumbling fool?

He pushed himself up from the steering wheel where he had been leaning and saw Joanie walking toward the doughnut shop. She had not seen him, he was certain, or she would have sought him out.

Her long chestnut hair fell in loose curls over her shoulders. Her movement with each step was confident and poised; he could only compare it to that of a dancer. Her beauty struck Brandon in a way that he could not explain. She was so much more than pretty. She sparkled and shone as though there was something illuminating her from within.

With a sigh of resignation, Brandon stepped out of the Pathfinder and headed toward the doughnut shop. He had to go through with this; he just was not sure why.

☩　　　☩　　　☩

Brandon walked into the doughnut shop and looked around for Joanie. He spotted her sitting in a booth in the corner of the quiet shop, with her hands wrapped around a cappuccino.

She had ordered the drink when she walked in, but she was certain she would not be able to drink it; it was just there for security. Nervous though she was, her body language did not betray her. Experience as a performer and journalist had equipped her with skills to hide her anxiety.

Her face brightened at the sight of him, and a warm and friendly smile lifted from the corners of her mouth. Brandon could feel himself being drawn into Joanie's simple charm; he had no will to resist. Without ordering anything to drink, he came over and took a seat across from her.

Her deep-brown eyes met his piercing blue eyes. There was something there between them, an energy that they both felt. This was new territory for both Brandon and Joanie, for neither one of them had ever felt drawn to the heart of another person. They sat for a few moments, neither of them knowing how to break the silence.

Please, Jesus, give me Your words, was the prayer Joanie kept repeating in her heart.

Joanie's eyes closed, and she began to speak, but she really was not sure from one word to the next what she would be saying. It was steady; it was calm. As she lifted her eyes to face Brandon, she could see he was listening, and his look urged her on.

"I've never really known anyone like you before, Brandon, and I suspect the experience is mutual. I feel like we're on battleships from two different worlds, and we just keep colliding. But I don't want to be at war with you. I want to work out a peace treaty of some kind. I just think that there's so much more to be gained for both of us to be fighting on the same side."

"That means one of us will have to be conquered," his voice calmly returned her analogy.

"Well, no . . . I mean . . . it was a poor analogy." She struggled with the incertitude she was experiencing in dealing with Brandon.

"No, I think the analogy was perfect." He leaned forward across the table and met her, eye to eye. "Do you have any idea what kind of life I have led?"

It struck Joanie as significant that Brandon had separated himself from his past. She did not want to stop him, so she took the question as rhetorical and waited.

"I'm a lone wolf, Joanie. I've learned to survive by looking out for number one. I've never really cared about anyone. I've never loved a girl—but I've been with more than I could ever name. And I've gotten along just fine—no commitments, no obligations, no worries."

That's not exactly true, he thought to himself. After all, since the night he had walked out on Ashley, he had suddenly become concerned about the risk of STDs in his life. He had gone for testing that following week. Blood tests and swabs—it was not a pretty procedure. There was something so grossly humiliating in having to be tested to find out just how dirty you had become.

So far, all of the tests had come back clear. But he had been advised to come back for regular testing over the next few months. Some of these things could take awhile to show up in the testing. From his last potential risk of contact, it would take up to three months before an HIV antibody test would show positive. Even after he had been treated for Chlamydia two years back, he still had never taken to heart how much his lifestyle was not worry-free.

Now, suddenly the innocence of this girl had him questioning everything. He could not bring himself to live that lifestyle anymore. For the first time in his life he was being tortured by his own conscience. He looked back up at Joanie's eyes: they were such a deep, dark brown and so animated. There was a pureness about her that left him in awe.

Had he an ounce of manhood within him, he would have walked out now and left her for a decent man: one of those church-boys he had seen there at the concert. Surely Joanie's beauty had struck them before now. This girl could have whomever she wanted. *I'm sure none of those guys are worried about sexually transmitted diseases.*

But Brandon had become completely captivated by Joanie and everything she represented in his life. That emptiness and deep longing seemed less threatening to him as he sat here with her. He could not pull himself away from her presence.

Joanie waited patiently. She could feel Brandon's penetrating gaze, and she wondered if he would continue talking or not. Finally he did go on, rather sheepishly.

"All of a sudden I'm faced with you, and my whole world has turned upside down. I can't stand who—or what—I am anymore. . . . I feel like I'm going crazy." Brandon's voice trailed off.

He closed his eyes and sank his forehead into his hands; his elbows were firmly planted on the table. There was no way he could begin to communicate to this girl the disgust and contempt with which he held himself. A shudder ran through him that made Joanie start.

She reached over with both hands and gently caressed his arms with her delicate fingers. The warmth and softness of her touch had an effect on Brandon that he could not understand. The simplest of gestures from her seemed so overwhelming to him. It was like there was an energy in this girl that flowed out of her and right through him. He sat there, lost in her touch. Soon the intensity of the previous moment subsided.

It was not until Brandon opened his eyes and looked down at her hands that Joanie realized how seemingly bold that gesture had been. It was such an instinctive response, yet she now felt awkward and embarrassed.

As she began to pull back, Brandon reached down and smoothly drew her hands into his own, pulling her towards him. Joanie was forced to lean on her elbows in order to keep her balance. She could not believe that twice she had allowed this situation to evolve: first at the concert and now here.

Her heart pounded, and her mind raced. Why did every encounter with Brandon seem to bring her into this new realm of emotions? She was a strong and self-disciplined young woman. She was not accustomed to having emotions run away with her. With the skill of a rider reining in a run-away, Joanie fixed her heart on Jesus and prayed.

Help me hold my heart, Lord, so I don't get lost in these feelings for Brandon. Help me to lead him to You. Let me see and think clearly and love purely.

Brandon's motion to hold Joanie's hands had simply been a reaction, but now he could see in Joanie's eyes the discomfort of the situation. As much as he wanted to keep those precious hands in his own, he could not bring himself to force the situation any further. He gently lay her hands back down on the table and offered a sincere apology.

She wrapped her hands around her coffee cup and gave him an affectionate smile. She reflected over the fact that he was much more selfless and caring than he realized. It was in him, she just was not sure how to make him see it or believe it.

"Brandon, nothing you could tell me about your past could ever convince me that you are no good. I know the value of every person and you are no exception. And pardon me for getting religious on you, but God just doesn't make junk."

Her manner was so matter-of-fact and unpretentious. He wanted her to go on, because everything within him wanted what she was saying to be true.

"I know you think I'm some inexperienced kid that just fell off the apple cart. And you'd be right in thinking that." She smiled up at him sweetly. "But I'd bet my bottom dollar that I have a much bigger picture of reality than you do. Your reality ends where you can no longer see or understand something. My reality begins there.

"Faith is so much bigger than we are that it can only come as a gift from God. There's no explaining it. If I could talk you into faith, someone else would come along and talk you out of it. But having faith changes everything, Brandon.

"I'm sure your life has been filled with one pleasure-seeking thrill after another. But pleasure is not a goal to be pursued. It's empty, in and of itself. I've had my share of pleasures in my life—although I'm quite sure they're of a different variety than what you've experienced. But pleasure comes as a bonus to many things. My life in Christ has so much more than mere pleasure.

"It's full and rich and each moment offers the promise of something new and exciting. It's a wonderful adventure, filled with joys and sufferings, successes and even failures. But each experience is real. It has meaning, and it moves me forward to the real purpose of my existence.

"We were not created for this world, but for something so great and wonderful and . . . unattainable . . . except through Jesus. He transforms it all because He calls us to join Him in a new life. And Brandon, believe me, once you've had a taste of that new life, you won't ever want to go back to your old ways."

Brandon mused at the fact that already he could not go back to his old ways. But now what? There had to be something better than this emotional limbo in which he now found himself living.

Joanie had paused to give Brandon a chance to respond. He was silent. As she searched his eyes, she could see that he knew what she was saying was true, but he was not able to believe it—at least, not yet.

She continued, slowly but firmly.

"When I look at you I can't help but see a wonderful and cherished soul that is lost. I see in you an amazing young man whose tenderness breaks through that tough façade at times you least expect. A fearful man, who would rather take control of every situation in life than to run the risk of being hurt. A lonely man, whose talents and time have been wasted on meaningless pursuits—because worldly pleasures cannot satisfy the real emptiness that's inside of you.

"That emptiness is there for a reason. There's something, or rather Some-one, who wants to fill it for you. But He can't come in uninvited. So you have a choice, Brandon. You can go back to your miserable little world and ignore the real longings of your heart. Or, you can take the risk of placing God in control of your life and discovering who you really were meant to be."

Brandon shifted uneasily in his chair, but he did not say a thing. He was feeling the challenge she set before him. He looked up to meet her eyes confidently, bracing himself for her to continue.

"I know you saw something the night of the concert, or you would have never avoided me for the past three weeks. You can run, Brandon, but you can't hide. God wants you, and He'll spend your entire lifetime seeking you out. I know you're somehow blaming all this misery you're experiencing on me, as if it was something I did to you. But let me tell you, Brandon, this is not a 'Joanie thing', this is a 'Jesus thing'."

Brandon flashed his eyes at Joanie, wondering how she could have identified with such accuracy what he had experienced at the concert and since.

She hesitated a moment, took the cue from his expression, and continued, "I promise you, Brandon, that I could walk out that door right now and out of your life for good, and it wouldn't change a thing. Those haunting feelings, those inner longings will keep surfacing. Because, even though it was just a crack of light breaking through your wall of darkness, you'll never be the same for having seen it. And you'll never be satisfied until your life is filled with His light."

With that Joanie leaned onto her hands, pushed herself up from the table, stepped out of the booth, and began to walk away. Jolted by her sudden exit, Brandon jumped out from his seat and took Joanie by the arm. She stopped and looked at him. Realizing he had a hold of her again, he let go.

"Where are you going?" he asked, somewhat in shock.

"Out that door," she said, motioning her head sideways. Then a smile began to light up her face, like the rays of sun announcing the day at sunrise. Her eyebrows lifted in a playful way, and she added, "But you're welcome to join me."

With that she walked out of the shop.

Chapter 13

Brandon could not believe the sense of relief he felt, which was replacing the sudden panic he had just experienced. He quickly caught up to Joanie in the parking lot and matched his pace to hers.

"Let's walk down to the river," she said, plainly, as though it was something they did together all the time.

It was a beautiful summer evening and sitting indoors at a doughnut shop was not Joanie's idea of a good time. It had been the most convenient meeting place she could think of on the spur of the moment, which is why she had suggested it.

Now that she was outdoors she breathed deeply, absorbing every smell and sensation of the fresh evening. The aroma of petunias filled the air as they passed by a manicured flower garden in someone's yard. She briefly closed her eyes and slowed her pace, trying to take it all in. Strolling on calmly, she neatly held her hands together behind her back.

Brandon, on the other hand, was awkward and fidgety. He was like a fish out of water. He kept thinking about this girl beside him whom he wanted so much, yet he did not dare touch. He shifted his shoulders nervously as they walked, and grasped the air with his fingers, trying to figure out what to do with his hands.

This was new territory for a man who had controlled every relationship with girls through his smooth-moving and smooth-talking manner. The worst part was, Brandon had a sense that Joanie was really enjoying watching him squirm. But in spite of all his discomfort, Brandon thought to himself, *There isn't any place else I'd rather be than right here beside her.*

He looked down at Joanie who stood a whole head shorter than him. Her dark hair picked up the rays of the evening sun and was shimmering with golden-red streaks. Her shoulders were held back, and she carried herself tall and gracefully. As he observed her taking in the sensations of the world around her, he was struck by the genuineness of this girl's character.

She looked up at him and, smiling through closed lips, she pointed to some children at play in a yard. Her gaze returned to the children, and she giggled at their misadventures while they tried to pull a wagonload of stuffed toys.

It was like a scene she had witnessed a thousand times at home. Growing up the eldest child in a large family meant there were always little ones playing nearby. Joanie adored children and the affection was reciprocated universally. She had never met a child whom she did not like, nor one who did not like her in return.

She waved to them as they passed by and called out a friendly greeting. They smiled and waved back to the couple, then continued their play.

"Do you know those kids?" Brandon queried.

"Oh, no," she chuckled, "I just love kids." It was a simple answer, as unpretentious as the girl who had delivered it.

She reached up and grabbed his arm, turning him in the direction of another yard full of children at play. "See that house over there?" She pointed, enthusiastically. The small bungalow was well kept, but there was nothing truly note-worthy about it.

"Uh-hum," he responded, distracted by the fact that she was still holding on to him. It puzzled Brandon that she was so free to touch him, but he could not touch her. He was not about to protest the injustice of it, though, since he would take whatever he could get.

"I grew up in that house until I was ten. It got too small for our family, and we moved into a larger, older house. It really is quite grand, though. My dad's a real handy-man, and he's always building or repairing something. I don't think he'll ever be done renovating."

Her speech was candid and free. It occurred to Brandon that this was the first time Joanie had shared with him so openly about her personal life, apart from religious stuff.

He found he was intimidated by the mention of her father. Funny, how he had never stopped to think about a girl's dad before, as if the girl was just some isolated creature, designed solely for his pleasure. The thought of his lifestyle gave him a dirty, uncomfortable feeling. His annoyance became visible on his face, and his arm tightened under Joanie's gentle hands.

Sensing his discomfort, Joanie pulled back from him and walked on in silence. She was not sure what had happened, but she felt she should give Brandon his space. She had been pretty hard on him earlier in the doughnut shop, and she had not given him much of a chance to respond. That had been on purpose. She wanted to allow him time to absorb it all on his own, hoping that he would open up to her when he was ready.

What she wished to do now was just relax, spend some time together with him, and hopefully become his friend. Maybe, though, he was not interested in her offer of friendship. She had not really considered what to do about that possibility. Joanie truly desired to befriend this mysterious man in her life. She was certain that they had more in common than he realized. That was the ticket: she would meet him on common ground, and they could build a friendship from there.

"So, tell me about your music, Brandon." She jumped into the subject, changing gears so quickly that Brandon felt a jolt.

"How do you do that?" he questioned her, with astonishment in his voice.

"Do what?" Now she was the one taken aback.

"Change gears like that? One minute it's all God and then you get up and walk out on me. You're talking about your dad one moment, and next you're asking about music. Your thoughts are scattered all over the place, and I never know where you're going to come at me from next." His tone was severe and reproachful.

Joanie did not flinch; she just laughed and walked on. "Oh, that." She waved her hand in a gesture of disregard. "I do that all the time. My thoughts just come at me from everywhere inside my head. I never know myself where I'm going to come at you from next until I get there. If it bothers you, I could just be quiet and let you do the talking."

It was all so matter-of-fact.

"Amazing!" He shook his head, smiling. "Doesn't anything ever bother you?"

"Not usually," she answered truthfully, shrugging it off.

She was a sensitive girl regarding others' feelings, but she was not easily offended herself. Joanie was not normally emotional or sulky. She just handed over in prayer the things that really bothered her. It helped to develop her uncomplicated style. She was who she was; take it or leave it.

"My music?" He returned to the last proposed topic and pondered a moment as to what he would say. "What exactly do you mean by that?" he asked, somewhat confused.

"Oh, come on," she entreated him in a friendly manner. "Anyone who can explain the details of mixing music like I've heard you do at work has to be a musician himself. I can sense it in a person. Music is my life."

"I believe that," he commented, more to himself than to her. Then, with a deliberate tone, he pressed her, "But I thought *Jesus* was your life." He figured he had caught her in a clever little trap.

"Silly!" She flicked his arm with the back of her hand, playfully. "Who do you think I do the music for?"

He shook his head and laughed. "Fine, you win. Yeah, I play. Guitar's my thing—acoustic, bass, electric. I picked it up when I was ten. My old man showed up one day with a birthday present—three weeks late, mind you. He had seen this guitar at an auction and figured I might be interested. He really had no idea what I was into.

"I never saw him more than once or twice a year, and at that he never talked to me. He'd just pick me up in one of his fancy cars, take me out for supper at some restaurant and then drop me off. He'd done his duty, and I was just as glad not to have anything more to do with him. He was basically a jerk . . . like me, I suppose."

Brandon was reflective for a moment. Joanie had been listening attentively.

He continued, "Anyway, I had a friend at school, Mark, who was really into guitars, so it turned out to be a cool thing after all. Music became my life, too . . . I suppose."

As his voice trailed off, Joanie smiled up at Brandon. The idea struck them both at the same time: music was a passion they both possessed. Brandon did not return her enthusiasm for he was aware that while they shared this in common, there was a distinction of purpose. Joanie's music was for Jesus. Brandon's music was for himself. There was always that distance between them. He turned away from her upward gaze.

Joanie quickly stepped before Brandon on the sidewalk and placed both her hands on his strong arms. She gave him a slight shake and smiled. Her look was so compelling that he could not escape her eyes. She could sense he was feeling inadequate in her presence, and she wished she could shake that right out of him.

"Don't you see," she began, "we've got a wonderful place to begin building a friendship. Don't let anything spoil that. I want to be your friend so much. We can find a way to share our music together. I'm sure of it!"

She was sincere and entreating.

Brandon smiled down at her. Taking her face gently in his hands, he held her there, consuming her with his eyes. Had she been any other girl, he would have kissed her, but he could not bring himself to do that: she was far too precious to him. He held her there for just a moment and then let go. Stepping back from her, he turned and continued to walk down the street.

The whole scene played out for Joanie as though she were watching a movie in slow motion. She was certain that Brandon wanted to kiss her, and she was reproaching herself for so carelessly having placed herself in that situation. Why was she constantly misleading him, sending him mixed messages? She needed to learn to be more careful. This was not her cousin. He was not like one of the boys from church with whom she had grown up.

Brandon was virtually a stranger to her and his upbringing was completely foreign. He was experienced with girls, and she had never even been kissed. Joanie had many friends her age who were boys, and she knew how to handle those relationships quite easily. But that was just it:

they were all still boys to her. Brandon was a man, and she was certain he had never had a girl just as a friend before. She had to learn to respect his space.

Oh, Jesus, please help me out here! It was a desperate plea for heavenly intervention.

She was frozen in Brandon's hold, but her heart raced on. The fact was, she would have wanted Brandon to kiss her, if things had been different between them. Joanie was battling an inner conflict. She had ducked away from kisses before. But this time she was not entirely convinced that she wanted to duck away. Why was her resolve so weak in his presence? Brandon stirred such new emotions within her. She was attracted to him differently than she had been to any of those other boys. She was not really respecting her own need for space if she was truly trying to forge a friendship with this man.

Keep my hands to myself! she rebuked herself. Sure, her touches were innocent. She had never placed romantic intentions behind any of the times she had touched him. But every time she did, it led to this kind of confused and awkward situation. He was a man, and she was a woman: a woman who was dangerously attracted to him. She had to start seeing the parameters of their relationship within appropriate limits.

When he released her and moved on, she audibly heaved a sigh of relief. She quickly regained her composure and jogged a pace to catch up with Brandon. He shook his head back and forth with silent laughter and looked down at her with tender affection. Slipping his hands behind his back, he hooked his right hand on his left wrist, straightened his posture, and walked on, whistling.

He knew if he wanted to have Joanie for a friend he would have to learn to be a true gentleman. In that moment of decision, when he had chosen not to kiss her, he had come to the realization: *I'll do whatever it takes, just to be with her. She's worth it to me.*

Joanie's heart thrilled as she watched Brandon stroll along. That was twice tonight that he had laid down his own desires out of respect for her unspoken wishes. He was perceptive and kind, even if he did not recognize it.

She delighted in the thought of what a wonderful Christian man Brandon might make someday, and she prayed silently that she might have the joy of sharing in his conversion. Joanie wanted this for Brandon, because she knew all the joy that could be his. She also wanted it for herself now, for in her heart she knew she could love this man—if they only shared a common faith—but in God's time, not hers. She would have to learn to take each moment as it came and enjoy the beauty of it.

Slipping her hands behind her back, she hooked her right hand on her left wrist as he had done, and walked on, listening to Brandon's musical interlude.

By this time they had made it down to the river and were now following the beautiful Meewasin Trail that wound its way in and out of the trees along the banks of the South Saskatchewan River. People rode past them on bikes and roller blades, and the young couple met up with the occasional jogger.

They talked about work; they talked about music; they talked about doughnuts and cappuccino. Joanie shared about her family quite openly. Brandon listened with eager ears, searching for the key to unlock the mystery of this fascinating girl who had come into his life. But he was no longer trying to figure her out so that he could exploit her as another sexual conquest. He wanted to figure her out so that he could have whatever it was that made her so full of life.

They came upon an unoccupied bench and sat down to enjoy the sunset together. The billowy clouds were blushing from all the attention they were getting from the gallant setting sun. Joanie could feel Brandon's attentive gaze on her. She finally looked up to meet his eyes and humbly smiled back at him.

She was not used to being admired by a man, and she worried over how much she liked the feelings that were stirring within her. She cautioned her heart to slow down. She knew this was not going to be an easy relationship, and she silently prayed for protection and guidance.

As the light in the sky waned into the deeper colours of night, they headed back to the doughnut shop. Street lights were just beginning to blink on here and there. There was a charming feeling between this young couple. They chatted about small stuff.

Brandon told Joanie about the incident with Officer O'Neill and thanked her as he had been advised to do. Joanie laughed over the situation, but when she inquired as to where he had been headed at two in the morning at that speed, he looked down at her with a look that said, *Don't ask!*

She laughed and imitated Mr. O'Neill's lilting accent, deliberately emphasizing his choice of words, "I may not be lettin' you forget your debt there to me, Mr. Vaughn. After all, I did save ya!"

"More than you'll ever realize," he confessed.

Joanie looked at him inquisitively, but she could tell by the look on his face that he was not about to explain himself. She smiled sweetly, and he nodded reflectively. They strolled on, finally arriving back at the parking lot.

Brandon walked Joanie to her vehicle: a grey, ten-year-old Toyota Corolla that was showing signs of age. He held the door open as she got in. Leaning on the frame, he looked down at her and smiled.

"Thanks," he said, nodding. "I haven't spent so pleasant an evening for a very"—he stopped to correct himself—"ever!"

Her face lit up, not unlike a star in the heavens. She replied in her simple fashion, "That's what friends are for!" She winked and started up the vehicle.

Taking the cue, he pushed the door closed, winked down at her through a most alluring smile, and stepped back to allow her to drive past.

He watched until the car was out of sight then went back into the doughnut shop. He ordered some food and a coffee, then sat down at the same booth where he and Joanie had met earlier that evening. It was the first real meal that he had eaten in a few days. His eating patterns were irregular, not a fate uncommon to bachelors, but the anxiety of the past three weeks of his life had really messed him up. For the first time in a long time, Brandon realized that he was famished.

The satisfaction of a good meal on an empty stomach was nothing compared to the sensation of release he had experienced this evening. He felt comfortable and happy: feelings to which he was not sure he had ever really paid attention before now. But in contrast to the emotional torment which had interrupted his life since the night of the concert, "comfortable" and "happy" seemed like two long lost friends.

"Friends!" The word slipped out silently under his breath. Brandon sat there pondering the concept, as though he had discovered a new invention. Indeed life was full of surprises. He became aware that the emptiness and longing were no longer playing havoc with his insides.

He smiled and as he cleared off the table, he shot one last glance at the spot where Joanie had sat. He strolled out into the night with a tremendous sense of peace filling his entire being. Yes, life certainly was full of surprises!

✝   ✝   ✝

"Nine-fifty-eight," her father announced, as Joanie quietly came in from the front entry to the living room where he, Amie, Isaac, and Zack sat playing cards. "And that's our canasta of sevens. We're booked," he said to Amie, his partner.

Joanie listened to the table talk of the card players, as she walked up behind her father and slipped her arms around his neck to give him a hug.

She whispered in his ear, "Good-night, daddy," and kissed him on the cheek.

"It must have gone well, Sweet Pea. I'm glad for you." He looked up from his cards and nodded his approval. He was proud of his girl and well she knew it!

Joanie bumped into her mother upstairs who was just coming out of the nursery. This room had been the smallest of the four bedrooms upstairs and was used by Aaron and Jessie, since their bedtime was earlier than that of the other children. Their mother had finally settled the two little ones down for the second time that night. With a finger covering her lips, she indicated for Joanie to be quiet, and she motioned for them to meet in her bedroom.

Joanie was glowing as she shared with her mom how her evening had gone with Brandon. It was a wonderful moment for a mother and daughter to share.

As they spoke, Joanie asked her mother, "If Brandon did become a Christian, would you approve of us pursuing a relationship beyond friendship?"

Her mother smiled and tenderly pushed back the loose curls around Joanie's face. "I've never even met this young man, Joanie . . . so it's kind of hard for me to say. I certainly think you're ready in your life to consider a committed relationship with a man. But, given his past, Brandon may not be capable of a committed relationship. There's a lot of baggage that comes from having lived a worldly lifestyle."

Joanie sighed and thought about her mother's words. "Why do you suppose I feel so attracted to him, Mom? Am I just being shallow because a good-looking man has given me a lot of attention?"

Laughing, her mother answered, "Well, I think it's pretty normal for a girl to let her emotions get carried away in that kind of situation. But I have a question for you?"

"Yes?" Joanie asked.

"Have you kept Jesus at the centre of your heart through this whole relationship with Brandon?"

"I have, Mom," Joanie answered, sincerely. "I've done more praying over the past two months than at any other time in my life. And the strange thing is, Mom, the more I pray, the more I feel drawn to him. I've never experienced that with any other guy. I keep pushing Brandon out of my mind, and Jesus just seems to keep bringing him back into my heart. Does that make sense, or do you think I'm just fooling myself?"

"Joanie, the only way we can know God's will is through prayer," her mother reminded her. "Keep your heart and mind open and trust that in

His faithfulness He will lead you to know His will. I couldn't possibly know for sure what God is calling you to with Brandon, but I have been praying about the situation myself, very much. I have a tremendous peace over it all, in spite of Brandon's past."

Placing her hand affectionately on Joanie's shoulder, Judy continued, "Just keep praying for God to give you a clear sign of His direction. And until Brandon converts and begins to live his life for Jesus—well, it seems to me the answer will remain fairly obvious—he's not for you. On the other hand, if he does convert, well . . . then you'll have to just keep praying and seeking God's will. Some of the greatest saints were the worst sinners. You'll know the tree by its fruit, Joanie, but it takes time. And just because he may become a Christian, does not automatically mean God intends him for you. Allow yourself to be an instrument of God's love in Brandon's life—no strings attached!"

"It all sounds so easy in theory, Mom," Joanie confessed. "But I'm not sure how easily I could hold back my heart if Brandon were to become a Christian. And I know what you're going to say . . . that strength will have to come from God, not from me. I'll keep praying."

As Joanie and her mom left her parents' room, Jessie appeared in the hallway, half-asleep, rubbing her eyes. "I want Joanie to sing to me," she whimpered in her tiny, little voice.

"No, Jessie, you go back to bed. Joanie's tired," her mother replied, as she began to redirect Jessie to her room.

"Oh, no, that's okay, Mom," Joanie interjected, "I kinda feel like singing tonight anyway."

Joanie swept Jessie into her arms. The two sisters nestled themselves under a big blanket as they sank into the rocking chair that was kept in the nursery for just such occasions. Jessie's eyes closed dreamily. Her wispy, auburn hair framed her angelic, little face as the softness of sleep stole over her countenance.

Joanie's singing continued on for a long time after the small child had drifted off. There just did not seem to be enough words and ways to tell Jesus how much she loved Him and to thank Him for all His many blessings. Joanie's heart was very full and very happy!

Chapter 14

Monday morning brought about a new set of emotions for Joanie. Not having spoken to Brandon since Friday night, she worried that he might have slipped back into discouragement. Perhaps she had pushed God at him too hard. Maybe she had placed too many expectations on this relationship due to the strong attraction she felt toward him. Was she prepared to handle whatever his response to their conversation would be?

Please, dear Jesus, just give me a clear sign as to Your will in this relationship. I'm weak and I want a sign that would at least point me in the right direction. My heart is way too frail; please don't let it be led astray. Mary, help me to know your Son's will and to be humble enough to accept it, just as you accepted God's will in your life.

She remained deep in prayer the whole bus ride to work.

Even as she entered the station, she remained distracted to the point that she failed to return the usual morning greetings of her co-workers. Tessa wondered at Joanie's distant behaviour that morning and decided she would make a point of catching up with her at coffee.

Joanie stopped by her workstation, dropped off her purse and briefcase, and mindlessly turned on her computer. She slipped off to the lounge to grab a quick coffee. She really needed one this morning. Returning to her computer, she sat down and made her usual morning offering, looking up at the images of Jesus and Mary beside her calendar.

Suddenly, something caught her eye. She leaned forward to see what it was. Taped to the wall, just below the holy cards, was an envelope with her name on it. She took it down and carefully opened it—her heart racing and head pounding with emotion. She was almost afraid to look.

It was a letter from Brandon. Her hands affectionately caressed the defined strokes of his handwriting—it suited him. She said a quick prayer and began to read.

Dear Joanie,

I'm writing to you tonight, after our walk together. It's 1:30 a.m. and I can't get you off my mind. I was so moved by everything you said to me—and everything you didn't say spoke volumes as well. I've never known a girl like you and I'm at a loss here, I confess. You see, I don't know how to proceed with you. But something has happened inside of me, as well you know, and it's just like you said—everything has changed!

To be honest, I'm more than a little nervous. I'm not sure what comes next. But I do know I want whatever it is that you've got. Of course, I know you'd tell me that it's Jesus, and I'm convinced that you're right about that. He's real and He's powerful. So powerful that I found myself praying tonight—and I'm not a praying man! So if you were looking for miracles, there was a first.

I recognize that I am a sinful man. My conscience has not allowed me to return to my old lifestyle since the night of the concert. Yet until tonight, I really did not know where to turn. Now I see that I have to turn to Jesus!

As I struggle through all these thoughts and feelings that I can't understand, I realize I do need a friend. I want to take you up on your offer, but I know that I will just keep confusing my feelings for you.

The fact is, I want you for more than just a friend, but I won't go there yet. I want to make myself worthy of you, in every way, so that I can stand before your father, unintimidated, and ask his permission to date his daughter. Believe me—I have my work cut out for me! But you are worth it. . . and I've never said anything like that to any girl before in my life.

Every time I close my eyes I see your sweet face, your bright eyes, your endearing smiles and expressions. I've memorized every last detail. I hear your tender voice, and I feel your soft hands in mine. As I think about you now, I know that I could live and die for the love of a woman like you!

Ever yours,
Brandon.

Joy filled Joanie's heart as she read the letter over and over. She bit down on a trembling lip and in vain tried to hold back her tears. There was so much for which to be thankful.

Brandon had chosen Jesus, not for her sake, but for his own. And he wanted Joanie for more than a friend. Her heart was racing because, the truth was, she felt the very same way about him.

Dear Jesus, I prayed for a sign. I don't know if this is it . . . but I want it to be! Please keep my heart open so that I will know Your will. And thank You for opening up Brandon's heart to You. Keep him on the path of righteousness.

Work was exceptionally difficult to attend to that day. Joanie was grateful to be out on an assignment by mid-morning. It was easier to keep her mind off Brandon while she was out dealing with other people.

As she came back in that afternoon, Tessa caught up with her. The front area was quiet, and Tessa was alone at the desk. Joanie was aloof and still very much distracted.

The receptionist walked around the counter to meet her friend. Looking Joanie straight in the eyes, Tessa implored her for an explanation. "Joanie, what's up? I know that something's happened to you. I can just sense it. You're acting like . . ." then Tessa paused, because the most absurd thought was entering her mind. "Joanie," she continued, with a cautious tone in her voice, "are you seeing someone?"

Joanie blushed and closed her eyes, as if she could hide from the question.

"Girl, talk to me," Tessa pleaded. "'Cause if I didn't know any better, I'd say you were seeing . . . Brandon."

His name fell off the end of her statement, for the shock on Joanie's face said it all. Tessa was stunned; it was too ridiculous to conceive. Did Joanie have any idea what this guy was really like? He was not one with whom a nice girl like Joanie should be trifling. Joanie was way out of her league, and Tessa was sick at the thought of it. She loved Joanie like a little sister, and she could not help but feel protective toward her.

"Joanie, you're crazy! Do you have any idea what—"

Joanie put up a hand to cut Tessa off. "Tessa, you don't understand. I want you to hear me out on this one before you jump to conclusions."

Joanie did not know where to begin. She spoke nervously and her thoughts were all over the place. She had not been prepared to explain Brandon to anyone, yet. It was all so sudden since the letter that morning.

"The letter," she said to herself, out loud.

"What letter? What are you talking about?" Tessa was completely confused.

Joanie explained to her friend about her evening with Brandon on Friday. He had left a letter for her at her desk this morning. He had accepted the Lord into his heart. "He's found Jesus, Tessa. I'm still so in shock, I can hardly take it all in." Joanie's eyes were welling with tears.

Tessa held onto Joanie's hands and looked directly in her eyes. "You are such an angel! How could I have been so wrong about him? I'm sorry, Joanie." Tessa just kept shaking her head and gradually a laugh came up from within her, and she grabbed Joanie into a big hug.

"How did you figure it out, Tessa?" Joanie asked, still stunned that Tessa could have put it all together so easily.

"I don't know," Tessa explained. "I could tell there was something different about you, but for the life of me I don't know why I put it together with Brandon."

Joanie smiled at her friend. She closed her eyes and shook her head in disbelief. *I'm gonna have to stop looking for signs, Lord. Because the more signs I get, the more confused I become!*

"Pray for us, Tessa," Joanie entreated her friend. "I'm so afraid I'm going to wake up and find this is all a dream!"

"I will, dear girl!" Tessa responded, her voice full of emotion. "God bless you both!"

✟   ✟   ✟

That evening at home, Joanie told her parents, Maggie, and Amie about the letter and Brandon's decision to follow Jesus. They decided that they should make a novena to St. Joseph, asking him to help guide Brandon.

Alone with her mother and father, Joanie took the opportunity to seek out their guidance. "How do you feel about my obvious interest in Brandon?" she asked.

John looked steadily at his daughter as he prayed about the situation. After a moment he spoke, "Joanie, I have a great deal of trust in your judgment. I know you've been praying sincerely for the Lord's guidance throughout this relationship. It seems to me that He's been directing you toward Brandon for a reason. But I want you to take it slowly. Brandon has a long road ahead of him as he learns about Christianity. Sometimes people fall off the path and go back to their old lives. I sincerely hope that isn't the case with him."

Joanie listened, attentively taking in her father's words.

"And you know our family's position on courtship," he continued. "If Brandon is sincere in his interest for you, he'll be willing to agree to our expectations. If he has no respect for my authority on the matter, though, I'll be quick to put an end to it. You understand that, don't you?"

"Yes, Dad. And I trust you . . . right now, more than I trust my own judgment. I've never found myself so confused," Joanie admitted.

"Perhaps that's because you've never experienced these feelings for a man before," her mother suggested.

"Those feelings aren't bad," John stated. "They just can't be completely trusted. You need to balance it with sincere prayer and sound reason." Smiling affectionately at his daughter, he added. "And that's what you've been doing, Sweet Pea, which is why I'm not worried about this relationship. When he's ready, bring Brandon around to meet us. I'm looking forward to meeting him."

Joanie hugged her dad and mom and thanked them for their guidance and support. As she walked away, her heart was full and secure in her hope in the Lord. She knew that He would look after Brandon and keep him on the path of righteousness for His Name's sake!

Chapter 15

It was after two in the morning when Brandon laid down the pen. He had just finished writing the letter to Joanie. It had been a long day; so much had happened to him following their walk. As he pondered over all that Joanie had said to him, he soon found himself praying. At what point his heart had opened the door to Jesus, he was not sure, but all at once he knew he believed.

It was as though he was seeing his life, for the first time, with clear vision. With his back turned now on his past, all he wanted was to come to know Jesus as Joanie knew Him. He wanted to love Jesus with the same love he had seen in Joanie's eyes. . . . And he could no longer imagine his life without Joanie in it. He desired so much to share with her this peace and joy in Jesus to which she had led him.

Looking down at his letter to Joanie, he closed his eyes and prayed again. *Oh, Jesus, I don't know You. We've only just met. But I've seen enough to know You're real. I want You! I want to believe in You and to know You, like Joanie does. I've never been any good, but I know You can change that. I don't know how, but I know You will. I don't know where to begin. I don't know what's next. Jesus, please just show me the way. . . . Jesus.*

Brandon sat there, bathing his mind in the name of Jesus. The release from fears, and the hope welling within him, intensified each time he uttered the sweet name. He knew very little about who or what Jesus was. He knew some people called Him the Son of God, but what that meant was an entire mystery to Brandon. The only thing he knew for certain was there was power in the name of Jesus. So he just sat there and called upon that power.

It was just before daybreak Saturday when Brandon woke up. He had fallen asleep over the letter on the table. Rubbing his eyes, he became acutely aware of a peace that had settled over his entire being. He looked down at the letter and seeing Joanie's name, a smile crept over his face. He reached for an envelope in a nearby drawer and turning back to the table, he picked up the pen and wrote *Joanie Collins* on it.

Sealing the letter inside, he realized that he was not sure how he was going to deliver this letter to Joanie. He did not have the nerve to mail it to her. He had to be careful at work. He really did not want to see Joanie just yet. He needed time to prepare himself for her. Somehow he had to get the letter to her unnoticed. Placing it in the pocket of his brown leather jacket, he decided he would figure that out later.

Extending his strong arms to either side, he stretched out the fatigue in his back. He debated whether or not he should go to bed and get some real sleep, but something urged him to stay up.

"Well, if I'm up, then I'm going to get a coffee," he told himself. He decided to hit an early morning drive-thru. Slipping on the jacket, he grabbed his keys and left.

With no particular destination in mind, Brandon headed down the highway out of town. Rays of light were just beginning to shoot up over the horizon as the vast prairie sky was opening up to welcome the day. The darkness was being swept further and further away from the east, and the deep purple colours of the western horizon soon gave way to the luscious green tones of the earth. A few mare's tail clouds swept across the sky in a stroke of pink, as if a child had drawn with a crayon over a blue page. Before long, though, their colour faded to white in the full force of the morning sunlight.

Brandon pulled over to the side of the road and sipped his coffee. He rolled down his window so that he could fill his senses with every sound and smell. It was a glorious morning!

He closed his eyes and breathed in deeply. "God, it's good to be alive!"

Possessed by a sudden urge, Brandon jumped out of his vehicle. He reached his arms high above his head in a V-shape, and he released a sound that seemed to come up from the bottom of his feet. "Waahooooo!"

His laugh was full and robust, and he knew that he could not contain all the life that was within him.

"God, it is so good to be alive!"

From where any of this was coming, he did not know. He had never been the impulsive type, but he had no will to hold it back.

He stood on the edge of the wheat field and looked out across it. At the prompting of the cool morning breeze, the tall stocks of grain had formed together in a united motion, resembling the gentle waves of the ocean.

Brandon was so animated with the power of the Holy Spirit that all he wanted to do was praise God. He waved to a few vehicles as they passed by, and he laughed out loud, "I'm crazy! I'm absolutely mad! But I'm in love with Joanie, and I've found Jesus Christ!"

✝   ✝   ✝

When Brandon re-entered his condo later that morning, he was overcome with disgust. He recalled the depression in which he had been immersed over the past three weeks. Now that he was seeing life through new eyes, this view would never do. He dived into cleaning up the mess that was all around him. He threw out anything that he found which had been a part of his old lifestyle. He was a new man, making a clean start. There was a tremendous sense of freedom that came from cleaning out the trash.

After a few hours, Brandon sat down in his favourite chair. There was a pleasant, tired feeling settling in his body. He reclined the rocker, closed his eyes, and fell into a deep and peaceful sleep.

It was three hours later when he awoke. Mid-afternoon by now, he wondered what he should do for the rest of the day.

He saw his acoustic guitar in its usual corner by the fireplace. It looked back at him invitingly, like a long lost pal. He went over and picked it up. With the tenderness of a father holding his child, Brandon's hands moved over the dark wooden grain of the instrument. Taking comfort in the feeling of it against his body, he closed his eyes and let his fingers wander over the strings.

He was a skilled player, always challenging himself to a higher level, a truer tone, a greater expression of self. As he played, the music moved him in a new and unfamiliar way. It was alive and it filled the room with such peace.

His mind drifted back to his conversation with Joanie about music. All at once it hit him: his music had changed because he was now playing for Jesus. It seemed to Brandon, in that moment, that there could be no greater expression of self than that.

✞   ✞   ✞

Sunday morning came with Brandon sleeping in very late. He was exhausted physically, emotionally, and even spiritually. Waking up at noon, he lay in bed for a long time, not wanting to move or to think. He eventually drifted back into a rather restless sleep and woke up again at about two o'clock. He was agitated and unfocussed.

He showered and decided that what he needed was some exercise. He would go down to the gym in his condo complex and do a workout. As he was getting ready to go, something entered his mind that was awkward and foreign to him. Church.

It was Sunday, and didn't Christians go to church on Sunday? Was that what he was now: a Christian? The title felt funny. It was an identity which he had never before considered for himself. This was way too weird. Maybe he had bitten off more than he could chew. What would his friends think?

The commotion in his mind grew and grew. He could not sort it all out himself.

Where do I go from here? I can't go to Joanie, not yet. I'm not ready. I need some direction here ... Jesus! Yeah, Jesus, I guess I'm praying again. Funny, how that happens!

He shook his head, feeling a little awkward. He mocked himself out loud, "If my friends could only hear and see me now! They'd have me institutionalized for sure."

He went down to the gym and worked out like ten men and a boy. It felt good. His mind had become clear and his body had regained its strength, yet it had not made the gnawing feeling inside him go away. He was aware that something was missing. Brandon resolved to make sure he corrected that next Sunday.

✚   ✚   ✚

Brandon was up bright and early Monday morning. He knew he had to beat Joanie to work in order to make his special delivery. He placed his hand into his jacket pocket to be sure the letter was still there. This was the boldest thing Brandon had ever done in his life.

Writing the letter was easy; it was all true. But handing it over was now laying his heart on the line. He had never taken that kind of risk before. Thinking back to the look in Joanie's eyes on Friday night, he felt certain that she would not reject him. He took courage in that thought, and in his simple praying style, he handed it over to God.

Take it from here, Jesus. I've done my part.

Grateful that Joanie had tape on her desk, Brandon tore off a piece and looked for a place to leave the envelope. It had to be inconspicuous, so as not to draw attention, but obvious enough for her to find.

The images of Jesus and Mary seemed to appear out of nowhere. "Perfect!" He smiled at the thought of how consistent everything was about Joanie.

"I'm sure you'll find it there, Church-Girl!" he murmured to himself as he walked away.

✚   ✚   ✚

By Wednesday afternoon Joanie realized that Brandon was not going to be surfacing in the near future. She understood his need for time and space, but she worried all the same.

With Brandon being so recent a defector from one side to the other in the spiritual battle, she knew it would be just a matter of time before Satan tried to lure him back. Being alone was not an ideal scenario for a new Christian. He had no armour yet with which to defend himself.

With this in mind, Joanie made a phone call to Catholic Campus Evangelization. They were a dynamic group of Catholics who evangelized on campuses in order to lead students to a deeper and more personal relationship with Jesus. They were solid and well formed in the Church's teachings, offering Bible studies and all kinds of fun, social gatherings, helping to bring faith alive to young adults.

The connection to C.C.E. for Joanie was very strong. Her parents had supported the ministry for years, and many of the staff members from C.C.E. went to their parish. During university, Joanie had been very involved with C.C.E. In fact, she had spent one summer in Peru with her sister, Maggie, doing missionary work through the ministry.

On her way home from work that evening, Joanie stopped at Catholic Campus Evangelization. She walked up to the small office located on the second floor of the rather drab office building. When she entered through the open door, she smiled at the change of atmosphere this obscure office presented in contrast to its environs. It was inviting and charming, even though it was overcrowded and modestly furnished.

Perched on a high counter off to one side was an oscillating fan, blowing air across the small room at Joanie. It felt good in the heat of the afternoon to have the soft air brush past her face as the fan made its path back and forth. Joanie called out a greeting which was answered by a hearty male voice from the back room.

It was Bill Curran; he was the director of C.C.E. The father of a family from their parish, Joanie had known him for years, and she knew he could be trusted. He was not much taller than Joanie, but his jovial demeanour and outgoing personality made him seem much bigger than he was.

He came forward and welcomed the young visitor to the office. Even though it was the end of the work day, he had waited for her after her call. Everyone else had already left.

She shared with him about Brandon, their relationship, and his recent decision to follow Jesus. She explained how Brandon had requested some time and space to sort things out, which is why she had come here for direction. Mr. Curran gathered up some literature into a neat little folder for her to pass on to Brandon, with the C.C.E. number and address on it. He suggested she write him a note and encourage Brandon to give the office a call and ask for Bill.

"I'll be happy to meet with him and answer any questions he has. And Joanie," he added, encouragingly, "I'm really impressed with your fortitude. I'm sure it can't be easy to step back and give Brandon the space he's asking for. But I know God will bless you for it. I can't wait to meet him."

✞   ✞   ✞

The next morning, Joanie stopped at the front desk on her way in to work to speak with Tessa. Joanie explained the contents of the package she was carrying and asked if her friend would be able to deliver it to Brandon. She hoped that he would not mind the fact that Joanie had taken Tessa into her confidence.

Tessa assured her she would get it to him. "Don't worry, kiddo, I'll place it into his hands myself."

✞   ✞   ✞

Tessa entered the production area on the third floor and spied Brandon's small office across the large open room. She worked her way through the maze of equipment and employees and stood at Brandon's open door, watching him for a moment. He was engaged in his work on his computer, sitting at his desk in his well ordered work space. He had on a headset and was busily manipulating on the computer screen images that Tessa could not even recognize. It was fascinating to watch as the patterns changed swiftly at the touch of his hand on the mouse.

Finally, she knocked on the open door, and Brandon turned around from his work and looked up. A smile illuminated his face at the sight of Tessa. It was not her habit to pay him visits, and he could only surmise that it had to do with Joanie. Taking off the headset, he walked over to meet Tessa at the door.

"What the heck are you doing here, Tessa?" Brandon asked, with the tone of greeting an old friend. Putting his hands on her shoulders, he gave her a curious look, with his usual tilted smile and one eyebrow cocked.

Tessa was not at all awkward with Brandon's friendliness. In fact, she was relieved to feel the warmth he now exuded. It was refreshing and reaffirmed for her the power of the Lord. She remembered what an arrogant man Brandon had once been. This was not the same man standing before her now.

She returned a smile to him and, without looking down from his eyes, presented him with the small package that had been entrusted to her care.

"I have something to deliver to you . . . from somebody on the second floor." She winked at him and walked out.

It gave Tessa a thrill to be a part of this secret love affair. It was just like something out of an old movie.

Brandon looked down at the package, stunned by the unexpected delivery. He closed his office door and sat down, staring at his name, *Brandon Vaughn*, which had been scripted on the top in beautiful calligraphy.

He had the feeling of holding something sacred in his hands: it was from Joanie.

He slowly opened it, not at all knowing what to expect. Inside there was a letter taped to a folder. He carefully opened the envelope to find a card with a picture of Mary, like the one he had seen on Joanie's cubicle wall. He opened it and read.

Dear Brandon,

I could never find words to communicate to you the joy that is in my heart. Your letter was the most beautiful gift I have ever received!

I confess, too, that my feelings for you have gone beyond that of mere friendship. So I gratefully accept your decision to allow some space between us for the time being. Be assured that you are constantly in my heart, and I pray for you unceasingly.

But I have tremendous concerns for you as you enter into new and unknown territories. It is one thing to experience Jesus as real, but that can leave a person hanging there, wondering: what's next?

I hope you don't mind my intervention here, but I went to the Catholic Campus Evangelization office yesterday and spoke with a dear friend of our family, Bill Curran. He's the director, an awesome man. I'm sure you'll be impressed by him. He told me to tell you to call the office and ask for him. He will meet with you any time. He'll answer any questions you have and give you sound advice.

I want so much to be with you again, in a new and wonderful way. But I will not initiate anymore contact with you. I feel you need to have space to explore for yourself the things that God is revealing to you. I fear that my presence would serve as a distraction from your own journey with Christ. We all must learn to walk with Christ in the way that He has called us.

I pray that He will bring our paths together again, when the time is right. Until that day . . .

I remain faithfully yours,
Joanie.

Brandon turned the card over, and on the backside noticed a prayer, scripted in calligraphy, like his name on the package had been.

He read it out loud., "Hail Mary, full of grace, the Lord is with thee. Blessed art thou among women, and blessed is the fruit of thy womb, Jesus. Holy Mary, Mother of God, pray for us sinners, now and at the hour of our death. Amen."

Under the prayer was a little note, in Joanie's handwriting:

When you feel lost or need help, ask Mary.
She always leads her children to her Son.
She will never fail you!

He smiled and thought of Joanie. He wanted to be with her again so much that his heart ached. Never before had his heart ached for a girl!

He turned the card back over to the front and stared for a long time at the picture of Mary. He liked it. Having a close relationship with his own mother, it somehow brought Brandon comfort to imagine that the Mother of Jesus was praying for him.

He proceeded to leaf through the folder from C.C.E. There were several brochures inside. Leaning back in his office chair, he picked up Bill Curran's business card and played with it between his fingers as he reread Joanie's letter. Funny, how she knew that he was feeling lost and unsure of the next step.

Well, I guess this is the answer to my prayer, Jesus. Here goes nothing, he said to himself, picking up the phone, *or then again . . . maybe here goes everything!*

Chapter 16

Friday nights had become a real challenge for Brandon. This would be the fourth weekend in a row that he had totally ignored his friends and their invitations to party. Actually, Brandon had turned the ringer off his phone, annoyed with all the calls that were coming in.

He would check the answering machine for messages and return the important calls, like from his mom. But as for his friends, he just could not bring himself to face them or their questions or their mocking him. How could he explain what was happening in his life?

Mark was different, though. Mark had been Brandon's best friend since the third grade. He knew everything there was to know about Brandon's life, until now. Each time Brandon heard Mark's voice on the answering machine, he got a sick feeling inside. Brandon wanted to tell Mark. But how?

Picking up his guitar, he tried to play, but there was a terrible restlessness inside of him. Brandon decided to pray.

Jesus, I don't want to lose Mark's friendship, but I'm afraid he's going to lead me back into my old ways. So, help me sort this one out.

Thinking about Joanie's letter, he reached into his pocket and pulled out the card. He needed to read the words of the prayer to Mary, so he kept it handy. Besides, he felt closer to Joanie by just having it in his pocket. He finished praying and closed his eyes to think about things.

The buzz of the apartment door startled him back to reality. Getting up quickly, he failed to notice that he had dropped the card on the floor.

An uneasy feeling was coming over him as he weighed out in his mind whether or not to answer the door. His Pathfinder was parked out front; any of his friends would know that he was home. With reluctance, he pressed the answer button of the intercom pad on the wall.

"Yeah," he said, completely without expression.

"Man, where the hell've you been? Let me in, already!" It was Mark's voice . . . and was he angry!

"Time to face the music," Brandon said to himself, as he unlocked the door. He unlatched the dead bolt of his apartment and stood back against the wall across from the door, guitar propped up in front of him, almost as a shield.

The door banged open, and Mark stormed in. "What the hell's going on here? It's been three weeks since I've heard from you. D'ya fall off the face of the earth or something? Ever hear of telephones?"

Mark glanced over at the answering machine, flashing "11".

"Eleven messages, probably ten of them from me! What gives?" His eyes were flaming with anger, and he was not going to leave without an explanation.

Brandon might have said something in response to Mark's onslaught, but just behind Mark, Justine and Tracey slipped into the apartment. The sight of the girls there made Brandon feel awkward and even irritated.

"Hi, Brandon," Tracey smiled, coyly. "You become a hermit or something?" Tracey was a hot number, to be sure. Sensuality exuded from every aspect of her svelte figure. She fixed her dark, dangerous eyes on Brandon in a penetrating way, making the blood run cold in his veins. She was on a mission, and she had her sights set on Brandon.

The prospect of what she proposed to him was utterly repulsive; yet, a short month earlier he had lived his life in pursuit of that very pleasure. His look was cold and severe, and he offered her no response.

Justine jumped in, trying to ease some tension. Her voice was gentle and friendly. "Look, Brandon, we were thinking of heading out to *Shooters* tonight. How about you joining us for some fun?" She slid her arm around Mark's waist and motioned her head sideways to Brandon, invitingly.

"Thanks, but no thanks," Brandon replied, politely, with a slight edge in his voice.

Tracey approached Brandon. Her attire was anything but modest, and her movements were provocative. All in all, she had a look to kill, and she was closing in on her prey. Brandon put his hand up in a motion to tell her to keep her distance. She ignored it and hooking her fingers through his, she took his hand and pulled herself up under his chin, not unlike a dance move. She was seductive, and she knew how to use her charm.

"Now how you gonna get lucky tonight with an attitude like that?" she whispered enticingly to him. Her eyes were working at capturing his glance, but she could not hook him in.

"Enough," he said, pushing her back, abruptly, but without force. His voice was severe, and he kept his eyes fixed on Mark's, completely avoiding either girl.

"Fine!" Tracey's tone was as sharp as a knife. "Leave him behind. There's plenty of fish out there. He can rot in hell, for all I care!"

She grabbed Justine's arm and began to pull her toward the door. "Aren't you coming, Mark?" she called back, in a commanding tone.

Mark motioned for the girls to leave. He tossed Justine his keys, and in a cool tone he instructed them, "Head on without me girls. I'll catch up to you later. I've got my cell on me."

Tracey marched out, without looking back. Justine fixed her affable eyes on Brandon as she left and in a mild tone whispered, "Good-night, boys." She shut the door gently behind her.

"So, are you gonna talk now? What's up with that?" Mark's voice was still annoyed, but he had cooled down substantially from his explosive entry. He grabbed Brandon's guitar out of his hands and walked over to the living room to sit down.

Something on the floor caught his eye. Without drawing attention to his actions, he moved the footstool over to get a better view.

"Nothing's up with anything. So, why don't you just catch up to the girls and go enjoy yourself." Brandon knew there was not much hope of that happening.

Mark's entire demeanour began to change. He became cool, like a detective on a case. "It's 'Church-Girl', isn't it?"

Brandon winced at that reference to Joanie. A shameful feeling came up from deep within, as he recalled the first time he had mentioned Joanie to Mark. He had called her "Church-Girl" and had bragged that when he finally got her, he would etch a cross instead of the usual notch onto his bedpost, since she had presented such a new and intriguing challenge to him.

"I don't know what you're referring to." Brandon acted dumb and walked off to the kitchen to grab a couple of beers.

"She's gotten to you, hasn't she?" Mark called out, amazement in his tone. "I know the type. I grew up going to church, remember? They're all the same those religious ones. You should never have messed with her, buddy!"

Mark was almost laughing; the thought of it was so absurd. He would bring Brandon back to his senses.

Brandon came back into the room, tossed a can to Mark and stood off to the side, leaning his elbow on the fireplace mantel. "You're daft," he said, indignantly.

"Brandon?" Mark was beginning to realize the seriousness of the situation. "You've gone and gotten religious on us. Haven't you?" he stated in disbelief, as he set aside the guitar.

"No, I haven't! Now get off the subject already!" He was stern and not to be messed with.

"Then," pulling the card up off the floor to reveal it to Brandon, Mark asked calmly, "explain this. It seems to me, if I remember anything from fifteen years of being dragged off to church every Sunday, there should be a cock crowing just about now."

Brandon could not make any sense out of Mark's off-handed scriptural reference, and the look on his face showed it.

"Man, you don't even know what I'm talking about—and I'm a bloody atheist!" Mark had a tone of determination in his voice. He was going to knock Brandon back to his senses, if he had to take a fist to his head to do it. "You're out of your league, man. You've found yourself in the wrong pond, and it's time to swim back home where you belong." Waving the card in Brandon's face, he added, "You don't belong in this world."

Brandon reached out and grabbed the card. He pushed it into his back pocket and turned away from Mark. He could not look at the card, he could not face Mark. He felt like a fool, embarrassed to have been trapped in his own lie.

"Brandon . . . come on, man . . . come to your senses!" Mark was calm and reassuring. He could sense Brandon was on the edge.

"Look, Mark," Brandon's voice was sincere and apologetic, "I don't know if I can talk about this yet. I'm sorry, I . . . I couldn't tell you what was going on and I still need some time to figure it all out."

Mark sat there in silence. He was stunned, to say the least. The situation was much worse than he ever could have imagined, and he wondered how it could have gotten so out of hand. One day Brandon was an average, fun-loving, all-round great kind of guy. The next day, he was living like a ruddy priest. Mark just shook his head in disbelief.

Brandon struggled inside for words. He felt like a heel. He wanted to offer Mark some sort of explanation, but he just could not make the words come out. The silence hung heavily over the room.

Brandon closed his eyes and rubbed his forehead. Suddenly, the image of Joanie flashed before his eyes. His heart pulled at him, and he began to ask for courage. It was time to pray.

Jesus, give me courage or I'm gonna lose it all here tonight. And I don't want to lose it. I don't want to lose You, and I don't want to lose Joanie. I can't do this alone, Jesus. Help!

Brandon looked around at Mark, nervously wondering if Mark could tell he had been praying.

"You remember when we were growing up, Mark, and I used to always make fun of you for getting dragged off to church with your folks on Sundays?" Brandon began, nostalgically.

"Yeah, what about it?"

"I was so proud of you the day you told them you weren't going anymore. If they wanted you to live at home, then they'd have to back off, or you were hittin' the road. You were bold and brave, and I thought we had it made."

His voice was stirring and he shook his fist in the air in a gesture of victory.

Mark made some sort of grunting noise and waited for Brandon to continue.

"A few weeks back, I headed out for what I thought was a date, or at least an opportunity. I was interested in Joanie and figured I could reel her in better if I moved in closer to her pond. You know what I mean.

"She had invited me out to some praise night at a church. I . . . I had no idea what I was walking into. I just can't explain it. There I was, sitting like an idiot in a church basement auditorium, and there she was—singing like an angel up on the stage. I don't know what it was for sure, but something happened to me there. I found myself really listening, and my insides were just spinning 'round and . . ."

His voice faded out. He was looking into space, remembering the night, trying to find words to express what had happened. But he could not; he just shook his head, shrugged his shoulders and kept his eyes fixed in the distance.

"Is she worth it?" Mark asked, simply.

"Oh, man." Brandon released a small chuckle under his breath, thinking of Joanie in those terms. "She's everything to me, now, Mark." Brandon looked up and straight into Mark's eyes. "I'd die for that girl. And I can't tell you why—or what it is about her that moves me that way—but I want her more than anything. Anything."

It was as simple as that.

"And so you're gonna fake some religious attitude, just to win her over." Mark's tone was accusing.

"No, Mark, it isn't like that. I wanted to resist all that Jesus stuff, but it just hit me so hard. I don't know how! I'm just as shocked as you are, but it's real. It's—He's real, man, and I've gotta have Him in my life. Everything's changed—completely changed."

Brandon's speech was uncontrived. Mark believed him, in-as-much as he did not believe it himself, but he believed that Brandon believed it.

"So, what about me? Am I out of your picture now—*completely*?" He stressed the last word, as if to throw it back in Brandon's face.

"No, Mark. No! I just didn't know how to tell you. I'm still figuring out all this God stuff myself. I'm not going to tell you what to do, but I'm not going to let you sit here and try to talk me out of it either."

Brandon was emphatic, not opening the door to compromise.

"Yeah, great," snarled Mark, slamming down the beer and getting up to leave. "I'll be leaving now, Brandon. Lot's of luck to you, buddy."

"Mark, wait!" Brandon's voice was compelling.

"Wait! For what?" The anger had returned, and Mark's face betrayed his hurt. "Wait for you to come along and try to convert me? Wait for you to look down on everything I do—everything *you* used to do with me—everything that ever mattered to us? Just sit around and watch Brandon turn into some sort of saint before my eyes . . . water turning into wine."

He threw a disgusted look at Brandon, since Brandon still had no idea that Mark was drawing reference from the Bible, and he continued, "You won't have any place for me in your life with your little church-going girlfriend. The wineskin'll burst, my friend . . . just like it says in the Good Book!"

With that Mark picked up the guitar beside him to walk past, tossed it across the room in a chest pass to Brandon, and walked out.

Brandon cringed at the sound of the door slamming behind Mark. He set the guitar down in front of him, sat at the edge of the couch, leaned his elbows on his knees, and sank his face into his hands.

"That couldn't have gone worse!" he uttered quietly to himself.

✝   ✝   ✝

At two o'clock in the afternoon of the following day, Brandon found himself walking into the Catholic Campus Evangelization office to meet with Bill Curran. Brandon was grateful for the opportunity to get out and do something. He was going stir crazy, having cooped himself up in his condo for the past four weekends.

Bill greeted Brandon enthusiastically. He reached out and offered a firm handshake. It was a quick character appraisal that these two men made of each other.

Brandon was impressed with the genuineness of Bill's expression. He instantly felt comfortable in his presence. Bill was impressed with the confidence with which Brandon presented himself. He could sense the true quality of Brandon's character. Bill could see why Joanie was attracted to him.

"Take a seat, Brandon," Bill welcomed his guest, gesturing to a chair at a table in the corner of the office.

The whirring of the fan on the counter behind Brandon was the only noise in the quiet office building on this Saturday afternoon.

"Thank you, sir," Brandon replied respectfully, taking in his surroundings as he sat down.

The office was humbly furnished and obviously too small for the ministry. But Brandon liked the simplicity of the setting, and it boosted his confidence in the integrity of the man he had come to meet.

"Well, you've managed to get yourself hooked up with quite a gal, Brandon. I can't begin to tell you how much I like Joanie and her family. She's like a daughter to me. I imagine you've come to appreciate just how special she is."

Bill was frank and forward. He did not want to leave Brandon fumbling awkwardly over the subject of Joanie. Brandon nodded; the glimmer of a smile appeared on his face. He waited for Bill to go on.

"I have a question for you. What do you suppose brought you out here this afternoon?"

"Sir?" Brandon queried, not quite sure how to respond.

"I mean, you're a fine looking, healthy young man, and it's a beautiful summer day out there. Surely you have other things to be doing rather than meeting with some middle-aged man in a dingy little office to talk about God."

Brandon was confused: had he come to the right place? He fidgeted uncomfortably in his seat.

Bill gave a little laugh, but continued in a serious manner. "Do you think it was your feelings for Joanie that brought you out here, or your curiosity to learn about Jesus?"

"Well, sir," Brandon paused for consideration, "I guess I'd have to say both."

Bill nodded with approval. "That's good. It's an honest answer and I appreciate your integrity, Brandon. You see, sometimes a man can find it confusing when he's attracted to a young woman who has brought him to Christ. But I don't see anything wrong with it. You know the saying, I'm sure, 'The Lord moves in mysterious ways.'"

"Yes, sir," Brandon replied.

"Well, that's just one of His mysterious ways. And it's a powerful one, to be sure!"

Brandon chuckled at the understatement.

"You see, we were not created as isolated beings. We're social beings. We need to be surrounded by other people, interdependently sharing our gifts in order to survive and thrive as a society. And one of the most important relationships that exists is that between a man and a woman. And it's a good thing, Brandon, you know. The Lord created that natural attraction for a reason."

Funny, Brandon had never considered the Lord mixed up in all that stuff before.

"But everything in its proper order, Brandon. The love that grows between a man and a woman should flow out of the love that exists between each of them and God. Otherwise we tend to cause an awful lot of pain and suffering. The world's full of that because it's full of people who love for selfish reasons which, of course, is not really love at all. So when you tell me you've come here for both reasons, well I consider that a noble thing."

Changing directions slightly, Bill put the question to Brandon, "So, what do you want from me here this afternoon?"

"Well, sir," Brandon began, "I don't know a thing about God, Jesus, the Bible, going to church, anything. It's all new to me. The only thing I know for sure is that I've experienced Jesus in a powerful way, and I'm filled with a burning desire to learn all I can about Him. I appreciated the pamphlets you gave me. I think I've read them through about ten times each. But I want more!"

Bill stood up and rifled through the papers on his desk, looking for something. He produced a book which had been sitting on the top of a pile off to the side and, smiling warmly, he brought it back to Brandon, saying, "Well, here's a starting point. This is a great book, with answers to all kinds of questions."

Brandon looked down at the book Bill had passed over to him: *The Holy Bible.* He smiled and chuckled to himself, appreciating Bill's sense of humour.

"But there's so much to learn about God, you just can't do it overnight. There are no crash courses. It's a journey that lasts a lifetime, and we're all on it together—at different points, of course. What you need to do is get involved in a worshipping community. Meet other Christians and talk to them. It's like I said, Brandon, we're social beings. We can't learn about God in isolation."

Brandon shifted his posture, displaying a certain awkwardness and asked, "Where would you suggest I go?"

"St. James Church, of course. Why, I would think you'd want to go to church with Joanie," he said, at first startled by the question. Then Bill recalled that Joanie had mentioned Brandon's request for space to sort out his life.

"Well, sir," explained Brandon, "I'm not really seeing Joanie right now. What I mean is, I thought it best that I stay away, get my life in order, and well, to be honest with you, make myself a better man before I . . ."

Brandon's voice trailed off, and Bill jumped in. "Before you what? I didn't suggest you propose to her or anything. Look Brandon, pardon me for saying so, but I think you've got it all wrong there. I suppose you're worried about your feelings for Joanie taking over your ability to have a solid friendship with her. But if you want to pursue those feelings someday, you'd better take the time to lay down the foundation of a friendship first. And yeah, I agree, attraction can be a mighty powerful thing. But that's where the practice of virtues comes in: self-control, self-discipline, self-mastery."

Bill looked perceptively at Brandon. "I suspect you're a man who has acted upon drives and instincts in your past relationships with women."

Brandon cast down his gaze, nodded, and looked back up to meet Bill's eyes.

"But that was in the past, Brandon, you're a new man now. You've got to trust the work that the Lord has begun in you. You've got to put your trust in Him and don't try to rely on your own strength, 'cause none of us can do it on our own. That's why He came to save us."

Bill paused and gave Brandon time to think on that. He could see how sincerely this young man was searching for truth.

It was inspiring to Bill. Times like this made all the hardships of missionary life worthwhile. *It's all for the love of souls,* the missionary thought to himself. There was no value he could place on the privilege it was to witness the work of God in someone's life. And it was humbling to be at the service of these people along their journey.

He stood up and smiled at the young man before him. "Look Brandon, you couldn't get hooked up with better people than the Collins family to learn about the faith. Take the opportunity to get to know them. I'm quite certain that they'll welcome you in. Joanie's father, John, will give you excellent direction, without compromising his moral standards. You'll be in good hands. In fact, if you impress John the way you've impressed me here today, I don't think you'll have to worry about a thing. Trust his authority as Joanie's father, and you won't go wrong!"

Brandon nodded, reflecting on what Bill was saying. It was true. Right now he had no other options for seeking out Christian companionship. Joanie was the only Christian that he really knew. There was no doubt that he wanted to be with her. And yet, he could honestly say that he was willing to set aside romantic feelings for the time being in order to have time to grow in his faith. The fact was, his longing to get to know Christ was even stronger than his longing to have Joanie as a girlfriend.

That was shocking enough to Brandon—a man whose life had once been dominated by the pursuit of physical intimacy with women. But even more shocking was the fact that he did not merely desire a physical relationship with Joanie. For the first time in his life, he wanted to give himself over in a committed relationship to one woman—and one woman only.

Brandon smiled at Bill and acknowledged his advice. "I'm so new at this Christianity business, I don't think I'll have any problem seeking the direction of Joanie's parents . . . that is, if I can get past my nervousness in meeting them."

"John and Judy Collins are two of the nicest people I've ever had the privilege to know. I'm sure you'll get along just fine!" Bill assured him.

"I'll be mindful of her father's authority, Bill. I have to admit, I've never respected a girl before, the way I do Joanie. It's actually kind of a relief to know that there's someone watching out for her, so that I can't mess up!"

Bill laughed. Brandon's sincerity came through in every word. He was not putting on an act to win a girl—this man's heart was in the right place, with Jesus at the centre.

"Mass time is Sunday morning at ten-thirty at St. James," Bill told him. "My family goes to that parish as well. I'll be watching for you."

They exchanged another solid handshake, both of them sensing the beginning of a wonderful adventure ahead.

Chapter 17

Brandon fumbled around nervously Sunday morning as he got ready to go. The peculiarity of the entire situation was not lost on him: Brandon Vaughn was going to church.

He worried about how Joanie's family would react to seeing him there. He considered calling Joanie to give her a "heads-up", rather than catching her by surprise. But he just could not bring himself to dial the phone.

He took out his card from her. By now he knew the prayer by heart, but he liked to look at the picture of Mary as he prayed. It helped him to stay focussed. He liked the way her heart was exposed with flames rising out of it.

"Oh, Mary, let my heart burn with love like that for Jesus!" he said, in hushed reverence.

He then opened the card and reread Joanie's letter. He began losing heart about going to church at St. James. Her letter did indicate a need for space. Maybe Bill was wrong.

Jesus, give me a sign so I know what I'm supposed to do here. I'm confused and afraid of making a mistake.

He wandered around his apartment for several minutes, half-expecting something to fall out of the sky and point him in the right direction.

"Anything, God," he said out loud, "any little sign from you, and I'll go." He felt a little ridiculous and somewhat childish, as he waited for a signal.

Lying down on his bed, he saw the Bible which Bill had given to him. It was still open where he had left it. Picking it up to read some more, he bumped the pages closed, exposing the inside front cover. At the bottom left corner there was a sticker attached, reading: *Donated to Catholic Campus Evangelization by St. James Roman Catholic Parish.*

"That'll do, God. Thanks!" Brandon grabbed his jean jacket and keys and flew out the door, before he lost his nerve.

☩   ☩   ☩

Sunday morning was always a circus at the Collins household: ten people to wake up, feed, get cleaned up, and dressed, with only three bathrooms. It was "Mass pandemonium", as their father would call it.

They had gotten better at it over the years, though. Joanie's mom attributed that to the fact that her older daughters had actually grown up to be quite helpful resources in the home. Judy could assign them each to a certain younger member of the family and, in a buddy system effort, they would generally make it to church just in time.

This Sunday morning, though, was the Sunday Joanie, her sisters, and Isaac sang with the youth choir at Mass. They had to arrive early enough to set up. On these Sundays the family took two vehicles.

✝   ✝   ✝

Brandon did not want to arrive too early for church, not quite knowing what he would do while he waited. He knew no one there except Joanie and Bill Curran. His steps were unhurried as he walked up to the front entry. He wanted to be here, but he was feeling apprehensive just the same. There were people coming in all around him, and he could feel himself being swept up with the crowd. He gave in to the momentum and was carried through the big open doors.

The large foyer was buzzing with the eager greetings of fellow parishioners catching up on the past week as they took off their jackets before going into the church. It was the children who caught Brandon's attention, darting in and out between the adult obstacles around them. Brandon smiled in amusement. It was a happy atmosphere, full of fellowship—not at all the image of church he had carried with him his whole life.

Brandon entered the church and looked about, taking in his surroundings. He saw Joanie up at the front. She was obviously involved with the music, and he did not want to disturb her. He took a step back, hoping she had not seen him, and slipped into the closest pew. As more people arrived, Brandon was pushed further down the pew to make room for a family coming in. Since there were already people at the other end, he found himself trapped with no way to run had he felt so inclined.

He watched as people genuflected before entering their pews. Even the little children displayed this outward sign of reverence. He observed people as they knelt in prayer. These simple actions stirred him to respect, for although he did not have the proper words or know the motions, Brandon's heart carried a deep reverence for the Lord. The young man could truly sense Jesus' presence as he sat in silence in this humble church setting. He was grateful that the Lord had brought him here this morning.

He looked up and saw the life-size crucifix that hung at the front of the church behind the altar. It was awesome. He could not take his eyes off it. He had read about Christ's sacrifice for the redemption of mankind in the brochures from C.C.E., but it was still a fairly abstract concept—one which he had not completely grasped. This was the first time Brandon had come face to face with the image of Christ's death on the cross.

He could see, in the sculpted image of Christ, the pain and suffering that Jesus must have experienced. Brandon wondered why it had been necessary, if Jesus had been God. Why was His death so important that the universal symbol of Christianity had become the cross? Surely His life had been more important than His death.

Yet as Brandon's eyes gazed upon the image of the Lord, he began to understand. The power of the outstretched arms of Jesus defied the vulnerability of Him in His crucifixion. Jesus did not have to be there—He was God—He had chosen to be there! It seemed to Brandon, in that moment of understanding, that the cross was truly a symbol of love in its finest expression.

He noticed that as people came in they would dip their hands in water and cross themselves. He remembered the first time he had seen Joanie crossing herself at the lunch table. Her beauty had certainly caught his eye, but it was that simple—yet bold—gesture which had distinguished her from all the other girls he had ever met. He chuckled to himself over how far he had come in so short a time.

An announcement was made, and Mass began. People picked up their hymnals and stood. Brandon had missed the number of the song and did not bother trying to find it. As the music started, he looked up to watch the choir. Joanie was mixed into the flock of young people, singing her heart out—just the way he had remembered her the night of the concert.

He could not keep his eyes off her; he wanted to be with her so much. She had grown even more beautiful in the ten days that had passed since he had last walked and talked with her. So distracted was he in thought that he had not noticed the song ending and everyone making the sign of the cross. It was the chorus of "Amen" from the congregation that tuned him back in to reality.

He watched, he listened, and he even tried to pray. But everything was so foreign to him.

He enjoyed the homily and judged the priest to be quite a fine speaker. Brandon figured the dynamic priest to be in his early thirties. He was a tall, good-looking young man. Brandon wondered at how a man like that had come to make the decision to give himself completely to the service of God in the Church. Reflecting upon the recent action of the Holy Spirit in his own life, Brandon realized how it could happen.

Then a disconcerting thought entered his mind. What if God was intending for *him* to become a priest? Would he be prepared to follow Jesus, even then? He closed his eyes and allowed the peace of God to calm his fears. He knew in his heart that he would follow wherever the Lord led him. God would supply him with the courage, just as He already had in order for Brandon to abandon his old life.

He looked up at Joanie, sitting with the choir. She was entirely his heart's desire. Brandon sighed, confident that he was not being called to the priesthood.

Brandon tried to follow the movement of the Mass, but he felt clumsy and awkward in the pew. He sheepishly watched the people kneel and rise, not knowing whether to follow along with them or to just stay put. In the end, he decided to sit and try not to draw attention to himself.

He closed his eyes and listened to the prayers. They were truly beautiful. Each word was so full of meaning. He was especially moved by the words that said: "On the night He was betrayed, Jesus took the bread . . ."

Brandon could not remember it all, but he reflected on the word "betrayed" for some time. He remembered the encounter with Mark on Friday night. Brandon was ashamed of himself for having betrayed Jesus so easily. In his heart, he begged the Lord to forgive him for having been such a fool!

✝   ✝   ✝

Joanie prayed intensely for Brandon throughout Mass. She wanted so much to share this with him: to be able to go to Mass together, to pray together, and to grow in faith together. She prayed earnestly for his intentions and asked Jesus to purify her heart so that her love for Brandon would reflect Christ's love for him.

It was not until Communion time that Joanie noticed her family. They were going up for Communion and Jessie, in her impish way, was waving at Joanie in the choir. Joanie waved back and smiled as she sang. She watched Jessie trot alongside her Dad, holding his hand all the way back to their pew.

Suddenly, Joanie's heart stopped, and she found herself lost for the words of the song. Her eyes opened wide, and her mouth hung open. What was *Brandon* doing there, sitting with her family? Someone in the choir nudged Joanie to keep singing, and Joanie fumbled to find her way back into the music.

Her heart was racing. The song ended, and she sat down. She had no idea what to make of the situation. She was fairly certain Brandon had no idea that he was sitting right next to her father. The irony of it all made her feel giddy inside.

She restlessly bounced her legs and grabbed nervously at the ringlets hanging down around her neck below her upswept hair. How was she going to deal with this? Her parents were cool, they would behave—well, for sure her mom would—but Joanie could not be sure that her dad would not give Brandon a hard time.

What was Brandon thinking, coming here? Joanie felt certain that he was not ready to meet her family, for his sake, not for hers. She just imagined poor Brandon, an only child, raised without a father, lost in a sea of Collinses.

Her heart raced on. She wanted to be with Brandon more than anything. She looked over at him, sitting with his eyes closed, in prayer, she surmised. He was so handsome. She closed her own eyes and thanked Jesus for having brought Brandon here this glorious Sunday morning.

The final song was like torture for Joanie to sing because now that she was aware of Brandon's presence, she could not keep her eyes away from him. He was watching her. Their eyes met and rested in each other's gaze. Joanie sang the song to Brandon, as though they were the only two people in the church.

Brandon stood there, lost in Joanie's consuming eyes. He had not meant to distract her this way, but now that she had found him, he could not help but indulge himself. He could sense her nervousness, and he felt badly that he had not forewarned her. But as they smiled at each other, he knew everything would be all right.

People began to leave their pews. Brandon just stood there. Should he go up to meet her or would she come to him? Joanie motioned for him to meet her at the back. He stepped out of the pew behind the family beside him and followed them into the foyer.

Joanie walked to the back, nervously trying to decide how to deal with this situation. When she entered the foyer she saw that Brandon was still close to her father. She took a deep breath and approached them.

Brandon smiled at her. He was gentleness mixed with confidence. All her apprehensions faded away in his presence. She smiled back but then turned away her gaze from him and looked up at her father, standing to the left of Brandon. She was aware that this diversion had given Brandon a start. Reaching out she took hold of his right arm.

Without looking back up at him, she turned Brandon to face her father, saying, "Daddy, I want you to meet Brandon Vaughn. Brandon, this is my father, John Collins."

Her voice was calm and collected and full of significance.

It was Brandon's mouth that fell open this time. He looked between Joanie and her father, recognizing the man beside whom he had sat during Mass. Regaining his composure with a swiftness that quite impressed Joanie, Brandon reached forward and offered Mr. Collins a firm handshake.

"Good to meet you, sir." Brandon's voice was steady and sincere.

"Well, Brandon, this is an unexpected pleasure." Mr. Collins's handshake was firm and he too had a sincere, although somewhat apprehensive, tone to his voice. "Joanie, you didn't tell your mother and me that Brandon would be here this morning, much less sitting right next to us."

"Well, that's because I didn't know Brandon would be here this morning, much less sitting right next to *you*, Daddy."

Her tone was not lost on Brandon.

Brandon laughed apologetically. He looked up and saw Bill Curran approaching them. "I wasn't sure that I was going to be here either, but you can blame it all on that guy, there." Brandon gestured to Bill, grateful for his timely entrance on the scene.

Bill gave a hearty laugh. He extended a handshake, first to John and next to Brandon. Putting his arm over Joanie's shoulder, he gave it a squeeze, saying, "Well, well, it is a small world, after all! I noticed you picked a good place to sit during Mass, Brandon." His voice revealed his amusement with the entire situation.

Brandon chuckled and looked down at Joanie who just closed her eyes and shook her head. *Unbelievable! I keep asking for signs, God, but every time You give me one, I never know how to interpret it. . . . But thank You for Brandon being here, anyway!*

"What's going on over here?" The question came playfully from a woman's voice entering the scene. "I have the distinct feeling I'm missing out on something good."

Joanie breathed in deeply and said, "Mom, this is Brandon Vaughn," and turning to Brandon, she added with feeling, "I want you to meet my mother, Judy Collins."

Judy gave Brandon a rich and beautiful smile. Brandon was struck instantly by this woman's warmth. He immediately liked her. She was not what he had expected, but just at that moment, he was not quite sure what he had expected.

For the mother of eight, she was a very attractive woman. Funny, how he had not thought that possible. He took her to be in her mid-forties, a slender woman of average height. She had the same hair and eye colour as Joanie. He could see Joanie in her features, especially in her smile and the way her eyes danced when she spoke.

"It's a tremendous honour to meet you, Mrs. Collins," he said with such charm and distinction that Joanie's heart took a leap.

"I've been looking forward to this moment for quite some time now," Judy said, still smiling. "And please, call me Judy. It's good to have you here, Brandon. You will come and join us for brunch at our house, won't you?"

The tone of her voice gave Brandon the impression that he should do as she said. "I'd like that very much," he replied, sincerely.

Joanie reached over, took Brandon's hand in hers, and began to lead him away. "If you'll excuse us," she acknowledged the group, smiling sweetly, "I'd like to talk to Brandon—alone."

She did not wait for a response.

It felt so good to hold Brandon's hand again. Joanie shut out every other sense so as not to be denied the thrill of his touch.

Leading him to a small room off the back of the church foyer, she looked up at him, still holding his hand and asked, "What on earth are you doing here?" Her voice revealed the shock of when she had first seen Brandon sitting beside her father.

Brandon explained about his meeting with Bill. Joanie smiled and listened, her eyes told Brandon to keep talking. She wanted to hear everything that had happened to him since they had last been together.

Motioning for him to sit in a chair, she sat facing him so as to keep him in her gaze. Reluctantly, she decided she should let go of his hand. Their relationship was new, and Joanie needed to guard herself, especially in light of the overwhelming attraction she had for this man.

They talked for over half an hour when, suddenly, Zack poked his little auburn head in the room and said, "Joanie, Mom sent me to tell you it's time to go home. She also said that you could go with Brandon to show him the way. Bye." He pulled his head back around the corner as quickly as it had appeared.

"That was Zack," Joanie laughed. "He's eight. And as we drive, I think I'd better review names and ages for you, or you'll be completely lost." They got up to leave.

Brandon laughed and said pensively, "Eight kids? Wow!"

Joanie returned the laugh and in a playfully patronizing way, added, "Honey, you ain't seen nothin' yet! When we get to my house, what d'you bet there are four or five other families over? There could be forty people there, no problem!"

Brandon choked down a swallow and looked at Joanie in disbelief, or terror; she was not quite sure which.

"Don't worry, Brandon, I'll take care of you!" She gave him a charming smile as they walked out of the church together.

Brandon wanted to take her hand, but sensed he should hold off. They strolled down the street together. Joanie was in no particular hurry. She figured the slower they went, the more time they would have to themselves.

"I'm so glad you came today, Brandon," she said.

"I'm sorry I didn't give you any warning," he apologized.

"The surprise was much better," she admitted. "I've missed you," she added, simply.

He looked down at her as he opened the door of the vehicle for her to get in. "I've never missed being with anyone as much as I've missed being with you these past ten days. I'm so glad Bill talked me into coming."

Chapter 18

A whole new set of emotions surged through Joanie as she got into Brandon's vehicle. The realization that she was taking Brandon home to meet her family seemed to strike her all at once. The fact that their relationship had transformed to this level since she had last seen him, suddenly seemed real.

She looked around the vehicle. It was just like Brandon: neat and tidy, bold and handsome, rugged and strong. She breathed deeply and smiled to herself: it even smelled good. As Brandon stepped in on his side, she caught a whiff of his cologne. It amazed her what powerful feelings scent could evoke. She kept her eyes closed for a moment, soaking up the whole experience.

Brandon smiled down at her, noticing how she always seemed to take such great delight in everything she did.

"How do you do that?" he asked, out of the blue.

"Do what?" she returned, opening her eyes, looking puzzled at his question.

"Breathe in life as though it could intoxicate you. You live each moment so full of joy. I've never known anyone like you before," he said in sheer amazement and wonder at this girl.

"I'm a one-of-a-kind kinda gal, Brandon," she returned, stretching both arms in front of her and smiling mysteriously. "So, if you want to figure me out, go ahead and try. But I warn you . . . it may take you a lifetime."

Still facing straight ahead, she looked over at him from the corner of her eye and waited for his response.

"That'd be just fine with me." And with that he put on his sunglasses, started up the vehicle, and pulled away. He never once took his eyes off the road, but he could feel Joanie smiling.

He was comfortable and relaxed in Joanie's presence, with such a tremendous sense of peace in his soul. He wondered at how life could have gone from being so ordinary to so extraordinary in one short month's time.

✞   ✞   ✞

Brandon pulled up into the driveway behind the Collins "Catholic Cadillac": a fifteen-seater, blue, Chevy van. As he turned to Joanie he had a look of consternation on his face.

Joanie just smiled at him and said, "Relax, Brandon. Mom invited you to *have* lunch with us, not to *be* lunch for us!" Then feigning concern, she added, "I just hope Mom let them know that."

She pointed Brandon's attention to the flood of children streaming across the front yard coming to greet them.

Brandon's eyes opened wide. He had never experienced what it was like to be around a large family. And, just as Joanie had warned him, there were over a dozen little kids charging at them. He pulled uncomfortably at his collar and shifted his head back and forth as if trying to clear breathing space.

"Where'd they all come from?" he asked in a tone of awe.

Joanie laughed and gave him a little push on the arm as she turned to get out of the vehicle. "Come on, big boy—don't tell me you're afraid of a bunch of little kids?"

Her laugh carried back to him, as he deliberated between getting out or running away. "Go ahead and laugh," he mumbled to himself, knowing what secret delight she must be experiencing, watching him squirm.

With open arms, Joanie received the hugs and kisses from her littlest siblings, cousins, and friends. Brandon walked to the front of the Pathfinder and leaned against the silver-grey fender.

He was taking in the whole scene. The love and affection among the members of this family and community was clearly evident. Brandon felt as though the mystery of Joanie was beginning to be unlocked, getting his first taste of her family life.

It did not take long before a few of the young boys threw themselves at Brandon, looking for a playful response. Brandon had had no previous experience with little children. His family life had consisted of himself and his mother. Now, as he stood victim to this wild mob, he was not quite sure how to react.

He threw a look at Joanie that clearly said, *Help!*

Joanie stepped in and shooed the boys away to go and play. "Give Brandon a chance to get inside the house. You'll scare him off before he ever sets foot through the door. Aaron, Daniel, Curtis—scoot. Brandon will play with you later."

The boys ran off and Brandon looked at Joanie, as anyone would look at the hero who had just rescued him, and said, "Thanks. Don't leave me alone like that again," he added, half-joking—but only half.

"Come on," she laughed at his forced expression of fear. She motioned with her head for him to follow her into the house, as she picked up Jessie and tossed her up in the air while she walked.

Brandon followed Joanie and a small herd of little ones in through the front door. He paused momentarily before crossing the threshold. This was definitely an occasion for him to mark in his memory. He knew that he was stepping into a whole new world and a whole new way of living.

The seventy-year-old house truly was a grand old place, just as Joanie had indicated to Brandon. The glassed-in front porch was cozy and inviting.

On either side of the room there was a wooden table, both of which were surrounded with comfortable-looking chairs. At one table a couple of teenage boys were playing backgammon, and there was a lively game of cards going on at the other table with four young girls.

As they entered the front door, there were hooks on the walls for hanging jackets and a beautiful wooden deacon's bench that just begged to be sat upon. The staircase to the second floor went up from the left side of the front hall. Off to the right side were French doors that opened up into a huge family room, which boasted a beautiful bay window facing the front yard.

On the other side of the living room was another set of French doors that opened up to the large dining room and open kitchen. There was a small back hallway that led out to a back entry with a washroom and laundry facility. A fairly narrow staircase descended to the basement from this room. The entire house, from outside to in, was a mixture of charming old character and creatively-designed renovations.

It was a practical home for such a large family. Brandon noted how well-kept and tidy it was. He found the children's drawings and artwork taped onto walls and doors to be delightful. Piles of books lined bookshelves in the kitchen, and he recalled Joanie talking about having been home-schooled. There were holy pictures all around and a crucifix in each room. There was no mistaking it: this was a Catholic home.

He followed Joanie through to the kitchen where the adults were all gathered. Brandon was relieved to see Bill Curran there, the only familiar face in this huge crowd. As Joanie was pulled away to help with lunch preparations, Bill made introductions quickly around the room.

There were aunts and uncles and older cousins and friends. Brandon's head was swirling in a sea of names, and everyone was enjoying the novelty of seeing this young man so overwhelmed. Someone offered Brandon a glass of wine, as was the family's custom while brunch was being prepared. He accepted it gratefully and looked around for a safe corner in which to take a seat and get out of the lime-light.

There was no such luck. John Collins grabbed him by the arm and pulled him into the current conversation of the group of adults standing around the dining room. Brandon smiled, feeling like a little boy who had just moved to a new school half-way through the year. He was not quite sure how or if he would ever fit in.

Despite Brandon's previous plea not to be left alone, Joanie had disappeared over in the kitchen area and had not returned.

Brandon's senses were so over-stimulated that when someone directed a question at him, he realized that he had no idea what that person had just asked. Awkwardly, he requested the young man before him to repeat the question.

"Don't worry, Brandon, I guess this would be fairly intimidating for you. I can only imagine what it must be like to stand on the outside of this crowd and be looking in. We probably seem pretty weird."

Brandon could not get over the confidence with which this young man addressed him. Brandon took him to be in his early twenties, for sure a few years younger than he was. He was tall and athletic looking, with a friendly face and a calm and natural voice.

"I wouldn't quite say weird, but definitely overwhelming," Brandon confessed, honestly.

Mike laughed and in an encouraging tone said, "Hang in there. If you survive today, you'll be able to survive anything."

Then changing the tone of the conversation, Mike reintroduced himself, offering Brandon a friendly handshake. "The name's Mike Ledoux. I'm Joanie's cousin and I play keyboards with *New Spring.*"

"Great music," Brandon responded, sincerely. "I can't tell you how impressed I was by your group at the concert I attended last month. You've really got something powerful there."

"It's a ministry and if it weren't so powerful to be a part of it, I'd probably have dropped out before now. It sure takes up a lot of time between rehearsals and gigs. I'm going into my fourth year of Commerce this fall. Every year it gets harder to manage our schedule. But if it's meant to be, it'll happen. Something will work out, I'm sure."

"I'm a Commerce grad, myself," Brandon informed him.

"Really, how'd you end up a commercial producer?" Mike asked, with interest.

Brandon looked curiously at his companion. How did Mike know his occupation? Obviously Brandon's name had worked its way around Joanie's family.

"I worked lots in radio while I was going to school, as a DJ and in the sound department. I had a foot in the door at the station. I've been there ten years now. Started as a volunteer in high school and worked my way up."

They moved their conversation to the living room where they were joined by a few older teens and young adults. They continued visiting until brunch was served.

Brandon was surprised to find how comfortable he felt in this crowd. He liked these people; they were truly likeable. While he could not say he felt at home in their midst yet, he definitely appreciated the effort they were making for him to feel welcome.

The family gathered to pray. This was completely foreign to Brandon. He stepped back and silently watched as they recited a few prayers. Even the littlest children knew the words and joined in. It made Brandon feel kind of stupid.

Then Joanie's father spoke out, concluding the prayers. "We thank You, Lord, for the opportunity You have given us to gather today as family and with friends. We ask for Your blessing on all our guests, but especially on Brandon as he joins us here for the first of what we hope will be many visits to come."

Brandon shrank back at the sound of his name and the sudden attention to himself that it had stirred. He had not been expecting that.

The look John directed toward Brandon as he prayed made Brandon realize that he was not just receiving God's blessing to be here, but John's as well.

The family concluded grace in making the sign of the cross. Brandon decided that he wanted to be sure to get Joanie to teach him how to do that whenever he got a chance to be alone with her. It occurred to him that he might not get that opportunity again here today.

After helping serve the smaller children, Joanie slipped through the line of people waiting to take their meals, buffet style. Stealing up beside Brandon's left arm, she gently set her hand on it.

He looked down at her, and she smiled back apologetically. "I'm sorry I got taken away from you. How are you doing?"

Her voice was hushed and private. Brandon carried on in that same manner, determining that this was about as much privacy as they would get. "Better . . . now." His eyes looked down where her hand was resting on his arm. Then he whispered, playfully, "I don't know if this is some sort of initiation process, but I hope I pass so that I can come back."

"Oh, you already have," she assured him, patting his arm. "My sisters, my cousins, my mom, and all the ladies in the kitchen are almost as crazy about you as I am!"

Her words were simple, but the effect was not lost on Brandon. They got their food and joined a group of young people for lunch.

After the meal, Judy announced, "Since the ladies did the prep, I guess that means you men are on cleaning detail. Have fun!"

She looked over at Brandon, and in an effort to make him feel at home, she tossed him a dishrag and playfully added, "I'm sure you must know what to do with that. The dish soap is under the sink."

The women had already retreated from the kitchen to make room for the men who were beginning to gather up dishes and put away food. Though taken by surprise by the informality of Joanie's mom, Brandon caught the dishrag and made his way to the sink to take his station.

He smiled at Judy as he passed by her and confessed, "I've never washed dishes for a crowd this size before, but I'll do my best."

She patted him on the shoulder and said, "I have a lot of confidence in your abilities, Brandon. I'm sure you'll do just fine."

Her eyes sparkled in a way that so reminded Brandon of Joanie's. He liked her and wondered at what a remarkable woman she must be.

Dish duty was an amusing time. The men and older boys joked around and made light conversation as they worked. Brandon was fascinated to see the way they all pitched in. With seemingly little effort, the job was done in no time at all.

Mission accomplished, Caleb, a red-headed, fifteen-year-old cousin of Joanie's, proposed that they all head down to the park at the end of the street to play some touch football. Brandon was happy to go along with that.

He figured he might feel a little more in his element there, having played football in high school. Brandon had not just played football. Like anything he did, he had been the best at it: captain of the football team and MVP all four years he had played.

What Brandon did not realize was that this game of football was going to involve everybody, right down to the three-year-olds. What was worse, the kids had decided to elect Brandon as one of the team captains. Mike, Joanie's cousin, was the opposing captain.

Brandon made some objections, but the kids were relentless. He was told to make first pick for his team.

In an act of sheer desperation he said, "Well, if I have to do this, I'm not doin' it alone. So I pick Joanie."

"Not me, silly," Joanie corrected him, with a smile. "We always pick from the littlest to the biggest."

"Yes, well nobody told me any rules." Smiling, he reached over and grabbed her arm, pulling her over to his side.

"Woooo-hooo," the kids sang out in spontaneous chorus, "Joanie's got a boyfriend!"

Joanie was not at all flustered by the teasing. Rolling her eyes, she scolded them, "Settle down, already." Turning to Brandon, she added, "You see what a commotion you've caused!" And she lightly hit him on the shoulder.

Brandon defended himself saying, "I don't know anybody else's name!"

Mike, picking up on the fun of the moment announced, "Well, Brandon can go ahead and pick his sissy-girlfriend, but as for me, I'm goin' for," he paused for dramatics and in a low, full tone said, "Jo-o-o-nah!"

Jonah was one of the younger Curran boys, four years old and built like a tank. Jumping for joy, he ran over to Mike and gave him a high-five.

Joanie shook her head at Mike's little production. "We pick Jessie." She reached out her arms for Jessie to come running, knowing how important it would be for Jessie to be on her team. "Of course I have to have my little angel on my side," Joanie said, looking straight into Jessie's bright eyes. Jessie beamed as Joanie lifted her up.

Joanie turned to Brandon with Jessie and, beginning to hand her over to him, said with great enthusiasm, "Check out this awesome player, Brandon!"

Brandon smiled and tried to look Jessie in the eye, but the three-year-old shied away and tucked her head into Joanie's shoulder.

Joanie assured her, "It's okay, Jessie. Brandon likes little girls with ponytails."

Jessie lifted her head slowly to take Brandon into her sideways glance. Deciding that maybe he was okay, she flipped her little ponytail around for him to admire.

"That's the prettiest ponytail I've ever seen, Jessie," Brandon whispered to her. Her face beamed with delight, and she reached over for Brandon to take her.

Realizing what had just happened, Brandon clumsily took the little girl in his arms. He had never held a child before—ever! His eyes begged Joanie for help.

Joanie just laughed and said, "I've got a team to pick. You just relax and get Jessie to teach you everybody's name."

Brandon shifted Jessie around until he finally found a comfortable hold for her. He enlisted her assistance, and the child rattled off the names of everyone there, two or three times over. She wrapped her little arm around his neck and used the other hand to point. Jessie was absolutely delightful, and Brandon took great satisfaction in her eager affection toward him.

He looked over at Joanie, picking out the team for him. She looked good in those cut-off blue jeans and tangerine T-shirt. The ball cap on her head gave evidence to her spunky nature. Yet the elegant curls, which had been pulled through the back loop, betrayed her gracefulness. They hung loosely down her back, shining in the bright afternoon light.

God, You sure outdid Yourself on that one! A smile crept up from his lips as he took in Joanie's beauty.

Her dynamic personality shone through every little thing she did. No one was left to feel unimportant when Joanie was around. From children to adults, she was respected and admired by all. Brandon was so proud of her. This exceptional woman was … was what? She was not his girlfriend, not yet. He still needed to ask permission from her father to date her.

Brandon had really not prepared himself for that today. He liked John Collins. And furthermore, he had the distinct impression that John had taken a liking to him. But looking around at all these amazing children, Brandon began to understand why a man would establish such protective boundaries around his family.

If I were John, would I allow Joanie to date a guy like me? Probably not. Brandon resigned himself to accept whatever John's decision would be.

You know how much I want her, Lord. But I know how much I don't deserve her. I'll let you sort out the difference.

Once the teams were picked, Joanie came and stood with Brandon again. There were ten children gathered around them by now, and enthusiasm was mounting.

It did not take Brandon long to adjust his thinking to this multi-age football match. The rules were announced by Mike: "You only get three downs to try and make a touchdown. On the third down you can try to make a touchdown, or kick the ball, without the other team knowing which you're gonna do. If you don't make a touchdown, the ball gets turned over to the other team after the third down. It's two-hand touch … that means no tackling, Josh and Zack!"

Everyone laughed. "After five Mississippi's the quarterback is live and can be rushed." Looking down at his watch, Mike announced, "It's three o'clock, let's play until four-thirty. Agreed?"

Taking in the general consensus, he continued, "Great! Well, let's do a rock-paper-scissors, Brandon, to see who starts. Winner takes the ball back twenty yards from centre, and his team does a kick-off. And," grabbing the ball cap off Isaac's dark head of hair, he threw it down on the field at approximately centre, "Isaac's cap's our marker."

Brandon lost the rock-paper-scissors, showing a rock to Mike's paper. Brandon conceded his shoulder to Mike's punch and, laughing, they took their teams to each side.

The game began with a tumbling kick-off by Eric Curran, a long-legged ten-year-old. The atmosphere was great fun. There was everything from impressive throws to fluky catches and the occasional awesome interception.

By half an hour or so into the game, Brandon was actually starting to sort out who was on his team—a helpful thing when you've been elected quarterback. Up until then he had only made one tactical error, throwing a beautiful pass to Joanie's sister, Katie, who had been pretending to be on his team. She glided down the side of the field, almost making a touchdown.

At four-twenty-three Brandon's team was at third down, twenty yards to go. The pressure was on with a score of twenty-eight to twenty-four against them. He called his team into a brief huddle and laid out the strategy. It was bold, but it just might work.

The hut was made, and Brandon caught the ball. Joanie ran past him, carrying her little brother, Aaron, in a piggy-back. Brandon passed the ball carefully, and Aaron made the catch. Then, with the swiftness of an eagle, Brandon flew forward to cross behind in Joanie's wake. He grabbed Aaron off her back and threw him over his shoulders. With the little tyke tightly gripping the ball, Brandon ran the distance to make a touchdown.

Their team cheered wildly as Brandon and Aaron crossed the end zone. Brandon set down the five-year-old boy and watched as Aaron threw down the football and proceeded to do a victory dance. It was an exciting end to a great game. Brandon lifted Aaron high on his shoulder and ran back up the field, soaking in the glory of their victory.

Joanie stood back and beamed.

After the game, the families went back to the Collinses' house for a cold drink. The guests were beginning to pack up their children and call it a day. Grown-ups were chatting, the children were hooting and hollering, and the whole house seemed to be buzzing with excitement.

Brandon leaned against the counter by the sink and observed the chaos. It was unlike anything he had ever experienced in his life, but he liked it. In fact, thinking back on the entire day, he could not remember when he had ever had so much wholesome fun.

He became aware of Joanie looking at him from across the room. Coming out of his trance, he smiled back at her and winked. Her eyes sparkled back at him, and he marvelled at this girl who was so full of life and love. Now he could see why.

Joanie slipped out to help her aunts and uncles and friends pack up little ones. Brandon followed to the doorway of the living room and watched. It was quite an ordeal, mobilizing these large families. Brandon was in awe. He wondered how they would sort out all the commotion, but within fifteen minutes or so, the house was quiet.

Most of the Collins family had followed the company outside. The younger children were jumping up and down waving goodbye as vehicles pulled away.

Brandon was left in the living room with Joanie's sisters. Amie sat down and began, most impressively, to play the piano. Katie had disappeared and returned with a sketch pad and pencil. She sat down on the couch to draw.

Maggie was making light conversation with Brandon as they stood in the doorway between the kitchen and the living room. They were discussing the football game and rehashing the fun moments. From her perch on the couch, Katie called out an apology for having tricked Brandon. He laughed and told her he would have done the same.

Realizing he was now the only guest left, an awkwardness began to steal over Brandon. He headed toward the front door, meeting Joanie and her folks as they re-entered the house. About to say good-bye and thank his gracious hosts, Brandon was interrupted by an invitation from John to go out and see his workshop. Brandon nodded his head respectfully and followed Joanie's father to the garage. Joanie did not go along.

Chapter 19

At six foot one, John Collins was a fairly tall man; still, Brandon stood a full inch taller. Brandon observed that this man carried himself in the same confident way that so characterized Joanie. He had a distinguished look: grey at the temples with a slightly receding hairline. Brandon guessed him to be in his late forties.

As they headed along the stone path to the garage, which was situated off to the back right corner of the yard, Brandon noticed the younger Collins children at play. It was a big yard with two rather imposing climbing trees in it. There was a tire swing hanging from the lower branches of the one willow. Near the other willow tree was a cinder block campfire pit with crudely made benches around it. It looked as though it had been well used.

Beautifully kept raised-bed gardens lined the side of the garage and the opposing fenced side of the yard. At the back corner of the yard was a play-house that was raised up above a sandbox full of toys. A ladder climbed up one side of the structure, and a slide came down from the other. There was an apple tree that stood near the back fence, extending its branches into the alley. The grass in the yard was patchy and showed the evidence of the children's many hours of play in this safe little haven.

Isaac was sitting barefoot in the lower branches of one of the willow trees. He had a discman on and was swinging his legs to the music as he whittled a long willow branch with a red pocket knife. He had the appearance of a mountain boy, displaced in the wrong century.

Zack and Aaron were wrestling, and John called out for the two boys to settle down or they would have to deal with him. He had the unmistakable voice of authority. The boys fell into line at once. They stopped their tussling and proceeded to get their bikes from the stand near the front of the yard.

✟   ✟   ✟

The workshop was an impressive sight to Brandon. It was well organized and a good size. There were tools of every description, each kept neatly in its place. A table saw took a prominent position in the middle of the shop. Three of the walls were lined with cupboards and counters full of hardware and power tools. One wall had shelving extending to the ceiling, with wood and other materials, neatly stacked, accessible for the finding.

John went over to a side cupboard and, opening it, he produced a wooden box about six inches wide by ten inches long and five inches deep. It was ornately decorated on the sides with the name "Katie" carved into the top.

"It's not quite done," John admitted as he opened it to reveal the little ballerina who had been hiding inside. "I still have to hook up the music box," he added, turning it over to show that the underside was unfinished. He pointed to the little music box mechanism still sitting on the shelf from where he had taken the wooden box.

Setting the box on the countertop, he took the mechanism down from the shelf and wound it up to play a pleasant old-time melody. *"In the Good Ol' Summer Time,"* he informed Brandon. "Katie's birthday is next week. . . . I've almost finished it for her. I made one for each of her older sisters when they had turned sixteen. It's become a kind of family tradition." John picked up the wooden box again as he spoke, examining the details of it for mistakes.

"It's a beautiful piece of work, sir," Brandon remarked, notably impressed. "May I?" he asked as he reached out to look at it.

"Yeah, you bet," John answered casually, handing it over.

Brandon was struck by the charm and beauty of this piece of artwork. It was such a simple gift, yet made with so much love, care, and attention. Brandon perceived this man to be quite a perfectionist: the kind of man who laboured over every detail of a job, leaving nothing out of his consideration.

As Brandon handed the music box back to John, he met his eyes straight on. Brandon breathed deeply, mustering up all the nerve he had within him to address Joanie's father.

"You know, sir, I'm quite taken with your daughter, Joanie," he began, "and I'm grateful for this opportunity alone with you to talk about—well I guess—to ask for your permission to date her."

He had done it. It was out. The worst was over, or so he hoped. He felt a sense of relief for having survived to this point.

"Well, Brandon, you know that's not an easy thing for me to do," John answered in a serious tone.

Brandon nodded, keeping his eyes fixed on the man before him.

"You see, Joanie's my little girl, and I'd die protecting her or any of my family for that matter. That's what being a dad and husband's all about. I don't know you yet; although, what I've seen here today, I've liked. Joanie has shared quite a bit with her mother and me regarding you and your relationship. It goes without saying that she's as taken with you as you are with her. But a man has more to take into consideration than just that."

He turned around, putting away the wooden box. Facing Brandon again, John leaned back comfortably against the counter and motioned for Brandon to make himself comfortable as well.

"You know we're a Catholic family and with that comes a whole way of living that I'm sure is quite foreign to you. I realize that you're going through some changes right now. I'm impressed with how you've responded to Jesus working in your life. I can see that you're eager to learn about God, not just to satisfy Joanie, but out of a real sense of being called. That impresses me," he said, nodding to himself. "But I gather that your past has been full of, well, shall we say, casual relationships."

Brandon looked down reflectively. That sense of not being good enough for Joanie was there again.

It was apparent that the next question was an awkward one for John to ask. "Would you be willing to tell me about your past, Brandon?"

Brandon met John's eyes straight on. He was not proud of his past; although, there had been a time in his life when he had boasted about all his conquests. It had been a fair question. Brandon searched for a place to begin.

"Well, sir, I became sexually active at seventeen. I've spent the last nine years of my life living a lifestyle that I'm ashamed of now. I've slept with a lot of women over those years. After I met Joanie, even before I came to believe in Jesus, something changed. I just couldn't go on living that way. . . . It's now been over a month since"—Brandon shook his head and made a stifled grunt—"I know it doesn't seem like much . . . but I'm sincere in my change, sir. I will *never* go back to that way of living again."

"I believe you, Brandon," John answered, nodding thoughtfully.

"I've been tested for STDs. As far as I know, I'm not carrying anything. I need to go back for ongoing testing for awhile yet, to be sure." Brandon shook his head and cast down his eyes.

"I know I don't deserve anyone as sweet and innocent as your daughter. I'm not pretending to be good enough for her, sir. But since I've found Jesus, Joanie's like the sun to me. I couldn't imagine a day in my life without her now. I'd give anything for her. She means everything to me. I can only give you my word, if you are willing to accept it, that I would never do anything to harm her in any way."

Brandon's words came slowly and deliberately as he pledged his honour to the guardian of the woman with whom he now desired to be, more than he desired life itself.

Looking the young suitor, eye to eye, the father nodded. "I believe you, son." Brandon started at the sound of that word coming from this man's deep voice. *Son.*

John went on, "You know, Brandon, I believe in the power of the Holy Spirit. I know God can make a new man out of anyone. I'm not about to judge you on your past, because we're all called to live in the present. And conversion is a powerful process. But it takes time, prayer, effort, and tremendous self-discipline not to fall back into old ways.

"Purity, like any virtue, is a direction we take in life. You've made the first step. You've turned your back on sin and your face toward God. Stay on that path, Brandon, and you'll find yourself growing in all the virtues. It takes time, though. Just keep your feet aimed in that direction and don't look back.

"I want to let you know that our family is more than happy to welcome you in and share with you our faith and be there to support you on your journey. But," he said, straightening his shoulders with purpose, "I'm not prepared to let you date my daughter."

Brandon stood there, silent, taking it all in. He made no motion, no effort to object to the man's decision.

"Brandon," the older man's clear voice drew Brandon's attention back, "I am, though, willing to allow you to *court* my daughter, if you're interested."

Brandon looked up, startled, his eyes full of confusion. "I'm afraid, sir, I'm not sure what you mean, when you say 'court'. Uh, pardon my ignorance, but what's the difference?"

"Well, son . . ."

There was that word again.

"There's a world of difference between dating and courtship. You see, when a couple dates, there's often no sense of direction and with that comes an attitude of no responsibility. You go out together. You spend extended periods of time, exclusively with one another. And for some folks that leads to some fairly involved physical relationships. Then, when you get tired of a person, after a few dates or a few years, you move on. You see, it sets a pattern, not for marriage and fidelity, but for marriage and divorce. When you're bored or overwhelmed, you high-tail it out of there.

"But courtship involves a whole different attitude. There's direction and with that comes a sense of responsibility and accountability. When a young couple courts, they take time to get to know each other in a solid friendship first.

"Now, I recognize your feelings for Joanie and her feelings for you have gone beyond that of mere friendship. It's going to take a great deal of self-discipline for both of you to go slow with your relationship. But it's an important stage—not to be skipped. I know people will see you as a couple—and since I'm giving you my permission to court—I guess that's what you'd be.

"But reserve your affection. Take your time and prove yourself to Joanie and to yourself. Test your own sincerity. Perhaps, after a time, one of you may find that the direction of your relationship should stay just as friends. . . .

There's nothing wrong with that. And if you've reserved your affection, there won't be any harm done.

"Please remember, Brandon, a woman's heart is a precious thing. It needs to be guarded—not used. Be honest and sincere, and treat her like gold. 'Cause let me tell you—once you've won it—a woman's heart is a priceless treasure."

The idea of just how cherished a prize Joanie's heart would be, brought a smile to Brandon's face. No sacrifice seemed too great for him to prove himself to her.

John allowed Brandon an opportunity to reflect on what he had said, before he went on.

"So where do you begin in a courtship? You spend time together, with each others' families. Believe me, family is important. If you end up married, you'll want to be able to get along with each other's family, or all kinds of hardships can arise. And you do things together—a variety of activities. You can spend a lot of time in each other's company—just not *exclusively* alone. Now, I'm not saying that you'd never get time alone with each other, but that time should be limited.

"And pardon my frankness, but location means everything. You don't go off to your apartment for an evening alone together and place yourselves in temptation's way. I trust Joanie, and I have the feeling I'll be able to trust you, but I'm no fool to human nature. Lots of good people, with good intentions, end up making mistakes.

"Sometimes people have the impression that if they're strong Christians, committed to chastity, they can throw common sense out the window. It doesn't work that way. You have to set guidelines that are practical.

"So you go out for walks. Go out for meals. Go out to the movies, if you can find a decent one. And you spend time doing things together. Because until you've seen each other in a variety of settings and functions, you won't really know if you're going to be compatible for marriage.

"You see, the purpose of courting, unlike dating, is to discern whether or not the Lord is calling you to marriage. And like I said, if one or both of you at any point in time feels that marriage is not in the course for you . . . well you can walk away from it. And you lose nothing. But if you grow in an understanding that marriage is your calling, then you'll have laid a beautiful foundation for it. You'll have made for yourself a best friend for a spouse. And that's a precious gift, Brandon. It'll last you a lifetime!"

John's look was kind and reflective. Brandon appreciated this man's openness and the way that he established, in no uncertain terms, the protective love that he had for his family. Brandon had nothing but respect for this man.

"Well, sir," Brandon began, "I'm willing to do whatever it takes. I really respect your guidelines, and I'll uphold my part."

"I'm sure you will, Brandon," John returned. "Now, please understand . . . the whole notion of accountability means that Joanie's mother and I will take opportunities to talk with you and Joanie about your relationship. I believe that the openness that will exist between us will serve to help both you and Joanie stay on course. It's not a question of trust; it's a matter of human nature. Accountability makes us all more responsible."

"I agree, sir," Brandon replied, thoughtfully. He had never seen an intimate relationship in those terms before. But it all made sense.

"Now I suggest you go ask Joanie yourself. She still has the right, you know, to turn you down!" John gave Brandon a friendly smile and patted him on the shoulder, inviting him to go back to the house.

Brandon paused and looked at John. "I'd just like to tell you how much I appreciate the kind of father you are. As awkward and difficult as this was for me, I'm grateful that Joanie has a father who loves her and protects her this way. You've raised a strong and confident daughter. She resisted every advance I ever made toward her. She always managed to turn the tables on me and disarm me every time. In nine years of living like a hedonist, she's the only one, sir, to have done that.

"I wish now that all those other girls would've had fathers who loved them and protected them the way you do your children. If they had, they never would have gotten messed up with a jerk like I was!"

Appreciating Brandon's comment, John interjected, "You know, Brandon, everyone has free will. We do our best as parents to raise our children to know right from wrong, but at a certain point we have to let them go to make their own decisions. I'm just grateful that Joanie has chosen to embrace our values . . . and that she was able to hold her own—even around *jerks*, like you once were!" The look in John's eyes, as he returned the young man's comment, let Brandon know that no offence was intended.

Nodding in acknowledgment of John's statement, Brandon went on, "Well, I admire the sweetness and innocence of Joanie, and I would never do anything to compromise that, I promise you."

John smiled with approval. After twenty-six years as a teacher, John was a good judge of character. He liked what he saw in Brandon.

"And I'd also like to thank you, sir, for having raised so bold a daughter. Her uncompromising faith is what brought me to know Jesus Christ. I owe a debt of gratitude to you all for that."

"I appreciate you speaking so openly, Brandon. I'm certainly convinced of the work the Lord is doing in your life. I'll keep praying for you."

The two men exchanged a look of mutual respect. John put his hand back on Brandon's shoulder and added, "By the way, Brandon, feel free to call me John." John's smile communicated volumes.

Brandon knew that this man would be, for him, a guide on his journey. He was determined to earn the trust of this man, Joanie's father . . . John. Brandon smiled back and replied, "Fine, John."

"Now, you might want to take Joanie out to dinner to discuss all this with her, alone. . . . I give you my permission, son."

With that he winked at Brandon and led the way out of the garage.

Chapter 20

The house had a true serenity to it as Brandon and John entered through the back door. Everyone seemed to have disappeared. The space had grown larger in the absence of all the activity. From the living room, the sound of piano music came floating freely through the house.

Where had the children gone? There was no one around. There was no noise to compete with the rich overtones of the old Heintzman upright. And so, the unimposing sound of a Chopin Waltz sweetly drew Brandon in the direction of the living room, as he took his leave of John.

Brandon was surprised to find that it was Joanie now playing, not Amie. He hesitated as he stepped up beside the piano and rested his elbow on the top of it. His presence had apparently not distracted the performer from the enthralment of the music.

The old piano was a vintage instrument, showing the signs of loving abuse from years of having been played by many children. An heirloom that had been passed down from generation to generation, it begged to be refinished. The ivory keys were jagged-edged. The ornate wooden designs, once impressive displays of true craftsmanship, were marred by scratches and chips, dug deeply into the dark wood finish.

There was a beauty in this time-worn instrument, the same kind of beauty one sees in the wrinkled face of an old woman. Having stood proudly through the storms of time, it had a wisdom all its own. There were countless stories it could tell, of love and sorrow, romance and pain, joy and suffering, death and new life.

It was a loved and cherished part of the family, as was the gift of music which it signified, transmitted through the generations: the birthright of each child.

The young man was captivated by the graceful movements of the pianist. Her hands glided effortlessly over the keyboard. Her arms seemed to be weightless, yet they fell into the keys with such depth that the rhythm of the waltz became completely animated. The final tone of the Chopin masterpiece hung in the air, characteristic of the Heintzman, a tribute to the talent of a commanding performer.

Joanie looked up at Brandon, somewhat shyly and in a quiet voice said, "Hello."

She had been aware of Brandon's presence, but years of training had taught her to play on, regardless of distractions. It was only upon finishing her piece that she felt the directed admiration of his gaze upon her. This uncomplicated girl was not at all familiar with this kind of attention. She liked it, but felt awkward with it all the same.

"I didn't realize that you played." His voice revealed how impressed he was by her talent.

"Well, I do," she responded. "That's Chopin's Waltz in C-sharp minor, from my grade nine exam. Some things just stick with you."

"I know what you mean," Brandon replied.

"But Amie's the real piano player around here. My passion is for singing." She smiled, turning herself on the bench to face Brandon straight on, leaning forward, her hands resting on her lap.

He met her eyes with tremendous affection. Joanie could feel her heart rebelling against her will to keep it contained. How easy it would be for her to lose herself forever in those blue eyes. She bit down on her bottom lip nervously, through a timid smile. When would she ever get used to these emotions?

"Would you like to go out for dinner?"

The question came as a welcome diversion from her internal reverie.

"I've already okayed it with your father," he added, for clarification.

Joanie giggled and nodded, "Give me a few minutes to get ready." With that she slipped out of the room, leaving Brandon alone.

He noticed a guitar in the corner and, hoping no one would mind, he sat down and began to play. Within minutes, the three youngest Collins children had appeared from nowhere and gathered around Brandon to listen. He wowed them all with his fun-filled blues style, and they cheered him on with their squeals of delight.

Soon Maggie, Amie, and Katie found their way into the living room. Amie slipped onto the piano bench and, picking up Brandon's lead, began to jam along with him. Maggie did not hesitate to pick up her violin and accentuate the jam session with various fun-filled strains. Katie got the little ones up dancing. And before too long, Isaac appeared with his snare drum and sticks.

Joanie's parents stood in the doorway between the kitchen and living room. Judy was snuggled up in John's arms, both of them taking in the whole scene. There was nothing unusual in the family jamming together, but they were impressed with how naturally Brandon fit in.

Joanie's few minutes turned out to be about twenty. Brandon was so wrapped up in the fun of the jam session, he had not paid any attention to the time. Joanie stepped into the room quietly and stood by the front entry, delighting in the scene. She was so proud of Brandon. Her mother smiled at her from across the room. They knew what each other was thinking.

Brandon looked up and saw Joanie standing there. She was beautiful. He could not fill his eyes enough with her. She had changed out of her football attire into a very simple, but stylish, summer dress. Her hair was pulled up, with little ringlets trailing around her neck. She wore a dainty chain with a golden medallion on it and simple dangling earrings. She smiled back, somewhat bashfully, at his obvious, attentive gaze.

Brandon stopped his playing and announced it was time to leave. The children sent up a cry of protest, begging him to stay and keep playing. He shook his head, regretfully, and handed the guitar over to Judy, who had stepped in to settle the children.

"I want to thank you, Judy, for the wonderful day. I don't know when I ever had so much fun!"

His gratitude was sincere and Judy smiled back with understanding. "You're welcome in our home any time, Brandon. Please, don't be a stranger."

The rest of the young couple's departure took much the same form as Brandon had witnessed earlier. Little ones were on the lawn, jumping and waving and calling out their farewells.

Brandon laughed as they pulled out of the driveway, "Are they always this happy?" he asked Joanie.

"I'm not sure about happy, but noisy . . . yes."

✞   ✞   ✞

That night as Brandon was getting ready for bed, he reflected on the entire day. His mind kept coming back to the feeling he had sitting in the restaurant, across from Joanie. It was the perfect ending to a perfect day.

She had agreed to the courtship, and they had discussed the details of that at great length. He would have to seek her father's permission to take her out alone, but they could be involved in group activities anytime.

She was comfortable with holding hands for now. But she felt they should be careful with other displays of affection. She knew it would be hard enough for her to keep a clear head in this relationship . . . all of the feelings were so new to her. Brandon had admitted to Joanie that these feelings were all new to him as well.

She made it very clear that there would be no kissing on the lips for the time being. Joanie had explained it in her uncomplicated way: "I only want to be kissed by the man that I will marry, and I don't want to have any regrets if things don't work out between us."

Brandon respected her boundaries; in fact, he respected everything about her. How was it that he could have gone his whole life treating women with such a lack of respect? It bothered him, but he prayed for God to take away those memories that chained him to his past and sinful ways.

He prayed that God would give him a new heart, that he might love Joanie purely and, as she expressed it, chastely.

Suddenly it seemed to Brandon that his whole life had been spent in emptiness, craving this kind of love. He had never known how to look for it until Joanie had brought him to Jesus. He thanked God for sending this girl into his life and, indeed, for saving him.

He got into bed and made the sign of the cross, as Joanie had taught him at dinner. He liked it. It seemed to be a prayer unto itself. Brandon felt a strengthening within, living now under the sign of the cross.

✞   ✞   ✞

By the time Joanie got in that night, the three youngest children were in bed. The house had that wonderful, peaceful, quiet feeling it gets at the end of a long, busy day. She found her parents, Maggie, Amie, Katie, and Isaac laughing around the big oak table, playing cards.

Their family did not watch a lot of television or waste countless hours in cyberspace. The children certainly had access to these things, but their parents were very strict about the use of them. While they objected to the content of most of these media influences, it was of equal concern for them to guard their family time together.

They always warned the children that all too soon they would grow up and move away from home. This valuable time they had together should be spent wisely. The children got along very well. They had to, or they would not have survived. They found all kinds of creative ways to occupy their time. Over the years they had become accomplished musicians, avid readers, creative writers, dynamic actors, skilled craftsmen, well-rounded athletes, and zealous card players.

Joanie pulled up a chair to watch the game. It was Honolulu Rummy and, as usual, Isaac was in the lead.

"How did your dinner go, Sweet Pea?" her father asked, as he arranged his hand.

"Joanie and Brandon went out on their first *real* date tonight," Katie sang out with delight. She could not resist anything romantic.

"Katie, don't you go picking on Joanie," her mother scolded.

"Oh, no, Mom, I think Brandon's wonderful!" Katie defended herself.

"Well, he's sure good-looking enough," added Amie.

"Isn't he a dream?" Katie carried on with her romantic swooning.

"How come everything good always happens to Joanie?" Amie complained.

"You'll have your chance soon enough," their father jumped in. "Too soon, for my liking."

"Joanie, do you think you'll marry Brandon?" asked Isaac who was obviously thinking things through. "'Cause if you do, then I'll have a big brother . . . and he's really good at sports. Do you think I could get Brandon to teach me how to play the guitar like that? He's got an amazing style." Isaac's mind was like that, scattered all over the place.

"Well, she won't be marrying him until he becomes Catholic," quipped Maggie, "or I won't have anything to do with it."

"Don't you like Brandon?" interjected Amie.

"I think he's wonderful! But Joanie always said she'd never marry outside of the faith . . . and I'm holding her to it!" Maggie stated, emphatically.

"Well—" Joanie made a futile attempt to get in on the conversation.

"Then it seems to me you've got a lot of praying to do, Margaret Mary," advised her mother.

"I have a feeling I'll be spending a lot of time on my knees. Once we marry off Joanie, I'll have all these other yahoos to pray into good marriages." She waved her hand, indicating the other siblings.

"Don't you think you'll marry?" asked her father, looking up at her with a pensive gaze.

"No," she said, in a matter-of-fact tone, while arranging her cards, "I won't ever marry. It's not my calling."

The mother and father exchanged a look that Joanie and Amie managed to get in on. They all knew that Maggie had a special quality that seemed to distinguish her from the other children. Ever since she was a small child she had been truly detached from worldly things. She was an absolutely delightful girl, admired and loved by all.

They instinctively had a sense of her being called to a religious vocation, but they had never pushed it. John and Judy felt that each of their children would have to discern for themselves God's calling. This was the first verbal indication Maggie had made to them in a long time of being called to religious life.

Soon, the family would be moving on: each of them with their own separate lives, living out their own dreams, responding to their own callings. Joanie, herself, was only still living at home at her parents' offer. She could pay down her student loan for a year, while paying room and board to them.

Closer to the heart, though, her reasons for still living here were asleep upstairs. Time had not afforded Joanie the luxury of being with her youngest siblings as much as she would have wanted. University and music study had occupied her much over the past four years. So now she was jealously guarding this time in her life, a brief period of grace before she was separated from this oasis of love.

As she looked around the table at the faces of those she loved the most, she thanked God for the gift of her family. Time and distance would never destroy the bond that had formed between each of them.

Joanie had a twinge of pain, realizing that the remainder of their days together were numbered. It was the only dark shadow that had interrupted this otherwise perfect day.

Chapter 21

When Brandon entered the staff lounge at lunch time on Monday, Joanie had a sudden panic rush through her. Up until now their personal relationship had not entered the workplace. Brandon walked over to the coffee pot, poured himself a cup, and made casual conversation with a few of the other employees.

Taylor called out across the room some remark about Brandon looking like he had scored big on the weekend.

Brandon just smiled and replied, "You have *no* idea how big, Taylor!"

The handsome young man walked over to the table where Tessa and Joanie were sitting and, in typical Brandon fashion, asked, "Is this seat taken, ladies, or may I join you?"

His look was calm and collected, and Joanie marvelled at how he could be so cool, while her heart was pounding in her throat.

Tessa answered, "You can join us, only if you care to explain that comment." Her tone was serious, but only to mask the situation. She did not want to blow the cover off this relationship.

"Well, Miss Farrow," he addressed Tessa, taking a seat, "I like to keep my private life . . . just that." He smiled and turned to Joanie. "And Miss Collins, I trust you had a good weekend? Anything exciting happen to you at church?"

His tone was so natural, just like the old arrogant Brandon whom Joanie had first met here, that it almost worried her. But his eyes betrayed his devotion and she raced through her mind to search for a response to suit the situation.

"Well, Mr. Vaughn, as a matter of fact, something rather exciting *did* happen. I met a wonderful new member of our congregation who, unlike you, is a perfect gentleman, is outrageously handsome, and is completely in love with the Lord." Her eyes looked dreamily at Brandon as she spoke.

Brandon shrugged his broad shoulders and, shaking his head a bit, he said, "I don't know, sounds too good to be true. I'd be careful there, Church-Girl."

"Well, I, for one, think it's wonderful," beamed Tessa. Then, turning to Brandon, she added in a scolding tone, "And it wouldn't hurt you, Brandon, to get a little Jesus in your life!"

Taylor, from across the room, burst out laughing and walked over to join the conversation. "Are you kidding, a devil like Brandon? Why, he's the last guy on earth that you'd ever find in a church."

"Well, Taylor," Joanie said, in an inviting way, "maybe you should spend some time there, yourself. You know, there's no sinner too big for God's mercy."

"You're wasting your time here, sweetheart," Taylor balked and waved his hand at them, adding, "I'm the second last guy you'd ever find there." With that he left the lounge.

The three co-workers sat and visited for the rest of lunch hour. Brandon was telling them about a new commercial he was producing. And so they passed the time quite amiably. To the onlooker, nothing here had changed. After awhile, Brandon took his leave of the girls, and they all returned to their workstations.

Joanie was grateful to be able to spend time with Brandon in this way. She knew this would be a wonderful opportunity to advance their relationship as friends, without any romantic pressures seeping in. And thus continued their courtship, incognito, at the workplace.

✝　　　　　　　✝　　　　　　　✝

Tuesday evening found Brandon heading over to the beach volleyball courts at the City Rec Centre. It had been four weeks since he had come out to a game, but he really wanted to connect again with Mark. The problem was, he would have to face all the other friends with whom they hung out, which included several past affairs.

Brandon was nervous after the confrontation he had had with Mark on the previous Friday. He made sure to get there early, hoping to talk with his friend before the match began. Brandon was relieved to see Mark's black Acura Integra in the parking lot when he arrived. Hopefully he could catch him alone in the change room.

Mark was closing his locker door when Brandon walked up. "Hey, Mark, can we talk?"

Mark's expression conveyed a certain reservation. "So, have you come to your senses? Or are you here to convert me?" His tone was neutral.

Brandon winced; it was so hard for him to be losing his oldest and closest friend. "I wanted to join the game tonight and spend some time with you."

"I wouldn't advise that, Brandon, unless things have changed with you. 'Cause nothing's changed with us. And I don't think you'll feel too welcome, not without first doing some serious grovelling. Tracey's fit to be tied. Ashley's got a big chip on her shoulder. And no one else is too impressed with the way you've brushed us all off, either."

"Well, it hasn't changed. And I'm not about to grovel; although, I've already told you that I'm sorry for having avoided you. I just want to be able to be your friend again, Mark," Brandon returned, sincerely.

"Sorry, buddy, no can do! I walked away from religion when I was fifteen, as you well remember, and I'm not about to go back for anything or anyone, not even you. So you see, it couldn't work. There's no more common ground here. I'll go on living for the next party, just like I always have. Meanwhile, you'll go off to church and get yourself married and settle down into some domestic life, with your pretty little wife and kids. The two worlds just don't meet. . . . See you 'round, Brandon."

Mark picked up his towel and began walking toward the door to the courts.

"Mark!" Brandon grabbed his friend's arm and turned him back to meet him, eye to eye. "You're wrong. I think there's a lot of common ground, still. But I guess you're right for now. Whenever you think you can put up with me, give me a call. I'd really like to see you again."

And with that, Brandon turned and left.

✞   ✞   ✞

Brandon's heart was heavy as he drove off. He felt quite isolated now. Before this all began he had done everything with these friends. They were fun and likeable people, all single and just looking for a good time. It was a simple life with very little meaning, as Brandon had come to see now, but it had filled his time.

Now he had Joanie and her family and, until he got to meet more people in this new world of his, that was it. He had made a decision. He had chosen Joanie and Jesus. There were no regrets over that. He just wished there could have been a way to have Joanie and Jesus, without having to give up everyone else in his life.

Restlessness became his companion for the evening. He was disinterested in television. Even his guitar could offer him no consolation; so, he put it down, regretfully. He prayed for a bit and asked Mary to help him sort everything out.

From the corner of his eye, the Bible caught his attention. Brandon had already spent many hours reading it. He did not understand it all, but he loved it. There was something about it that commanded his attention. While he could not explain why, he did feel closer to Jesus as he read it.

Rather than picking up where he had left off, he leafed through it aimlessly. He did not have the heart tonight to devote himself to reading, not even his treasured Bible. Without specifically searching for an answer, Brandon's eyes fell upon Luke's Gospel, chapter six, verse twenty-two:

Blessed are you when men hate you, and when they exclude you and revile you, and cast out your name as evil, on account of the Son of man! Rejoice in that day, and leap for joy, for behold, your reward is great in heaven; for so their fathers did to the prophets.

He read on to verse thirty-six:

Be merciful, even as your Father is merciful. Judge not, and you will not be judged; condemn not, and you will be not be condemned; forgive, and you will be forgiven; give, and it will be given to you; good measure, pressed down, shaken together, running over, will be put into your lap. For the measure you give will be the measure you get back.

Brandon put the Bible down on his lap, closed his eyes and prayed.

Oh, God, so far I have suffered very little persecution for my faith in You, and already You have given me so much.

He thought about Joanie and her family, his tremendous sense of peace, and the overwhelming joy that had filled him since he had let Jesus into his life.

I'm sorry for complaining, Lord. Keep my head and my heart focussed on You so that I might give glory to You in my life. Jesus, I don't know why You called me, but I'm sure You have Your reasons, and I thank You. I guess if You can change a good-for-nothing like me, well, You can do anything. So please help Mark and the rest of them. They need You, even if they don't know it.

Brandon made the sign of the cross and sat silently under it for a long time, aware that he was now marked as a Christian.

Chapter 22

When Brandon got home Wednesday after work, he found a message on his machine from Joanie. She wanted him to come out for a barbecue on Saturday with a group of friends from Catholic Campus Evangelization. It would be at someone's cabin at Wakaw Lake, about a forty-five minute drive from town.

It was so good to hear her voice away from work. There were no façades; the guard was let down and the tenderness of this girl came through in every word. He listened to the message a couple of times over before calling her back.

The young suitor was still a little nervous calling Joanie at home. It was a young boy who answered the phone, but Brandon could not hazard a guess which one of her brothers it was. Brandon asked for Joanie.

"Joanie, it's your *boyfriend,*" the little voice called out in a childishly teasing way.

It gave Brandon pause; he and Joanie had never used that term yet to identify themselves in this relationship.

"Hello, Brandon," Joanie's voice came on, sounding embarrassed at her brother's indiscretion.

"That's *boyfriend* to you," he laughed.

She chuckled at his playfulness. "Well, *boyfriend,* what can I do for you?"

"Can I pick you up Saturday at one to go to this barbecue?"

"That'd be great," she answered. "And don't forget your guitar."

"Oh, I don't know about that," he replied, with hesitation.

"Well, I do. So, please bring it." Her voice was entreating.

"I'll think about it. You know, you can't always get your way with me," he reproved her, affectionately.

"No . . . but I can try."

He could picture her smiling face. "I miss you," he said, softly.

Her heart melted. "I miss you too, Brandon." She paused, then added, "I know it was my family's idea that we court and you've been so good to go along with it, but it must seem terribly dull to you," she apologized. "It isn't as easy as I thought it would be. I . . . I hope you're not losing heart."

"Are you kidding? I think this whole courtship thing is the best thing that has ever happened to me. First of all, 'cause it's with you." His voice was full and rich, and he could feel her blushing on the other end of the phone. "But, secondly, because it's giving Jesus lots of time to work on me. And believe me, He's not missing a beat!"

She laughed softly. "I want you to tell me everything. I can't wait until Saturday. It's just too bad the lake wasn't further away."

"Careful there, little Missy!" His tone was playfully scolding. "I'm under some pretty strict guidelines with regards to being alone with you. You'd better not start disarming my defences now, or I'll have to take it up with your father!"

"Oh, please don't tell my daddy on me!" She sounded just like a child. Then she laughed and added, "I'll be good. There's too much at stake here and I don't want to blow it."

"Well, I think I'm the one who should be saying that," he said, emphatically.

"Don't be fooled, Brandon, by my tough exterior. Deep down, there's a fragile heart here that's terrified of being broken."

Acquiring a tone of knightly chivalry, he assured her, "It's safe with me, my lady. You have my word, on my honour as a gentleman."

"I believe you." She sighed heavily into the phone. "I'd better go; I was helping Mom with supper. Saturday at one—*with* your guitar!"

"I'll see you then," he said with finality.

✟   ✟   ✟

Brandon arrived to pick Joanie up at one o'clock sharp. Something was different about him; then Joanie realized, it was the first time she had ever seen him dressed in shorts and a T-shirt. His muscular arms and legs made Joanie realize just how powerful this man was. She felt small standing in front of him.

She picked up his left hand and turned his arm to check the time on his watch. Joanie noticed that Brandon was unfailingly punctual. She, on the other hand, was nowhere near ready to go.

"I'm sorry I'm not ready yet. I spent the morning helping with housecleaning, and I just got back from the park with Zack, Aaron, and Jessie," she explained, offering him an apologetic smile. "I'll hurry."

Brandon smiled down at her and winked. He gently reached up to her face and moved a strand of hair that was hanging over the corner of her left eye. "I'm in no hurry. Take your time."

Joanie's expression turned bashful under his attentive gaze. She thanked him for his patience and rushed off to get ready to go.

Brandon did not mind the wait at all. In fact, it gave him a chance to play with Isaac, Zack, Aaron, and Jessie. Brandon had sorted out all of their names last Sunday, and he was feeling pretty proud of himself for having attached the right name to the right child. For someone who had no previous experience with children, he was like a magnet to them. Brandon was beginning to realize that he loved all the attention he was getting from this little fan club.

When Joanie came down to leave, she found Brandon at the bottom of a pile of children. She laughed at the sight of it, and Brandon called out from underneath, "Apparently your brothers and sister don't want us to go."

Joanie tried to scold the kids, but she could not stop laughing at the sight.

Brandon called out, "Jessie, help me, I can't . . . breathe."

Jessie, rising to the call, jumped off the top of the pile and started hitting her brothers to get off. "Stop," she yelled out, "Bwandon can't bweathe! Get off!"

Isaac got off first and told Jessie to calm down. "Bwandon *can* bweathe," he imitated her little way of talking.

"Isaac, be charitable," Joanie scolded as she laughed, for he sounded just like Jessie.

By this time, Brandon was sitting on the floor, propped up against the couch, breathing heavily, "Thanks, Jessie, you saved my life!" he told her, looking straight into her big round eyes. Her auburn hair was all dishevelled around her adorable baby face.

Before he knew what was happening, the three-year-old jumped up at him. Throwing herself around his neck, she squeezed as hard as her little arms would let her. "I love you, Bwandon!" she said sweetly and sincerely, thoroughly warming his heart.

He returned the hug gently and said, "I love you too, Jessie!"

Brandon looked up at Joanie and smiled. There she stood, in charcoal shorts and a light grey T-shirt. It was a challenge for him not to look at her in a way that he knew would make her feel ill at ease. This new Christian did not want to ever communicate a lack of respect for her, even in his gaze. He was grateful that Joanie dressed modestly, for even at that it took discipline on his part to avoid her slim, graceful figure and keep his eyes focussed on her alluring smile.

As he gazed upon Jessie's biggest sister, he wondered when the day would come that he could hold her the same way he was holding Jessie and tell her what he had just told the child.

Joanie's heart took a picture of Jessie wrapped up in Brandon's strong arms. How she wished she could be three again, so that she, too, could throw her arms around Brandon and confess her love the same way. But that would have to wait awhile yet, because at twenty-two, one must guard the heart very carefully.

Thank you, Jesus, for letting Jessie tell Brandon for me.

✝   ✝   ✝

The first thing Joanie did when she hopped into Brandon's vehicle was to tune his radio to the local Christian station, Glory FM. "It's time you expanded your taste in music, Brandon," she asserted.

She closed her eyes and breathed in the smell of his cologne. It had such a wonderful effect on her. "I like your cologne," she said sweetly, opening one eye to look up at him and then closing it again, while she breathed deeply one more time.

Brandon smiled and shook his head. "You love life!" was all he said in response. This girl could find delight in the simplest things.

She giggled and looked straight at him. The station began playing an old favourite of Joanie's. "Oh, Brandon, this is such a wonderful song." She reached down and turned up the volume. Brandon listened as Joanie softly sang along with the radio. He thoroughly enjoyed the sound of her voice. He could have gone on that way for a long time, but when the song was over Joanie leaned forward and turned down the volume so they could talk.

With eyes sparkling, she commented, "I see you have your guitar back there."

"I do," he nodded, glancing over at her.

"Thank you." She smiled at him, in her sweet way.

"You know, I'll never be able to keep my eyes on the road, if you keep looking at me that way," he admonished her.

"What way?" she defended herself.

"That way that makes me want to stop everything I'm doing and gaze endlessly into those deep, dark eyes of yours."

She blushed.

"The only problem is, you can't help yourself. And I'm gonna have to learn to live with it, if I'm ever gonna get anything done around you," he said, mostly to himself.

"Well, here," she offered, putting on her sunglasses. "I can do like you and hide my eyes."

Brandon looked over at her and smiled. "Nah, it didn't work. I still find you irresistible, shades and all."

"Well, your sunglasses don't make you any less irresistible, yourself," she returned, affectionately. She pulled her sunglasses back up onto her hair. "Brandon," she changed the subject, "why don't you call me during the week? What keeps you so busy?"

He was surprised by the question. "Do you *want* me to call you?"

"Well, silly," she laughed, "how else are we supposed to get to know each other? I just thought that maybe you've been really busy."

Brandon went on to tell her how he had been spending most evenings at home alone. "I never miss the local news anymore," he teased her. "There's this hot little reporter that comes on. Dark, dazzling eyes and gorgeous, curly, dark hair. She's not even half-bad at what she does. It's the highlight of my evening."

"Seriously, Brandon," she prodded him on. "And I'll overlook the 'half-bad' comment for now," she added from underneath arched eyebrows.

He smiled. "But don't overlook the 'hot-looking' comment," he persisted, his eyebrow cocked up in a way that was so intriguing to Joanie.

"Really, what do you do?" she insisted, brushing off his flattery.

"Oh, my life is full of excitement these days," he confessed. "I go down to the gym for workouts, play the guitar, and read the Bible. Did I mention I play the guitar and go for workouts?" he added, to emphasize the mundane routine into which his life had fallen, since his old friends had now all abandoned him.

Joanie laughed. "Brandon," her voice revealed delightful surprise, "I had no idea you were reading Scripture. That's awesome!"

"Yeah," he nodded, genuinely, "Genesis and Exodus were great, but that Leviticus has got me baffled."

She chuckled at the idea of him floundering through the Book of Leviticus, "Well, I have a suggestion to make it easier for you. I have a Bible history video at home. It really helps you to understand what you're reading. We could watch it together, and I can give you this chart that helps you read through the historical sequence of the Bible. It makes it a lot easier for a first-time reading. And," she added as an afterthought, "that way I can get you over to my house to visit me."

"You've got me all wrong here, sweetheart!" He could feel her smile at the sound of that word. "I haven't been avoiding you because I *wanted* to. I just thought I was *supposed* to. You know, I don't know much about this courting business, and it seems to me that you've been holding back on some rather pertinent information here. You'd better not leave me out in the rain too long."

She shook her head with a little giggle and grabbed his hand, which had been resting on the gearshift. "I think you're wonderful," she stated, plainly.

"Thanks, but I know you're laughing at me, not with me."

"Not true. I just think it's awesome the way you've laid aside everything." She reflected on how he had turned his back so completely on his old life that it did not seem to be a part of who he was anymore.

"Yeah, well, I've been thinking a lot about that lately. It seems that God made sure to slam the door to my old life behind me . . . since all of my friends have now disowned me. I guess that was one way to be sure I wouldn't slip back into old ways—not that I've been tempted, mind you. I don't miss it at all, to be quite frank." Brandon glanced over at Joanie. "It was a pretty shallow existence. But—"

Joanie jumped in, "You must be going crazy cooped up all alone!"

"Crazy? I don't know, maybe. . . . All I know is that God's been doing some serious make-over work on me. To be honest, I haven't minded having the time alone . . . except that I miss you." He gave her hand a little squeeze, but kept his eyes on the road.

His speech had been playful, but Joanie could sense the awkwardness he felt with all the restrictions in their relationship. Returning to her earlier suggestion, she asked, "Well then, what do you say about coming over to watch those videos?"

He looked over at Joanie and laughed. "I'll be there. Just try to keep me away now!"

They drove on in silence for a few minutes.

"Tell me about your life," he asked her.

"What do you want to know?"

"Everything. What was it like to grow up in a large family, home-schooling, Catholic? I mean, everything about you is so completely foreign to me. It's like you're from some other planet."

She laughed and began talking about home-schooling; however, one topic led into another. The thing is, in a large, Catholic, home-schooling family, everything is so connected. Home-schooling becomes a way of life that allows a family to explore the depth and meaning of their faith. Their faith is the foundation that gives life and expression to everything they do. The relationship that exists between the members of the family forms and shapes who each of them becomes.

She shared with him funny stories of events in the family over the years, how they had struggled through difficulties and how they had celebrated achievements.

Brandon marvelled at the dynamics of this incredible family. He had absolutely no frame of reference by which he could relate to Joanie's experiences, yet he was moved by how animated she was by her love and devotion to both her family and faith.

With each detail of her life that Joanie shared with Brandon, a longing grew ever deeper within him to be a part of it. All at once he realized that he no longer felt out of place in Joanie's world. He knew he belonged there. Knowing Joanie was like holding a treasure map that would lead him to find that one, true, priceless treasure. And for the first time in his life, Brandon felt his heart longing for heaven.

As they got closer to Wakaw, they stopped talking. They watched the lake finally appear as they topped a hill. The trees that surrounded it created a cozy oasis in the midst of the prairie landscape.

Brandon reached over and took Joanie's hand in his own. His heart thrilled at sharing anything and everything with this girl. He felt like a child when he was with her, experiencing life for the first time. And indeed he was, for since he had become a Christian, he now was seeing the world through new eyes.

Chapter 23

Alex and Caitlyn Bolt were a young couple who had met during their first year at University through Catholic Campus Evangelization. They were now finished their schooling and had married just that past spring. It was Caitlyn's family cabin that they were using for the day.

The little cottage was of humble furnishings, but it had a large open room that accommodated a fair-sized crowd. There was a huge deck out front, surrounded by trees, where the group would be hanging out on this hot, summer day. They had a beautiful lakeside property with a large lawn area that would soon become the battleground for some intensely competitive tournaments of bocce ball and badminton.

Joanie's involvement with C.C.E. throughout her years on campus had been a wonderful experience. It had been a time of growing and maturing in her faith while having a whole lot of fun.

New Spring was closely connected to the ministry, receiving many of its gigs through C.C.E.-promoted functions. Most of the band was here today. Maggie was around somewhere. She had driven out with a group of friends and cousins. Amie had not been able to make it. And Joanie had decided to come alone with Brandon, for obvious reasons.

She went around with him, making introductions. This was a great opportunity to get Brandon connected with some fun-loving, dynamic, young Christians. She was awkward at first, walking around holding his hand. People teased them, and Joanie and Brandon just took it, as though they knew somehow they had been asking for it. But there were never any rude or unkind remarks. Brandon found that to be quite remarkable.

In fact, he saw how wrong he had been in his impression of Christians before his conversion. He had always figured they were a bunch of boring, stick-in-the-mud types. He would never have imagined them to have been this much fun. But here they were. They teased. They joked. They laughed. They played. But none of it was ever offensive. They had even brought out beer—which shocked him—but no one got drunk.

Brandon and Joanie sat down on a bench, built into the railing of the deck. Someone came over and offered them drinks. Joanie wanted a pop. Brandon hesitated at first, but then went for the beer. The cold drink felt very satisfying in the heat of the day. As he sat back and took in his surroundings, he lifted his heart in prayer.

Thank You, Jesus. Since I met You, life just keeps getting better and better.

He leaned back and his eyes closed. Unintentionally, he had squeezed Joanie's hand as he prayed. She looked over at him and seeing the serenity on his face, she surmised that he was praying. She returned the squeeze, and slowly he opened his eyes to meet her gentle gaze. He sighed and closed his eyes again.

"Hey Joanie, aren't you two going to get into the games?" Caitlyn called out as she approached to invite them to sign up for the tournaments.

Joanie lightly shook Brandon to get his attention. "What do you say, Brandon?"

"Whatever you want to do, sweetheart, I'm in," he returned without opening his eyes.

"We'll play in both. Brandon's getting way too relaxed on this bench. I'm afraid I'll never get him home tonight," she remarked, pointing to his peaceful countenance.

Caitlyn laughed, "Oh, we'll wake him up yet today. Don't worry, Joanie. He's too new on the scene to be *that* comfortable."

Brandon opened one eye and cocked his eyebrow, as if to say, *What did she mean by that?*

Joanie started tugging at his arm. "Take it easy, honey, I'm a-comin'," he drawled.

He stood up, stretched out his mighty arms, and raked his fingers through his hair. Without looking down at her, he put his arm around Joanie's waist. Feeling her straighten up, Brandon pulled his arm back. He took her hand instead. He smiled down at her apologetically. . . . This reserving affection business was not exactly natural to him. Joanie smiled up at him and received his silent apology. Laughing at themselves, they walked off the deck.

☩   ☩   ☩

Joanie shocked Brandon with her athletic ability. She was quite a skilled badminton player. She explained to him that it had been one of her family's favourite summertime activities.

"But watch out when we play Maggie, 'cause she's the best!"

Sure enough, by their fourth match, they played Maggie and their cousin Mike.

"So, we meet again on the battlefield, Mr. Vaughn," Mike addressed Brandon.

The two young men chuckled, genuinely enjoying each other's company. The play was fast and furious, but in the end Maggie and Mike beat them two games to one.

☩   ☩   ☩

Bocce ball is a lawn bowling game of skill and accuracy in aim. Once again, Joanie impressed Brandon with her adeptness. Her father had taught all his daughters, early in life, not to throw and aim like girls. He had trained them up well in many areas of sports, and she advised Brandon, "Stick with me, boy, we could go places."

Picking up on the innuendo, Brandon replied, "I'd follow you, girl, to the ends of the earth."

"Oooooh, Joanie, watch out for this fellow," Caitlyn piped in. "Those smooth-talking types can be dangerous."

Brandon and Joanie laughed, both thinking, *If only Caitlyn knew how true that statement would have been just a few weeks back.*

Joanie took Brandon's hand and said, "It's me that he'd better watch out for. You know, Caitlyn," she added, "those smooth-talking types just don't stand a chance around those devoted-Christian types."

"Now, ain't that the truth!" Brandon exclaimed.

✣　　　　✣　　　　✣

Deciding to go down to the lake for a swim, they made use of the cabin to get changed. Brandon waited for Joanie and then they walked down to the beach together. As they stepped out onto the old dock, Brandon grabbed Joanie's towel from her hand, tossed it over to Maggie, swept Joanie into his arms and threw her in. Joanie screamed as she flew out past the edge of the dock and sank down into the lake. Upon catching her breath, she began scolding Brandon who promptly dived over her head and splashed down into the water behind her.

What ensued was a lively water fight, as other people jumped off the dock and joined in with the young couple at play. A ball got tossed in and soon a variation of water polo began. Someone more accurately dubbed it "murder ball", since the rules of the match were very loose, and the competition got rather fierce.

Brandon deliberately chose not to be on Joanie's team so as to take advantage of the opportunities to guard her. Though Brandon could easily have managed to have kept Joanie from ever getting the ball, he was shrewd enough to let her receive a pass from time to time. He had realized that it was much more fun to steal the ball back from her. Joanie would have objected to Brandon's constant interference, had it not been so much fun to tussle with him.

When the game was over, Joanie's cousins, Mike and Ben, grabbed Brandon from behind and dunked him into the water. Brandon splashed back up. Though taken aback from the attack, he was laughing as he looked over at his adversaries.

Standing tall, with his hands upturned, Mike explained in an Italian accent, delivered through a clenched jaw, "Joanie . . . she's like a sister to us. We felt it was our duty to get some sort of revenge for her . . . warn you not to mess with the Catholic mafia. We take care of our own!"

Brandon smiled at the two young men. "Glad to hear it," he replied.

Joanie took Brandon's hand and pulled him along, heading back up to the cabin. He smiled down at her, and she met his gaze with a wink. "Thanks, boys," she called out over her shoulder to her cousins. "Rough him up a bit to keep him in line, if you have to. But don't scare him off entirely. It'd be a shame to lose such a good partner for badminton and bocce ball."

"It'd take a lot more than that to scare me off," Brandon said with amusement, looking down at the charming girl.

Her wet hair was forming soft curls around her face as it dried. Brandon picked up a perfect ringlet that was hanging over her shoulder and played with it in his fingers. Joanie returned his look with playful eyes. "I'm glad to hear it," she replied.

✟   ✟   ✟

They enjoyed a feast of barbecued burgers and great salads for supper. Everyone was hungry after all the exercise. They all chipped in to help with clean-up and then congregated down by the campfire pit at the edge of the property. It was nestled into the trees and provided the atmosphere for an ideal ending to a wonderful day at the cottage.

Joanie sat down by Brandon, but stood up and left after a few minutes. When she returned she was carrying his guitar. He looked at her with real amazement. She handed him the guitar from one hand, and from her other hand she dangled his set of keys in front of his eyes.

She leaned over and whispered in his ear, "I pick-pocketed them."

"Now is that appropriate behaviour for a good Catholic girl like you?" he questioned quietly in her ear, as she sat down.

"No, but I noticed they were almost falling out of your pocket while we were playing badminton, so I seized the opportunity and took them from you. Sorry." She smiled innocently at him.

He leaned back his head, shaking out his wonder, as he began to play. Everyone stopped their chatting and quickly got into the rhythm of his blues and started cheering him on.

Ben showed up with his guitar and joined in the jamming. Ben was twenty-one, average height, and of small build. With his dark hair and dark eyes he could have passed for Joanie's brother. They were close cousins, making him like a brother to her anyway. He was a popular guy in the group, a natural entertainer and a real crowd pleaser. Ben was a good guitar player and had a great voice for singing.

As the two young men played, it became obvious that Brandon was a superlative guitar player. He picked up on anything Ben led and accentuated it with adept improvisational picking.

After several minutes of the jam session, someone asked the boys to lead a singsong.

"Fortunately," Brandon said, changing his strum, "I spent three summers at camp when I was a kid. How about you, Ben?"

The look of shock on Joanie's face was worth the price of admission in itself, or so Brandon thought.

"I not only attended camp, I was a counsellor for three years as well," Ben returned, hinting a challenge across the campfire.

Brandon laughed and the two of them soon fell into a repertoire of campfire ditties and familiar tunes. Everyone joined in.

Joanie thrilled at the sound of Brandon's clear, baritone voice. *Where did that come from?* She wondered, amazed at this secret talent of his. She sang alongside him.

It gave her great satisfaction to know that they had so much in common. Soon she found her heart battling against her will again. She tuned out the world momentarily for a quick, but meaningful, heart to heart with the Lord.

Oh, sweet Jesus, I don't know how long I can hold back my heart from this man. You'd better give me some clear direction in this relationship, because I am falling deeper for Brandon all the time.

She looked over at Maggie and knew that Maggie had been reading her thoughts. The younger sister smiled knowingly at the older sister and formed her hands as if to pray. Joanie laughed inside.

Okay, Jesus, I'll persevere in prayer and wait for You to show what Your will is for Brandon and me.

The campfire went on for some time. They stopped and prayed for awhile and then Ben led some praise and worship tunes. Brandon followed along on guitar and even joined with the singing when he picked up on a repetitious line or chorus.

Joanie closed her eyes, her heart filled with wonder as she listened to his voice. She could not get enough of the sound of praise being sung from Brandon's lips. She felt as though she were in a dream and she was afraid of waking up.

Joanie invited Maggie to drive home with her and Brandon that night. She longed for Maggie and Brandon to get to know each other, and she knew that Maggie would appreciate the invitation. They talked the whole car ride home, answering Brandon's never-ending stream of questions on the Bible and the Church. Time flew by and before they knew it, they were home.

Maggie excused herself quickly and said good-night. Joanie did not linger, for she did not trust herself after all the emotions of the day. She reminded Brandon about Sunday Mass the next morning at ten-thirty and invited him to come and sit with her family as she did not have to do music.

They made their farewell brief. They both knew they were safer that way.

✞   ✞   ✞

Joanie did not crawl straight into bed that night; rather she knelt beside it to pray her rosary. She asked Mary to help her and Brandon to grow in virtue and in holiness.

Oh, dear heavenly Mother, you know I could never marry a man who does not share my faith. Please, if it be God's will, open Brandon's heart to the Catholic Church, that I might be free to love him completely. And if it is not God's will for me to marry Brandon, make me to see that soon. Keep me under your mantle of purity at all times, that I would never betray my love for Jesus. Amen.

She climbed into bed, feeling a tremendous peace settle over her. She fell asleep very easily that night.

✞   ✞   ✞

Brandon also prayed to Mary before bed that night.

Mary, mother of my Lord, I ask you to do whatever it takes in my life to bring me closer to your Son, Jesus. I have never cared about heaven before today, but now I long for it more than anything. Teach me all that I can learn so that I might be able to share fully in the life of Christ. And help me to have a pure and holy love for Joanie. Amen.

Like Joanie, Brandon had no trouble falling asleep that night.

✞   ✞   ✞

The moonlight streaming in through the bedroom window caused the wispy shadows of the willow tree to dance on the wall. The gentle breeze brought with it a fresh and wholesome feeling into the warm summer night.

The sound of her sisters' breathing was soothing and comforting to Maggie as she lay in bed praying. Her heart was a mixture of joy and sorrow, for she could feel time slipping away, just as sand passes through an hourglass.

Reflecting on the day she had spent up at the lake, Maggie prayed.

Dear sweet Jesus, my heart's only desire is to be in Your presence and to know You and to love You and to serve You all the days of my life.

This was how she always began her prayers.

I know You are calling Joanie to something else in life. As I watched her and Brandon together today, I knew in my heart that You have called them to be one, and You have blessed their love for each other. But my heart aches at the thought of leaving this grace-filled time of life as our family begins to separate, and we go out into the world.

Oh, Mary, my mother, please give me the grace to let go of these attachments, so that I might freely follow wherever Your Son will lead me. And give Brandon and Joanie the special graces that they will need to live fully in Jesus' love. Amen.

As Maggie prayed her rosary, she felt the comforting love of Mary, her mother. It was the love of someone who understood completely. Mary, in her earthly life, also had known the pain of letting go in order to experience the fullness of joy that came from living according to the Father's will.

Chapter 24

The Collins family had a most enjoyable day with Brandon that Sunday. It was not hard for them to like this young man, and he felt right at home in their midst. Following Mass he came over to the house and helped Joanie's mom make lunch. Judy had shooed everyone else out of the kitchen, including Joanie, in order to have the opportunity to get to know Brandon better.

After lunch he got into a fairly intense game of Kaiser with Isaac, Katie, and Amie. Later, Jessie, Aaron, and Zack made sure to drag Brandon and Joanie off to the park to play for an hour or so.

He stayed for supper with the family and joined in a singsong around the campfire before going home. Isaac, a guitar enthusiast, sat across from Brandon and eagerly learned what he could from this impressive musician.

"How did you come to play guitar like that, Brandon?" John inquired.

"In high school my best friend, Mark, and I played in a small band. We did a number of gigs around the city and local area. It was great fun. There were five of us in the group; I was lead guitar, Mark played bass. There were keyboards and drums, and we had a soundman," Brandon explained.

"Were you the lead singer?" Judy asked.

"Yeah, I was. Not 'cause I have such a great voice, but because all of the other guys were worse than me," Brandon confessed.

"Oh, I disagree," put in Maggie. "You've got an incredible voice, Brandon!"

Brandon smiled, humbly accepting the acclamation. The feeling of acceptance that he experienced from Joanie's family was a far greater reward than any praise they could have given him.

As he was saying good-night to the family, Joanie's father called out to Brandon, "If you're able to take in nine holes tomorrow morning, I've made a booking for five-thirty-eight at the Willow Creek Course."

"I'd like that very much, John. I'll be there. Thank you," he said, with real appreciation.

"I just hope you have enough good sense to let me beat you, at least the first time we go out together!" John called after him.

Brandon laughed and agreed to do his best or rather, not his best, if such be the case.

✝   ✝   ✝

It was a cool, fresh, August morning. The dew sparkled on the trees and in the grass giving the appearance of a fairyland to the golf course. John's favourite time of day was at dawn, and he especially loved it when he could enjoy it with a golf club in his hand. He was an exceptionally good golfer who not only played well but taught it well. John tried his best to pass that skill on to his family. He tried to get out every few weeks, or as the budget allowed. Each time he would take a different combination of children, or sometimes he would go alone with his wife. It was always a wonderful time of bonding.

Today though, John wanted to just spend the time alone with Brandon and he hoped that they would not be interrupted by any walk-ons at the course.

When John arrived, Brandon was already hitting a bucket of balls to warm-up. "Well, son," he commented, "it looks like you've got a mighty fine swing there. Be careful. You remember our agreement here, don't you?"

Brandon laughed and invited John to hit off the last four balls, so that he, too, could get warmed up. "I'm sure you'll beat me, John, but I just wanted to be able to keep you on your toes so that the game doesn't get boring," he remarked.

John looked up at him and nodded. Turning his attention back to the ball, he lined himself up. Then, in a perfectly fluid motion, he drew back the club and pulled it through. There was a clear, hollow sound as the club connected precisely on the sweet spot to send the ball sailing straight and true about three hundred yards.

Brandon was duly impressed. He watched the same scene repeat itself three times more, standing in silence so as not to disturb John's concentration. Somehow he felt proud of Joanie's father for being able to flex such muscle. It added to the respect he had for this man who was the guardian and protector of the woman whom he had come to love.

"Just remember, Brandon," John advised him, "the oldest bull still has the strongest horns."

"Yes, sir," Brandon acknowledged him, respectfully, "I see that quite well."

Called up to the first tee, they were both relieved when no one approached to join them. The game got off to a good start with both of them getting a birdie on the first hole. On the second hole John got a par, while Brandon slipped in a long putt for a birdie. John cocked his eyebrow at Brandon who just lifted his hands as if to say, *I'm as shocked as you are.*

"Can't let that happen too many times here," John commented.

Brandon seemed to have quite a talent for the game, reminding John of himself some twenty years earlier. "D'you play often?" John inquired, as they walked up the fairway.

"I used to play a lot more," Brandon replied, "but lately I've found myself too distracted to get into it."

"Well, a woman will do that to you for sure," laughed John. "Let me tell you, Joanie's a sweet girl, but I've tried for years to get her interested in golf, with no luck. She's got a good swing, and she putts real well, but she says it's just not her thing. Oh, she comes out from time to time to humour the ol' man. I suspect, though, that you might be a bigger drawing card for her. Maybe you can talk her into the game and then you'll be able to start getting out on the course more often, yourself."

"I'd like that," Brandon admitted.

They played on for another two holes, appreciating each other's skill. Then John inquired, "Tell me about yourself, Brandon."

"Where should I start, John?"

"Tell me about your family," John suggested.

Brandon hesitated. He did not have much for a family, nothing like the Collinses. "Well, sir, I grew up an only child. My mom, Caroline Taylor, lives out in Calgary now. She just remarried three years back. There really isn't much to say. She had been orphaned as a child when her parents died in a car accident. I don't have many relatives to speak of."

"What about your father? Did you ever know him?" John asked, in a caring tone.

"Not really, sir. You see, my father was a real . . ." he hesitated over the word, ". . . jerk. He fooled around a lot on my mother and when I was eight years old, he flew the coop. I never saw him much after that, and I don't really care if I ever see him again."

Brandon's tone was distant and low, full of pain.

They golfed on for another two holes in silence. At first Brandon's game seemed to be a bit off; faltering in his concentration, he ended up with a bogey on the next hole. John got his par. But the natural athlete in Brandon recovered his focus, and he, too, was back on par by the sixth.

John was praying for this young man. He knew that Brandon could not become a good husband and father until he had forgiven his own father for betraying and abandoning him.

Finally, on the seventh fairway, John commented, "You know, son, you need to do something about that situation with your father."

"Sir?" Brandon was unsure as to John's meaning.

"I'm sure you've heard of the Ten Commandments, haven't you?"

Brandon nodded.

"I don't expect that you know them by heart, but the fourth one says, 'Honour thy father and mother.' The Bible doesn't ever qualify that commandment according to the worthiness of our parents. We're all sinful and frail, Brandon. And we all make our share of mistakes, as you know from your own life.

"But you've experienced the tremendous grace and mercy of our Lord. It brought you out of a darkness that had not been your own choosing. Your father, well, you need to honour him, no matter what he's done . . . not for him having earned it but . . . because God chose *him* to be your father. When you can forgive him, son, you'll be free of all that pain that you've been carrying 'round all these years." John turned his attention back to the game.

The two played on, making small talk about the game until the last hole. Brandon and John were tied.

When they approached the tee, John looked up at him and said, "I'll be disappointed if you don't nail that ball on the head!" And with that he gave Brandon permission to beat him, which he did by one stroke. They laughed and shook hands as they left the ninth green.

"Do you have time for a coffee?" John asked Brandon, checking his watch. "Come on into the clubhouse. It's on me."

They chatted about weather and up-coming plans for the week. When Brandon got up to leave, he thanked John for the game and the coffee. "And thanks for the advice, John. I'll pray about what you said to me!"

"I'll pray for it too, son," John added, in a fatherly tone.

☦   ☦   ☦

That evening Brandon was restless, anxious about John's words, sensing the truth of them but unsure as to how to proceed with living them out. He opened the Bible, looked up the Ten Commandments and prayed over the text for quite some time.

He wondered if he were capable of forgiving his father. In many ways, it just seemed like too much to ask. He wanted to say he could forgive his father, but in reality his heart was still too full of hate toward the wretched man. He closed the Bible and set it on the couch beside him, discouraged by his lack of integrity.

Brandon got up and turned on the radio, which he now kept tuned to the local Christian station. He got ready to go down to the gym for a workout. As he passed back through the living room on his way out the door, something caught his attention.

There was a talk show on and some preacher man with a really thick Southern accent was being interviewed. Brandon had no idea of the context of the conversation, but suddenly the man's words shot out an arrow, aimed at Brandon's heart.

"Remember, we're told in Romans five, verse nine, that God shows His love for us in that, while we were yet sinners Christ died for us . . ."

Brandon stopped, dead in his tracks. He could not hold back his tears. He walked away from the door, went over and turned off the radio. He had heard enough. That was the message that he knew Jesus wanted him to hear. He went down on his knees. How could he have been so proud and so unforgiving when Christ had shown, in His own love for Brandon, such mercy? Brandon thought about the wretched sinner that he had been when God brought Joanie into his life to light a way for him to find Jesus.

He remembered the feeling of release when his heart had been washed over by the power of the Holy Spirit and was filled with praise and thanksgiving to God. Brandon had not earned these graces. He had done everything in his life to avoid these graces. But God's mercy knows no bounds.

With new resolve, Brandon stood up and went to the phone. Taking out his address book, he looked up his father. He was not even sure if it was the correct number. His father moved around quite a bit, and Brandon had not spoken to him in almost two years.

He punched in the numbers on the keypad and waited. With each ring of the phone, his heart pounded louder. He was relieved when it was the answering machine that picked up.

At the sound of his father's voice, a wave of forgiveness flooded Brandon's heart. His mind was transported briefly to an incident in childhood. Brandon was six at the time, and he remembered his father down on the floor, helping him put together the train set he had gotten for Christmas. It was one of the very few memories Brandon had of his father and him happy together. Brandon remembered feeling love in his heart for his father at that moment.

All at once the message ended, and the beep in his ear brought Brandon back to reality. He fumbled at first for words and then continued with a message. "Hi, Dad, yeah, it's Brandon. I . . . I just wanted to let you know I've been thinking about you lately. And I guess I thought it'd be good to get together with you sometime and catch up. Give me a call, nine two nine, three six nine four. Bye."

He hung up the phone and realized he was sweating. His hands were all clammy, and his heart was racing. He sat down and picked up his rosary from the side table. Joanie had taught Brandon to pray the rosary, and he had enjoyed the spiritual exercise of meditating on the life of Christ. Using a prayer card to guide him through the sorrowful mysteries, he offered up a rosary for the healing of his relationship with his dad.

For the first time in his life, he felt a release from the anger within him. It was like John had said—he was being set free from the burden of pain which he had carried around his whole life. Brandon marvelled at the goodness of God. He realized now that he had not been capable of forgiving his father on his own. It was only through the grace and mercy of Jesus that he could unshackle the chains of hate that had bound his heart. In releasing his father through forgiveness, Brandon, too, had been set free.

Brandon went down for his much needed workout. It felt good to release all of the physical tension that had settled in his muscles. He prayed silently for his dad as he worked through his routine.

A few hours later the phone rang, and Brandon saw on his call display that it was his father. Brandon made a quick prayer to St. Joseph for guidance and answered the phone.

"Brandon?" his father's deep voice rang out. "Is everything all right? I haven't heard from you in two years."

"Yeah, Dad, everything's great. Better than great. Life's been ... really good lately. I just wanted to connect with you, because ... well it's been two years."

Brandon's voice was full of hesitation. He was deliberating whether or not to explain to his father about Joanie and his conversion. Somehow it was not something he could share over the phone.

"Sometime, Dad, when you come to town, look me up. I'd like to see you again."

"Well, I'd really like that, Brandon. In fact, I have business there at the end of the week. How about I check in with you then? I'll take you out to supper."

Brandon chuckled to himself: it was the only thing he and his father ever did together.

"Yeah, Dad, that would be great," he returned sincerely.

✞   ✞   ✞

When Brandon got home Thursday from work, there was a message on his machine from his father. He would be at *Antonio's* at six-thirty, if Brandon still wanted to meet with him.

Brandon smiled. It had taken him a long time to arrive at this point in his life. He sat down and prepared himself in prayer before going.

✞   ✞   ✞

Antonio's was a small restaurant. The cozy booths were dimly lit and very private. The music was neither here nor there, but the food was really quite good.

As Brandon walked in, he looked furtively for his father. Spying him at a booth on the other side of the restaurant, he swallowed deeply and headed across the open room. His feet felt heavy as he struggled to lift them confidently. He worked to relax his shoulders. Every sound around him seemed to fade into a blurred white noise, like a radio dial tuned into lost airspace. He reached the table. His father, a tall and handsome man, put down the menu and looked up at Brandon, then smiled through eyes as blue as the sea. It was obvious that Brandon had taken his looks from this man. He motioned for Brandon to sit down and offered him a drink. Brandon gratefully accepted.

His father, James Vaughn, was a successful business man who had spent the last twenty years of his life making wealth and enjoying it indiscriminately. He had made his start in real estate but moved on into the technology industry, coming into real money when he pioneered internet marketing for Canadian businesses.

He looked across the table at Brandon and could not help but experience a sense of pride in his son. Though he had had little involvement in Brandon's upbringing, he was still his flesh and blood. Brandon had grown to be a successful commercial producer, a handsome and talented young man. There was a pang of guilt and regret that gripped James' heart. But he could not turn back the hands of time. It was best to let bygones be bygones.

James ordered a beer for his son when the waitress returned.

The waitress smiled coyly at Brandon, obviously taken with his good looks. It was a look with which Brandon was all too familiar. He shuddered at the thought of how many one night stands from his past had begun with a look just like that. His father, picking up on the waitress's signal, commented that Brandon might just get lucky tonight with that girl.

Brandon was suddenly overwhelmed by the situation. It was off to a typical start. He wondered why he had expected it to somehow be different tonight with his father. Then, with a burst of heavenly inspiration, he asked St. Joseph for assistance and the sensation of futility passed.

"So tell me what's new, son," his father began. Brandon had never liked it when his father called him "son" because their relationship had never reflected that kind of intimacy. Somehow tonight it did not bother him. In fact, he felt encouraged by it.

"A lot, Dad," Brandon asserted. He drew deeply for strength, then setting his mind on course he began. "I met a girl."

"Nothing new about that, son. It's been my impression that you've met a lot of girls in your lifetime. Kind of a chip off the old block," he remarked, rather proudly.

"Well, it's not like that, Dad." Brandon struggled not to be derailed by his father's casualness. He had to remind himself that it was shamefully true.

He remembered Joanie's gentle assertion from St. Augustine: "But for the grace of God, there go I."

Brandon continued, "This one's different, Dad. She's . . ." he faltered for words.

His father looked at him, suddenly sensing a change, and with a tone of encouragement, he said, "Go on, son, I'm listening."

"Well, she's changed everything in my life." Brandon closed his eyes and brought Joanie's face to mind. He knew he could do it. "She's a Christian and a really strong one." He chuckled at what an understatement that seemed. "She won me over for Christ, Dad, and I've turned my life around. I go to church now and pray lots and read the Bible and . . . well you get the picture."

"So you're a Christian," his father muttered, almost to himself.

"Yeah, Dad, I am." Brandon paused, waiting for whatever would come next.

His father sized him up in a thoughtful look, then asked, "So what do you want from me, Brandon?"

"I don't know," Brandon confessed. "I guess I just wanted you to know since . . . you're an important part of my life." Even as the words came out, Brandon knew that they were true, but had not ever expected that he would have said them.

"Yeah, well I guess I've been a real screw-up for a dad and a real jerk most of my life. I can't say I've blamed you for not wanting anything to do with me. But I'm a little confused now, son. I'm not sure that I can be anymore of a father to you now than what I was when I had the chance the first time." He was sincere and non-threatening.

"I think I just wanted to tell you, Dad, that I . . ." he paused, sensing the significance of what he was about to say, "I forgive you, Dad."

His father looked at him, silent and somewhat awkward.

Brandon went on, "I'm not expecting you to become a Christian. I'm not here to convert you. I'll leave that between you and God. But it's important for me to let you know that . . . I've let go of all the hate I'd been carrying around toward you. And I think it'd be good to begin again in our relationship. Who knows, maybe we could even become friends after all these years."

His father sat there, speechless. This was the most Brandon had ever opened up to him in his entire life. He felt justly accused by Brandon's assertion of hate and overwhelmingly moved by Brandon's attempt to make amends. He had never given the relationship much thought, knowing that he had not merited anything but Brandon's animosity. And so he had never placed any expectation there. Now here was his son, offering him forgiveness and reconciliation out of the blue. It was a lot to take in.

Fortunately the waitress came back to take their orders and rescue

James from his vulnerable state of mind. They ordered, not at all interested in what they would eat.

There was silence between them now, and Brandon used the opportunity to pray, invoking the Holy Spirit to touch his father's heart in some way.

Finally James smiled. Looking straight into Brandon's eyes, he said, "I'm in, son. I'd very much like to get to know you again, or for that matter, for the first time. And by the way, thanks. It means a lot to me that you would . . . well that . . . that you forgive me. And I want you to believe me when I tell you that I am sorry for everything."

Brandon returned his father's look with genuine love. For the first time in his life he knew that he was keeping the fourth commandment. His heart became filled with a tremendous consolation.

✠   ✠   ✠

That next Sunday after Mass, Brandon was at the Collinses. While brunch was being fixed up in the kitchen, Brandon sought out John and asked him how his woodworking projects were going. John took the cue and invited Brandon out to the garage for a look.

As they examined the details of John's latest undertaking, John asked Brandon, "So what's on your mind, son?"

Brandon smiled at the intuitiveness of the fatherly figure before him. He replied, "I just wanted to thank you for steering me in the right direction with my father."

"Joanie told us you met with your dad after two years of not having seen each other. I was happy to hear about that, Brandon. How do you feel about things now?"

"Well, sir, I think that I stand before you today a freer man. I never realized how consuming hate could be," Brandon answered, thoughtfully.

"And I bet you never realized how much freedom there was in living God's laws. Funny, the paradox, eh? So many people think that religious convictions confine and restrain a person from being who they *want* to be. But in reality, they free us to be who we were *created* to be. And once we've discovered that, there's no end to the possibilities. Fear, hate, and selfishness no longer hold us back from living life to the fullest. There's true peace and freedom there for those who choose it."

"I agree, sir."

"I'm proud of you, Brandon," John stated, with real affirmation.

He put his hand on Brandon's shoulder, and together they walked back to the house, just in time for brunch.

Chapter 25

"So how's that new set of legs doing, Brandon?" Paul inquired one afternoon, as they were working alone together in an editing suite.

Brandon looked over at Paul from under raised eyebrows, smiling. He had not discussed his and Joanie's relationship with anybody at work, but he knew Paul had figured it out. Paul had seen the whole thing coming. "Which new set of legs are you referring to, Paul?"

"Is there more than one new set of legs in your life these days?" Paul returned. "'Cause I'd be kind of shocked if Joanie would put up with that sort of thing."

"Has she said something to you?" Brandon asked, carefully guarding what information he was willing to disclose.

"She says lots of things to me . . . but it's the way she's been behaving that speaks volumes," Paul told him.

"Like?" Brandon inquired.

"Well, it's not much different from you these past few weeks. She smiles an awful lot, even more than usual. She's got that I'm-in-love-and-I-just-can't-help-myself look about her. You know what I mean! Surely, you've noticed by now." The cameraman had stopped working at the equipment and had turned to face Brandon.

"Good for her. I'm glad to hear it."

"You're not going to cave in and talk to me, are you?" Paul asked, with disappointment.

Brandon laughed at his friend. "I guess since you've already figured us out, it's safe to tell you. But I'd appreciate it if you kept this under your hat, Paul. Joanie and I have agreed to leave our relationship completely out of the work place."

"Your secret's safe with me . . . like it has been all along, Brandon." In his own way Paul was reminding Brandon that he had already proven himself in this matter.

"Thanks, Paul." The commercial producer looked at his friend with a real sense of appreciation.

"Seems like there was more to that girl than just a nice set of legs after all," Paul bantered, without coming right out and saying: *I told you so!*

"Yeah," Brandon said, thoughtfully, "she's the genuine article, Paul, just like you said. And what's more, she's made a Christian out of me."

Paul smiled. Though he had no strong religious convictions of his own, he appreciated what Christ had done in Brandon's life. Paul had seen the changes in his friend, and he liked what he was seeing. "Funny, how things happen! The first time you pointed Joanie out to me, I just had a feeling you had met your match. I'm so glad for you that I was right!"

Brandon patted Paul on the shoulder. "So am I, Paul. So am I. . . . Come on, let's get back to work."

✜   ✜   ✜

Joanie could sense Paul had something on his mind as they drove off to a location for a shoot. He had a curious smile about him, but he was being uncharacteristically quiet. Finally he broke the silence. "Brandon's sure been looking better these days," he threw out at her and waited for her reaction.

"Has he now?" she inquired, with interest.

"Yeah, it turns out I was right about him all along," Paul boasted. "It seems he has met his match."

"Really?" Joanie was very interested. "What has he said to you?"

"Oh, only that some beautiful girl with great legs has managed to turn his whole life around. In fact, it seems *he's* become a Christian," Paul continued, hoping for some sort of reaction from the young reporter.

"Great legs?" she asked. "Did *he* say that?"

"Oh, long before she ever got under his skin. Yeah, he had his sights set on her right from the start. But you know, she just kept her cool with him, stuck to her morals and—wham! Brandon, the hunter, got caught in his own trap!"

Joanie began laughing over Paul's dramatic interpretation of events. "Okay, Paul. Enough. What did Brandon really say?"

"Most of what I said, but I just say it with such flair!" He looked at her, from over his sunglasses. "I'm happy that things have worked out between you. I think you're the best thing that could ever have happened to that man! And for that matter, so does he."

Joanie breathed deeply and smiled back at Paul. "Thanks. You're not going to spill the beans on us here at work, are you?"

"Are you kidding? And spoil all the fun I'm having watching this secret love affair unfold?" He threw her a friendly look as he pulled the station van in to the location of their shoot.

"Paul, I think you're a wonderful man!" Joanie said sincerely, as she patted him on the shoulder.

"Well, Joanie, I think you are an amazing woman!" He turned off the van, took off his sunglasses and hooked them on the driver-side visor.

As she stepped out of the van, she looked across the vehicle at Paul from her door. "Great legs?"

"Those were his words, Joanie. I wouldn't have noticed. I'm a happily married man!" Paul replied, smiling through those black, friendly eyes of his.

She laughed and closed the van door. Somehow, though, Paul was certain that Joanie was carrying herself just a little taller than usual for the rest of the afternoon.

✟   ✟   ✟

That evening Joanie and Brandon took the little ones to the playground. While Zack, Aaron, and Jessie were running around out of earshot, Joanie took the opportunity to ask Brandon a few questions. "So, what's this I hear about 'great legs'?"

Brandon threw a sideways glance at her, sitting beside him on the park bench. "You've been talking to Paul, I take it."

"Maybe," she replied, rather coyly. She was sitting forward with her legs tucked under the park bench.

Brandon leaned forward and looked down at Joanie's legs. "Well," he asserted, with a twinkle in his eyes, "they are that!"

Joanie laughed and hit him on the shoulder. "Thanks . . . I think," she replied. "Just don't go comparing them with other legs."

"I haven't seen another pair of legs in weeks, Joanie. And I can guarantee you that I won't be noticing any other legs from now on," he declared, rather soberly. "I'm a one-woman man, you know!"

He took Joanie's hand in his, and she sat back beside him. She smiled. She liked being his girl. "Well, I'm sure glad that I'm that one woman, Brandon."

"My one and only," he confessed. "I'm a reformed man, Joanie. I have eyes for you and for you alone!"

She gave a little giggle and stated, "Well, it seems that in spite of yourself, the message of chastity came through that ridiculous advertising campaign after all."

"In the biggest way!" he admitted. Then, assuming his old arrogant tone, he asserted, "And if I'm not mistaken here, you just might be spared the fate of becoming an old spinster, knitting away in a parlour."

Joanie continued the bantering. "And you know I was pretty worried about that, too, considering what a prude I was and all!"

He laughed and leaned forward, bracing his elbows on his knees. He was still holding her hand, playing with her fingers as he spoke. "How did you ever look past all that crap and find me?"

Joanie leaned forward to meet him eye to eye. "Because when you dropped that awful façade, and I could catch a glimpse of who you really were . . . I liked what I saw. When I was with you, there was something about you that made me feel like I'd never felt before. And as much as that terrified me, it made me want to find the real man behind the mask. I'm so glad I didn't give up on you." Her words came out softly, almost in a whisper.

Looking deeply into her eyes, he implored her, "Please don't ever give up on me."

"I won't," she assured him. "I'm content to walk this road with you as far as the Lord takes us."

How he wanted to take her in his arms. Never before had he cared for a girl like he cared for Joanie. Ironically, the best way for him to show it to her was to not show it to her at all—at least in terms of physical affection. Instead, the self-control it took to withhold his affection communicated with absolute clarity the respect and admiration he had for this woman.

As they let the silence breathe between them, Joanie reflected on her feelings for Brandon. Brandon was just about everything she had ever prayed for in a man. He was sincere in his love for the Lord; he was enthusiastic about learning the faith and putting it into practice in his life. He was an incredible musician and singer. He was gentle and kind, strong and stable. He was fun, and he had come to love children as much as she did. He treated her with nothing but respect, and she felt completely cherished by him. The fact that he was outrageously handsome was just a bonus. There was only one thing missing—and he was so close to it. She did not feel anxious about it, though. God had brought Brandon along this far. There was just one more step for Brandon to make . . . but in God's time.

Their quiet moment in the park came to an end when Zack and Aaron attacked Brandon from behind. He jumped up off the bench and began chasing the two little would-be-assassins around the playground. They climbed the monkey bars and Brandon followed up behind them. He grabbed hold of Aaron and began tickling until the five-year-old begged for mercy. Next, Brandon got hold of Zack and hung the eight-year-old upside down from the top of the monkey bars until he, too, begged for mercy.

With the line of authority re-established among the troops, the boys coaxed Brandon into popping some high flies with the bat for them so they could practise their catching. Joanie got Jessie from the sandbox and the two girls followed the boys out to the open park area to watch. After a half-hour, Brandon packed them all into his Pathfinder and took them out for ice cream cones.

✝   ✝   ✝

Life seemed to pick up pace over the next few weeks. Brandon spent most evenings and free time with Joanie. Except for the nights when she had band rehearsals or other commitments, he attended weekday Mass with her at St. James. They got involved with friends through C.C.E. and took in whatever activities were happening over the summer. They went out for walks, played tennis, and they even managed a few games of golf. John was right that Joanie's interest in the game would be sparked by Brandon.

The young couple entertained, or were entertained by, Joanie's younger siblings at pools, parks, and such. Having an older brother in the family was a real novelty. Isaac, Zack, and Aaron could not believe their good fortune. And Joanie suspected that Brandon was having just as much fun playing as were the little boys.

Very often at the end of the evening Joanie and Brandon would spend time studying the faith through video and audio tapes at her house. Brandon was amazed at what a wealth of resources her family had. They had more books on theology, saints, miracles, and teachings of the Church than Brandon ever could have imagined existed.

He was up late every night reading. Bright and early each morning, he would be right back at it. He just could not get enough. His appetite for learning about the faith had become insatiable; the more he read, the more he wanted to know.

Summer was drawing to a close. *New Spring* was enjoying a short reprieve from its hectic performance schedule. The band had much to discuss regarding fall bookings and commitments. They plugged on, week by week, trying to discern the direction they would be taking.

Work was going extremely well for Joanie. She loved the atmosphere at the station; she got along well with all her co-workers. Her enthusiasm for reporting had increased with each new assignment. Had Brandon not been such a distraction in her life outside of office hours, she would have found it hard not to become a workaholic.

✠   ✠   ✠

Joanie was surprised one afternoon when Mr. Lemay came to her cubicle and with a certain awkwardness asked her to come to his office for a meeting. Her surprise turned to shock when she saw Brandon standing there, waiting for them. Brandon just looked back at her in his calm, collected way. They had been so careful not to allow any of their relationship to spill over into the workplace. Joanie's mind raced to try to figure out the meaning of the situation.

"Take a seat, kids," Mr. Lemay said, inviting them to sit side by side in front of his desk. He took his seat across from them and continued. "I have to say that I'm feeling rather awkward about this meeting here. You see, we have a company policy that does not allow for dating among employees. I've heard from a reliable source that you two have been seeing each other for some time now."

Joanie shifted around in her seat, feeling, she imagined, like a child who had been called into the principal's office. This situation was worse, though, since both her job and Brandon's were at stake here.

Brandon did not flinch. He remained perfectly composed.

"Now I'm not sure what to do in this situation. I . . . I can't very well tell you not to date, but as long as you're both employed here . . . well, I can't allow it to go on, which doesn't leave me with very many options in the matter. Frankly, I don't know what to do. I respect and appreciate the work that both of you do here at the station." His look was sincere. He was disappointed and uncomfortable. *Sometimes being the boss really sucks!* He heaved a sigh, picked up a pen from his desk and began to click it.

"Well, sir," Brandon began, "with all due respect, I'd like to suggest a loophole in this situation."

"Please do, if you can," Mr. Lemay responded, without much hope.

"Well, while it's true that Joanie and I have been seeing each other this past summer, we have *not* been dating."

"How so, Brandon?" Wariness filled Mr. Lemay's voice. He set the pen back down.

"You see, we've been *courting,* sir. And if the policy does not allow for *'dating',* maybe we've got our loophole there." Brandon had the air of a lawyer as he spoke.

"I fail to see the difference," Mr. Lemay said, with disappointment apparent in his expression. He picked up the pen again, clicking it.

"Begging your pardon, Mr. Lemay, but believe me, there's a world of difference!" Brandon stated, rather emphatically. "Joanie and I have been spending a great deal of time together with her family, going to church . . . I've been studying to become Catholic, sir."

Joanie's heart skipped a beat. Never before had she heard Brandon make any such profession of faith.

"But I guarantee you, Mr. Lemay, our relationship has *not* been physical," Brandon continued. "We've been spending this time discerning about our relationship with regards to marriage. So you see, in accordance with the wishes of Joanie's father, we've been courting, not dating. And believe me," he added, with great conviction, "coming from a man who's life has completely changed over the past two months, there's a world of difference between courtship and dating."

Joanie squirmed some more, unsure as to what to say, so she prayed silently while Brandon boldly defended their relationship. She was so proud of him.

"Is this true, Joanie?" Mr. Lemay addressed her, setting the pen aside.

"Yes, sir," she answered, as confidently as possible. "In fact, it would be all right with me if you wanted to call my father and discuss it with him."

Mr. Lemay released a heartfelt laugh. He jumped up from his seat and walked around the table, extending his hand out to Brandon. "Well done, young man! I'm impressed. And since there's been no interference on the job, I'm willing to go to bat for you two should someone want to take you to task over this. You see, I heard about you two through Bill Curran. No one at work has ever mentioned it. So let's just leave it to rest." He motioned that they were free to leave.

"Thank you, sir," Brandon stated, almost in shock as he headed toward the office door.

"Yes, thank you, Mr. Lemay. I don't know what to say, but I'm terribly grateful," Joanie said, with apparent relief.

"That's fine. But I suggest you thank Brandon later for his quick thinking. And," turning to Brandon, he added, "I suggest you thank Joanie. There's nothing like the love of a good woman to make a better man out of you, is there, son?"

"You can say that again," Brandon concurred, looking at Joanie.

They all laughed and the meeting ended.

Mr. Lemay stood at his office door in amazement. He was well aware of Brandon's reputation as a womanizer. It had been a concern at the time he had hired Brandon on fulltime at the station. Had he not been so impressed with the high standards and professionalism of the young man, he would never have given him a chance. Joanie was the last person he would ever have imagined to have become mixed up with a man like that.

I guess I underestimated the strength of that girl's character . . . to have taken a guy like Brandon and to have transformed him into what I just saw here today. Courting? If I hadn't seen it with my own eyes, I would never have believed it. I may just have to rethink our family's policy on dating.

"Hmm . . . maybe there's hope for my children yet!" he said under his breath as he shut the door, thinking about his fourteen and sixteen-year-old daughters.

✝   ✝   ✝

That night at the Collinses, Brandon thanked John for the excellent guidance he had given to the young couple regarding courtship. The whole family was thoroughly amused over the entire situation.

John was quick to point out to all his children, sitting around listening, "Just remember, father knows best!"

✠　　　✠　　　✠

Later that evening Joanie and Brandon went out for a walk. They strolled down to the river and found an obscure, quiet path to take through the thicker part of the trees.

Brandon noticed that Joanie had a pensiveness about her. He decided not to interrupt her thoughts. She would let him know what was on her mind when she was ready. They walked on, holding hands. Brandon was whistling a familiar melody.

"Brandon," Joanie's voice interrupted the tune, "what did you mean, when you told Mr. Lemay that you were studying to become Catholic?"

"Just that," he replied, without explanation.

"Brandon, talk to me." Joanie stopped walking and turned to face him. "I know you've been studying whatever you can get your hands on to learn about the faith. But you've never once said anything about becoming Catholic."

"Well, Tuesday nights when you've had band rehearsals, I've been meeting with Fr. Steve. I decided quite some time ago to become Catholic."

Joanie stepped back. Her face had a mixture of expressions that Brandon could not quite read.

"Why have you never said anything about becoming Catholic to me before now?" she questioned him, her dark eyes wide open, entreating him for an answer.

There they stood, the river slowly murmuring behind them. The evening light was sparkling in her hair. The soft wind whispered in the trees. It was the moment of truth.

"Because," he said, taking her hands into his own, "I want to become a Catholic, not just because I have fallen in love with one. And I wanted you to have a chance to fall in love with me . . . not just because I'm becoming a Catholic."

She stared up into his eyes. Never before had either one of them openly professed their love to each other. It was there between them. They both knew it and felt it, as though it had a life of its own. But they had avoided discussing it in order to allow time to discern the direction their relationship was to take.

Joanie breathed deeply, not knowing how to respond to what Brandon had just said.

"Joanie," he said, lifting her hands up and kissing them gently. She felt the warmth of his lips on her fingers and she closed her eyes. The moment was so big and so full, there was no way her senses could take it all in. Brandon waited for her to look back up at him. He could have stood gazing down upon her angelic face forever, waiting for her response. It made no difference to him. Time stood still as he kissed her hands again.

Finally, she looked up directly into his eyes, as though she were seeing his very soul.

In a voice, full and rich, he professed, "I love you!"

Her eyes were watery, and a tear slowly began to trickle down her cheek. Softly, he wiped it off her smooth skin. With great tenderness, he drew her up close and held her in his arms. It was the first time he had ever taken her into his arms, and he did so with all the sensitivity of holding a delicate flower. He could feel the pounding of her heart against his body.

Joanie wrapped her arms around Brandon and stayed there for a few minutes. She could not talk; she could not think. All she could do was feel the love that was within her, welling up so that she could no longer contain it.

Lifting her face, she whispered in his ear, "I love you, Brandon!"

He pulled back his head from hers and drew her back into his gaze.

She repeated herself, as she took into her heart every aspect of this man for whom she was professing her love. "I love you." Her voice was soft, and the words were simple, but the moment was absolutely divine.

They stood there in silence. They did not kiss, though they both ardently desired to do so. That would be for another time. It was enough, for now, to rest in the assurance of each other's love.

Gradually a smile began to take form on Brandon's face. He stepped back from Joanie, and in an act of sheer release, he hollered out, "Waahooooo!" Then turning back to her, he picked her up around the waist and twirled her around.

"Brandon! You've gone crazy!" she scolded him, looking around to see if anyone had been watching.

"I don't care who sees," he told her, as he set her down. "I could tell the whole world—I love Joanie Collins, and Joanie loves me!"

She blushed at his foolishness and bashfully pulled away from him.

He pulled her back, lifting her off the ground again and said, "You are the *only* woman I've ever told that to, Joanie. And you're the only one I ever will!"

She buried her face into his shoulder, her tears pouring freely now.

Softly, she spoke, "I've held my heart for so long, waiting for this moment. I'm giving it to you now, Brandon. Please take care of it for me!"

"I will," he solemnly vowed. "I promise I will."

Chapter 26

September rolled around with its usual whirlwind of activity. The Collins household became animated by the academic scene as the children re-established themselves in their home-schooling routines. John was back at work, teaching at Sacred Heart High School, and Judy was busy trying to schedule all the children's activities for the fall. Outside of work hours, Joanie began an intensive practice schedule at home. She was preparing for her Associate exam in voice and her grade four counterpoint exam, the last of the written requirements for her to complete her music degree. Both exams would be in the spring. Maggie was back at university for her third year of Education. She worked part-time in a nursing home as well. Amie had taken on a half-time position at their church doing youth ministry. She was continuing an intensive course of music study, working on her Associate level for piano and two of her written components for her degree. She also taught fifteen students piano lessons from home.

With all this activity the house was noisy and lively, which at times drove everyone a little bit crazy. But when Brandon came around, he found the hustle and bustle of the Collinses' home absolutely refreshing to his soul. He loved to watch how this family survived in all the commotion, dealt with situations, solved their problems, and reconciled disagreements. It was the warmth and love of this family that most characterized their home life to him.

There were always friends and relatives stopping in to visit. It seemed that this house could never become too full: as though the walls expanded to make room for everyone.

The love that Brandon experienced in the Collins family was the most beautiful testimony to the Catholic faith that he could have possibly witnessed. He wanted so much to have what they all shared. He could not express enough his gratitude to them, for having taken him into their hearts and making him feel like one of the family.

✞   ✞   ✞

One evening while Brandon was alone at his place reading, the phone rang. It was his mother, Caroline. Brandon had a certain awkwardness talking to his mother ever since his conversion. So far he had avoided telling her about Joanie and the fact that he had become a Christian. Caroline had a great distaste for religion. Though he never really understood it, Brandon knew it had something to do with her parents' deaths when she was a child. He just did not know how to bring up the subject with her. So now, every conversation with her was guarded.

"Brandon, what's with you lately?" his mother asked.

"What do you mean, Mom?" The tentative tone in his voice could not be hidden from his mother.

"There's something up, and I know it. You've changed. Every conversation we've had over the past few months has been like this. . . . Personally, I think you've got yourself a girl." The tone of Caroline's voice was very emphatic. She knew she was right, and she was not about to let Brandon deny it.

"You're sure that's not just wishful thinking on your part, Mom?" Brandon returned, playfully.

"No, it's not, Brandon. It's called motherly intuition. And if you don't come through this time and tell me what's up, I'll drive to Saskatoon and find out for myself!"

Brandon laughed and replied, "Okay, okay. What took you so long to figure me out?"

"I figured you out long ago, son. I was just waiting for you to come out and tell me yourself. But you sure are tight-lipped about this relationship. . . . She must be awfully special." The softness of his mother's voice was a welcome and familiar sound. He had a great deal of love for this heroic woman in his life—the only woman he had ever loved, until Joanie.

"Well, she is really special, Mom. Her name is Joanie Collins, and we've been seeing each other now since July," he began.

"Which would account for why you were too busy all summer to come and visit me," she pointed out, as only a mother would do.

"Sorry, Mom," he apologized. "I guess I have been rather preoccupied."

"Are you living together?"

The question caught Brandon by surprise. It had been a natural question, given his former lifestyle. Suddenly Brandon was reminded of just how far he had come since he met Joanie. How would his mother understand that he had never even kissed Joanie, let alone that he had never slept with her? He really did not want to open up the whole Christianity debate with his mom just yet: it was too sensitive an issue.

Searching for an appropriate response, he said, "No, Mom. She's not that type. Look, I can't see myself getting out to Calgary before Christmas. Life's been pretty busy with work and all. But I'll get out to visit you at that time, and I'll try to bring Joanie with me then."

"She must be something, Brandon, if you still intend to be seeing her at Christmastime. I've never heard you speak of a long-term relationship with a girl before. I'm glad to hear you're finally growing up, son," she teased.

Brandon laughed. "Tell me, Mom, how'd you know there was a girl—beyond your motherly intuition?"

"Brandon, there's nothing like the love of a good woman to change a man. And you've changed. . . . I've heard it in the gentleness of your voice, in the way you'd talk about some things, and in the way you no longer talked about other things. Love shows in little ways. I'm happy for you, son."

"Thank you, Mom. I've never been happier in my life, and I can't wait for you to meet the woman responsible for that!" That was the truth. He figured that the best time to share his conversion with his mother would be once she had met and fallen in love with Joanie for herself.

Their conversation ended with some small talk. When Brandon hung up he decided to offer up a rosary for his mother. It would take much prayer to open up her heart to his new-found faith—of that he was certain.

✠   ✠   ✠

The second Friday of September found Joanie and Brandon again at a *Praise Event* concert at St. James' Parish. It had been only two months earlier that Joanie had invited Brandon to come . . . that fateful night. They marvelled at how much life had changed for both of them since that time.

Brandon came early to help Joanie and the band set up. He had heard them perform many times over the summer at weddings and gigs, but this was different. He was coming back to where it had all begun for him. Brandon had a tremendous sense of gratitude as they entered the church.

Squeezing Joanie's hand in his, Brandon leaned over and whispered, "Thank you!"

She knew exactly what he meant.

They went down to the auditorium and Brandon gave Mike a hand hooking up the sound equipment. Joanie watched as the two men laughed and joked around on the stage. She knew how it had hurt Brandon to have lost the friendship and camaraderie that he had once shared with Mark, his friend from childhood. She was so grateful that he now had Mike for a friend.

The friendship that had developed between these two men had made Mike the natural choice to be Brandon's sponsor in the Rite of Christian Initiation for Adults, the program he would follow as he prepared himself for entering the Church. Mike was a strong, dedicated Christian man. While there was much Brandon could learn from him, Mike was in turn deeply inspired by Brandon's conversion. Their relationship was a mutual blessing as they challenged each other to grow in faith.

When all was set up, the performers met in the side room to pray before the concert began. Brandon joined them. They prayed for the Holy Spirit to fill the hearts of all those who would come out to praise and worship. They asked for the intercession of St. Cecilia, the patron saint of musicians, that their music be blessed for the work of the Kingdom. They prayed that the Blessed Mother would draw all of their hearts closer to her Son that they might truly give glory to His most Holy Name.

As they left the side room, Brandon took Joanie by the arm and led her to a row of chairs. He had thrown his jacket down, reserving the spot where they had sat together two months earlier. Joanie laughed as they took their seats.

Brandon reached over and took her hand in his. She closed her eyes, noticing how wonderful it still felt to hold hands with this man. She remembered the new and exciting feelings that her heart had first experienced that wondrous night. She prayed that she would never grow dull to the thrill of Brandon's touch.

When she opened her eyes Brandon was looking down at her. He mouthed the words, "I love you."

She laid her head on his shoulder and whispered back, softly, "I love you, too!"

They sat there quietly praying, until the concert began. Then Joanie lifted her head, smiled up at Brandon, and left him to join the band.

The concert began with the usual upbeat praise music that got people on their feet, singing and clapping. Brandon laughed, in spite of himself, as he joined the throng of people in praise. Not only was his heart one with theirs this time, but he actually knew many of the songs, and he freely sang out. It was spiritually exhilarating and emotionally freeing to be here in this atmosphere of Christian fellowship and praise.

After their set, Joanie came back to take her place with Brandon. The love between this young couple was so powerful that they could hardly have found words to express it. Yet standing there, side by side, their voices lifted in praise, they knew they were of one heart in the Lord. They did not need to say a thing.

Then, to Joanie's surprise, Brandon excused himself and got up to leave. She questioned him, but he just looked back at her and winked, motioning for her to stay where she was. She watched him slip out to the back as she sat there, perplexed to the point of distraction.

The group leading praise finished their set and her cousin, Mike, stood up to the microphone. Still distracted, she did not pay attention to him leading the people in prayer.

All of a sudden she noticed Brandon, guitar in hand, approaching the stage. He pulled up a stool to the microphone and sat down. Joanie's heart was racing as she listened to Brandon's deep, rich voice.

"Two months ago I came out to this concert a perfect heathen. I only came because I was attracted to a beautiful young lady who was going to be here. But Jesus touched my heart that night and since then, nothing's been the same.

"I was a sinful man, full of selfishness and pride. But through His grace and His mercy, He has given me a new life . . . a life that has been filled with joys and blessings far more abundant than I could have ever dreamed. So it is to this awesome God and Saviour that I dedicate this song."

Tears were streaming down Joanie's face. She could scarcely breathe. Her heart pounded so that she was afraid she would not be able to hear. All at once she felt an arm over her shoulder, and she looked up. It was Mike. She had not noticed him come to sit with her.

He smiled and handed her a tissue. "Thought you might be needing that just about now," he whispered. She laughed and thanked him, taking the tissue.

Brandon gently cradled his guitar. His fingers moved over the strings with such tenderness. The entire audience was hushed in prayerful awe. The young man lifted his head, and the words welled up from his heart.

Amazing Grace, how sweet the sound,
That saved a wretch like me,
I once was lost, but now am found,
Was blind, but now I see.

'Twas Grace that taught my heart to fear,
And Grace my fears relieved.
How precious did that Grace appear,
The hour I first believed.

The crowd of people were held captive by Brandon's performance. The words of the song were so compelling, coming from this humble man.

Through many dangers, toils and snares,
I have already come,
'Tis Grace hath brought me safe thus far,
And Grace will lead me home.

Gradually, through the next two verses, the audience joined in singing. Brandon's clear voice floated above the worshipping crowd, inspiring them all to greater praise for the goodness of the Lord.

The Lord has promised good to me,
My hope, His Word secures.
He will my cup and portion be,
As long as life endures.

When we've been there ten thousand years,
Bright shining as the sun.
We've no less days to sing God's praise,
Then when we'd first begun.

When the song was finished, there was an awesome silence that settled over everyone present. Slowly, someone began clapping, and within moments every person was on their feet, with the sound of applause like roaring thunder.

Brandon humbly stepped down, laying his guitar off to the side, never once looking up to the standing ovation.

He came to take his place by Joanie. When he reached her side, she threw her arms around his neck and held on to him for a very long time. He closed his eyes and cried with her.

The concert moved on in majestic praise. It was as though everyone was singing with that much more conviction after Brandon's testimonial.

Joanie joined with the band to finish the closing set. Her face revealed the love that was consuming her heart. Love for Brandon. Love for the Lord.

Brandon watched her, saying to himself, *Someday, I'm gonna marry that girl. Praise be to Jesus!*

✟   ✟   ✟

Band practice on Tuesday night, following that concert, presented an interesting turn of events. Ben came in late that evening, and as he made his grand entrance, everyone sensed that something was up.

"I've got good news and bad news," Ben announced. "What'll it be first?"

"Give us the good news first," his cousin, Annie, answered him.

"Well, I've got an awesome job opportunity," he began, almost not able to contain his excitement. "I've been offered a part to play guitar back-up for a band in a movie that is being filmed in Calgary. They start shooting in October. I'll be gone for at least four months. It's the chance of a lifetime." Everyone sat, speechless.

"So, you can guess what the bad news is . . . I'm leaving the band." His tone was more controlled. "But I've also come with a great solution to that problem. Based on what we witnessed Friday night, I think there's really only one natural choice for a replacement."

He aimed both his hands at Brandon who was sitting beside Joanie. There was a general uproar of enthusiastic acceptance from the group. Brandon was a little awkward with all the sudden attention.

"Come on, Brandon, you'd be perfect. You're ten times the guitar player that I am," confessed Ben. "'Sides, you're here at just about every practice now anyway."

"It wouldn't take you anytime to learn the repertoire," added Mike who had sat back, rather pensively, throughout the announcement.

"I . . . I'd love to!" he answered, looking over at Joanie to be sure she was okay with it.

"You'll be awesome," she said, with a smile that conveyed the pride she felt for him.

"So, it's settled," Ben cut back into the discussion. "You see, I promised to return the call tonight, so I'm taking off." He punched Brandon on the shoulder in a friendly way and added, "Tag, man, you're it!"

Brandon nodded and asked, "Is there a guitar here for me to use?"

"Here, use mine," Ben said, handing it over to his substitute. "I brought it for you, just in case. You can drop it off on your way home. I'm out of here. See you all Sunday."

Brandon set himself up in Ben's spot and asked for some music. As rehearsal unfolded Brandon displayed his amazing talent. He could sight-read with ease and he had a gift for strumming and rhythm that was truly inspiring. It was almost distracting to the band, because of the temptation his playing presented for everyone to cut out and just listen.

There was a great sense of peace for everyone in this new arrangement.

Brandon laughed at himself, remembering his years playing in a rock band as a teenager. What a contrast this was. God certainly must have a sense of humour for him to be here now, using his music to evangelize. It was pure blessing.

Chapter 27

"Brandon Vaughn here," his clear voice spoke into the receiver.

"Hello, son." Brandon was startled to recognize his father's voice on the other end of the line.

"Dad?" Brandon asked, with hesitation.

"How's it going these days, Brandon?" James continued.

Brandon could hear the awkwardness in his father's voice. That was reasonable. Brandon was feeling very awkward on his end. "Fine Dad. How about you?"

"Just fine. So are you still together with that new girlfriend of yours?"

Brandon was struck by how funny it sounded to have Joanie referred to as his "new girlfriend". She was so much more to him than that. "Yeah, Dad, Joanie and I are still together. . . . What can I do for you?"

"Well, I was hoping to take the two of you out for dinner tonight. I'm in town, and I sure am curious to meet the girl who managed to reform my son." James' voice grew more relaxed with each moment that passed. He was struggling to know where to begin again with Brandon. *How does a father start over after twenty-six years of having been a screw-up for a dad?* Going out for supper was the only thing that felt sort of natural in this relationship, so far.

"That would be great, Dad. Look, I'll have to confirm with Joanie, but I'm sure we can manage it. I'm really looking forward to the two of you meeting each other," Brandon replied.

James was relieved to hear the enthusiasm in his son's voice. Maybe this was not such an impossible thing to achieve after all. They set a time and place for dinner.

☦   ☦   ☦

Brandon proceeded to dial Joanie's direct line. He had never called her at work before. It was just something they had both decided they would not do.

"Joanie Collins, CNB news, how can I help you?" she answered in her bright, cheery, telephone voice.

"You already have helped me so much, sweetheart!" Brandon teased her.

Joanie's voice got hushed as she looked around then ducked down into her cubicle. "What are you doing? I thought I told you never to call me here!" The tone of her voice quickly went from shock to playfulness.

"I couldn't help myself, you're just on my mind all day long." Brandon was starting to enjoy the luxury this call was affording him.

"Cut it out. Something must be up, or you never would have called me at work," she scolded him.

"I love you," he persisted, playfully.

"That's fine," she said, still scolding him. "You get to sit there in that quiet office of yours with the door closed. Meanwhile, I'm stuck out here in the middle of the newsroom with people all around me."

"But I still love you," he said, with great affection.

"I do, too. I'm just not going to give you the satisfaction of hearing me say it under these circumstances!" She had that certain intensity to her voice, and he could just picture her eyes all fiery—the way she always got when she was all worked up over something.

"My dad just called to invite us out for dinner tonight. Can you make it? Please say yes." His voice had become serious.

"You haven't spoken with your dad since that night, have you?"

"This was the first time. . . . I really want you to be there, Joanie. Dad wants to meet you, and I'd feel better if I had you by my side." His voice was openly entreating.

"Now what girl could resist an invitation like that?" she responded, smiling at the thought of Brandon. "I'll be there. I'll have to cancel something I had arranged with Katie tonight, but I don't think it'll be a big deal."

"Thank you, beautiful. . . . I love you," his voice was warm and tender.

Joanie sighed heavily into the phone. "I'll see you tonight. What time are you picking me up?"

"Six-thirty sound okay?" he asked.

"I'll be ready," she stated. "Now I should get off the line, I really feel awkward talking to you here."

"Thanks for understanding. I'll see you later."

"Good-bye," she said, softly. As she hung up the phone, she looked around. In spite of her awkwardness, no one had taken any particular notice of her secret call.

Brandon hung up the phone, closed his eyes, and said a quick prayer to St. Joseph for his Dad and for their new-found relationship.

And thank You, Jesus, for my Joanie!

✚　　　✚　　　✚

Joanie was a little nervous entering the restaurant, but when she felt the tension in Brandon's arm, she decided one of them had better relax. She held her head confidently and walked on, in noble fashion.

Brandon led her over to the table where his father was sitting. James looked up and watched the young couple approach. As Brandon held Joanie's chair for her, his father stood up to greet the young lady.

"Well, you must be Joanie. I'm impressed, Brandon. She's a real looker."

Joanie struggled not to lose her composure. She had not expected such a forward greeting.

"Dad," Brandon cut in, embarrassed at his father's bluntness, "this is Joanie Collins. Joanie, this is my father, James Vaughn."

"James . . . like *your* middle name," she smiled as she put the two together. "It's wonderful to finally meet you, Mr. Vaughn."

She held herself regally as she extended her hand to greet Brandon's father. Brandon's heart swelled with pride, and his nervousness faded away.

"Call me James, please," his father asserted, in his friendly manner. "Mr. Vaughn makes me feel like an old man, and I don't intend to get old before my time!"

"Fine, James," she agreed with a smile. She took him in perceptively. He impressed her to be like a boy who had never quite grown up. He was a terribly handsome man, with Brandon's light brown hair and piercing blue eyes. The resemblance was almost eerie.

"Sorry for my forwardness with you," James went on, apologetically. He was beginning to be taken in by the classiness of this young lady. He liked her charm. "I'm not used to thinking about religious girls as being so attractive. I guess that's one way for me to have avoided getting messed up with one, like my son so clumsily did." His tone was full of good humour, and his smile was warm.

Joanie picked up on the fun and responded in kind. "Well then, it's a good thing for me that your son only inherited your good looks and not your narrow-mindedness."

"Oooh," Brandon winced. He had never expected Joanie to deliver such a well aimed shot.

The three of them laughed, and the evening got off to a very friendly start. Joanie had established herself with Brandon's father, and he, in turn, found himself drawn to respecting and admiring her very much.

They parted on excellent terms at the end of the evening. Brandon confessed to Joanie on the way home that he had never known so much about his father. Joanie had prompted James to share all sorts of details of his life that Brandon had just never cared to learn.

His father had come from a broken home, with his own father an alcoholic, and his mother struggling to put food on the table. His life had been quite miserable growing up. He had one older brother who had run away from home at the age of sixteen, and James had never seen him since. James was a lone wolf. He had made his way in the business world with hard work and determination. He never wanted to suffer poverty again. James told them how his father had been a wife beater. When James had found himself starting to repeat that pattern with Brandon's mom, he decided it was time to high-tail it out of that relationship, rather than to make Brandon and his mother suffer anymore from him. He felt that Brandon was better off alone with his mother who was a very good woman. He figured that by staying out of the picture, for the most part, Brandon might have a chance at a decent life. He had missed being a part of Brandon's life though, and he was grateful to have a second chance.

It was a lot for Brandon to mull over. It felt as though pieces of a puzzle—which was his life—were falling into place. He had never intended to put that puzzle together. It was Joanie's natural curiosity that was leading him there.

He held Joanie's hand as they drove home in silence. She could sense he was deep in thought and she did not want to interrupt. When they got back to her house she excused herself quickly, determining that Brandon probably needed some time alone.

He walked her to the front porch and stood, holding the door open.

"Thanks, Joanie . . . for being you!"

She smiled and brushed her hand gently across his cheek.

"And by the way," he added, "Dad was right about you being a real looker!"

He took her hand in his, kissed it gently, and said good-night.

Chapter 28

The busy routines of fall had settled in. Both Joanie and Brandon had become so occupied with work and studying, prayer meetings and band rehearsals, that it was a challenge to find time alone for each other.

Brandon was now a regular fixture in the Collins abode. His presence was warmly welcomed by all. He would often help out by carting children off to sports and lessons. It was a wonderful arrangement because, while it helped the family, it also gave Brandon the chance to really get to know everyone.

But the young couple longed for time alone together. Whenever they could, they would steal away a few hours from their busy schedules and go out for a walk or for dinner.

On one such evening in late September, Brandon and Joanie had gone out to a quiet restaurant. They were just leaving when they were met by Mark and Justine walking in. Joanie of course did not recognize them, but the look on Brandon's face said it all.

Justine grabbed Brandon's arm and greeted him warmly. "Brandon, it's so good to see you again. Isn't it Mark?"

Everyone could feel the tension as these two men locked eyes.

Mark did not answer, and Justine went on, desperately trying not to lose this opportunity. "You must be Brandon's girlfriend. I recognize you from the CNB news. You're Joanie Collins, right? I'm Justine Foster, and this is—"

"Mark Jacobs," Joanie said, smiling in her amiable and unassuming way. "I'm so happy you stopped us, Justine. It's a pleasure to meet you both."

Brandon stood there stiffly.

Joanie knew how difficult it was for these two old friends. Mark was the closest thing Brandon had to a brother. There was so much hurt there. She prayed intently for the grace of reconciliation between them.

Finally, with tremendous effort, Brandon said something. "Mark, Justine, I'm . . . I'm so happy to see you, again. It's great to have you finally meet Joanie."

Mark nodded his head, acknowledging Joanie, and awkwardly answered, "Nice to meet you, Joanie. Look, I apologize for standing here like such an idiot, it's just . . . you see, the last time I spoke to Brandon I was a real jerk."

His eyes had turned away from Joanie. He was looking straight at Brandon. "I'm sorry, Brandon. I was wrong."

The stiffness lifted from Brandon, like a heavy yoke that had been oppressing him. He reached out and grabbed Mark by the shoulders, saying, "I'm sorry too, Mark. Please forgive me for everything."

Mark laughed and shook his head, as if in disbelief and retorted, "Still on that religious stuff, are you?" He smiled over at Joanie, to show he meant no offence. "I *forgive* you," he blurted out, unceremoniously.

The two young couples stood there laughing. It was a great moment of reconciliation, and they all sensed the opportunity for a new beginning.

Brandon spoke out, "You two are coming over to my place. We'll get caught up."

"We haven't eaten yet," Mark said, pointing to the restaurant.

"Oh, don't worry about that," Justine stated, emphatically. "We'll grab a burger on the way, Brandon, and we'll meet you there in about twenty minutes."

✟ ✟ ✟

In the car on the way over, Joanie gave Brandon a look that he could not interpret.

"What?" he asked her, confused.

"You're forgetting something, darling," she said, politely.

"What?" he repeated, his brain frantically searching for her point. Then it hit him. "Your father. Oh, man, I've got to call your dad and ask if you can come back to my place."

"Bingo!"

"Do you think he'll let you come? Joanie, I need you there, honey, I can't do this alone." He was talking more to himself than to her.

He reached down and grabbed his cell phone from under the seat. Punching in the Collinses' number on speed dial, he waited.

"Hi, Judy, it's Brandon. . . . Yeah, everything's all right. I just need to talk to John, if that's okay. . . . Thanks. . . . John, it's Brandon. . . . Fine, sir. I was just calling to get your permission to take Joanie over to my place this evening. . . . Well, you see, we ran into some old friends of mine at the restaurant as we were leaving, and I invited them over. I guess I wasn't thinking much, but I . . . well, sir, I would really appreciate it if Joanie were there to help me explain, you know . . . Yeah, all that Christianity stuff is a little beyond these people. I . . . Yes, sir, two a.m. Thank you, John. You have my word. . . . Good-night."

He breathed a sigh of relief and threw a look at Joanie that said, *See how much I love you!*

Joanie laughed, taking the phone from him, and said, "I love you, too, Brandon! And you do look especially cute when you're begging my father."

He rolled his eyes at her and said, "Just you wait, girl, someday you'll be begging me!"

"For what?" Joanie asked.

"I have no idea, but it just wouldn't be fair if it never happened."

Joanie laughed as she took his hand in hers.

✝   ✝   ✝

Mark and Justine showed up shortly after Brandon and Joanie.

Mark came walking in, carrying a case of beer. "Here," he said, shoving it into Brandon's hands, "I wasn't sure if you still served drinks around here, and I didn't want to go dry tonight."

Brandon put the case in the refrigerator. There was always room in his bachelor's fridge. He pulled out a couple of cold beers and called out to Justine, asking what she wanted to drink.

"I'll have a beer too, Brandon. Thanks," she replied.

"I've got some coolers here as well," he informed her.

Justine looked over at Joanie with a smile and said, "Great, I'll have a cooler." Joanie smiled back.

Justine watched Joanie setting up CDs on the stereo across the room. She liked the look of Joanie, simple and unpretentious. She was even prettier in real life than what Justine had remembered of her from the television. Justine could certainly see why Brandon had been attracted to Joanie. But there was more to Joanie than just her good looks. She carried herself in such a graceful way, sparkling with an inner beauty that was truly compelling.

Brandon came back into the room with the beers and coolers. He passed the drinks to Mark and Justine. Justine thanked him, asking, "When did you start stocking coolers in your fridge, Brandon?"

He just smiled and winked. Walking over to Joanie he handed her the cooler and set his hand on her shoulder. Joanie could sense his nervousness. She, too, was uncomfortable in this unfamiliar territory.

"Would you girls like a glass for your drinks?" he asked her.

"No, we're fine. Thanks," Joanie said, as she slipped her hand around his waist to reassure him.

The group of four exchanged some pleasantries with each other, every one of them experiencing the awkwardness of the situation. Searching for a way to break the tension, Joanie asked, "Is anyone up for cards?"

That was the ticket: just enough of a diversion to provide them with the opportunity to begin building this new relationship on common ground.

"Great," Joanie said, as she took Justine by the arm and led her to the table, "'cause Justine and I are going to whup your sorry little butts at Canasta here tonight, boys!"

They all laughed, caught off guard by Joanie's informality.

Justine protested that she did not know how to play, but Joanie shrugged it off, saying, "Then it's time you learned."

Brandon got out his Canasta cards which, since knowing the Collins family, he now owned. The game was fun, the conversation was light, and the evening went by without a glitch.

Brandon and Mark got caught up in the competitiveness of the game and soon re-established a camaraderie between them. Justine and Joanie watched and smiled at each other, both of them pleased to see the progress in the restoration of this friendship.

The game ended with a narrow win by the girls, but they soaked up their victory just the same. Having finished the last hand, the group retired to the sofa and loveseat, and each couple settled in for a relaxed visit.

Joanie was very impressed with Justine. Piecing together information from conversations, Joanie had figured Justine to be twenty-four years old. Justine was stunningly beautiful. She looked like a movie star: not a hair out of place, her make-up perfect, her dress very fashionable. Joanie might have found that all intimidating, except that Justine had a wonderfully warm and gentle personality. Joanie had the distinct feeling that they would become very good friends.

Joanie liked Mark, too. He just had that thing about him that made him easy to like. He possessed that same bold and confident nature that Brandon had displayed when she had first met him. And Mark's uncanny sense of humour made him able to find the joke in any situation. Joanie found that a little intimidating though, since much of the humour was off-colour, and she was bashfully aware that her naïveté was obvious to the group. Brandon just kept her hand in his and sat close by her side in a protective manner. She felt safe and secure with him.

"Well, I for one have to say that I am so impressed with the change in you, Brandon," Justine piped up, during a lull in the conversation. "I don't know what you did, Joanie, but Brandon is a new man. And I like what I see!"

Joanie, at a loss for words, looked up at Brandon.

He gazed into Joanie's eyes for a moment and then, looking back at Justine, he responded, "Yes, well, I thank Joanie every day for having saved me from myself!" His tone was sincere, yet light.

"I don't get it," Mark interjected, "I've known this lug-head for eighteen years now. I've seen him woo the girls and win the girls, but I've never seen one that had him eating out of the palm of her hand before. So what's your secret Joanie, are you some sort of hypnotist?"

"No," Joanie laughed at the very idea, "I just . . . I just prayed for him."

Her honesty was so sweet that Mark could not poke fun at her.

She continued, "You see, I could never have fallen in love with a man who wasn't a Christian . . . and I wanted to be able to fall in love with Brandon, so . . . the Lord took care of the rest."

"And how!" Brandon exclaimed. "But—I've never been happier in my entire life." He too was sincere, with no intention of pushing religion on anybody, but with no apologies, either.

"You know, I was baptized Catholic, too," Justine stated. "In fact, I went to church until I was confirmed at twelve. My mother let us choose after that, since my father rarely went to church. I don't know, I guess I never really thought it was that meaningful, so I quit going. I miss it sometimes, though." Her voice trailed off.

"Oh, man, don't tell me you're going to get religious on me now, too," Mark protested.

"Relax, Mark, no one's making *you* go to church," Justine reassured him.

Joanie looked down at her watch. It was after one a.m. She yawned, in order to send a hint to Brandon.

"Holy smokes," he exclaimed, looking at the time, "I've got to get Joanie home."

"I guess that's what you get for robbing the cradle, buddy," Mark mocked, in fun.

"Yeah, yeah," Brandon brushed off the comment, giving Mark a shot in the shoulder on his way by. "How about a game of tennis tomorrow?"

"Yeah, sure," Mark agreed. They set a time and place and everyone left.

✞   ✞   ✞

Driving home that night Mark was silent. The impression of the new Brandon was strongly imprinted on his mind. Mark was happy to see Brandon again, and Brandon seemed genuinely happy, but he had changed, to be sure. Mark was not quite sure if he liked the new Brandon or not. He would reserve judgment for the time being. Maybe the tennis game tomorrow would bring out the old Brandon.

Justine broke the silence of the car ride, commenting, "I've never seen Brandon so gentle and peaceful. He's really a changed man."

"Well, don't make too much of it," Mark grumbled back.

"You don't like the change?" Justine inquired.

"I don't like the way *you* like it," he returned, his tone betraying a certain frustration.

Justine sat there reflecting on the situation. "You know," she said, speaking her thoughts out loud, "Joanie has managed to get something from Brandon that no other girl has ever gotten."

"Well, you can be sure Brandon isn't getting much from her!" he responded, crassly.

"Not that, Mark," Justine spoke in a disgruntled tone. "What I mean is that Joanie has won Brandon's respect."

"Brandon has always treated his girls well and given them what they wanted," Mark asserted.

"That's not the same, Mark. Brandon has *never* had respect for a girl he's dated, or he would never have dated so many at the same time," Justine observed, emphatically.

"Yeah? Well, I respect you." His tone was defensive.

"In some ways you do, but . . . I guess, if I had respected myself more, I would've been able to have demanded that kind of respect from the men I've dated."

Her words reflected the deeply pensive mood she was in. Mark decided not to push the issue, lest he should have to suffer the same fate as poor old Brandon: trapped in a world controlled by religious ideologies, and living—in his prime—like a priest!

Chapter 29

Brandon and Joanie were reflective, too, on the way home. It was Brandon who broke their silence. "Joanie?"

"Uh-hum?"

"How come you never ask me about my . . . my past?" He was hesitant, unsure if he should bring up the topic.

"What do you mean? I've asked about your family and growing up. You've told me all about Mark and your friendship, before. I'm—"

"Not that," he cut in, "I mean, well, other girlfriends and stuff."

Joanie was silent. She had avoided that subject deliberately, since she was not at all sure if she was prepared to deal with the information that it might bring.

"Yes," she said, plainly, "it does."

"You know, for someone who makes her living as a research-reporter, you suffer from a deplorable lack of curiosity in this matter," he admonished her.

He looked over at Joanie, searching her out as best he could. Why was she so reluctant to discuss this? It was important. There were obvious implications for their relationship.

With his last comment, Joanie had stiffened up in her seat. She was searching, too, to understand her own feelings. The whole idea of Brandon's past evoked a painful confusion within her.

He pressed the issue further. "Have you never worried about diseases? You've never asked me about it. I'd think that would be a real concern for you."

"No," he answered. The coolness in Joanie's voice hurt him, but he could not blame her. It was he, himself, who was at fault here. She was just an innocent victim of his past. "I've been tested a couple of times now. By the mercy of God, I'm not carrying any STDs."

The sound of that term roused such anger in Joanie. She should have been grateful for what he had just told her; instead, she was angry that it ever needed to have been mentioned. She accused herself for being so selfish. In her heart she had forgiven Brandon long ago for his past. Why bring it up now? She gripped her pant legs and set her jaw firmly, as she turned to look out the window.

Silence fell between them for a few minutes.

Had Joanie not been so caught up in her own anger and pain, she might have noticed how Brandon was struggling. The more he felt her pain, the more he hated himself for his past. He wished he had never brought up the subject. Maybe it was better left unmentioned. Maybe it was enough to ignore it and pretend it had never happened.

He prayed for guidance. He prayed for forgiveness. He prayed for healing.

Looking over at Joanie, her eyes fixed in the distance, he offered, "Look, Joanie, if you don't want to talk about it, I can close the subject now."

The gentleness of his voice broke through and began to melt the coldness that had stolen over her heart.

"No, Brandon," she replied tenderly. "The thing is, I don't know what I need to know and what's best left unsaid." She looked up at him, able to meet him again eye to eye. "You are a new man in Jesus. I want to know you and love you as the man you are today. I'm afraid that if you fill my mind with images of who you were and the things you once did, I might not be able to—"

"Forgive me?" he interjected.

"No. It's not that. I do forgive you. I forgave you long ago. You didn't have Jesus in your life then and you do now. It's just that . . . I might not be able to look at you the same way. Or maybe I could, but I don't trust myself not to let your past influence how I see you.

"You see, when God forgives our sins, His love is so perfect that He no longer sees the sins. He just sees us as we are—forgiven. But I'm not God, Brandon, and my love is far from perfect."

Her words were honest, and he could feel the depth of her love. But the pain that his past brought to her was like a knife in his side.

"Joanie, if I could relive my life," he began, his voice faltering under the weight of emotion, "I would *never* have done all those things. I would have kept myself completely for you. I never realized how much I was hurting . . . so many people."

His voice faded away and a tear rolled down his cheek. He pulled the vehicle over to the side of the road and, parking it, he buried his face in his hands and wept.

Joanie put her hand on Brandon's back and tenderly caressed him. Her eyes, too, filled with tears. Her heart ached for this man, whom she loved so much. She closed her eyes and prayed for him, silently.

Then slowly and gently she spoke. "Allow God's forgiveness to wash it all away, Brandon. Don't keep living in the pain from past sins. The Bible tells us, 'Whatever is true, whatever is honourable, whatever is just, whatever is pure, lovely, and gracious . . . think about these things.'

"Can't you see, it's Satan who wants you to be brought down by the guilt of your past? God desires you to live fully in this moment. And I'm content to leave your past where it belongs.

"I want to experience everything in our love and in our life together as new and good and true and beautiful—the way God intends the love of a man and woman to be. No matter who was in your past, or what you may have done with those women, I know that I am your heart's desire. I believed you when you professed your love for me, because you are now a godly man, Brandon!"

He rubbed his eyes and lifted his head. Turning to meet her gaze, he said, "You *are* my heart's desire, Joanie. I could never thank Jesus enough for bringing you into my life. And I could never thank you enough for bringing Jesus into my heart."

He smiled through his tears and reaching over, he gently touched her face. "Let's get you home."

Chapter 30

Mark was impatient, waiting for Brandon to arrive at the tennis courts. Brandon could sense, as he drove up, that this was going to be a critical moment in their relationship. Brandon had to be able to somehow disarm Mark's apprehensions about Brandon's newly found religious convictions, while not betraying his faith. He wanted desperately for Mark to see that they could still be friends and have fun. More than anything, though, he yearned for Mark to come to know Jesus as he now did. Brandon was praying the whole way there and did not stop until he actually stood face to face with Mark.

The tennis courts were not busy when they arrived. The autumn evening was cool and a breeze was beginning to pick up, but the courts were surrounded by a wall of trees just outside the wire fences along all sides, so they were well sheltered.

The two old friends got right into the game. Mark did not seem to be in much of a mood for socializing. The game was fast-paced and furious. Brandon had a sense that Mark was taking out an awful lot of frustration on that poor little tennis ball. They played three matches, all of which Mark won. He had always been a better tennis player than Brandon. But they had been close matches, keeping the game interesting.

"How about a beer at my place?" Brandon asked, as they walked off the court together.

"Yeah, that'd be okay," Mark responded, his frame of mind hard for Brandon to interpret.

✤   ✤   ✤

While Brandon got the beers out of the fridge, Mark restlessly walked around the apartment. It bothered him to no end to see Brandon's newly acquired treasures lying about.

There was a Bible, left open with obvious signs of having been read. There was a cross up on his wall. Funny, how Mark had not noticed that the night before. There was a rosary sitting on the end table by Brandon's favourite chair with a prayer book opened and turned face down beside it.

It all added up to the fact that Brandon had turned into some sort of Jesus-freak and there was not much hope, in Mark's mind, of bringing Brandon back to the world in which he belonged.

Brandon handed Mark the beer and they sat down across from each other. Silence hung over them like a dark cloud. Brandon prayed intensely for some way of communicating effectively to Mark. He was not here to push religion down Mark's throat. He really just wanted to re-establish their friendship.

Grasping for something to say, Brandon asked, "So what do you think of Joanie?"

"She's a nice girl, Brandon . . . too nice for me. To be honest, she makes me uncomfortable. I found I was watching everything I said around her," Mark admitted.

"I know what you mean," Brandon laughed. "She's got a sweetness and an innocence about her that sometimes just leaves me in awe. Frankly, I never knew that they made them like that anymore. Her whole family's like something that walked off the pages of a history book."

"I don't get it, Brandon. Why are you with her? I mean, I've known you practically your whole life, and I know which century you belong in." Mark's tone indicated a real confusion.

"'Cause I love her, Mark. And you know me better than anybody. Have you ever heard me say that about any other girl?" Brandon's manner was frank and unassuming.

Mark sat there, shaking his head, lost in thought. After a few moments he looked up at Brandon and smiled. "She's a beautiful girl, Brandon. I'm happy for you, buddy. And," after a thoughtful pause, he added, "I guess it wouldn't hurt me to be around somebody who causes me to lift my language out of the gutter." His tone was lightly sophisticated and definitely jovial.

"Well, I'm living proof that it won't kill you!" Brandon laughed, in spite of himself.

"I have noticed how refined your manners have become," Mark bantered with him. Then changing his expression, he added, "The only problem I have now is how to deal with Justine."

"What's the problem? You two've been together now for over three years. Isn't it time she made an honest man out of you?" Brandon prodded him.

"That's just the point. I wasn't looking to be made into an honest man. I had no intention of being changed by anybody. But after last night, Justine has new ideas for our relationship . . . which means that if I want to keep her, I'm suddenly gonna have to work for her."

Mark stood up and walked over to the fireplace mantle, placing his elbow on it. His face was contorted by his deliberations. "I don't know if she's worth it to me or not," he confessed. "I mean, she's just become a habit for me. Maybe it's time I moved on to greener pastures. I don't know."

Brandon was now the one shifting around uncomfortably. He knew what he wanted to say, but he did not know how far to push the matter. On one hand, Mark was his oldest friend. On the other hand, Brandon wondered if he was secure enough yet in the re-establishment of their friendship to challenge Mark. And Brandon did not want to turn Mark off entirely from God.

Lord, give me a green light to proceed or a red light to know when to stop.

Mark was silent and obviously deeply disturbed by this decision that lay before him. After a moment he looked over at Brandon and asked, "What should I do, buddy?"

Brandon took the signal, but proceeded with caution. "Mark, Justine's a beautiful woman. I've always liked her and respected her more than any girl that I ever dated."

Mark noted how accurately Justine had assessed Brandon the night before.

Brandon continued, "She's sincere and kind. She'd do anything to help another person. She's fun to be with. I mean, it's your decision, man, but I'd say she's worth it. And if she's demanding more from you than the crappy deal you've offered her so far, it shows she's made out of something worthwhile.

"I know she loves you, Mark. She's always given more to you than she ever got in return. It's time you stopped taking, and started giving. . . . That is, if she's worth it to you. You'll have to search out your own heart to decide that.

"Just remember, the love of a good woman can make you a very happy man—but it requires sacrifice. No pain, no gain!"

Mark was quiet. He knew Brandon was right and he knew what he needed to do. He patted Brandon on the shoulder, saying, "Thanks for the beer, buddy," and he left.

Brandon picked up his rosary and offered it up for Mark and Justine.

Chapter 31

Tessa was preoccupied with her wedding, which was set for the last Saturday of September. Lunch hours and coffee breaks when Joanie was around were spent with the two girls excitedly discussing plans and the details of the upcoming nuptials. Tessa had asked Joanie to sing for the ceremony, and of course Joanie and Brandon would be going to the reception and dance, along with other people from work.

Brandon did not show up often. When he did pass through the staff lounge, he did not always stop to talk, but he never left the room without telling Joanie he loved her. Tessa loved to watch the secret exchanges that would take place between these two lovers-in-disguise.

One day, though, Brandon stopped over at the table where Tessa and Joanie were sitting eating their lunches. He waved a white flower-embossed envelope in the air and said, "Thanks, Tessa, for the invite."

"You're welcome, Brandon," she replied, wondering what he was up to. Of course he knew he would be coming to the wedding.

"You know," he said, making himself comfortable on a chair across the table from the girls, "I notice it's made out 'To Brandon and escort'."

"That is the standard format for an invitation, Brandon," Tessa responded, still confused.

"Well, I was just thinking, since you probably sent one 'To Joanie and escort', how about we save you two meals, and I'll take Joanie for my escort?" he suggested.

"Wait a minute," Joanie spoke up. "Don't I have a say in this? Why ask *her*? And if I were going to go with you, I'd want you to be *my* escort, not vice versa."

"Fair enough," Brandon jumped at the chance, "I accept. I'll pick you up for the wedding at two. Dress nicely, eh?" With that, he walked out of the lunchroom, mission accomplished. Now everyone at work would know why they would be coming in together and why he would be dancing with her so much.

Joanie dropped her mouth open over that last comment he had made. "Dress nicely?" She turned to Tessa who was laughing.

Joanie was not used to Brandon being so casual with her, and he could still get her going with his arrogant ways when he was putting on an act at work. She made up her mind to get back at him later for that one.

✟   ✟   ✟

Finally, the wedding day arrived. Though Joanie had sung at many weddings, this one was particularly close to her heart because of her friendship with Tessa, and because it was the first wedding that she and Brandon would attend together as a couple. They would still have to guard themselves, though, so as not to attract the attention of their co-workers.

It was a bright and crisp fall day, with a freshness in the air that was wonderful to breathe in. It was a charming little church, filled with joy and excitement as Tessa and Karl were about to be joined together in Christ. When Joanie saw Tessa coming down the aisle, her heart skipped a beat. Tessa was a perfect bride, and the joy that was within her made her absolutely stunning.

During the ceremony, Joanie slipped down from the choir to go sit beside Brandon who was in a nearby pew. She daintily slipped her hand into his and thrilled at the thought that this was the man she hoped to someday marry. They did not dare look at each other, but their hands communicated the love that was between them.

✟   ✟   ✟

At the reception, they sat with a group of co-workers and genuinely enjoyed the friendly exchanges. It was hard for Joanie and Brandon to be so close to each other and not to betray their feelings. Still, Joanie found Brandon under the table and, slipping off her shoe, she carefully snuck her foot around his leg. The amusement of the entire situation was lost on their table companions as Brandon tried to remain composed, with Joanie playing footsie with him!

When the dance began, Brandon had to think of a clever way of being with Joanie without giving themselves away to their colleagues. He danced with all the ladies he knew from work and finally came around to Joanie who had been keeping herself occupied on the dance floor with the other men.

Their first dance was easy enough since it was upbeat, but the music slowed down on the next song, and Brandon could not let Joanie walk off the dance floor. He reached out and gently pulled her back by the hand. In a smooth and confident motion, he manoeuvred her back into his arms. A startled look appeared on her face. Brandon was being awfully bold, considering the circumstances.

He smiled down at her in a disarming way, saying, "That's it, sweetheart. Look like you don't want me doing this, and just maybe we'll get away with it in everyone else's eyes."

Joanie was almost frightened by how casual Brandon's tone could be. He may have become a new man, but his ability to put on the old role at will was most alarming.

She scolded him with her eyes, and he pulled her in even closer and said, "Perfect, just keep resisting me, and I'll just play the jerk. Let them all think I've had too much to drink." He laughed and danced on.

The irony of it was that since Brandon had hooked up with Joanie he had never gotten drunk. Tonight was no exception. He had only had a couple of glasses of wine over the evening. How was anyone to know he had been getting plain pop for himself and Joanie at the bar?

Joanie might have laughed along with Brandon over the situation had she not been so nervous. However, it did not take her long to stop resisting him. All at once she found herself lost in Brandon's arms. It was a beautiful dance, and Brandon did not say another thing. Joanie closed her eyes and tried to concentrate on the words of the song.

Soon the music disappeared as she gave in to shutting out the world around them. All she could think about was the feeling of her head on Brandon's shoulder, the warmth of his arm around her waist, and the touch of his fingers as he caressed her hand. She could feel the beating of his heart as he pressed her hand against his chest. The scent of his cologne filled her head, intoxicating her mind with the love she felt for this man. It was so thrilling and so peaceful all at the same time.

The dance ended. Reluctantly, Brandon pulled away from Joanie and, giving her a look of caution, he led her back to the table to sit down and cool off.

Taylor spoke out at the sight of them coming back to join the group, "I'm warning you Brandon, stay away from that girl. She's got a lot of religion, and if you don't watch out, you'll end up here yourself. And what a shame that would be!"

Brandon laughed at the insinuation and commented that Joanie was far too classy a gal for a jerk like him. She was just good enough to humour his ego. They all laughed, and the conversation moved on to other things.

Brandon and Joanie managed to sneak in a few more dances throughout the evening, each one as thrilling as the one before. By one o'clock the dance was shutting down, and they said their good-byes and left.

Joanie kept her head on Brandon's shoulder the whole way home. She had a wonderful tired feeling all over, the kind that comes at the end of an eventful day. Neither of them spoke much. They just savoured the moment of seclusion. Finally hidden away from the eyes of their co-workers, they could be themselves again.

Brandon pulled up the vehicle into the driveway at the Collinses. Joanie lifted her head from his shoulder, and with a sigh she sat up and began to undo her seatbelt. As she did, Brandon grabbed hold of her hand. A startled Joanie looked up at him, confusion all over her face.

"Play footsie with me, will you?"

"Oh," she responded; her smile was shy. "I guess I shouldn't have been teasing you like that . . . but I couldn't resist." She had that alluring air of innocence about her that Brandon found so hard to resist.

"I could kiss you right now." His voice had suddenly changed from its playfulness.

Oh, did she ever want to be kissed by him. She fixed her eyes on his, trying to determine whether or not he was going to follow through with it.

Tipping her chin gently, he pulled her face up closer to his. With the back of his hand he softly swept away the loose curls that framed her delicate face. His hand rested on her cheek. She closed her eyes and nestled her face into his warm, strong hand.

Kissing her tenderly on the other cheek, he whispered, "But I'll wait until the time is right. I love you, Joanie."

She breathed deeply, and a smile lifted contentedly from the corners of her mouth. She knew she could not have resisted Brandon had he truly intended to kiss her. She was way too tired and way too emotionally spent from the day to remember why it was they did not kiss each other yet.

Softly, she pressed her lips against his cheek and kissed him, then murmured, "That's why I love you so much, Brandon, because you know how to love me so well."

He got out of the vehicle and stepped around to open the door for her. They walked up to the house together with the cool evening air surrounding them. Brandon put his arm around Joanie's waist and pulled her close to his side. He held the front porch door for her as she went in.

Gently kissing her hand before they parted, he winked up at her. The sound of a soft giggle lay hidden beneath her bashful smile. He stepped back from the porch door and closed it gently. She stood there watching him as he got back into the vehicle and drove away.

Reaching up to the rosary which Joanie had hung from his rear-view mirror, Brandon took it down and began to pray.

✞   ✞   ✞

The next day, following Sunday Mass, Brandon came over to the Collinses' house as usual. There was a reserve about him that did not go unnoticed by Joanie, nor by her parents. After lunch he got permission from John to take Joanie out for a walk. It was a cool, crisp fall day, and the riverbank was very beautiful with the changing colours.

As they walked along, Joanie sensed something was really bothering Brandon, and it concerned her. They went on in silence, finally arriving at their favourite spot: the spot where he had first professed his love to her.

Brandon's distracted manner caused Joanie to move from concern to worry. When he finally spoke, Joanie braced herself for the worst.

He began slowly and deliberately. "Joanie, I think we need to talk about things."

"What would you like to talk about, Brandon?"

Her voice was soft, and he could sense her insecurity. "Joanie, I'm sorry if I've given you the impression that—"

"You want to break up with me," she blurted out. The fear which had been mounting within her could not be held back any longer.

"Never!" he asserted. Taking both her hands in his, he tried to catch her eyes, but they were downcast. Tears were rolling down her cheeks. "Joanie . . . I've given you the wrong impression today, and I'm sorry for that. I couldn't break up with you anymore than I could live without my own heart!"

She looked up at him through tear-filled eyes. "Then what is it? I'm really confused, Brandon. You've been acting so strange all day."

He closed his eyes and breathed heavily. What he had to say was not exactly easy. *Just say it!* he urged himself on. "Joanie, I think we need to reconsider our relationship in terms of how we're expressing our affection. Now, don't get me wrong, here . . . I want your affection more than anything, believe me! But I think that even though the actions have been innocent, in and of themselves, we've been stirring passions that would best be left, well . . . until . . ."

"Certain passions only belong in marriage, don't they?" she murmured softly, filling in for his awkwardness.

"There was a time in my life—and not that long ago—when I wouldn't have said so, but . . . yeah!" He looked down at Joanie, whose tears had dried.

She laughed at herself, feeling a little foolish in front of Brandon. Sensing her embarrassment, he added, "Joanie, I want you to know, as far as I'm concerned, there's no other woman in the world for me but you. But in all fairness to you, I'm not ready to ask you to marry me, yet. I just feel I need to put more distance between my past and our future before I'd ever ask you to consider marriage."

"Well, I might consider it," she offered, sweetly.

He chuckled at her timid response. "No. . . . It's not the time for that. When I ask you to marry me, I don't want you to have to consider it. I want you to know beyond the shadow of a doubt that marriage is for us.

"But," he continued, "we do have this time for growing in our relationship and for discerning God's will for us. Give me a chance to prove myself worthy of your affection, Joanie. There's no rush. I'll be around. . . . I'm not going anywhere—that is, unless you send me packing!"

"Fat chance of that, Mr. Vaughn!" she replied, giving his hands a little squeeze. Then acquiring a more sober expression, she added, "I'm sorry for playing footsie with you at the reception last night. That was hardly appropriate behaviour, all things considered."

"I can't say that I'm entirely sorry that you did," he returned, smiling. "And I can't honestly say that I'm sorry for holding you so close to me while we were dancing. I promise you, there's no one else I'd rather have in my arms. But the Lord has certainly given me the conviction to back off for the time being.

"I know that it's only been little kisses on the cheek or affectionate caress-es. Those things are innocent enough on their own. But the reality is, they make me want more than what is mine to have right now in our relationship. And I don't want to run the risk of compromising you in any way, Joanie, and possibly spoiling what I hope will be ours to share someday. . . . Last night was a wake-up call for me. I don't know about you, but I sure had a hard time reining in my instincts when we were alone in my vehicle—"

"But you *did*," she affirmed. Before he could make any objections, she raised her hand and added, "But I know that's *not* the point. It's best not to head down a path that we really can't follow . . . at least not yet." She smiled at him, shyly. "I would not have resisted you kissing me last night, at all. And the worst part is—it never even bothered me that my guard has come down so far. . . . So, I guess that's exactly the point you're trying to make, isn't it?"

Brandon nodded, smiling that irresistible smile of his.

☨   ☨   ☨

When Brandon and Joanie returned to the house, John and Judy took the opportunity to talk with the young couple in private. Sensing the tension from earlier, they wanted to be sure everything was still as it should be.

Joanie and Brandon shared openly about their new conclusions in their relationship. This was not the first time they had discussed things with John and Judy, and it certainly would not be the last. The accountability which they had established with Joanie's parents had given rise to a beautiful and open relationship among them.

"To be quite honest," John concluded, "we're learning about this whole courtship process along with you kids."

"What do you mean?" Brandon inquired.

"Judy and I never courted," he explained. "We dated, got engaged, and got married."

"But both of us had come from strong Catholic families," Judy added. "And although there were many people discarding their morals in our day, we didn't have the same pressures to go against our Christian upbringing the way young people have today."

"The whole concept of honourable courtship has been resurfacing among Christians for some time now," John continued. "We believed in it strongly . . . but I'm afraid Joanie is our guinea pig."

"Gee, thanks, Dad," she said, shaking her head at him. She walked over and kissed him lightly on the cheek.

As he wrapped his arms around his daughter, John winked at Brandon. "Now this is where you should still be getting your hugs and kisses, Sweet Pea!"

Brandon chuckled, enjoying the beauty of the relationship that existed between Joanie and her father.

Chapter 32

Winter settled in early that year. By the end of October there was a snowfall that never did melt away. It had transformed the city overnight into a winter wonderland. The trees hung heavily under the burden of snow on leaves that had not yet fallen. The snow crunched under every footstep, and all around the sounds of the city seemed to be muffled.

The ritual of pulling out winter wear and finding boots to fit everyone was an annual event in the Collins household, one which set the children buzzing. They just could not concentrate on school; they had to get out there and play. It was as if winter could not possibly stay around long enough for them to enjoy all the fun it promised.

Joanie loved each change of season, but especially now, for it was another first to share with Brandon: having snowball fights, helping the younger children build snowmen and forts, going tobogganing and skating.

Brandon enjoyed the play almost as much as the little ones did. Every outdoor adventure was followed by drinking hot chocolate around the kitchen table, with Jessie perched on one knee and Aaron perched on the other. This ritual became even better by the fact that Joanie's parents would often join in the amusement around the table. Soon stories would begin to come out. Brandon loved to listen to the Collins family stories.

He could not relate to such a happy home from his own childhood. Here he witnessed the affection that was shared so freely. What impressed him the most was the playfulness that existed between John and Judy. They truly loved each other. After almost twenty-four years of marriage and eight children, Brandon figured that was quite a remarkable feat. His parents had not lasted nine years, and they hated each other to this day.

Brandon wondered what made a couple's love grow and strengthen as did John and Judy's. He knew enough to realize that the answer lay in their faith. Experience had brought him to understand now that all true joy was rooted in love for God. Brandon had seen this in Joanie's parents' relationship and indeed in the relationships of her uncles and aunts and other married couples from church. He prayed that God would bless his and Joanie's love with such timeless joy.

✣   ✣   ✣

Advent was a completely new experience for Brandon. He loved it. This season of preparation was so rich in anticipation of Christ. He understood the longing of the people of Israel for a saviour. He himself was waiting for the coming of Christ in his own life through the Sacraments of the Church.

He ardently desired rebirth through Baptism and the gifts of the Holy Spirit through Confirmation. He longed for the spiritual strengthening that comes from the Sacrament of Reconciliation, and his heart literally ached to be able to receive Jesus in the Holy Eucharist.

How he longed for the day when he could walk up, along with Joanie, to receive Jesus in this Sacrament. Each time he attended Mass he would pray fervently, as he watched Joanie go to Communion:

Oh, God, how awesome You truly are that You came to us humbly, taking on our flesh so that we might become heirs to Your Kingdom. And still You come to us through the miracle of each Mass. Prepare my heart to receive You, humbly.

The mysteries of the faith were all beyond Brandon's comprehension, yet his faith was securely grounded on the rock of the Church, and it was unshakeable.

✟   ✟   ✟

Christmas was a particularly joyous event. Brandon joined the family for Christmas Eve Mass which was followed at the Collins home by *Réveillon* which went into the wee hours of the morning.

It was a French Catholic tradition to celebrate after Midnight Mass with all kinds of wonderful food and drink, songs and festivities. Though they now attended an earlier Mass on Christmas Eve to accomodate the younger children, Judy Ledoux, who was of French background, kept alive this *Réveillon* tradition within their home. And she surely made a mighty fine *tourtière!* Brandon had never before tasted this French Canadian favourite. The savoury taste of the meat pie, blended with herbs and spices, and baked to perfection, topped with Judy's homemade relish, was indeed a taste sensation.

Everyone gathered round as Grandpa Ledoux, a robust, bald-headed man, pulled out his accordion and led the family in one Christmas carol after the other. Isaac slipped out of the room and soon returned with guitar in hand. Eagerly, the twelve-year-old presented the instrument to Brandon. Brandon looked up at Grandpa who nodded him on, and the young man skilfully followed the old master's lead.

As Brandon played along with this gentle old soul, he was inspired by the beauty of the man before him. Grandpa's bright blue eyes, which shone with such childish delight, in no way revealed the life of struggles and hardships which he had endured. He had survived the Dirty Thirties, riding the rails looking for work and food. He had served overseas during

World War II, leaving behind a wife and child. He had worked hard his whole life, alongside this same loving wife, to provide for their family of nine children. He had suffered, at the side of that amazing woman, the deaths of three of their children in childhood. Yet the hardships of life had not diminished the love and faith of this dear old man, nor that of his beautiful bride.

Brandon looked around the room with the family gathered about their grandfather who was leading them all in chorus. He could see how the gift of faith had been transmitted so powerfully through the generations. Brandon realized that he, too, had become a beneficiary of the generous love that had been passed down in this family. He paused for a moment to thank God and prayed that he would, in his own life, be as devout and dedicated a man as Grandpa Ledoux.

Grandpa winked at Brandon and cajoled him, "You're pretty good there on that guitar, Brandon, but let's see if you can keep up with a seventy-six-year-old Frenchman." With that, Grandpa picked up the beat and began to play some traditional French jigging music. Brandon followed along, rising to the challenge.

Grandma Ledoux jumped up and said, "Let's see if any of you youngsters can keep up with an old lady!" A spry and slender woman, she was not much for size, but she packed about as much energy as a stick of dynamite. Her dark eyes sparkled under her snowy white curls, as she began to jig in the French Canadian tradition of dance. She lifted the bottom edge of her skirt to reveal her feet, skilfully and swiftly moving to the rhythm of the music.

The children all got up and formed a circle with Grandma at the head of it. Feet were kicking out in every direction as they frantically tried to follow her quick moves. Although the children abounded with energy, it was clear that none of them could out-jig the experienced feet of Grandma.

After a few minutes Grandma called out, "Grandpa, you'd better stop now, or you'll be carrying me out on a stretcher!"

She fell back onto the couch, panting for breath. The children flocked around her excitedly and she affectionately took the little ones into her arms.

Judy spoke out, "Mom, you shouldn't do that to yourself!"

"Oh, Judith," her mother returned, in French accent, "that's what keeps me young!"

Grandpa piped up, "Well, Grandma, the children might be able to outlast you on the dance floor, but you still have the nicest set of legs out there by a long shot!"

The children giggled as Grandma waved her hand to scold Grandpa.

Grandpa waved his finger at Grandma and said, "Just remember, *Ma Belle*, that's what keeps me young!" He waggled his eyebrows at his wife, who turned her head away in a scoff and joined in laughing with the rest of the family.

Brandon caught Joanie's eye and winked at her. She chuckled with amazement, wondering how she had managed to find a man so close at heart to her own Grandpa.

Slowing things down, John announced it was time for Joanie, Maggie, Amie, and Katie to sing his favourite carol. Though not a Frenchman by birth, he had come to love *Minuit Chrétiens,* and each Christmas at midnight he got his daughters to sing it for him.

Judy went to the piano to accompany them. Brandon sat back and admired these four girls whose clear voices rang out in rich and beautiful harmony together. When the French version of the carol was finished, John joined his family in singing the English, *O Holy Night.*

The evening wore on at this relaxed pace. Grandpa Ledoux was always good for a few stories of the olden days. The children hung on to his every word. Though they had heard each story many times before, they could never tire of hearing them again, told by this expert story-teller. For Brandon, it was the first time he was hearing the family tales, and he wondered at what a privilege it was to be a part of such a gracious, happy family.

Grandma and Grandpa had planned to stay the night, since they knew the party would go quite late. That way they would be there for the morning gift opening.

By three a.m. Judy offered Brandon to take the couch, if he did not mind children jumping all over him at seven o'clock, ready to open gifts. Brandon gratefully accepted the invitation and heeded the warning.

☦   ☦   ☦

Christmas morning was brought in just as Judy had indicated—bright and early with Isaac, Zack, and Aaron attacking Brandon with pillows. Brandon put up a pretty good pillow fight for a man who had only had three and a half hours of sleep, and who was outnumbered three to one.

With all the commotion, Jessie came running in and joined on Brandon's side of the battle. Soon the entire family was down in the living room, ready for opening presents. Joanie brought Brandon a coffee and manoeuvred her way in through the maze of children to sit beside him on the couch.

It was a happy time. Brandon could not think of a Christmas that he had ever enjoyed so much. He said a silent prayer for all those people who would spend this Christmas torn by a broken home, like so many he had experienced. He did not allow that to bring him down, but he did slip away to phone his mother in Calgary.

His mother was busy getting Christmas dinner ready for her new family. Her heart was warmed by the sound of her son's voice. He had promised to come out for a visit the following weekend, and he would be bringing Joanie. Caroline was dying to meet the girl that had managed to capture the heart of her son.

When Brandon returned to the living room, there was one gift left under the tree that was the centre of a great deal of excitement. It was a huge parcel tagged: *To Joanie and her family. Love, Brandon.*

Zack and Aaron dragged it over to Joanie and, with Jessie's help, they ripped away the paper. Inside there was a box in which they found a host of little gifts, all neatly wrapped. Joanie had helped Brandon with Christmas shopping, and there was something for everybody.

Brandon apologized to Grandma for her gift, saying, "If I had known, Grandma, I would have gotten you a new set of jigging shoes, instead."

"Oh, that's fine, Brandon, I'm quite happy with the candles. . . . If I have too many more nights like last night, you may just need to use these candles for my wake!"

Grandpa lifted up the bottle of wine that had been for him, saying, "And this wine will come in handy, Brandon. . . . I can serve it at Grandma's wake, just so people don't get too gloomy in that candle-lit room!"

Brandon chuckled. "Well, what I had in mind was a romantic candle-lit dinner for you two lovebirds," he commented, "but go ahead and use them for whatever suits your fancy."

Grandpa snuck his arm over Grandma's shoulder and replied, "Well, that's almost worth sticking around for a little while longer. Wouldn't you say, *Ma Belle?*"

"Thanks, Brandon, like the old fool needs any encouragement," Grandma retorted. "After fifty-two years you'd think he'd be bored with romance. He's worse now than he was when we first got married."

"That's 'cause after fifty-two years, we finally have the house all to ourselves again! And you have just gotten more beautiful with each passing day," Grandpa confessed, sneaking a kiss from his wife.

"You see what I mean?" Grandma complained, pushing Grandpa away playfully, though her dark eyes betrayed her affection. "I can't get a minute to myself anymore. . . . On second thought, Brandon, maybe you should have gotten me a pair of running shoes, so I can get away from this man when I need to."

The familiar laughter of the family filled the room.

Brandon could not help but picture in his mind Grandpa chasing Grandma around the house, with her in a pair of sneakers. The feisty old woman that she was, she'd keep him on the chase until her dying day, too! He marvelled at how the love had never diminished between these remarkable lovers.

Looking over at Joanie, he thought to himself, *I'm gonna enjoy growing old with you—my feisty woman!*

Jessie unwrapped a beautiful doll. She ran over to Brandon and gave him an enormous hug and many little kisses on the cheek. There were toys for Zack and Aaron and Christian CDs for Katie and Isaac. Maggie and Amie each got a sweater.

For Judy and John there was a framed print of Millet's famous painting, *The Angelus.* On the back Brandon had written: *John and Judy, Thank you for teaching me, through word and example, what it means to be a Christian. Brandon Vaughn.*

Judy walked over and gave Brandon a warm and motherly embrace, whispering in his ear, "I thank Jesus each day for bringing you into our family." She kissed him gently on the cheek and Brandon returned the kiss.

John stepped forward and offered Brandon a hug as well.

For Joanie there was a beautiful gold watch with the inscription on the back: *Yours, Joanie, 'til the end of time, B.J.V.*

Joanie read it aloud, and Jessie asked, with a look of amazement on her face, "Does that mean you get to keep the watch foweveh, Joanie?"

"Yes, it does," Joanie assured the child.

"It's so beautiful," Jessie exclaimed. "Bwandon?" the child turned to question him, in all her simplicity, "if Joanie doesn't marwy you, will you marwy me?"

Brandon tapped Jessie on the nose with a great deal of affection and answered her, "That's a deal, sweetie."

Jessie turned back to Joanie, her face revealing an expression of delight. "Then I'll get a nice new watch, too, Joanie."

"You sure will, Jessie," Joanie agreed, as she lifted Jessie on her knee to allow the child to admire the watch.

Chapter 33

Three days after Christmas, Joanie and Brandon were off to Calgary to visit his mother. Joanie was nervous about meeting Brandon's mother, but the idea of having Brandon all to herself for the six-hour drive was adequate compensation.

There was a snug and cozy feeling in the car as they drove along through the winter prairie landscape. They plugged in CDs and sang praise songs. They listened to talks and discussed issues of the faith. And time flew by, much faster than either of them wanted.

The house where his mother lived was in a fairly well-to-do area of Calgary. It was a beautiful split-level home with plenty of rooms. Brandon laughed to himself as he recalled his mother's reaction to his request for separate bedrooms for Joanie and himself.

He did not bother to share with Joanie his mother's shock. Brandon wanted to avoid any awkward situations. He knew his mom's curiosity was going to be especially heightened, now. What kind of girl was Joanie that she could have turned Brandon's lifestyle around like that? He could not wait for his mom to find out just what an amazing woman Joanie was.

Upon arrival, they were greeted with overwhelming enthusiasm. Brandon's mother, Caroline, was about the same age as Joanie's mother. She was a lovely woman with such distinctly fine features. She had rich auburn hair and stunning green eyes that were kind and welcoming.

She and Joanie hit it off immediately, both impressed with the warmth and charisma of the other. They dived into conversation and Brandon sat back, not able to get a word in edgewise. He did not mind, though. Here sat before him the two most important persons in his life.

Joanie begged Caroline for stories about Brandon's childhood and Caroline happily obliged. From thumb-sucking to braces, Caroline backed up every embarrassing story with pictures from photo albums. Brandon wondered why Joanie had been nervous about meeting his mother; he should have been the nervous one. Joanie enjoyed every amusing tale and told Brandon it was now her turn to laugh at him, since her family had not withheld exposing all the embarrassing moments from her life.

Caroline's husband, Dan, had been out when the young couple arrived, but he showed up a few hours later. He had been visiting at his daughter's house, enjoying a new grandchild. Brandon introduced Joanie to Dan.

Dan Taylor was a heavy set, jovial man, irresistibly likeable. He would have made a good Santa Claus in a red suit and white beard. Brandon sincerely appreciated Dan. An honest and caring man, he had been a good husband to Caroline.

He had been widowed several years back and was the father of four adult children and grandfather of seven. It had been a new and intimidating experience for Caroline when they married, to suddenly have so much family in her life. But she was happier now than Brandon had ever remembered her to be.

The foursome enjoyed a wonderful meal. Brandon felt good being near his mother again. Everything was going very well, until Dan asked Brandon about the medal he was wearing. It was a miraculous medal which Joanie had given him for Christmas. Brandon briefly explained the history and significance of it to Dan, while his mother sat in silence.

When Brandon was done, his mother directed the question at him, "Are you becoming Catholic, son?"

"Yes, Mom, I'll be joining the Church at Easter," he answered, anticipating her reaction.

Caroline looked at Joanie, then back at Brandon. She excused herself from the table and left the room. Joanie was shocked. Her eyes searched desperately for an explanation from Brandon. Brandon lifted his hand, motioning for Joanie to wait for him as he left the table to follow his mother. Joanie looked at Dan awkwardly, not really knowing what had just happened.

ф   ф   ф

"Brandon has obviously neglected to tell you about his mother's background," Dan observed. He paused, searching for the proper wording as he moved his big hand through his thick silvery hair. He looked back up at Joanie, then proceeded.

"Caroline was baptized in the Catholic Church. But at the age of twelve both her parents died tragically in a car accident. She and her two younger sisters were divided up amongst relatives. It was an unimaginably painful time for Caroline. The relatives she went to live with were unkind and treated her harshly. She pretty well worked as a servant in their home. Her sisters, Mary and Sharon, ended up with kind relatives, and they had good lives. But Caroline suffered in isolation, and she became very bitter towards God.

"She got pregnant with Brandon at eighteen and married his father just before Brandon was born. It was a terrible marriage and, as you know, they split up when Brandon was just eight. Caroline was a self-determined, hardworking woman. She put herself through school and became a nurse. She provided a good living for herself and her son. Brandon's father helped out financially, but otherwise had very little involvement. Caroline managed just fine on her own, though. She's a strong woman.

"Because she had to rely on her own strength throughout her life, she turned her back on God and refused to allow Brandon to have anything to do with religion. When we met, I was wavering myself with faith. I had stopped going to church after my wife died. Two of my kids still go, they're Born-Again Christians. But Caroline and I . . . I guess we've both been satisfied to just have each other and not to bother with God.

"I know that must sound strange to you, because I take it you've had a lot of religion in your life, Joanie. But Caroline felt betrayed by God. Hearing Brandon talk about becoming Catholic . . . well you can imagine the awful memories that stirs up for her. Don't fret it, though," Dan assured her, "she's a good woman, and she'll come around. There's just so much pain. She's had an awfully hard life, Joanie."

Joanie thanked Dan for the explanation and sat there in silence. In her heart she was offering up many Hail Marys for Brandon and his mother.

✞   ✞   ✞

Brandon found his mother in her room. She invited him to come in. Sitting on her bed, holding her forehead in her hand, she was deep in thought. Caroline was a strong woman; she was not one to give in to tears. Brandon sat beside her and put his arm around her shoulder. He prayed for assistance before talking to his mother.

"I'm sorry I walked out on you and Joanie there, son," she said, quietly.

"I'm sorry I hadn't told you about all this sooner. I just didn't know how to bring up the subject. I know how strongly you feel about it and I was hoping to find the right opportunity . . . I don't think that was it." His tone was sincerely apologetic.

"You're a big boy now, Brandon. You can make these decisions on your own. I shouldn't have reacted that way. It's just so painful to remember anything about my life before the accident." Her voice faded, and she struggled for control.

Acknowledging the confusion on her son's face, Caroline stood and went to her closet. She reached up and brought down an old shoebox from the top shelf. Gently wiping the dust from the top, she came back to the bed and set it down between herself and Brandon.

"I saved this all these years. I don't really know why. I can hardly bring myself to open it." She pushed it toward Brandon, indicating for him to look inside.

He carefully lifted the lid off the box. There he found a wooden crucifix, two rosaries, a pocket Bible, a Baptismal candle, a prayer book, a handful of holy cards and a jewellery case. He opened the soft velvety case and there in it lay a beautiful, golden miraculous medal. He looked up at his mother, his eyes begging for an explanation of the contents.

"These are my *holy trappings,*" his mother offered, by means of a simple explanation. "They were all the little gifts I had received as a child before my parents died. That miraculous medal you're holding there is the last gift I ever received from my parents. It was only two months before the accident that they gave me that for my Confirmation."

Her voice quavered, and her eyes welled up with tears. The pain associated with the memory of that time in her life came flooding back in a torrent of emotions. Brandon reached out and took his mother into his strong arms and held her close as she began to weep. Never before had he seen his mother cry. Even the few times when his father had hit her, she had held herself proudly and had never succumbed to tears.

But this was the burden of her heart—a burden that she had carried, hidden away for thirty-two years. It had locked away all her faith and all her hope, leaving her an empty, lonely soul. Brandon's tears fell freely, as he held his mother gently in his embrace. He knew the pain that comes with release, and he prayed for his mother. They remained that way for some time.

As her tears subsided, she pulled back from Brandon. She tried to regain her composure as best she could. Reaching out to the box, she ran her fingers gently over each of the secret treasures.

She spoke softly, "I was such a happy child, Brandon. My parents were wonderful, and my sisters and I were so close. We went to church together every Sunday, and we prayed together every night.

"After the accident, I hated God for taking them all away from me. First Mom, then Dad, then my sisters. Right after the accident, we three girls all lived together with one family, but then we got separated. The relatives I was sent to live with were awful. And though I tried to keep in contact with my sisters, we drifted apart. They had kept their faith. I had lost mine. Even as adults, there's always been that distance between us. How many times did you ever see your aunts when you were growing up? It wasn't often. They tried, at times harder than I, but . . . it just got more difficult as the years went on.

"I blamed God for leaving me with nothing in life—nothing but pain and suffering—until you came along." Caroline paused and smiled at her son, gently placing her hand on his cheek. "You were the only good thing that ever happened to me. I intended to protect you from everything I had gone through. I couldn't let you build false hopes in a God who could not hear, or just simply chose to ignore the prayers of a child. I couldn't let you know the pain of being let down by a God who was so distant and uncaring.

"I think I only kept this stuff, hoping someday, somehow, it would make me feel closer to Mom, Dad, Mary, and Sharon. But every time I tried to open it, it just brought back so much pain and anger." Her voice was strained with emotion. "I would just turn to ice inside. I couldn't cope with it."

Brandon spoke softly, "I had no idea, Mom. I don't know how I never knew all this about you. I knew you were orphaned, but I . . . I never saw the pain that you went through. I'm so sorry that you had to bear it all alone."

"It wasn't your place, son, to bear that burden for me," she said with firmness.

"No, it wasn't," Brandon agreed. "But it is the place of someone I know." He gathered up his courage in this sensitive moment. Reaching down to the crucifix, he lifted it up to his mother and said, "He bore my burden, forgave all my sins, and set me free, Mom. And I owe my life to Him."

He paused, allowing her to take the crucifix and hold it. Her fingers traced over the outstretched arms.

He continued, "This is *your* heritage, Mom. It's *who* you are! And it's the only way that you will ever find peace and joy in your life. I know, because it happened to me. Mom, I have so much joy now, sometimes I think I'm going to explode. Jesus gave that to me, when I gave Him my life."

Caroline kept her eyes fixed on the crucifix. "My daddy, as he was dying in the hospital, asked me to make a promise to keep my faith. And I couldn't do it . . ." her voice broke off. The tears stung, as they burned their path down her cheeks.

"I wanted to do it for him," she continued, "because I loved my dad so much, but I just couldn't do it. It would have meant that I had accepted their deaths and I could never accept that. . . . I lost all my faith, Brandon. No matter how much I want it back now, I don't know where to begin. It's been too long. I don't know how to believe anymore."

Brandon knelt down on one knee before his mother. He took her hand in his, looked deeply into her eyes, and said, "Just ask Jesus to help you. He knows your burden. Let *Him* carry it for you. He'll show you the way back home, Mom."

With a soft chuckle, he added, "I had no idea where I had come from or where I was going in life, but He brought me to the Catholic Church. And now I find out that's where I belonged in the first place."

Caroline reached out and stroked her son's face with her soft hand. "It was your rightful inheritance, son. Somehow your Grandfather, clever Irishman that he was, found a way to make sure this family heirloom was not going to be lost forever."

She smiled and sighed heavily. "I love you so much, Brandon," she said. "Thank you. I don't feel so afraid of believing anymore, knowing there's someone there who loves me."

Brandon hugged his mother, like only a son can. She could feel an energy touching her, stirring her heart so profoundly that she could not ignore it.

She cried again, such sweet release this time, and she whispered through her sobs, "Oh, Jesus, please bring me back home to You."

Brandon stayed with his mother a while longer. They did not speak. Instead, he prayed silently for her, knowing that she needed time to reflect on all that was happening in her life. In his heart he thanked God for the gift it was to be a part of his mother's conversion.

✝   ✝   ✝

Brandon found Joanie and Dan doing dishes and talking. Dan had been asking Joanie questions about Brandon's conversion. The older man's manner toward her conveyed an obvious respect for this young couple's convictions.

Caroline joined the group in the living room, where they had gone after the dishes were done. She was surprisingly animated in her expression, radiating peace and joy in her entire being. She smiled and snuggled up on the couch beside Dan. She took his hand in hers and she announced, "Tomorrow is Sunday, and I would like to go to church with you all."

Dan's eyes widened, but he did not say a thing. Brandon nodded to his mother and looked at her, as much as to say, *I understand. I've been there.*

Caroline looked at her husband and added, "Of course, I'd love for you to come with us, Dan, but I understand if you choose not to. I know this is all so sudden for you, but I need to go."

He shook his head gently and said, "No, it isn't all that sudden, dear. I've seen it coming now for a long time. You've been searching, and you've had a restlessness about you. Each time my kids would talk about Jesus, you'd get a faraway look in your eyes. I was wrong to have walked away from God after Laura died, but when I met you I guess I figured it was just as well, considering all the pain in your past. Now I see that I was wrong in letting you hide away from all that pain. I just wish I could have been the one to have pointed you back to Jesus.

"No, Caroline, I would be honoured to stand by your side, as you go home after thirty-two years. I wouldn't miss being there for anything." He put his arm around her and held her close.

Silently, tears rolled down her face. She closed her eyes and wrapped her arms around her husband. It was beautiful to see the love between them. Brandon reached over and held Joanie's hand.

Reaching into her pocket, Caroline produced the two rosaries that had been in her shoebox. She passed one to Brandon and asked, "Would you lead us in the rosary, son? I used to pray it as a child with my family, but I've forgotten how."

Brandon nodded his head slowly. His gentle eyes closed and with a clear, rich voice he began, "In the name of the Father, and of the Son, and of the Holy Spirit."

"Amen."

Chapter 34

Brandon was up early on Sunday morning. He went down to the kitchen and dug around until he found what he needed to put on the coffee. While it was brewing he took a phone book, looked up the Catholic parishes, and began phoning around for Sunday Mass times.

Joanie was the next one up. She walked over to Brandon while he was still on the phone. He hung up and smiled, greeting her, "Good morning, beautiful."

She smiled affectionately and leaned back against the counter, facing him.

"That's twice this week I've awakened to see your smile first thing in the morning. I could get used to this," he remarked.

She sighed through a smile and replied, "I could get used to this too, honey." Joanie was not talkative; she was simply enjoying the feeling of being with Brandon. How she wished she could have every morning to share with him.

After a moment he walked over and got them both a coffee, doctoring hers up just right: plenty of cream and a heaping teaspoon of sugar. He always found that so amusing.

"A little coffee with your cream and sugar," he teased, handing her the cup. "You can't even get one vice right," he added, winking at her, as he took a sip of his strong, black brew. Brandon never started the day without a hefty coffee to wake himself.

Joanie quipped back, "I'm afraid too much coffee over time would turn my halo yellow."

"I can't imagine anything tarnishing that halo," he responded, taking in her angelic appearance.

She smiled back at him, feeling the warmth of his love. Changing the topic she inquired about Mass times. He had found a few options. They would have to decide once his mother and Dan got up.

"I'm sure she had a hard time sleeping," Joanie remarked.

"Actually, not too bad at all." The voice was bright and cheerful. Brandon and Joanie looked up to see Caroline, in her bathrobe, standing in the doorway of the kitchen with a particularly gentle smile on her face. She entered the room and thanked Brandon for making coffee. Pouring herself a cup, she joined the couple sitting at the table.

"I feel like a new woman this morning, kids. And Joanie, I need to thank you for that."

"Why me?" Joanie's voice showed her surprise.

"Because you brought Jesus into Brandon's life, and that gave me the courage to face God after thirty-two years of shutting Him out of my own life. I've wanted so many times to go back and make peace with God, but I couldn't. Last night, when I realized Brandon had become a Christian— that set me free. I no longer bore the guilt of having denied Brandon faith when he was growing up."

She reached up to her neck and showed Brandon and Joanie the miraculous medal. "This reminds me that I made a commitment to my God and my Church when I was confirmed. It's time I followed through with that commitment."

Her expression changed, with a faraway look stealing over her eyes. "Last night, as we were praying the rosary, so much of it came back to me—all those things my parents had taught me about God. And I dreamt about my childhood before the accident, for the first time ever."

She was positively transformed. Her eyes were glowing as a few tears trickled down her cheeks. "I'm so at peace, I can't begin to explain how good it feels. . . ." She ran out of words and just sat there, lost in the silence.

Joanie got up, went and knelt in front of Caroline, and said, "Praise be to Jesus."

They hugged. Joanie felt so privileged to share in this wonderful woman's conversion. She whispered to Caroline, "Thank you, by the way—for Brandon. He's changed my life, too."

They moved apart and fixed their eyes upon each other. Blessing Joanie with her loving gaze, Caroline reflected, "My dad used to always say, 'God has His reasons for everything.' I think I'm beginning to understand that now."

Tenderly, Caroline touched Joanie's face. There was a powerful bond forming between these two women, and they both felt it.

✜   ✜   ✜

When Dan got up, they decided on a ten o'clock Mass at a nearby parish. They quickly got ready to go. There was a hushed feeling in the car; no one wanted to break the silence. So they drove on quietly, each one of them praying in their own way.

Dan took Caroline's hand, and they followed in behind Brandon and Joanie. Dan and Caroline had never entered a church together, not even to get married. This was an occasion, and Dan was proud to share it with his wife. They both sensed a new beginning in their life, and with that, a tremendous peace.

Brandon sat between Joanie and Caroline. He prayed for his mother and also for Dan. He was so grateful to God that Dan was such a good and supportive husband. He knew the changes that lay ahead of them would require a great deal of faith. Brandon prayed that their faith would be confirmed and fortified in this Mass.

Caroline marvelled at how familiar everything was, from the sensation of the holy water on her fingertips and forehead, to the posture of genuflecting before she sat in the pew. She looked around for the red sanctuary light which she found off to the side, behind the altar. There, beside it, was the Tabernacle.

Her mind floated back to childhood. She remembered how her father, the faithful Irish Catholic that he was, would take her and her sisters before the Tabernacle. They would all kneel together.

She could still remember the lilting sound of his voice, hushed in reverence. "You see in there, girls, Jesus is waiting for you to come and visit Him. I know you can talk to Jesus anywhere else, for His Spirit is everywhere. But in the Tabernacle is the Holy Eucharist. Jesus chose to make Himself truly present to us in the Bread of Life. He told us He would be with us always, and *here* He is. And He's waiting and longing for each one of us to come and share with Him all our joys and sorrows. He has answers for our questions. But we must be very still and listen with our hearts."

Then her father would close his eyes and pray. Caroline remembered how beautiful her father looked to her when he prayed. She loved him with such great affection.

Caroline closed her eyes now, too. She prayed to Jesus in the Holy Eucharist who was waiting for her in the Tabernacle.

I know You've waited a long time for me to come back, Jesus. But I'm here now, and I know You forgive me. Please, show me the way.

She sat, silencing her heart and listening very attentively for Jesus to speak to her.

Brandon could feel the peace that had settled over his mother as she prayed. He remembered the first time he had prayed in a church. The experience of Jesus' presence was so real to him. He could not find words to express it, but he had felt it.

Later, Joanie told him about the meaning of the Real Presence of Jesus in the Eucharist. Brandon had no trouble believing the Church's teaching, for he had experienced it to be true.

From that time on, he longed to receive Holy Communion. But he knew he must wait until he was fully a member of God's family in the Church, through Baptism. He was okay with that, for the waiting strengthened his desire and his faith. It was much like waiting for Joanie until they were married. He could not even imagine now betraying that love or spoiling it in any way. It was sacred and holy. He could see how faith interconnects every aspect of a man's life to make him whole.

Mass began. Caroline was awkward in the responses. The last Mass she had attended had been in Latin. But she loved it all the same, just as she had loved it as a child attending alongside her parents and sisters. She was overwhelmed with the beauty of the Mass and how meaningful each prayer was to her. She could not sing; there were far too many emotions stirring within her. But as she listened and thrilled at the sound of her son's voice lifted in praise, her heart rested in the feeling of gratitude.

When it came time for Communion, Brandon, Caroline, and Dan remained seated in the pew. Dan was confused as to why Caroline did not go to Communion.

After Mass, in the car on the way out for brunch, Dan asked about it. "I know why Brandon and I didn't go to Communion, Caroline, but you're a Catholic. Why didn't you go?"

Caroline smiled and looked back at Joanie and Brandon in the back seat. She stroked the back of Dan's neck, affectionately. She was completely at peace as she answered him.

"I was baptized Catholic and I was raised and confirmed in the Church. But I remember enough about my faith to know that if I've been living outside of the Church's teachings, then I'm going to have to reconcile my life with God before I return to Communion."

"What's to reconcile?" Dan asked, confused.

"Well, first of all, I need to go to Confession, Dan. I'm thirty-two years overdue!" She laughed at the sound of it. The fact was, though, her heart was yearning for the grace of that wonderful sacrament of healing and forgiveness.

Then, appearing somewhat tentative, she added, "And I have to find out what to do about our marriage, dear."

"What about it?" Dan's voice was slightly defensive, but more puzzled.

"Joanie, Brandon, could you help me out here? I'm a little blurry on the details," she petitioned the couple behind her.

Brandon looked at Joanie as much as to say, *You're on.*

Joanie explained, with great sensitivity, that the Church upholds Christ's teaching on the indissolubility of marriage. Therefore, due to Caroline's divorce, she was not allowed to remarry in the Church unless she had received an annulment. The annulment would be granted after a Church tribunal researched the circumstances at the time of her marriage to Brandon's father. It would have to be determined that the marriage had been invalid from the beginning.

The annulment would state that, while there had been a civil marriage, there never had existed a Christian marriage. This process would allow for Caroline to marry in the Church. Then her civil marriage with Dan could be blessed by a priest and would be accepted by the Church as valid.

Dan was silent, taking it all in. Finally, he asked, "How come it has to be so complicated? Maybe we should just go to my old church, Caroline. There's no legal red-tape like that to have to go through. It's pretty simple—if you come, you're in."

He was not at all angry. He was not meaning to be antagonistic. He was just confused by all the fuss.

Caroline kept rubbing the back of his neck and smiled, looking straight ahead as they drove.

She simply replied, "No, Dan. God's calling me back home and that's where I'm going." Then she thought for a moment and added, "But you don't have to become Catholic, dear. I don't want you to feel pushed into it just because I'm choosing to make that commitment."

Dan smiled: my how he had grown to love this woman. He was filled with gratitude for the peace that she was experiencing. Now, for the first time since this had all begun, he realized he was no longer angry with God, either.

He shook his head in a friendly manner and said, "I'll go with you, dear, wherever you want me to go. I'll stand by your side, whatever happens. And who knows," he chuckled, "maybe someday God'll call me to become Catholic as well."

✝   ✝   ✝

The following three days in Calgary were absolutely delightful. They went to the mountains to ski one day, something Joanie had done only a few times before in her life. But it had never been so much fun, because she had never had Brandon for an instructor before.

Joanie and Caroline spent another day shopping. Caroline told her that since she had no daughter of her own to spoil, she intended to have fun spoiling Joanie. When they got back, Joanie put on a fashion show for the men. Brandon could not hide his pleasure as he watched his beautiful Joanie model, with such grace, all the treasures of the day's shopping spree.

Since it was December thirty-first they had supper that night with all of Dan's children and grandchildren, and together they brought in the

New Year. It was a happy occasion. The house was full of life, with all of the little ones running around. Brandon told Joanie it was making him homesick for her family.

After the countdown to midnight and the usual New Year's hoopla, Dan got up and made a toast. "It seems to me that this is an appropriate time for a new beginning in our life. I want to toast my beautiful wife and thank her for inspiring me back to faith in Jesus Christ. It's been a long journey, Caroline, and I have a feeling it's only just begun. I can't tell you what an honour and privilege it is for me to be on this journey with you! To Caroline!"

Everyone joined in the toast. From that point several more toasts were made, blessing each other in the coming year. There was a great deal of love and affection within this family, and Joanie and Brandon were happy to know that Caroline had this kind of support in her life, after so many lonely years.

Dan's two Born-Again daughters were thrilled over the news of Caroline's conversion. The fact that their father was once again a believer was a great relief to them. And they could not get over the change in Brandon, which automatically drew Joanie into their affection.

The two sons who had no religious affiliations were somewhat uncomfortable in the excitement of all the discussions. Still, they could appreciate the transformations they had seen in Caroline and Brandon and were duly impressed.

Wednesday afternoon, Brandon and Joanie packed up to leave. Caroline was sorry to see them going. It had been such an eventful visit, and she did not want to see it end.

She had concerns about how to proceed in learning more about the faith. Where does one begin? But that morning, after the New Year's Day Mass, Brandon had encouraged his mother to speak with the parish priest, which she did. She set up an appointment for her and Dan to meet with the him again.

Joanie also gave Caroline the name and number of her aunt and uncle who lived in Calgary. She had phoned them the day before. They said they would be more than happy to meet with Caroline and Dan and to support them in any way. Like Joanie's family, they were loaded with all kinds of books and audio resources for learning about the faith. Brandon told his mother to prepare herself for the adventure of a lifetime.

Caroline and Dan were also planning to come to Saskatoon for Easter to be with Brandon at his Baptism and to meet Joanie's family. So it was with great anticipation and joy that they made their farewells.

Joanie and Brandon were physically and emotionally spent from the previous four days. They listened to their music, prayed a rosary, held hands, and enjoyed the solitude that the drive afforded them.

They marvelled over the work of God in and through their lives. It was humbling.

✠   ✠   ✠

After Brandon and Joanie left, Caroline did something she had not done in a long time. She picked up the phone and called her sisters, Mary and Sharon. It was the final step in coming home.

Her sisters received Caroline's calls with tremendous joy, for they had both been praying for Caroline throughout the years. Her loss of faith had left her so bitter and had been the source of so much suffering in her life. Now, finally, after all those years, they were once again united in faith.

Her sisters were both living in Edmonton, a few hours north of Calgary. It was decided that the three of them would meet in a week's time and have a family reunion.

Caroline hung up the phone after talking to Sharon and sank back down into her rocking chair. "Daddy," she said, softly, "I understand now why you wanted me to keep my faith. It would have saved me so much suffering if I had only trusted in God. . . . I see that now. Thank you, Mom and Dad, for praying me back to Jesus. Someday, Daddy, we're all gonna be together again in heaven . . . just like you said."

She smiled, and a single tear trickled down her cheek. It was a tear of joy. "And thank you, Jesus . . . for having sent Joanie into our lives to light the way back home!"

Caroline closed her eyes and pictured Brandon and Joanie together. A smile illuminated her face as she realized this young couple would keep the torch of faith burning brightly in their family. Something stirred again in Caroline's heart that day that she had not felt for a great many years: hope!

Chapter 35

Brandon and Joanie had the rest of the week booked off for holidays. It was good to have so much free time to spend together.

One evening Brandon hosted the entire Collins family at his condo for supper. The littlest ones ate around his table, and everyone else sat wherever they could fit. His apartment had never felt so small.

Brandon surprised them all, including Joanie, with his culinary skills. He explained that it was a talent which he had acquired from his mother. Making fancy meals together was something they used to love to do. "I just never had to prepare food in such large quantities," he confessed. "I've got enough leftover lasagne to feed me for a week! So, if you don't mind taking most of it home, I'd really appreciate that."

"That's awfully kind of you, Brandon, but—" Judy began to protest.

"No, really," he interjected, "you'll be doing me a favour. I like lasagne, but not that much!"

John stepped into the conversation, having savoured a bite of dessert. "You make an excellent cheesecake there, Brandon."

"It's not hard to follow a recipe," Brandon said, brushing off the praise.

"No, it isn't," admitted Judy. "What impresses me is that you bothered to in the first place."

"I'd say that boy's gonna make a mighty fine husband for some woman, someday!" John returned to Judy.

"If not, he can come live at our house and cook for me," Judy replied.

Isaac, Zack, and Aaron picked up on that idea and responded with a great deal of enthusiasm.

"Well," Brandon got back into the conversation, "if I can't find any woman who's interested in me, at least for my cooking talents, I'll take you up on that offer, Judy."

Joanie had avoided eye contact with anyone during this pointed conversation. She served out the cheesecake with Brandon and kept quiet.

After supper they enjoyed a singsong, with Brandon on his twelve-string, and Isaac following along on the acoustic guitar. It was great fun, and the time passed by quickly. Soon, cranky little ones let them know that all good things come to an end, and the Collinses packed up and left.

Joanie stayed to help clean, with Brandon assuring her folks that he would have her home in a couple of hours. John and Judy had come to trust Brandon explicitly with their daughter. Brandon had never once failed to meet a curfew and the way he was living out his faith was absolutely exemplary. They counted themselves blessed for Joanie to have found so good and trustworthy a man.

The fact that John still established curfews for Joanie, at twenty-two years of age, had nothing to do with a lack of trust for either her or Brandon. What it provided was a framework within which Joanie and Brandon could practise self-discipline. It was, for Brandon, a question of honour. He would never argue with his boss at work over a deadline. He just made sure that he met it. Likewise, he was not about to question John, a man for whom he had undying respect. If John established a limit, Brandon would meet it.

Brandon was mature enough in his Christianity to realize that it was important not to give rise to scandal. Though he and Joanie were not doing anything immoral, and he knew that John and Judy trusted them in that regard, it was important not to give the impression that they were. Keeping Joanie out all night—just to talk—would look the same to the neighbours and to her younger siblings as though they had spent the night otherwise. Brandon had become far too honourable as a Christian man to ever bring that kind of disgrace to Joanie or to her family name.

After everyone had left, Joanie began washing the dishes, while Brandon set into cleaning up the rest of the mess. It really did not take that long and, in fact, the time spent together at the sink was most amusing.

Brandon was drying, and so he took many opportunities to thwack Joanie with his tea-towel on the backside. It never hurt, but she was getting annoyed with his persistence.

"Cut that out, Brandon," she scolded him.

He ignored her as he twisted his wrist, rolling the tea-towel to snap it back for another playful hit.

"You're such a little boy at times, Brandon. Stop it. I'm warning you," she threatened him.

"I'm not worried," he returned, thwacking her again. "Besides, I'm not hurting you. Now if I wanted to hurt you, you'd know it."

"I didn't say you were hurting me. You're annoying me!" She turned to look at him. "You think just 'cause you're so handsome, and your eyes are so blue, you can get away with anything you want with me?"

"No, *not* 'cause I'm handsome, and not because my *eyes are so blue* . . . but because you love me so much." He raised his eyebrows at her. "And I do love it when you flash those fiery eyes at me," he teased her.

Joanie made a stifled noise under her breath and turned back to the sink. The dishes were almost done, and she filled a cup with water. Next thing Brandon knew, he was standing there dripping wet.

There was a tentative pause, after which Joanie realized she had better get out of there—posthaste. Brandon refilled the cup and went after her. His apartment did not afford her much place to run and hide. After a few laps around the furniture he doused her with water and tackled her, pulling her down over the back of the couch to land on it. After some tickling and screaming and begging for mercy, Brandon finally let her go. They laughed and lay back against the couch to catch their breath.

"Look at me, now," she complained, pulling at her sweatshirt, which was soaking wet.

"It seems to me that you asked for that, babe," he retorted.

"No more than you had it coming to you," she returned.

He laughed as he brushed back the strands of hair that were hanging down around her face from all the tussling. "Even mussed up and soaking wet, you're still the most beautiful woman I know," he said, gently, admiringly.

Joanie got quiet and moved away from Brandon. All of a sudden, this situation was way too close for comfort.

Picking up on the signal, Brandon got up and led her by the hand. "Come on, I'll find you something to put on. I have to get changed anyway."

Joanie felt awkward following Brandon into his bedroom and when she hesitated at the door, he stopped and laughed. Turning to her with a feigned look of injury, he asked, "After all this time, you don't trust me?"

"No," Joanie replied, with real sincerity, "after all this time, I don't trust *me!*"

He looked at her tenderly and assured her, "Well, I do. But I respect your boundaries, and I will fetch something for you to wear." He went into his room and got her a top. He apologized that he had no pants to offer her.

Joanie laughed and said, "If your pants fit me, I think I'd die! Besides, mine aren't too bad; it was the sweatshirt that got soaked."

She got changed and came out of the bathroom, all snuggled up in Brandon's U of S bunny hug, hands tucked into the front pouch.

"I haven't worn that thing in years," he commented.

"It's wonderful," Joanie remarked, pulling at the dark green hooded sweatshirt.

Brandon smiled and remarked, "You look good in my clothes, but I'm not too sure that your parents would agree with me."

His eyes conveyed his admiration for her beauty, and Joanie felt a little shy in front of him. She picked up his guitar and sat down at the couch to play.

Brandon loved to hear Joanie play, not because she was exceptionally good, but because it amazed him just how much music seemed to flow out of her. She sang like an angel, played the piano with tremendous grace, dabbled on the guitar, and occasionally treated him to a tune on the fiddle.

He picked up the twelve-string and joined her, singing and playing. She followed along as he taught her some strumming and picking techniques. He was a good teacher and, before too long, his soft voice, his gentle nature, and his patient attitude were all drawing Joanie into a battle with temptation. She was grateful to have two guitars in between them as she struggled against her desire for physical intimacy with this man.

Brandon was apparently oblivious to her inner turmoil as he carried on in conversation.

"So tomorrow night we do it again with Mark and Justine," he remarked.

"Oh, yeah, I forgot about that. How are they doing now?" Joanie asked, relieved to have her mind taken off the present situation.

"I'm not sure how to read it," Brandon commented. "Mark's been doing some real soul-searching, and he doesn't like that very much. Justine's still been showing up at C.C.E. talks on campus and has really seemed to make a commitment to Jesus in her life. That part's awesome. I see her more now than I do Mark.

"But when Mark and I played racquetball last week, he was sounding better. I know he's struggling. He loves Justine, and he isn't prepared to lose her, but all this religious stuff has him pretty intimidated. I told him I think that Justine finding Jesus is the best thing that could have ever happened to him—speaking from experience—because *you* are the best thing that has ever happened to me!"

"Just like you're the best thing that has ever happened to me!" Joanie returned. She paused for a moment, the smile fading from her face. Once again she was brought back into the awareness of being all alone with Brandon. She realized that it simply was too hard to be in this circumstance and not to have feelings stir within her that otherwise would not have been an issue. She leaned back against the couch and sighed.

Brandon smiled at her as she bit down on her bottom lip. "Come on," he said, getting up to put away the guitars, "I'll have enough explaining to do with you in my clothes, let alone being late in getting you home."

Joanie was grateful for Brandon's good judgment as he tuned in to her awkwardness. She was finding it harder and harder to resist the temptation toward a physical relationship with him. Once the floodgates opened a crack, she feared she would not be able to hold back the tide. It was now easy for her to understand how it was that good people got into trouble.

"Let's pray a rosary together on the way home," she suggested, "for Mark and Justine and . . . for us . . ."

Brandon looked at her, curiously.

She finished, ". . . to be strong, because lately . . . I've been feeling really weak." She was standing, leaning against the door, waiting for Brandon to shut off lights and get his keys.

As he approached her, he took his rosary out of his pocket, saying, "That's why we don't rely on our own strength, Joanie. It's funny, when I was weak, you were strong and now that you're feeling weak . . . I'm feeling like a fortress!" He directed his gaze toward her in a reassuring way. "But that power comes from God. . . . So," he took her by the hand to go, "let's pray."

"Brandon?" she hesitated at the door.

He paused and turned back to her. "I think I know what you're going to say," he responded, gently holding onto her hand.

"I can't be here alone with you anymore—you do understand?" She felt awkward with her own insecurity. She was a strong Christian woman, why was it so hard to fight back these desires within her?

"Joanie," Brandon began, apologetically, "I'm sorry for having created a situation of temptation for you here tonight. That was never my intention—you know that. I'm just feeling so strong spiritually right now, which we both know is not my own strength . . . it's God's grace. But just because I've been feeling strong doesn't make it right for me to overlook what you've been experiencing. I realize now that I haven't been entirely fair to you."

Joanie closed her eyes. A tear rolled down her cheek. She felt ashamed of her weakness.

"Hey," Brandon's voice was soft and compassionate. He placed his hands gently on her shoulders. "Don't feel bad, Joanie. . . . I'm sorry that I wasn't being sensitive to your needs. I have no intention of placing your purity at stake."

He stepped back from Joanie to look her in the eye. She reached up and wiped away her tears, laughing at herself. "I'm sorry. . . . I never realized until tonight how easily I could be tempted. I was fine until we were alone together."

Taking Brandon's hands in her own, she continued, "You know I love you and that you're the only one I want to be with. I trust God in the direction He's taking our relationship. But, for the time being, I need for us to establish appropriate limits to our time alone together . . . just because I have come to love you and to want you so much."

"The feeling is mutual, you realize," he returned playfully. "I wouldn't want you to go away thinking that I don't desire you, Joanie. Because I do! And I have struggled with this at times, too. I'm not some superman, you know. But you know what keeps me on track?" he asked.

She shook her head and silently waited for him to continue.

"Well, aside from the fact that I love you too much to ever hurt you like that... what helps to keep me on track is... *accountability!*" He laughed over the word. "Knowing that I'll have to face your father the next time I see him and answer for my actions with you, helps to keep me an honest man. There is no way I could lie to your father. And there is no way that I would ever be able to hide the truth from him if we were to spend an evening together... well... doing what I'd love to do with you if we were married."

Joanie laughed at Brandon's subtle frankness.

"You're all I want, Joanie. And I promise you . . . our day will come." He gave her hand a little squeeze.

"I know it will, Brandon." Acquiring a serious tone again, she stated, "And I can wait patiently, but I don't want to be in this kind of situation again. Tonight was hard!"

Brandon nodded and smiled at her in a reassuring way. "You know your father once told me to be sincere and honest with you, to guard your heart, and to treat you like gold. . . ."

"You've done all those things, unfailingly," she reminded him.

He shook his head, regretfully. "I know I could have guarded your heart more carefully tonight. I'm sorry that in my playfulness I overstepped the boundaries that we both had agreed upon in our relationship. I'll guard your heart better from now on, Joanie . . . I promise."

She looked at him, her eyes filled with so much love. "I'm so grateful I can trust you to be the knight in shining armour that I had always dreamed of falling in love with." A radiant smile lit up her face.

Brandon stood up straight, offered her his arm in a noble fashion and replied, "My lady, I place myself entirely at your service, according to God's purposes. I will protect your honour, guard your purity, and defend your integrity with all that I am."

Joanie laughed at Brandon's chivalrous display and took his arm. "And I promise to behave as I should, dear sir." Motioning to the door for them to leave, she entreated him, "Now would you please lead us in that much needed rosary?"

"With all my heart."

As he made the sign of the cross, he turned his heart to the Lord and asked for guidance to live up to the calling of being a righteous Christian man . . . in love.

Chapter 36

Mark and Justine were clearly uncomfortable with each other when they arrived at Brandon's apartment for supper. The tension grew throughout the evening. Joanie tried to set Justine at ease with small talk, but Mark was obviously miserable.

Finally, Brandon could not take it any longer. "Out with it, Mark. What's on your mind? You're driving us all nuts here with your attitude."

Mark glared at Brandon and an intense silence spread over the group.

It was Justine who spoke out. "Mark is upset with me because," she looked at him to see if he would stop her from talking, but he did not, "because he asked me to marry him . . . and I turned him down."

"What?" Brandon could not believe his ears.

Justine went on, "I turned him down, only temporarily," she explained. "You see, Brandon, I took your advice and went and met with Fr. Steve today. After we talked, he heard my confession of twelve years. I made a decision there to clean up my life and return to church.

"I have a lot to learn I realize; I've forgotten so much. But I love the C.C.E. Bible studies and Mr. Curran has been awesome in providing me with books and tapes. So considering all the changes and everything, I think Mark and I need time now to think—so we can be sure that marriage is right for us."

"You didn't tell them all the changes," Mark prompted her on, with real disdain in his voice.

"No. I guess I didn't," she admitted, nervously. "I'm moving back home with my parents tomorrow. Well, actually, tonight. I asked Mark to take me there to sleep. But I'll be going back to pack my things tomorrow."

She fixed her gaze on Mark, and in an effort to explain, she went on, "It's the only way I can think of for us to know if we really are ready for marriage, Mark. It's just too easy to go from living together to getting married, without really appreciating the differences between the two. I've seen the statistics, and it generally doesn't last.

"I want to start out in married life right. And you're going to have to decide whether or not you can accept the Catholic Church's teachings on marriage, because it isn't how we've been living. I refuse to contracept anymore, Mark. It's all changed. And maybe you won't want me once you've weighed it all out."

"I told you I don't care about that stuff. I was willing to go along with it, get married, and make it work out. I thought you loved me enough to make some of the concessions. I guess I was wrong." His voice was cold and full of anger.

Brandon could relate to the struggle Mark was experiencing. The difference was, Mark had not yet found Jesus in his life to fill the hole that was causing so much pain.

"I do love you, Mark. I told you that. And I believe you love me, too. But I think we need to prove to ourselves just how much we really do love each other." Justine's voice was faltering. This was very difficult, and she was desperately hoping Brandon and Joanie would offer some help.

"Mark," Brandon cut in, cautiously, "trust me, buddy. It's not easy to live out what Justine's asking from you. In fact, it's impossible except for . . ." He was unsure whether or not to say it. The look on Justine's and Joanie's faces told him to go on; the look on Mark's face gave him a chill.

"Except for *what?*" Mark's voice was strained with anxiety.

"Except for . . . Jesus."

"There! I *knew* you were going to say that!" Mark threw his arm up in the air. "It was just a matter of time, Brandon, before you'd try to convert me. All of you," he spit out his words with great fury, "you're all in on it together. 'Let's gang up on Mark next and turn him into one of us!'"

He slammed down his beer, grabbed his coat, and walked out. "Well, there's no bloody way!" he called out over his shoulder, as the door crashed behind him.

The loud thud of the slamming door shook throughout the condo. Justine started to cry. Brandon walked over and put his hand on her shoulder. "It's gonna be okay," he assured her. "You're doing the right thing."

"Absolutely," Joanie piped in. "I'm so happy for you, Justine. You've found Jesus. Don't let Mark's anger diminish your joy in that. It'll all work out. Trust God to get you through this."

"Would you both pray with me?" Justine asked, her voice weak and fearful. "I've never stood up to Mark or anybody before in my life. I'm afraid of losing him altogether, and I don't want that. But I'm so afraid I'll lose my nerve and cave in. Then I'll have nothing."

Brandon brought her over to the couch to sit down, and together the three of them offered up intentions for Mark and Justine. Then Brandon handed Justine a rosary, and he led them in prayer.

He could sense Justine's tension subsiding as they prayed. Brandon, himself, was familiar with the peace that came whenever he invited Mary to petition her Son on his behalf. His love for the Blessed Mother came out of the richness of knowing and feeling her unfailing maternal care.

✟   ✟   ✟

Mark went out into the night and walked and walked and walked. He could not move his legs fast enough to work out all his anger. He had no particular destination in mind, nor did he know if he would ever come back for Justine. All he knew was anger: powerful and hateful anger.

After fifteen minutes at this hard pace he began to slow down and, with the easing of his stride, he felt the anger subside. Snow was falling in thick, soft flakes. Had Mark not been so distracted in thought, he might have noticed what a beautiful display the snow made shimmering through the street lights. Instead he walked on at a controlled pace now, completely oblivious to the outside world. There was a storm going on within that was consuming all his energy and attention.

The screeching of tires startled Mark back to reality. He looked up to find himself in the middle of the street, with a car's headlights staring him down. He turned his eyes away from the glare, as the driver jumped out to meet him. There was something vaguely familiar about the tall, willowy man coming toward him.

"Are you okay, young man? I almost ran you over. You didn't even see me coming!" There was real concern in the man's controlled voice.

"I'm sorry, sir," Mark spoke through a dazed expression. "It was my fault. I'll pay attention from now—"

"Mark?"

"Yes, sir," Mark responded, his wits not fully about him, yet.

"Mark Jacobs! I recognize you now!" The man's expression was warm and fatherly. He put his hand on Mark's shoulder and shook him gently. "I'm Pastor Kline. You went to my church until you were about fifteen or sixteen. I know your parents well. They still attend, you know!"

"Pastor Kline," Mark's voice revealed that he was gradually returning to the real world. "Sure, I remember you." He shook the pastor's hand. "Thank you for not running me over," he said sincerely.

"Is everything all right, son, or would you like to talk to someone? I could drive you back to my office if you'd like."

Pastor Kline's tone was completely non-threatening to Mark. For whatever reason, he actually found himself accepting the invitation and getting into the kindly man's car.

The two men spent over an hour together. Mark told the pastor all about Brandon's conversion and Justine's new-found faith. He was angry. He was hurt. But he was mostly confused, for he could not understand what it was about this Jesus that made everyone so willing to turn their lives upside down.

Pastor Kline listened attentively. He liked Mark. He had always liked Mark. He had a great deal of respect for Mark's parents. He knew how they had suffered over Mark's loss of faith, and he knew the vigilance of their prayers for him. Pastor Kline prayed intently while Mark spoke, asking Jesus to give him words to somehow reach Mark through all the confusion and to guide his footsteps home.

Mark stopped talking and silently looked at the older man before him. Pastor Kline's hair had once been light brown, but now it was a distinguished silvery-grey. He had aged since Mark had known him, but he still had the same kind eyes that Mark had trusted as a child.

Pastor Kline took Mark's silence as a cue and began. "Mark, until you experience Jesus in a real way in your own life, you will never understand what it is that makes people so crazy when they finally meet him.

"You know, in the early days of Christianity people walked *joyfully* into the lions' den. They desired only to make a testimony of their lives for Jesus. That commitment, that faith, was what caused Christianity to spread like wildfire throughout civilization. You can read about it in the history books, but until you meet Jesus and accept him into your own heart, you will *never* understand it.

"It seems to me that God has been placing people in your life, and very significant ones, to bear witness to Jesus for you. You are watching your friends lay down everything in their lives for Jesus. It's not unlike the people who watched the early Christian martyrs and were converted by the example of their faith. True, your friends are not marching into the lions' den. But there are times, I'm sure, when it must seem just as hard for them.

"Take Justine, for example. It sounds to me as though she really loves you, Mark. But she's willing to give up everything, and she is risking losing you for a love that is even greater. Sounds like she's a pretty amazing woman."

He paused to let Mark think about it for a moment. Mark nodded his head in agreement. Justine was an amazing woman. Funny, how he was just starting to realize that about her.

Pastor Kline went on. "Mark, do you remember the day you decided to stop going to church?"

"Yes, sir, I do," Mark answered.

"So do I, son. I remember your parents coming to see me. Your mother was a wreck, afraid of pushing you too hard and having you leave home altogether. Your father was ready to crucify you himself. I can still picture them sitting here, where you are right now.

"And I have such a clear memory of you before that day. You had been so bright and enthusiastic. You always were at the top of your Bible study classes. You had a real knack for learning and memorizing Scripture. I remember watching you at Bible Trivia nights. The other kids begged to be on your team because your team always won.

"But then one day you announced that that was it. Your parents were both convinced your friendship with Brandon was at the heart of your disobedience to them and your disinterest in God. Funny, eh? Now Brandon is the one who is leading you back to God."

Mark sat there silently. He remembered the hurt that his parents went through back then. He thought about how they still carried that hurt to this day. He thought about Brandon and how he had changed from the basic heathen he had always been to some insanely happy Christian. It was almost sickening to Mark to see how happy Brandon now was.

A change of feeling came over Mark as he thought about Justine and how much he did not want to lose her. Gradually he could feel the anger inside of him begin to soften.

He was not quite sure who it was that he was fighting. Why had he grown cold to God? Why had he walked out all those years ago? He really had never hated church. It was like Pastor Kline said: he had been popular and had fun at church youth nights.

It was Brandon. Brandon was not allowed to attend church with Mark on account of his mother's disdain for religion. Brandon had coaxed and convinced Mark to free himself of the chains of church so that the two of them could have more time together—getting into trouble mostly.

Now it was Brandon trying to convince Mark that he could only find peace and happiness with Jesus. If he did not love Brandon so much as a brother, he would have hated him for having caused so much grief in his life.

Mark sat there mutely; an obvious change in demeanour had come over him. Pastor Kline waited silently in prayer for Mark.

Focussing his attention back on the sincere man before him, Mark finally said, "Look, I'm not saying I believe in God anymore now than I did two hours ago. But I think that maybe I should give God a chance to prove Himself to me so that I could believe. What I mean is, I really have nothing to lose now in trying. But if I don't give God a chance, I have an awful lot to lose that I'm not willing to give up that easily."

"That's a fair statement, Mark, and a good start," the pastor assured him. "I think you need to go back to your friends now and begin from there. I'm sure they must be worried about you. I'd be happy to drive you back."

Mark gratefully accepted the ride. He thanked the pastor for his time and advice. As he stepped out of the car, he added, "And what the hell, Pastor, why don't you pray for me?"

"I'll do just that!" Pastor Kline answered, with a hearty laugh. "Goodnight, Mark."

✟   ✟   ✟

When the buzzer went off in Brandon's apartment, Justine just about jumped through the ceiling. Mark walked in. There was a tentative moment for everyone. Then Justine, perceiving a certain calmness about Mark, went over and hugged him warmly.

Mark returned her hug and whispered in her ear, "I'll take you home now . . . to your parents' house. I'm ready to try."

Justine started crying and kissed Mark, tenderly.

Brandon and Joanie stood back, watching and praying for their friends. Brandon offered for them to stay and talk, but Mark insisted he was exhausted and was going home to bed. He would call Brandon tomorrow and tell him what had happened.

"Let's just say," Mark commented, as he and Justine were leaving, "I know you people were praying for me tonight. Good-night and thanks."

Brandon and Joanie were left standing in awe, wondering what the Lord could have done to have effected that kind of comment from Mark.

Brandon looked down at Joanie with a particularly gentle expression and said, "I guess our evening's over. I need to take you home now."

Joanie smiled, grateful for Brandon's determination to keep their commitment to not being alone together at his place. He got her jacket, helped her put it on, and they left.

As they drove home, they talked about the evening and offered up more prayers for Justine and Mark. Joanie and Brandon were both so thankful for the love that God had given them and for the gift of each other. They were aware of the blessing of being of one mind in faith.

Their hearts went out to Mark and Justine, knowing the challenges that they would face. At the same time, they rejoiced at the possibilities that lay ahead, unbeknown to Mark and Justine, when they would finally be able to put Jesus at the centre of their love.

After walking her to the front porch, Brandon kissed Joanie's hand and winked at her in that way that always set her heart aglow. He was indeed her chivalrous knight.

She picked up his hand, gently kissed his fingers, and whispered, "I love you . . . too."

Chapter 37

John and Judy had been very supportive of Joanie and Brandon's relationship. They were impressed with the responsibility that the young couple demonstrated and their determination to keep the rules of courtship upon which they had agreed. They had nothing but respect for Brandon, inspired by his commitment to his faith and his obvious sense of direction in life.

The time had come to discuss certain matters alone with their daughter. It was just another spot check on the road of romance in order to be sure she was still on track. New emotions that a person encounters along the path of love can sometimes confuse and blur the vision.

Joanie knew the significance of the invitation to go out one evening in late January to a small café for dessert and cappuccino. She was grateful for the opportunity to discuss things with her parents. They settled themselves into a small booth in a corner of the quiet café.

"Joanie, what have you and Brandon discussed about marriage?" Judy wrapped her hands around her cappuccino, as if warming herself by a fire.

Shrugging her shoulders, Joanie answered, "Very little, Mom. We've only ever mentioned it in a handful of conversations. We both know that's the direction our relationship is taking. But we kind of avoid discussing it, to allow our relationship time to grow naturally, without a lot of pressure. Why?"

"Well, what are your plans for the future?" John asked, noticing that his daughter was now hugging her cappuccino in the same way as her mother. *If you two were any more alike, you'd be twins.*

The smile from her dad was warm and affectionate. Joanie had so much love for this hero in her life. Guarding and protecting her until the day he would die, she would always be daddy's little girl.

She hesitated a moment, before answering. "I have my work at the station. My voice degree will be completed in June." Joanie's eyes began to sparkle, leaning herself forward. "You know how I've always wanted to record Christian music. It's now my dream to be able to do that with Brandon. And more than anything, I want for us to get married and have a family together."

John and Judy sat there nodding, but they kept so quiet Joanie could hardly read them.

Finally, a smile stole over her mother's face, gently, with understanding. "I could have guessed that would be your dream, Joanie. I think you and Brandon would make beautiful music and beautiful children together, because I know that your first desire in both is to serve the Lord."

Judy's eyes looked through Joanie. Only a mother can look at her daughter and see in her the adult and the infant, the teenager and the toddler, all at once. It had been almost twenty-three years since she had taken this precious baby into her arms for the first time, but that moment would be forever imprinted on her heart.

A lifetime of unconditional love had brought them to this moment. It was just a small speck in time, set against the backdrop of eternity, but for the mother it was absolutely timeless.

John began to speak, slowly and thoughtfully, "Your dream certainly is understandable, given your talents and your love for the Lord and for Brandon. But are you thinking about how marriage and family will restrict you from living out that dream of recording? Perhaps you and Brandon should step back and cool off a bit to allow you to live out some of that dream before you get too serious?"

"Daddy, I'm not sure when Brandon and I will decide to get married, but I'm not afraid of missing out on anything. I can always pursue some of that dream, even while we're having children. I realize it would be more challenging that way. But I really trust Brandon's sense of timing. I know I'll be ready when he's ready to ask.

"Maybe it would be different if Brandon and I didn't share the same dream with our music. But we do. And I think we can live out that dream beautifully together. I'm so confident of that calling in our lives. I've trusted God to reveal His will to me throughout this entire relationship. I believe He's guiding us on safe paths."

She paused for a moment to look at her parents. Their lives had been an exemplary model of married love. She knew what she was seeking in a good marriage. The struggles and sacrifices were not unknown to Joanie, but she also saw the joys and rewards.

Why she hesitated about what she wanted to say next, Joanie did not know. She knew she could share anything with her mom and dad.

"To be honest, I'm not so sure that I really want to wait a long time before we get married. I'm . . . well, I'm really starting to understand the virtue and discipline involved with chastity. It's a lot easier to practise when there's no one in your life to distract you."

Joanie looked at her parents to see if she was conveying herself appropriately.

"I really do desire to be married to Brandon. I mean we've never even kissed, but there's an awful lot of energy there that I find hard at times to contain. I'm so grateful that we don't spend a lot of time alone together. In fact, we've agreed to really guard ourselves from circumstances that would possibly," she smiled over her hesitation, "lead us into temptation . . . like being alone at his place."

Joanie's reference to the Lord's prayer brought forth a chuckle from her parents. They understood the challenges of chastity. Just because abstinence is the most loving response for an unmarried couple, that doesn't make it easy. Even after a couple is married, abstaining can present a real challenge at times. But then again, a mature Christian understands that another word for love is sacrifice.

Joanie went on, "I'm just finding that as our emotional intimacy grows, I'm struggling more and more with myself. Everything you used to warn me about guarding my purity makes so much more sense now. Avoiding situations of temptation is a lot easier than putting all that energy into practising self-control. Our commitment to our Christian principles is really helping me to stay on track. And Brandon," by the look in Joanie's eyes, it was obvious that she had brought his face to mind, "well, he's wonderful! He never even tries to tempt me. He really does have strong convictions. Sometimes I trust him more than I trust myself."

Her mother laughed, "I understand, Joanie. But don't worry, we trust you, too."

"We really do, Sweet Pea," her father added. "We're very proud of your sense of commitment, your fidelity to Christ, and your desire to live according to God's laws. And," he added, taking a deep breath, smiling across at his daughter, "some day, in the not so distant future, I'm sure there will be a young man seeking my permission to ask for your hand in marriage. Your mother and I just wanted to be sure that we knew your heart and your mind on the matter before permission was granted."

"Well, if it's Brandon, for goodness sake, don't say no!" Joanie returned, playfully. For clarification, she added, with a glimmer in her eye, "I just want to be sure that you *do* know my heart and my mind on the matter."

"I read you loud and clear," her father assured her.

Softly, Joanie giggled. "I'm so glad I have you for parents. It feels good knowing you're watching out for me, even at my age."

They finished off their visit, talking about other family matters. There was a sense among them, as they talked, that their relationship had undergone great change. When had it happened? Their little girl had grown up . . . and John and Judy were proud of the woman she had become.

Chapter 38

Time seemed to pass by in a flurry of activity. *New Spring* had a number of gigs through January and February. The rehearsal schedule was tight. Brandon had brought many new ideas to the band and had been able to rig them up with better sound equipment than they had ever used before. The instrumental parts were developing, and their repertoire was expanding.

All together there were fifteen people in the band. They now had a sound man, Paul Delainey, a friend from the parish. In spite of his heavy schedule at university, Mike Ledoux had made the commitment to continue with the band. He still did electric keyboards and, along with Joanie and Brandon, did the arranging. Joanie remained the lead singer. Brandon played acoustic and electric lead guitar and was their lead male vocalist. David Bander, from their parish, played bass and sang as well. His younger brother, Kyle, was their amazing drummer. Caleb Ledoux now played acoustic guitar and sang as well. Leah and Maggie still played violins and did back-up vocals. Amie played piano and sang. Their vocal section had expanded, including Annie and Jocelyn Ledoux, Katie Collins and two guys from the parish, John Delainey and Daniel Schultz.

Their sound was good, and their style was accentuated by the level of talent these young musicians possessed. They were all committed to the evangelical opportunity that their music provided. It was clearly evident that the Holy Spirit had blessed their work, for many people were drawn to the Lord through their ministry.

The second Friday *Praise Event* at St. James' Parish had become a huge success. The enthusiasm of the other musicians getting up to lead praise and worship was inspiring. Young people were coming out and getting on fire for their faith.

Brandon and Joanie loved the opportunity that *New Spring* gave them to use their music together for the Lord. Practices were never a chore, and performances were always a blessing. The energy on stage between these two was electric. Joanie and Brandon had worked on a few Christian love songs that they did together for wedding dances and concerts. No one could hear them perform and not be moved by the love that existed between them.

After one such performance, a guest from the wedding approached Brandon between sets.

"That's quite a group you have there, young man," the older gentleman began, offering Brandon his hand. Brandon was impressed with the firm handshake the silver-haired man gave him. "The name's Charles Gerbrandt."

"Nice to meet you, Charles. I'm Brandon Vaughn." Joanie walked up just then and taking her hand, Brandon introduced her to the gentleman.

"The pleasure is all mine, Joanie," Charles stated, emphatically.

Joanie greeted the distinguished man, her eyes dancing the way they always did.

Charles went on, "You two put across a powerful message in your music."

"Thank you," Brandon received the compliment.

"Not just because the music is excellent. It is that. But you two have something special there. Are you married?" Charles was leading to something, but neither Brandon nor Joanie knew just what.

Joanie smiled at the question, but she let Brandon answer. "No, sir. I have not yet had the honour of that blessing in my life."

Charles laughed. He was a big man and his face was so angular and business-like that the joviality of his laughter seemed out of place at first. "I take your meaning there, Brandon. Hang on to her, though, she's a real keeper, that one."

Joanie looked up at Brandon, a little awkward with all the attention. "Thank you," she returned to Charles, humbly.

"You know, the reason I'm interested in you two is because I'm involved in the recording industry myself. I'm from Calgary. Our company, *Music Alive*, works with up-and-coming recording artists in Christian music. We try to help them get a foot in the door. It's a big industry, and it's growing all the time. We like to help our Canadian artists along—recording, promoting them, distributing music, setting up concert tours."

Brandon was taking in everything Charles said. "I'm not sure what your interest is in us, sir."

"I'd just like for the two of you to keep me in mind." He reached into his pocket and offered Brandon his card. "Sometime in the future, near or far, if you think that's the direction you're being called, well, don't hesitate to contact me. I'll remember you.

"I'd be interested in this whole band for that matter. Your sound is tight and clean. You've got something here. But sometimes these pick-up bands are made up of people filling time on their way to a different dream.

"There's no rush. Think about it. Like I said, the industry's big and growing. If there's a calling for someone, it'll still be there a few years down the road."

He offered his hand again, noticing the band beginning to assemble for another set. "It's been a pleasure meeting you two. I hope to hear from you someday. And I hope you stay together. It'd be a shame for a couple with your dynamics to split up."

As Charles walked away, Brandon turned to catch Joanie's eye. She smiled up at him, waiting for his reaction.

"That was pretty sound advice he had there for us," Brandon commented.

"About music?" Joanie asked, innocently.

"About sticking together. Let the music sort itself out, in time." He fixed her in his steady gaze.

"It's awfully tempting," she stated.

"What, sticking together?" he asked, pointedly.

"Recording music, silly. The other will sort itself out, in time," she winked at him, as she teased.

Brandon laughed at her playfulness. The love between them was obvious and the energy of that love could be felt by all. Their desire to be together was so powerful that they needed to guard themselves in their expression of physical affection now more than ever. Joanie appreciated not only how Brandon kept that distance, but how he still found so many little ways of making her feel cherished. They stood there, absorbed in each other's loving gaze.

"That's close enough, you two," Mike called out, on his way by. "We've got a few more sets to get through tonight. . . . And if you two get any closer, you'll start to steam up the stage."

Joanie laughed and punched Mike in the arm on his way by. He was as close to her as a brother and just as fresh. They all took their places on stage to continue with the wedding dance.

✟   ✟   ✟

On the way home that night Brandon and Joanie discussed the opportunity that Charles Gerbrandt had presented to them. Brandon flipped the business card around in his fingers as he drove, thoughtfully pondering the entire situation.

Finally, he said, "I think we should wait on this. You're just starting your career at the station, and you've got your music degree to finish. I think this would be a big distraction right now. *New Spring* is a big enough commitment for us for the time being, and it's been a powerful ministry. . . . And Charles is right—if the calling is there, it'll wait for us."

"I feel the same way," she agreed.

He slipped the business card back into his pocket and picked up Joanie's hand in his. Gently caressing her soft hand with his fingers, he held it over the gearshift while he drove. Still his touch had the effect of thrilling her.

The lightly scented floral perfume that Joanie was wearing rose up to fill his every breath. It was as soft and sweet as the girl who wore it. Brandon wanted what was best for Joanie in their relationship. As much as he desired to have her for his wife, he knew that the time was not right, yet. But tonight had confirmed for them both a direction they had been discerning in their lives.

In time, he thought to himself, *in time*.

Chapter 39

Having been deprived of a family life when he was growing up, Brandon appreciated the opportunity to be a part of the Collins family. He came around as often as he could, while being careful not to wear out his welcome.

One afternoon in February, Brandon left work early in order to get to the Collinses before Joanie. He never drove her home from work, as they carefully guarded the cover they kept at the station.

He called out a greeting as he walked in, smiling at the sound of Judy singing away in the kitchen. He found her washing dishes at the sink. He washed up before grabbing a tea towel to help.

"Put that down," Judy reprimanded him. "I was letting God dry those dishes." She smiled at him as she took the towel and patted him on the back. "Here," she said, getting him a coffee, "I'd much rather enjoy a visit with you."

"Thank you," he said. "It smells good in here. What's for supper?"

"*Sgabetti,*" she said very seriously.

"Ahhh," he acknowledged. "It was Jessie's turn to pick tonight, was it?"

"Uh-hum," Judy laughed. It was so easy to be familiar with Brandon, because he had such an appreciation for all the children in their family.

"So, how did I manage to find you here, all alone?" he asked, looking around. "Your children are conspicuous by their absence," he teased her.

"I should say. It's so quiet in here, I can hardly think!" They laughed at the irony of it. "I sent them all off with Amie and Katie to the pool. They were so wild, I figured they needed the exercise to work off some energy. And after all the yelling I was doing, I figured they needed a break from me!"

"You? Yelling?" he questioned her.

"Oh, yes, me!" she asserted. "Don't be fooled by the good behaviour I put on when you're around, Brandon. Underneath this composed exterior lurks a haggard old mother."

"You're hardly haggard, Judy," he corrected her. "You're an amazing mother. And you will never be old—you're far too young at heart." His voice was openly sincere.

"Thanks, Brandon. But some days I really do feel old. And I have my fair share of faults; just ask Joanie. But you know," she said, walking over to him from the stove and putting a hand on his shoulder, "having you around so much has made a much better person out of me. It helps to keep me on my better behaviour."

He put his hand on hers and commented, "Well, if that's true, I'll have to come around more often."

She smiled down at him.

Brandon leaned against the back of the counter stool. He looked up at this woman, taking in the whole of her at once. He liked her so very much. He could see the mother's personality reflected in the daughter, which helped him to picture Joanie twenty-some years down the road.

Thinking about it, he realized Judy was a pretty feisty woman. Brandon tried to remember if he had ever seen her truly lose her cool. The incident of Isaac having used her good towels for an experiment with molasses and paints last summer came to mind. She had been pretty heated over that one, especially when she had threatened to turn Isaac into a science experiment himself. Brandon thought of Joanie with the same fiery spirit when she got worked up over something. They were women of passion, for sure.

Judy was, to Brandon, a tower of strength combined with true maternal gentleness. She had a firm sense of discipline, yet she was so much fun to be with. And he loved the way she freely played with her children. Judy's enthusiasm for life was absolutely contagious.

Their home was filled with music and laughter, interspersed with arguments and typical squabbles and the occasional row between Zack and Isaac. This was not a perfect family, just a family who knew how to love and how to forgive when they did not love as they ought.

He smiled up at Judy with one eyebrow raised, and his eyes piercing through her.

She shook her head and laughed. "There's that smile that made my daughter fall in love with you. You know, if I hadn't come to love you so much myself, I'd be afraid of you."

"Me?" he queried, defensively.

"Yes, *you!* With that handsome face and magnetic personality . . . my, you must have gotten into a lot of trouble in your past," she remarked, honestly and perceptively.

Brandon cast down his gaze. His demeanour revealed a certain shameful awareness.

Judy lifted his chin and met his eyes, lovingly as a mother does her child, and said softly, "I'm sorry. I didn't mean that the way it sounded. Do you know what makes goodness in a man so praiseworthy, Brandon? It's all the badness that he has to overcome through virtue. You, my dear young man, have demonstrated incredible virtue. And I trust you explicitly with my daughter because you have proven yourself to be so trustworthy."

Brandon fixed his eyes on Judy. He wanted so much to please her and to prove himself to her. He could never bring himself to betray her trust.

"Thank you, Judy. I'm sure it wasn't easy at first for you to let me into your family—what with my past and all."

"Actually, Brandon, it was easy to let you in, because I saw in you the spark of greatness. I didn't trust you back then, like I do now. And I have to admit, I have often wondered about your past, mostly for the sake of my daughter. Joanie has never talked about it with me. I worry about that sometimes."

"That's because she won't talk about it with me," Brandon stated, apparently frustrated over the subject. "I've tried to bring it up a few times. It's hard. I don't want to hurt her with it, but it's still there." He paused, reflectively. "Judy, if I could relive my life, I would have done things very differently. You know that, don't you?"

"Of course I do, Brandon," she affirmed him. "But praise be to God, He found you when He did."

"Thanks to Joanie," Brandon commented. Then with a certain determination, he asked, "What would you like to know about my past, Judy?"

"I'm not sure," she answered, not prepared for the question.

"You're just as bad as your daughter," he reprimanded respectfully, with a smile. "What concerns do you have for Joanie?"

"Well, Brandon," she began, pensively, "I suppose I'm mostly concerned about disease.... I'm quite aware that you've had numerous sexual partners in your past."

The words were like bullets in his chest. How he resented the truth of them. He looked Judy in the eye, as best he could. He knew the loving concern she had for her daughter, but it was her affection for him that helped him to get past his own shame.

"I've been to a doctor and have had the standard testing done, blood work and all. By the grace of God, all the tests have come back clear. I'll tell you this much, Judy . . . it was not for my sake, but for Joanie's, that I know God has spared me. I'll spend a lifetime making reparation for my past, but—somehow, miraculously—I'm not carrying any of those diseases."

Judy's eyes were full of love for Brandon. She knew how hard this was on him, and she appreciated his honesty and integrity in being able to discuss it with her openly. "Praise God," she said, softly. "Joanie knows this, does she?"

"She does," Brandon acknowledged.

"Well, Brandon, I've come to the conviction that your past is no longer what defines your character. I want you to know that. I see you now as the new and wonderful man that you have become in Christ. I know Joanie does as well. She'll deal with what she needs to from your past when she has to. She's strong in the Lord, and she's strong in her love for you."

Judy leaned down and kissed his cheek and said, "And I couldn't love you more if you were my own son!"

He was relieved to have finally discussed these things openly with Judy. Returning her affection, he replied, "I love you too, *Mom!*"

"Good," she said, returning to her pot at the stove. "Perhaps someday we can come to some sort of arrangement." She threw a glance over her shoulder at him, and he laughed at her innuendo.

"So, what's new with you these days?" she asked, changing the subject.

"Well," he said, leaning his forearms onto the island, "I was hoping to find a moment alone with you today to talk about Joanie's birthday on Saturday."

"Yes," her voice trailed off, as her thoughts were transported in time. "Twenty-three years old. My baby!" She smiled and looked over at Brandon. "Time flies by, Brandon. Make each moment worthwhile."

"I know," he commented, "I'm discovering that." He paused to allow her a moment of reminiscence.

Proceeding, he stated, "*New Spring* has a gig booked for Valentine's Day—Friday night. But, believe it or not, Saturday we're not booked. So what do you say if I take the whole family out to dinner to a really fancy restaurant that night?"

"Oh, no, Brandon, that's too much," she said, shaking her head.

"No, it isn't," he returned emphatically. "Judy, I have money and no one to spend it on, yet." Looking her straight in the eye, he said, "I want to do this . . . please."

She sighed and thought for a moment. "Fine," she answered, "if you think we can get Zack to eat with utensils. And if you can get John to agree to it."

"Yes, well, I won't worry about Zack's unusual eating style if you don't." He laughed, thinking of how the eight-year-old was able to find so many amusing ways to entertain himself with food as he dawdled through each meal. "And . . . I was kinda hoping you'd help me out with convincing John," he implored.

She laughed and agreed. Together they decided on a restaurant, a time and a plan to surprise Joanie. Brandon would pick Joanie up for dinner. But before taking her to the restaurant they would make a stop for something. That would give time for her family to get to the restaurant first, for the surprise.

Brandon insisted that Grandma and Grandpa Ledoux come as well. He loved to be around Judy's parents; they were an absolute inspiration to him.

All was set and Judy smoothed over the arrangements with John later that night.

Chapter 40

Brandon arrived at five-thirty sharp on Saturday to pick up Joanie. She was absolutely stunning with her hair pulled up and her elegant frame accentuated by a straight cut, crimson red dress. It was one of the dresses his mother had bought for her in Calgary at Christmastime. Red was her colour. He knew he would not be able to take his eyes off her, but then again, whenever could he? Her earrings hung down delicately, drawing attention to her distinctive jaw line and dainty neck. Wispy curls played around her face, neck and shoulders, framing her like the masterpiece she was.

Brandon stood there in his navy blue suit and tie. What a handsome couple they made. He smiled, speechlessly, but everyone in the room could sense his admiration for this girl's beauty. Finally, he mouthed, "Happy Birthday, beautiful!"

Joanie smiled shyly, as she always did when she felt herself holding Brandon's attentive gaze. She liked how he looked at her. It was never disrespectful or lustful. She felt loved and cherished by him and held highly in his esteem. Still, she was awkward receiving so much attention.

"Let's go," she said, softly. Brandon helped her slip on her coat and then pulled on his own. They made their good-byes quickly and left.

When Brandon pulled up to St. James Church, Joanie smiled. They often stopped at the church to pray before the Blessed Sacrament when they went out alone together. As they walked up to the church, Joanie drew her winter coat snugly around her. There was a sharp bite in the air this cold February night.

They stepped inside, took off their coats, and went into the church where they knelt down to pray in a pew near the front. After ten minutes or so of silence, Brandon took her hand in his and led them in prayer.

"Dear Jesus, I thank You for the many gifts You have given me in my life. I deserve none, but You have chosen to bless me in Your mercy with all these graces. Help me to use these gifts for Your glory, that You might use me to bring others to the light of Your truth. I'm nothing apart from Your love, Lord. I ask You to never let my heart grow proud, but to boast only in Your saving grace.

"I thank You especially, dear Jesus, for Your daughter, Joanie. Bless her on her birthday. Help me to love and cherish her always according to Your will. Keep us holy in our love. Keep us on the path of purity. Show us how to serve You through our love for each other that You would bring us both one day to Your heavenly kingdom. Amen."

"Amen." Joanie looked up at Brandon and smiled. The spiritual leadership he demonstrated in their relationship was something she had always prayed for in her future husband. It still amazed her at times that God could have taken such a perfect heathen and formed him into such an upright Christian man. God's power can never be underestimated!

Sitting back down on the pew, Brandon reached into his pocket and took out a small package, elegantly wrapped. He placed it into her hands and said, "Happy Birthday."

Joanie carefully peeled back the tape and opened the package. Inside there was a jeweller's box, long and narrow. On the top was a note in Brandon's writing which said: *Thank you for showing me where to find the pearl of great price.*

She looked at him inquisitively and opened the lid. Inside the box lay a delicate string of pearls.

"Oh, Brandon," she breathlessly said his name, "this is too much."

"No, it isn't. It's nothing compared to the pearl you gave me," he gently asserted. He took the string of pearls out of the box and carefully placed them around her graceful neck.

Brandon took her hand again in his. Softly, he spoke. "I love you, Joanie. I'd give my life for you. I gave you this gift because I want you to think of the Kingdom of Heaven each time you feel those pearls around your neck ... 'cause someday ... we're gonna be there together. And if it hadn't been for your love in my life, I might have missed out on that."

Tears softly rolled down her cheeks. Gently, he wiped them away. She reached up and took his hand. Bringing it to her lips, she kissed it softly. His heart warmed at her affection. She filled his life so full of love that there was not one thing he would not have done for her.

"Come on," he said, motioning with his head for them to get going. "I've got reservations for us at a restaurant." Turning back to the Blessed Sacrament, they each said a silent prayer, made the sign of the cross, and got up to leave.

✝   ✝   ✝

The restaurant was very elegant, and Joanie felt like a princess entering on the arm of her handsome prince. She was very aware of the blessing it was to have a man like Brandon who treated her like gold.

She reached up and touched the string of pearls laying delicately around her neck. A smile stole over her face as she dreamily lost herself in the thought of spending eternity with Brandon in the presence of the Lord.

So distracted was she that when the waiter led them up to their table, Joanie did not even recognize her family at first. The children were delighted to see that they had actually managed to surprise the birthday girl. Recovering from the start they had given her, she went over to kiss her grandparents, mother, and father.

John lifted the pearl necklace and held it between his fingers for a moment. With a look that took in his eldest daughter's beauty, he said to Brandon, "Someday, son, some young man might come along and put a string of pearls around your baby's neck. It's an occasion. And it's a good thing I'm so fond of you, boy!"

He threw a glance at Brandon that made Brandon stand a little taller, intimating that the father was still a factor in this girl's life and to keep that in mind.

Grandpa Ledoux watched the scene with great amusement and spoke across the table to Grandma. "Do you remember that day when some young man came along and swept off with our baby?"

"I do," Grandma answered, smiling at John who returned her look with a familiar wink.

Grandpa continued, reminiscently, "I don't recall a string of pearls, but I do remember it was an occasion."

"Oh, it certainly was, Grandpa," she agreed, adding, "especially when you took after him with that shotgun!"

Everyone laughed at the idea of it.

Grandpa Ledoux added, as an afterthought, "Come to think of it, it was an awfully good thing that I was fond of that boy . . . or I might just have used that gun!"

There was a rousing chorus of laughter around the table.

Brandon escorted Joanie to her seat and held out the chair for her to sit down.

"My, you're dashing!" exclaimed Katie, always the romantic. "I hope someday I find a man with such good manners and such good taste in jewellery!"

Brandon smiled at Katie and replied, "I have every confidence, Katie, that you will win the heart of any man of your choosing."

Katie's face lit up, her bright blue eyes shining out in stunning contrast to her dark hair. From her aristocratic nose to her perfectly poised manners, she had all the charm and grace of a noblewoman. Everyone knew that Brandon's words rang dangerously true.

Jessie piped up, "I'm not sitting over here acwoss fwom Joanie and Bwandon." She struggled to get out of her big chair. Brandon jumped to the rescue and went to the four-year-old's assistance. He swept her up in his strong arms, commenting on her beautiful dress and hairdo. She hugged him warmly and kissed him sweetly.

"You will sit here between us," Brandon announced to the little princess. "And I will sit here between you and Aaron. Right, buddy?"

Aaron nodded in agreement and gave Brandon a high-five.

The meal was a true adventure. Brandon watched with amusement as the younger children attempted to read the menu, pick meals, and discover the proper utensil for the appropriate course. Brandon had never before seen these children on such good behaviour. Their manners were truly impeccable, even Zack's, and Brandon marvelled at how they were all so able to rise to the occasion.

Grandma and Grandpa Ledoux entertained them all with stories of their childhood, how they had met and had fallen in love. Even Jessie was kept captivated as she crawled onto Brandon's knee and cuddled up to listen to the marvellous tales.

After the meal, Judy and John invited Brandon and the grandparents back to their house to have some birthday cake and keep the party going. Joanie went with her family to allow Isaac, Zack, Aaron, and Jessie to have a ride in Brandon's Pathfinder. They loved to go driving with him, especially when he would let them move the gearshift. Zack got to sit in the front seat this time, so that was his privilege.

After cake was served, Brandon caught John's attention and asked if they could speak in private. John nodded and they went downstairs to the music room. It was too cold to go out to his shop on a night like tonight.

"John," Brandon began, "I believe I owe you an apology, sir."

John looked at Brandon thoughtfully and allowed him to go on.

"I recognize now that it was an oversight on my part not to have consulted with you before giving that gift to Joanie."

John smiled and nodded, responding, "I accept your apology, Brandon."

"I want you to understand," Brandon explained, "that the monetary value of that gift means nothing to me. I have money, John. My father put me through school, bought me my first car. I live debt free. Now, I don't want to give you the impression that I throw around money on whims. But giving Joanie those pearls was symbolic of an even greater gift that I've received from her. It was not intended to be a status symbol of any kind."

"I appreciate that, Brandon," John replied.

"The love I share with Joanie, the friendship and warmth that I've felt in your home from your family, the mentoring I've received from you, John, is worth more to me than any string of pearls. I value these things far more than money." Brandon looked John squarely in the eyes.

"You know," John commented, "I had a sense, right from the first time we met, that God was working powerfully in your life, Brandon. I still stand in awe when I see what a transformation there's been in your life since your conversion."

"You do realize, of course, that *that* is completely a gift of God's grace. I'm not sure why He has fortified me with such spiritual convictions. But I'm not about to question Him on it either." Brandon laughed with John and went on. "As far as I see it, God has blessed me with this strength for Joanie's sake. I was so completely undeserving of her love. But God supplies that for which I lack . . . and I'm so grateful He has chosen me to be in her life. She's an amazing woman, and I assure you, John, my intentions are still honourable regarding your daughter."

John's smile communicated his confidence in Brandon's integrity. Acquiring a serious look, John asked, "I'm curious, Brandon. . . ."

"Go ahead," Brandon nodded the older man on.

"You know I trust you with Joanie; that goes without saying. But do you ever struggle with sexual temptations now in your life?"

Brandon appreciated the boldness of Joanie's father. His protective love for his family caused him to never shy away from important issues. "That depends on what you mean when you say 'sexual temptations'. If you're wondering if I'm ever tempted back to my old lifestyle, the answer is . . . no!" Brandon replied, humbly. "I know that might seem hard to believe when you take into account my past. But it's true. I'm so repulsed by the notion of sexual sin now, that it doesn't tempt me in the slightest.

"Don't get me wrong. I still have sexual desires. . . . I'm a man. And I do struggle at times with impure thoughts. When I least expect it, images will come into my head that I have to fight to be rid of. There are times I wake up from dreams at night that just leave me in tears. . . . It makes me so ashamed now that I ever lived like that, John. I wish I could remove every memory. But those memories never tempt me back to sin. If anything, they keep me on track because I never want to be that kind of man again.

"To be honest, my greatest struggle is my desire for Joanie. I have to remind myself that as long as she is not my wife, I'm not at liberty to imagine what it'll be like when she finally is, someday. It's a challenge to be pure in heart—I don't know if I'll ever get there, John!"

John laughed at Brandon's frankness. "Well, Brandon, to be honest with you, I still struggle with that virtue myself. I'm a man as well, so I understand what you're talking about. But it's only in recognizing our weaknesses that we ever come to depend on God for strength. If we keep handing it over in prayer, honestly confessing our sins to God, and if we sincerely seek His righteousness . . . someday, He assures us, we will be pure in heart. We won't see God face to face until we are."

Brandon nodded, appreciating the support he felt from John. "I won't stop working at it. And let me assure you, John, my love for Joanie is far greater than my desire for her physically. I could never bring myself to sin against her purity or to go against the love that God has shown me and called me to in my life."

"I don't doubt your integrity in that matter at all, Brandon," John assured the young man. "You know, I've often wondered how you were able to turn your back and walk away from your old life the way you did."

Brandon shook his head in amusement, thinking back on his conversion. "It took me almost a whole month, just to wake up to what God was doing in my life—"

"A month?" John cut in. "You do realize that it takes many people years? And at that, some still don't get it!"

Brandon's eyes revealed his humility; there was no pride on his part in this matter. "I suppose," he acknowledged John's statement. "But a month of that turmoil was more than enough for me! And once the Holy Spirit finally broke through my dullness and opened my eyes to the truth, there was no turning back. Do you want to know what it's like? I'll tell you what I compare it to. . . .

"A boy that's been brought up to become a Nazi soldier can't really understand how sinful the deeds are that he carries out under orders. Sure, there's got to be an inkling, but he might not experience any regret for his actions. But then one day God opens his eyes to the truth. That soldier can no longer go on being a Nazi. So he runs away, escapes with his life and begins to live for God. He can't undo his past, no matter how much remorse he has now. But is he ever tempted to go back and commit those sins again? Never!

"I know the analogy isn't perfect, but I assure you, in my opinion, the sins I committed in my life were just as offensive to God as those of that Nazi soldier. I know God's completely forgiven me for my past. And I have to remind myself that no one is deserving of His mercy, so it's not for me to question it. . . . I just accept it, as humbly as I can. You know what makes God's grace so amazing? It's that He pours it out on undeserving wretches like me!"

John put his hand on Brandon's shoulder. "Once again, Brandon, you've managed to inspire me with your faith."

Brandon's eyes revealed a certain shock. "I don't understand, John."

"Brandon, you have no idea how you inspire us all with your pursuit of holiness. We're all on this journey together. Sometimes the fuel that sparks a conversion like yours propels a man down that path at record speed. It's hard for the rest of us to keep up with you." John chuckled at the young man before him, still so on fire with the power of the Holy Spirit. "Sure, you've got maturing to do in your faith. We all do. But your determination is what reminds us all to try harder for the Lord each day. You've blessed us so much, Brandon, and I thank you for that."

Brandon had been looking down, humbly receiving John's acclamation. Lifting his eyes back up to the man before him, he said, quietly, "Thank you, John."

"And just so that we're clear on the matter," John questioned, pointing toward Brandon in a clarifying manner, "in the event that you and Joanie break up someday, are you telling me that I'm free to hock those pearls to help pay down my mortgage?"

Shaking his head and chuckling, Brandon replied, "Whatever you do with the money you get from them is between you and Joanie!" He put his hands up before him so as to absolve himself from any responsibility in the matter. Smiling, he added, "I just hope it never comes to that."

"I'll drink to that!" John agreed wholeheartedly. "Come on. Let's get back up there; we've got a birthday party waiting for us." John opened the door of the music room and motioned for Brandon to go ahead. They returned upstairs to a lively singsong in the living room, with Grandpa entertaining the troops.

Soon everyone took a turn in the spotlight, prompted by John to perform. There was no shortage of talent in that crowd. Different children sang and played instruments for the family audience. Even Jessie got in on the act. Standing proudly, she imitated her older siblings, singing right in tune, even though she did not pronounce all the words correctly. Then together the family sang some old-time songs, until Judy finally announced bedtime for the little ones.

Grandma and Grandpa headed home.

Jessie and Aaron whined and complained about bedtime until Brandon promised piggyback rides for the youngest members of the Collins household once they were ready for bed. He carried them up and tucked them in, blessing them each on the forehead, as he did. Joanie joined him, and they led the younger children in bedtime prayers. It was inspiring for Brandon to witness the beauty and simplicity of faith that he saw in these children.

Joanie and Brandon rejoined the older half of the family for a drink, card games, and more stories. The evening grew quite late and Judy said to Brandon, "It's such a cold winter night. Now, I know you have that fancy remote start and all, but you're welcome to stay over—if sleeping on the couch appeals to you."

Brandon accepted the gracious offer, and she gave him some bedding and some towels.

John shook Brandon's hand and thanked him once more for the excellent evening. They all said their good-nights, and everyone went off to bed.

☦   ☦   ☦

Joanie lay awake for some time, reliving the events of the day. Softly, she heard Maggie's voice in the darkness, "Joanie are you still awake?"

"Uh-huh," Joanie replied.

"So am I," Amie said.

"Me, too," Katie called out from her top bunk.

"Thank you," Maggie went on, "for bringing Brandon into the family. I don't think I could bear the thought of you getting married to someone who didn't love the rest of us the way Brandon does."

"I know what you mean," Amie agreed. "He's the best big brother any girl could ever ask for!"

"He's so much fun to have around," Katie added.

Joanie lay in the darkness of the room, smiling to herself. It meant everything to her that Brandon was now considered a part of their family. She responded to her sisters, "Thank you for making Brandon so welcome in our home."

"Are you going to get married soon?" Amie inquired.

"I don't know," Joanie answered, truthfully. "To be honest, we haven't discussed it that much yet. We know that we both want it. It's just, well, we're trying to live in the present and not get preoccupied by the future."

"Have you and Brandon ever kissed?" Katie's curiosity was getting the better of her.

"Not on the lips," Joanie answered.

"Good for you!" Maggie rejoined the conversation with enthusiasm. "I mean if I were ever to fall in love, I would make him wait a long time, too. I think it increases a man's attention to a woman when he has to really earn her affection."

"For a girl who never wants to get married," Joanie remarked, "you sure have done a lot of thinking on the subject, Maggie."

"I've been watching you and Brandon for some time now. I think it's wonderful the way the two of you are together. I've never sensed so much love between a boyfriend and girlfriend before. And I've come to the conclusion it's because all that energy isn't being spent on, you know—physical stuff.

"You've got all that love and attention and respect from your man,

Joanie, because you pour out your love for each other in simple ways. There's a look here or holding hands there, you sneak in a little peck on the cheek from time to time. But it's never done selfishly.

"Don't compromise that, Joanie. You and Brandon have the makings for a lifetime of happiness. I just know God has blessed you both for your faithfulness. I'm proud of you." Maggie's voice was full, as she spoke slowly and thoughtfully.

Joanie got out of bed and went to Maggie's bedside and hugged her sister. "Maggie, I don't think I would be able to consider marrying Brandon if he hadn't become such a part of our family. Thank you for blessing us with your love!"

They held on, both of them sensing time lurking at the door, waiting for the opportunity to steal them away from each other. By this time Amie and Katie had joined them, and Joanie pulled them in for a group hug.

"My love for you all is what keeps me on the right track. I would never betray the confidence you have in me. I thank God for each day we have left together in this home." On the verge of tears, all four girls soon found themselves laughing.

Judy stood outside the bedroom door. She had been wakened by the noise and had come to see what the problem was. When she realized what was happening, she did not want to interrupt the scene.

She crawled back into bed and snuggled up to John who wrapped his arm around her and sleepily asked, "Is everything all right?"

Judy smiled and kissed him on the chest where her head was lying, and murmured dreamily, "Everything is perfect, dear. Praise be to Jesus."

Her heart swelled with maternal love as she brought to mind the picture of her daughters. A tear rolled slowly down her cheek. She knew exactly how they all felt.

Chapter 41

The next morning Brandon was up bright and early, wakened by the enthusiastic greetings of Zack, Aaron, and Jessie. It was the price to be paid for sleeping over, but he did not mind at all. After Aaron and Zack's failed attempts to draw Brandon into a pillow fight, Jessie snuggled up beside him on the couch.

Brandon managed to convince the boys to go play across the room with some toys. Somewhere in the course of conversation Zack got into a show and tell session, proudly displaying the warts on his feet. Katie came walking into the room and saw Zack showing off his warts to Brandon.

"Zack, stop being so disgusting! Brandon doesn't want to see your warts," she reprimanded the child, her face distorted by repulsion.

"It's okay," Brandon assured her, "boys are disgusting, Katie. We can't help ourselves."

"That's true for these boys, but you are hardly disgusting, Brandon," Katie returned.

"Not as much as I used to be," he laughed. "But then again, it's been years since I had warts."

Katie smiled at Brandon. Still repulsed by the wart show, she led Zack out of the room to ensure that he washed his hands.

Brandon laughed as he began to get up off the couch. It was the little things of family life that were so amusing to him.

Joanie came down to join them. As she stood at the door of the living room, Brandon looked up to greet her and sat back down on the couch. Her hair hung down loosely over her shoulders. She had on a T-shirt and blue jeans, but she still looked like a queen to her admirer.

"Good-morning, beautiful," he greeted her.

A smile lit up her face, as fresh and beautiful as any sunrise. She came over to the couch to sit beside him, taking Jessie onto her knee. Joanie lightly kissed Brandon on the cheek and softly said, "Good-morning, handsome."

"I'm not so sure about that," he confessed. "I could really use a shower."

"Shower or not, you can't help but be handsome," she returned, her eyes sparkling up at him.

"Beauty is in the eyes of the beholder," he reminded her.

"In your case Brandon, I wish that were true, but it isn't," she stated. He looked at her questioningly. She added, "I'm afraid women will always find you temptingly handsome."

"I'm not interested in other women," he assured her.

"No, but they'll be interested in you, all the same," she said, plainly.

He pondered Joanie's statement for a moment. He watched as Jessie climbed down off Joanie's knee and began to play with Aaron and Zack who had returned from washing his hands. Brandon looked down at Joanie and asked, "Does that bother you?"

"Sometimes," Joanie confessed. "Good looks can be a curse, Brandon, as you know from your past."

Brandon was surprised that Joanie would make that reference. Maybe she had spoken with her mother. He was not sure. Taking her hand in his, he questioned her, "Are you afraid I'll regress in my convictions?"

"Heavens, no!" Joanie exclaimed, looking up at him. "I thank God that He's given you such a strong faith. Any man as handsome as you has to be strong in the Lord . . . and you are." She held onto his hand with both of hers and put her head on his shoulder.

Brandon sat quietly for a moment. It was true what Joanie had said. Women had always made themselves easily available to Brandon, merely based on his looks. He thought about his past, how empty and shallow all those relationships had been. It was like looking at someone else's life now—Brandon was so disassociated with that lifestyle. It amazed him that he ever could have been so blind.

He wondered if Joanie did not completely trust him, but as he felt the weight of her head leaning on his shoulder, he relaxed. She trusted him absolutely; he knew that. She had simply stated a fact. He turned and gently kissed the top of her head. He looked forward to the day when he would wake up every morning to have her by his side.

"I love you," he whispered.

She turned her face up to meet his gaze and murmured softly, "I love you, too, handsome!" She winked at him, assuring him of her confidence.

"Well, as much as I hate to do this, I've got to go," he stated.

"So soon?" she asked, disappointment apparent in her voice.

"I've got to get home, shave and shower for church. Did you forget it's Sunday morning?" he teased her.

"No," she answered, distractedly. She lightly touched her fingers to his grizzly chin. "It's a shame you have to shave, though," she said, enjoying that rugged, unshaven look.

He turned and pushed her hand away with his rough chin. "If you don't cut that out, I'll give you a whisker rub," he scolded her.

"Cut what out?" Judy's voice entered the scene.

The young couple looked up to see Judy standing in the large doorway between the front hall and living room. She was trying to look severe with her hands on her hips, but her brilliant eyes gave away her playfulness.

With a twinkle in his eyes, Brandon answered her, "I hate to inform you, Mrs. Collins, but your daughter is a tease."

Judy laughed and shook her head. "Like mother, like daughter, Brandon. But go ahead—give her a whisker rub anyway."

"Mom!" Joanie exclaimed, jumping sideways on the couch to get out of Brandon's reach.

Brandon grabbed her by the arm and pulled her back. Joanie struggled to keep her face away from his. He finally managed to give her a small and gentle whisker rub.

Judy shook her head with disappointment and said, "Now Brandon, how's that ever gonna teach her not to tease again? You're such a softy." She winked and continued on into the kitchen.

Joanie punched Brandon on the shoulder, but he just laughed and took her into his arms for a gentle hug. She could never stay angry, even playfully angry, with this man.

"I'm leaving now. I'll see you at church in a few hours," he said as he got up to leave.

☦   ☦   ☦

The first Sunday of Lent was a particularly important milestone along Brandon's journey into the Catholic Church. According to the R.C.I.A. program this was the Sunday that all of the Catechumens gathered with the bishop for the Rite of Election. Mike stood with Brandon. All of the Ledoux family and the Collins family had come out for the event.

Bishop Alphonse spoke beautifully, explaining how the history of Lent was very much connected to the process of initiation into the Church. The early Christians first observed a Lenten penitential season in preparation for Baptism.

Since then, Lent had become a practice in the Church for spiritual renewal of all the faithful. Through prayer, fasting, and almsgiving, Christians made the effort to place God at the centre of their lives and to turn away from the selfish tendencies of fallen human nature. It was in imitation of Christ who faithfully battled with Satan in the desert, that Christians engaged in a period of self-denial and purification.

So the Catechumens were initiated into the period of Enlightenment and of Purification. The bishop spoke eloquently, challenging the Catechumens, and indeed all Christians, to embrace the truth of the faith.

"Truth is not a mere ideology, but a person. That person is Jesus Christ. Embrace Truth," he exhorted them. "Live in Truth and defend Truth, knowing that you are embracing Jesus Christ, living in Jesus Christ, and

defending Jesus Christ. It's in this way that your faith will be real . . . and it will be personal . . . and your lives will be filled with joy and light. And the light of Truth in you will draw people to Jesus."

Mike and his family joined the Collinses that night for supper, celebrating the fact that Brandon was now one step closer to full initiation into the Church. It was a grace-filled time for all.

Through Brandon's eyes, they appreciated so much more what they already had in Baptism. Through Brandon's humility, they all felt the challenge to daily conversion of the heart. And through Brandon's enthusiasm to grow in holiness, they all became more focussed on living each moment for Christ.

Chapter 42

Monday night racquetball was boys' night out. Brandon and Mark were like brothers; they always had been. With all the strains in their relationship over the past several months, Brandon guarded this night together even more.

Each week he could see an improvement in Mark's disposition. Gradually the bitterness of Justine's conversion was wearing off, and Mark had grown to be more relaxed in the company of his friends.

Mark had not been thrilled at first about dating Justine from her parents' home. He had never gotten along with the Fosters. Her parents had resented Mark for shacking up with their daughter and—he had come to realize—rightfully so. There was a lot of history between Mark and this family, and much healing was in order. But over time, he found he was no longer forcing the effort to get along with Justine's folks. A genuine relationship had begun to form.

Mark and Justine were making an effort to spend much more time together with both their families. Mark had come to admire Justine's sense of commitment to her parents and her sister. In turn, the young man had discovered a renewed respect and appreciation for his own parents and his younger brother. It was like he was getting to know them all for the first time. He was now able to see just how warm and rich the love between his parents really was—it was inspiring.

Mark was also beginning to discover all kinds of things about himself. When Justine had cut off the physical relationship, he had worried that they would no longer have any interest in each other. Instead, he found that he and Justine really did have a lot in common. They were now enjoying doing so many more things together than they had ever done before. Overall, Mark was happier than he had ever anticipated he could be under these circumstances.

What impressed Brandon the most was a certain nobility in Mark that was surfacing. In his effort to prove himself to Justine and her family, he was becoming a much more responsible person. Like what had happened to Brandon, Mark was growing up!

Brandon did not push the religion thing too much. He knew this was a sensitive issue between Mark and himself. But one Monday night, after a gruelling game of racquetball, Mark gave his friend a complete shock. He invited Brandon and Joanie to come out to a dance sponsored by his parents' church. The Jacobs really wanted Mark and Justine to come, but Mark felt awkward about it, not knowing anybody else there. He was looking for support from the only Christian friends he had. Brandon was more than happy to accept the invitation.

✝   ✝   ✝

Arriving at Rosedale Community Church, the two young couples went inside for the dance. It amused his friends to watch Mark's tentative behaviour. Justine held onto his arm and pulled him along. They all knew that the temptation for him to bolt was very real.

Brandon laughed and slapped Mark on the back, "Hang in there, buddy. Christians don't normally feed pagans to the lions!"

Mark looked curiously at Brandon, remembering the conversation he had had with Pastor Kline the night he had stormed out. He had never told Brandon the details of that conversation.

Strange emotions stirred in him at the memory of Pastor Kline's uncanny intervention in his life. Things had changed that night, for sure. Mark was now a different man. He had not really stopped to reflect on that until Brandon's off-handed comment had brought it to the forefront of his mind.

"Are you okay, pal?" Brandon asked, sensing Mark's preoccupation.

Mark shook off the distraction and stammered something. Brandon exchanged a look with the two girls; they all sensed that the Holy Spirit was at work here.

They entered the beautifully decorated hall attached to the church. There was music playing and a wonderful atmosphere of fellowship filled the room.

Pastor Kline came over at once to greet Mark and meet his friends. Mark began the introductions, but when he got to Brandon the kindly pastor smiled and took Brandon's hand, saying, "Brandon, I remember you well! Welcome, son."

"Well, try not to remember me too well from back then," Brandon implored him, with a lightness in his voice. "It's good to see you again, too, Pastor."

Brandon had a quick flashback of the pastor and his wife visiting at the Jacobs' home when Brandon was about fourteen: Brandon and Mark were out in the back, looking at some dirty magazines that they had won in a poker game from some older boys. He pushed the memory out of his mind and quickly thanked God for having delivered him from that meaningless existence.

The group walked in and sat at a table near the front of the hall. There were only a few people up on the dance floor, but that did not intimidate Justine. She grabbed Mark's hand and led him out to dance.

Joanie wanted to dance as well, but Brandon stopped her. He pulled her close and motioned for her to sit back and watch.

Justine was a well trained ballroom dancer and had introduced Mark to the art. It was something they loved to do together and they did it well. They truly were poetry in motion on the dance floor. It was wonderful to see Mark wrapped up again in Justine's charm. Brandon prayed that Mark would continue to grow in a pure and holy love for this graceful woman.

Joanie's heart delighted at the sight of this inspiring couple. She could sense Mark shedding off the hurtful burden that had clouded his perception of Justine's new life in Christ. Justine was so exquisitely beautiful and so naturally graceful. Her eyes shone like diamonds and her love for Mark was most apparent in the way she fixed her gaze upon him.

It was good to see the love rekindled between these two, only it was no longer a selfish and insecure love. It was deep and wholesome, and there was a mutual respect that had transformed their old relationship. Joanie prayed intensely for them.

After a few dances Brandon took Joanie by the hand and led her out to the dance floor. He whispered apologetically into her ear, "I can't show you off like Mark does Justine, but I'd be honoured if you would dance with me anyway."

"That's okay," Joanie confessed, "I don't dance like Justine. But if you don't mind mingling with an amateur like me, I'd be happy to dance with you for the rest of my life."

He swept her up into his arms and softly held her in his embrace. The feeling of Joanie's small frame held close to him stirred all kinds of protective and sheltering instincts in Brandon. He wanted so much to marry her and take her into his home, fill it with their children and build a life together.

Joanie was lost in Brandon's piercing blue eyes. She saw in him all the nobility and greatness he possessed. Desiring nothing more than to pour out her love on him completely, she longed for the day when they would be united as one in Christ.

After a few dance numbers, a praise song that they recognized began. They sang out and soon they were both transported into the realm of worship. Mark and Justine had taken a break, and they sat back, observing. The floor, by now, was filled with many people, children and adults alike. Mark had never experienced anything like this before. For him, the sight of these people caught up in praise was unbelievably moving.

He set his eyes on Brandon and Joanie in particular. Whatever it was that Brandon had discovered in his new-found faith, Mark could see that it was real. He knew this man well, and what Mark witnessed in Brandon's expression was not put on. He sincerely was praising God. Joanie was absolutely radiant. And when Mark glanced at Justine—who sat sweetly at his side, holding his hand—her eyes revealed that she, too, had been swept away in the spirit of the praising throng.

Mark looked down at her hand in his. Funny, how they now held hands again. It seemed that their love had become completely new. In the warmth and affection that she freely poured out on him, he had come to realize that he did not miss the sexual relationship as much as he thought he would. While he still desired Justine, he was now committed to waiting for her until marriage.

The engagement ring on her finger sparkled up at him. A smile stole over his face at the thought that Justine would soon be his wife. Mark had grown in a real appreciation for the value of the marital covenant after he and Justine had attended a C.C.E. course on Christian marriage. Justine had accepted his proposal because Mark had proven to her that he understood and was willing to live according to the Church's teachings. He would never again ask her to compromise her faith.

While Mark could not give his assent of faith, he had come to accept the rational arguments presented by the Church against premarital sex and contraception. In his own experience, so far, he acknowledged the difference in his respect for Justine since they had begun to abstain. He knew that he truly had grown in love for her.

What he had come to realize was that abstinence demands respect, self-control, self-discipline, maturity, and responsibility. The fruit of all these things, he recognized, would be fidelity and, as some couples referred to it, 'stick-with-it-ness' in tough times.

He knew his parents had a good marriage, even though they did not practise Natural Family Planning. But he was shocked to find out that a little more than fifty percent of Christian marriages ended up in divorce. Christians were doing no better than the general population in this regard. Meanwhile, couples who practised Natural Family Planning had a less than five percent divorce rate.

Mark was an engineer; he knew that with the correct formula any job was made easier. He saw the Catholic Church's teaching on marriage in that light. It was simple math, and he was willing to apply the formula. He did not want for Justine and him to end up as a divorce statistic. Furthermore, if he wanted Justine for a wife, which he now did with all his heart, he knew there would be no compromising on this matter.

Mark had truly come to admire the changes he had witnessed in Justine since her conversion. She was warmer and more affectionate with him than before. Her character had taken on a new strength that was truly admirable. Mark knew that this strength came from her faith in Jesus. At times he jealously wished that he could share in it with her.

As his thoughts turned back to the people on the dance floor, he experienced a revelation. He admired Justine, Brandon, Joanie, and his parents for their faith. He marvelled at it and had even jealously desired it at times. But he had never once tried to pray to ask Jesus for it. Indeed, he felt he would have been a hypocrite to pray to someone in whom he did not believe. It dawned on him now that he would never get to the point of knowing if Jesus was real if he did not pray to ask Jesus to reveal Himself.

Mark's entire being was suddenly flooded by an overwhelming desire to pray. He closed his eyes and began.

Jesus, if You are real, please give me the faith to believe in You!

It was a simple prayer, but it was sincere and from the heart. He could not form any more words. He was compelled to an interior peace which shut out the entire world around him. Mark rested in that peace, his eyes still closed.

What happened to Mark just then was something that he could not easily understand. He just knew that Jesus was real and that Jesus was calling him to believe. There were no words that he heard. There was no voice that spoke to him. Yet in that silence, Mark felt God's presence, and something changed inside of him.

Mark had always relied on his intellect to know and understand things. For the first time in his life Mark became aware that there was something within him more powerful than the mind itself. As he felt his will drawn toward faith in Jesus, he realized that the intellectual understanding of that faith was secondary. That would follow. What was important now was to seek out truth with all his heart and with all his mind. And Mark had come to believe, in that moment of revelation, that truth was to be found in Jesus Christ.

Justine had felt Mark's hand loosen on her own, and she looked up at him. His eyes were closed, and she saw on his face a peace that she knew could only come from the Lord. Her heart leapt within her, and she immediately began to pray for Mark. She begged Jesus to pour out His love into Mark's heart and to make him new, just as she had been made new in His love.

After a short time, Mark opened his eyes and looked at Justine. She was watching him, with intense emotion. He smiled at her, and she knew that he had been touched by the power of the Holy Spirit. She threw her arms around his neck, and he held her tightly.

Whispering softly, he said, "I never tried to pray before. But Jesus answered my prayer, and I know now that He's real."

Justine was crying when Brandon and Joanie returned to the table. Brandon made a quick summation that the tears were of joy. The expression on Mark's face told him that something had changed. Brandon returned a look to Mark that told him he understood, for he too had met his Creator in a wonderful moment of revelation.

Changing his demeanour, Mark shot a look at them all, with his usual wit and calmness and asked, "Why did none of you ever suggest to me to try praying?"

Brandon laughed and grabbed Mark's hand in a handshake and said, "Welcome aboard, mate!"

The two couples enjoyed an evening of celebration. The dance had been wonderful. The praise and worship had been awesome. And there was a real solidarity in their midst, for as they left the hall that night, they knew that they were now united in faith.

✝   ✝   ✝

Sunday morning found a new man sitting in the pews of St. James Church. Justine held onto Mark's hand as they attended Mass together for the first time. Mark laughed, in spite of himself, for he truly did feel at home here.

While he did not understand much about what was happening in the Mass, Mark was genuinely moved by the music. He resolved, though, to take some time to study about the Mass, since he knew that if he wanted to attend church with his bride, this was where it would be.

He appreciated the Scripture readings and the homily. He reminisced over childhood Bible study classes and decided he would get a Bible and read it. He also determined that he should attend a Bible study with Justine. He loved the thrill of academic pursuit, but now that Jesus was real to him, there was a personal reason for studying Scripture.

Joanie and Brandon joined up with Mark and Justine after Mass and introduced them to Joanie's family. They stayed and visited for awhile, but Mark and Justine had promised to spend the day with her family, and so they left.

After they were gone, Brandon took Joanie by the hand, and they went back into the church to pray before the Tabernacle. It was their custom to spend quiet time after each Mass to thank God for the gift of Christ in the Eucharist. Today, they also prayed in thanksgiving for Mark's conversion.

✝   ✝   ✝

That Thursday afternoon at work, Taylor, the resident self-proclaimed hedonist, walked into the lunchroom with an obvious bone to pick with Brandon.

"So, Brandon," he began his offence, "what keeps a guy like you busy after working hours, lately? I mean, I never hear you talk about your wild weekends anymore. In fact you seem to have slipped off the face of the earth. You don't show up much, and when you do you've got nothing to boast about." He waited for a response.

Brandon was taken aback, wondering what it was that Taylor had figured out about him. Was it religion, or Joanie, or both? "I'm not sure why you're asking, Taylor," Brandon responded, displaying his typical calmness.

"I have a cousin who goes to the Rosedale Community Church," Taylor went on.

Brandon was listening and nodding.

"She tells me she met a couple from the station Saturday night there at a dance. And it turns out to have been you and Joanie. You remember, that hot little number that started here at the station last June."

Brandon winced interiorly at the boorishness of that reference to Joanie, which *he* had first made to Taylor when Joanie had begun working at the station.

"So 'fess up, boy, I'm listening." Taylor stood facing Brandon, his legs set in a bold stance, arms crossed proudly over his chest. His dark eyes flashed like lightning under the crop of bleach-streaked hair that poked up in gelled peaks on top of his head.

"Well," Brandon began, grateful that Joanie was out on an assignment and not there to bear the brunt of the attack. By this time several other co-workers, including Shelly Lesichyn, had gathered around. Their curiosity was peaked by Taylor's explosive entrance. "Your cousin was right. We were there," Brandon acknowledged.

"Details, man! Did you go and get yourself messed up with that Christian troublemaker, after all my warnings?" Taylor's voice conveyed real disappointment in Brandon.

"Yes, Taylor, I did. And it's worse than that, because I've become a Christian now, too. So what can I say?" Brandon was calm and cool, unruffled by Taylor's dramatic display.

At this point Shelly stepped into the conversation, saying, "I think it's wonderful, Brandon. Welcome to the family." As she left the lunchroom, she gave Brandon a look that told him not to worry about company policy: he had her blessing, as Senior Producer at the station.

Brandon returned a look of acknowledgment to Shelly. Then, in an attempt to calm Taylor, Brandon commented, "I didn't bother telling you, 'cause I figured you wouldn't be interested. But I'd be happy to share with you anything about the faith that you want to know."

"Bahhh!" Taylor waved his arm past Brandon's face, somewhat discouraged that he had not managed to shake Brandon at all. Then a wily smile took claim of his face, and he added in a taunting voice, "So Brandon and Joanie, the Christian couple. No wonder you've got nothing to boast about. You've been cut off—and in your prime!"

Brandon shook his head in disagreement, "No, Taylor, I'm just finally beginning to live."

With that he left the lunchroom and headed back to his office.

☩ ☩ ☩

Later that afternoon, a knock at his office door interrupted Brandon from his work.

"I guess the jig's up!" The man's voice came from across the room.

Brandon turned to see Paul, standing in the doorway, smiling. "So it seems," Brandon concurred, smiling in his usual way.

"Well, it's about time," Paul stated, leaning comfortably against the door frame.

"How so?" Brandon asked.

"Your love affair with Joanie was far too good to keep it a secret for too long. Personally, I'm glad Taylor exposed you—although, diplomacy was never really his forte!" Paul shook his head, laughing over the thought of the spiky-haired technician.

"No, it sure isn't," Brandon agreed, with a laugh. "But, I'm grateful too," he added. "Does Joanie know yet?" Brandon asked.

"Tessa greeted us with the news when we got back from our shoot a little while ago," Paul explained.

"How'd she take it?" Brandon inquired, with concern.

"Like the trooper that she is," Paul smiled. "She was a little nervous at first, but when Tessa explained that Shelly had been there and had offered her approval, Joanie relaxed."

Brandon nodded, thoughtfully.

"And I warned her," Paul continued, lifting his finger in the air playfully reproving, "I don't want to find the two of you smooching in the corners around here—now that you no longer need to keep a cover on things."

Brandon shook his head, "No fear of that, my friend," he asserted.

"Apparently not," Paul added, reaching up to his shoulder. "I've got a bruise here where Joanie hit me to prove that!"

"That's my little spitfire!" Brandon acknowledged proudly. "Don't mess with her, Paul—she's a real feisty one!"

"So I've learned," the cameraman stated, rubbing his shoulder. "But then again, I suppose a girl with any less personality than that would never have brought you along as far as she has, my one-time hedonistic colleague."

"Admittedly so, Paul," Brandon replied. "She keeps me on my toes, that's for sure. And I wouldn't have it any other way, now that I've found her."

"Well, I've come to a real appreciation for the new and improved Brandon myself," Paul said with open admiration. Motioning his intention to leave he said, "But I'd better let you get back to your work. Catch you around, lover boy!"

"See you 'round, Paul," Brandon chuckled, shaking his head at his friend. Turning back to his work he wondered how Joanie was doing with all this sudden attention. It felt good not to have to hide his relationship with her anymore. Still he decided that it would be best to continue their policy of keeping a low profile as a couple at work and that way keep the pressure off themselves.

As he reflected on the entire situation, there was a feeling of liberation that came over him. He realized that Taylor, through his boisterousness, had freed Brandon to be himself at work: a Christian. He welcomed the opportunity to bear witness to the Gospel.

Leaning back in his chair and locking his fingers together behind his head, he uttered, "God bless you, Taylor!"

Chapter 43

Lent was quickly drawing to a close. A few weeks before Holy Week, Brandon decided to spend two days in a silent retreat at a nearby monastery. He wanted the opportunity to turn off all the distractions of the world in order to focus on the meaning of the new life in which he would soon partake through his Baptism. He collected some excellent reading materials and set off early one Saturday morning for his adventure in solitude.

The monastery was a magnificent place. It was located on a hill, situated in the middle of a beautiful property covered in trees that stretched out over ten acres of land. There were beautifully carved-out paths through the woods. These led to any number of little nooks and openings which offered opportunities for seclusion and quiet reflection.

It was mid-March now, and there had been a snowfall overnight that had left a shimmering white blanket over all of creation. It made everything seem fresh and beautiful, almost surreal. The whole scene lay out before Brandon like a make-believe world in a faraway land. He felt that here he was truly removed from the fast-pace of society. Even the trees had a lazy charm about them as they glistened under the cover of new-fallen snow in the morning light.

He breathed in deeply the fresh, frosty air. Brandon was ready to enter into the mysterious new realm of solitude in this idyllic little sanctuary.

That for which he was not prepared, was how much effort it would take for him to shut off the outside world. Before too long he discovered that he was more distracted here than he had been back in the city. He anxiously walked about, hoping that the next path might bring him to a place where he could truly find calmness and peace. Yet no place offered that desired reward.

Finally, he came back indoors, hoping that time spent in the quiet of the chapel before the Blessed Sacrament would give him the sought-after release. To his disappointment he fidgeted and nervously shifted about as he desperately tried to find a moment of silence in his soul. The more he worked at it, the more it evaded him.

He got up and walked around the building. It was a beautiful piece of architecture. The antiquated features of the woodwork, contrasted with the simplicity of the furnishings, only added to the charm and mystique of the monastery. The long corridors were brightly lit, with natural light flooding in through tall windows that gave a view of the beautiful surrounding premises.

Brandon was agitated; he paced the hallways, impatient with himself. He could not understand why he felt so distant from God in a place where he should have been able to be completely focussed on Him.

The worst thing of all was that every sinful and disgusting thing that he had ever done in his life was now haunting his thoughts. Brandon felt dirty, and he despised himself for his weaknesses. He became frustrated.

Frustration soon gave way to anger at the foolish waste of time that the whole thing was turning out to be. In fact, maybe the whole experience of conversion had been something he had conjured up in his own mind in order to impress a good-looking girl. Maybe none of it had been real. Maybe he was discovering that fact just in the nick of time, before he made a bigger fool of himself in becoming Catholic.

Brandon was in this state of anger and confusion when he came across an elderly monk strolling down one of the corridors. This was the first person Brandon had encountered since he had registered at the monastery five hours earlier. Brandon paused to greet the old priest. Suddenly, he felt compelled to ask the cleric if he would kindly give him some spiritual advice.

The old monk smiled meekly through a wrinkled, weathered face. The top of his head was as white as the snow-covered hill that Brandon could see through the hallway window. Yet despite his age, the eyes of this old priest were as bright and alive as any eyes that Brandon had ever seen. Brandon knew he was standing in the presence of a very holy man.

The old cleric led Brandon to a sunny sitting room. He asked Brandon to share about himself, for he was impressed with the sincerity of Brandon's faith. Brandon was shocked that the priest would make such a statement. Indeed, Brandon was feeling very weak in his faith at that moment.

They talked for awhile, with Brandon sharing every detail of his life that he could bring to mind. He was ashamed of all the sins he had committed in his past. There were so many sins of impurity, and the consequences of those sins had hurt a great many people. He was remorseful for the hate which he had borne his father for so many years. He told the priest about Joanie, his conversion, their relationship, and his intention to marry her. His voice conveyed the joy he had in the anticipation of being baptized and receiving Holy Communion at Easter.

The priest listened and at times questioned Brandon. He was reflective, and his experienced ears missed no detail of Brandon's discourse.

Finally, at the end of it, the old priest raised his gnarled and bony hand and laid it on Brandon's head. There was power in that misshapen old hand. Brandon could sense the incredible spiritual strength of the old priest, in spite of his physical frailty. It sent a wave of energy through Brandon's being. The monk spoke slowly, through a heavy European accent. His voice was old, but unfaltering and compassionate.

"You have searched your conscience sincerely. You have confessed your sins honestly, and you have made a firm purpose of amendment in your life. On the day when you are reborn in the waters of Baptism, all of these sins will be washed away and absolved. You will be a new creation in Christ, and your life will be made new in Him. Go, son, and may the peace of Christ fill your life. And," he added, almost as an afterthought, "when you return to your room, look up Matthew chapter four, verses one to eleven."

Brandon was speechless as he watched the old priest stand up and leave. The burdens of his heart had been lifted. He realized that he had confessed them to Christ through this humble minister of the Church. Brandon knew that he had not received absolution for his sins, but the blessing of the priest reminded him of the power of the Sacraments he was preparing to receive.

He looked up at the clock on the wall; it was just after three o'clock: the hour of mercy. Brandon's mind began to go over the events of the day, and he recognized that Satan had been plaguing his thoughts from the very start, trying to weaken his resolve, making him feel that he was not able to rise above his past.

Satan wanted Brandon to focus on his own weak nature and to forget that it was Jesus who now sustained his life. It was Jesus who lifted him above the dirt and gave him strength to fight against sin. It was Jesus whom Brandon would soon be receiving through the Sacraments of the Church at Easter. Brandon prayed to Jesus and rebuked Satan's power. He felt a tremendous peace settle over him.

He left the sitting room and returned to his sleeping chamber. He picked up his Bible and turned to Matthew's Gospel, just as the old priest had advised. There he read the story of the temptation of Christ in the desert. Battling with Satan was just part of the adventure of solitude; now Brandon could move on. As he finished the passage he smiled, reflecting on the wisdom and gentleness of the old priest.

God bless and keep our priests! he said, as he went back to the chapel and prayed his chaplet of Divine Mercy.

He was now able to focus completely on Christ in his prayer. Brandon sat in peaceful stillness for a long time, absorbed in Christ's Sacrificial Presence there in the Blessed Sacrament.

Chapter 44

"Get out of the way, Isaac!" Joanie pushed by the thirteen-year-old who was blocking the door to the music room.

"What's *your* problem?" he snarled back. "I just came in to get my guitar."

"Oh—just leave me alone!" she returned in a disgusted tone of voice as she headed up the stairs. Joanie had been fidgety and irritable all day. She walked around the house avoiding everyone and annoyed by everything. The house, which normally felt large, had become crowded and confining. At times like these she wondered why she still lived at home. How was it possible for little children to be so obnoxious?

She had turned to vacuuming, hoping that if she kept herself busy everyone would leave her alone. Besides, the noise of the vacuum would maybe block out the world around her. She tackled the job but soon began to sink deeper into a spirit of resentment as she picked up toys, books, and clothes lying around the hallways and rooms.

Why was she always doing the cleaning? She certainly was not the one making the mess. Those little brothers made more mess than their fair share. But did they ever help clean? No. They were downstairs wrestling—again.

It occurred to Joanie that boys were, by nature, irresponsible and destructive. No wonder the world was so full of problems. Boys, who had never completely grown up, were running it—irresponsibly and destructively. What a better world it would be if people would learn to take a little more responsibility and pick up after themselves! But since it was only ever the big sisters of the world doing any of the clean-up, she yielded to a certain despondency regarding the fate of humanity.

Jessie came running up to Joanie to ask the big sister to help her change her dress.

"Again?" Joanie snapped back at the four-year-old pioneer girl who now wanted to become a princess. "I just helped you put on that dress and petticoat. I'm busy, and I don't want to help you again. Go get Katie or Amie to help you."

"But Joanie, I don't know where they are," Jessie whined.

"Stop whining! That is so annoying!"

Jessie dissolved into tears. Joanie felt like a heel. She picked up the small, deflated child and carried her upstairs. Though her heart had by no means softened toward the distressed child's plight, Joanie knew that she would never get rid of Jessie if she did not help her.

She walked into the nursery only to find dresses pulled down all over the floor. Joanie could have screamed. Actually, she did. "Jessie, clean up this mess right now! I'm not helping you get changed until it's all cleaned up. Honestly, you'd think this house was full of pigs instead of children!" Jessie began to sob and threw herself onto her bed. Now Joanie really did feel awful. She was taking out her frustration on Jessie who at this moment resembled a fragile flower that had been carelessly trampled underfoot. With a softened and contrite heart, Joanie walked to the bedside of the whimpering child and put her hand gently on Jessie's head. Lightly running her fingers through the soft auburn hair, Joanie apologized to her sister.

"Jessie, I'm sorry. I shouldn't have yelled at you. I know I hurt your feelings. Do you forgive me?"

Jessie looked up from her pillow and in a reluctant tone, she grunted, "I fowgive you!" Though her heart was not in it, she knew the formula well.

Joanie smiled down at her precious sister. Jessie, sensing Joanie's sincerity, rolled onto her back and raised her arms to hug her big sister. Joanie held Jessie tenderly.

"You know what, Jessie? I'll help you clean up. We'll get it done before Mom finds your room like this."

"Yeah, 'cause then I would get a spanking, wight Joanie?" Jessie's expression was very serious.

"Probably! And you don't want that!" Joanie confirmed. "When we're all done, I'll help you put on your princess dress, and you can go find Mommy and Daddy and show them how pretty you are."

Jessie smiled and quickly began picking things up. Within minutes the room was in order. Joanie helped the little princess don her regal garments: a flouncy dress with many layers of shimmering pink skirts that floated out in perfect circles around her as she twirled. There were also sparkling golden slippers with dainty little heels and white studded gloves. Joanie pulled up the fine auburn hair into a bun and wrapped it with a pink scrunchy. Finally, she crowned the young princess with a jewel-studded tiara.

Jessie delighted in the praise of her parents, as Joanie paraded her into the kitchen. The four-year-old princess twirled round and round until she toppled over. Gracefully, she threw out her arms as if she had planned to fall down in the first place, with her skirt puffed out all around her.

Their father exclaimed, "Jessie you are such a princess . . . *my* little princess!" He walked over and swept the little beauty into his big arms, hugging her warmly. Then he turned to her older sister, adding, "It doesn't seem like it was that long ago when Joanie was dancing for us like a princess."

Joanie chuckled and excused herself from the kitchen.

The irritability had not completely subsided, and she was not really in the mood for conversation. What she needed was to get out, so she could be by herself for awhile. Maybe going for a walk would settle her nerves. She went up to her room to get changed, relieved to have avoided any further interactions with family members. If the little kids had known she was going out, she would have had to take them with her.

Entering her bedroom, Joanie found Maggie kneeling by the bed with a rosary in her hand. Is that all that Maggie ever did? Pray? Sometimes Joanie was completely confounded by her sister's piety!

Maggie looked up at Joanie and, with complete simplicity, said, "You realize *he's* under attack right now."

Joanie covered her face with her hands. It all made sense now. Why was she so slow and dull not to have realized that her restlessness was not about her? It was about Brandon. Brandon had gone away on a retreat, and here she was being so ugly to everyone all day. Sometimes, she was a really lousy Christian.

Sorry, Jesus!

Joanie took out the rosary from her pocket and knelt beside Maggie to pray.

Maggie pointed to the clock and said, "It's the hour of mercy, he doesn't have much more to suffer now."

The two sisters prayed a chaplet of Divine Mercy. They prayed for Brandon to be released from the attack of Satan so that he could make a good retreat and be strengthened in his faith.

When they were done praying, Joanie looked up at Maggie with awe. "How did you know?" she asked the young prayer warrior. "How do you always know?"

Maggie smiled. This uncontrived girl exuded such a compelling and humble spirituality. She looked at Joanie with eyes that had wisdom far beyond her twenty-one years and said, "Because, like you, Joanie, I'm in love. And I know what my lover is thinking at times. It's not very different from you being able to know what Brandon is feeling or thinking when you're together. And I long to be with Jesus, just as you long to be with Brandon. In time we'll both be married, Joanie, just in different ways."

Joanie hugged her sister. She loved Maggie so much. She could never be like Maggie. The vocations that God had called them to were distinctly different, yet there was so much in common. They knew their lives would bless each other as they lived out fully their calls from God. They sat at peace in each other's company, silent for awhile. Then Joanie began reminiscing with Maggie, and soon they were transported back into the world of childhood pleasures and fun.

It did not take long before their bedroom door opened to the invasion of their other siblings. Joanie and Maggie's laughter had first attracted Zack and Aaron. As the noise level grew, all the other kids, one by one, found their way up to the bedroom. Soon they were all caught up in the game of "remember when". The younger children relentlessly begged for one story after another. There seemed to be no end to the family tales and in no time the afternoon had slipped away.

Their mom came in and joined the fun for awhile. Finally, she broke herself away from the camp meeting in order to "rustle up" some grub to feed her crew. Judy left her children together at play and went downstairs to the kitchen. She did not ask for help with the supper preparation that day.

She knew very well that times such as this were like precious gems for her children. They were part of the many riches of family life that money could never buy and that busy schedules often threatened to steal. These treasures were stored up in the hearts of her children as investments in their future. The best thing was, these investments were guaranteed . . . with amazing returns. And her children would be able to withdraw them at any time—without penalty.

✝ ✝ ✝

Brandon showed up Sunday evening at the Collins abode, having just gotten back to town from his retreat. He longed to share with this family his experiences and to be in their company once again.

John and Judy were sitting together in the front room enjoying some quiet time after a long day. Some of the children were downstairs watching a show. The others were around . . . somewhere. The house was uncharacteristically calm.

Brandon commented that after two days of silence he was disappointed to find everything so tranquil at the Collins house. Snuggled up to her husband, Judy warned Brandon not to mess with a good thing. He promised to be on his best behaviour.

"What's with the beard there, Brandon? D'your razor break?" John asked with amusement.

Brandon ran his fingers over the three-day growth of beard on his chin and laughed.

"Oh, that," he said, remembering the fact that he had decided not to bother shaving while he was away. "I thought I'd give Joanie a thrill."

He winked at Judy who nodded her agreement.

"Well, she hasn't seen you now in two days, so don't get her too excited," John warned the rugged young suitor.

They all laughed, and Judy sent Brandon on in to look for Joanie downstairs.

Brandon first checked out the television room in the basement where he found the boys and Jessie watching a movie. As soon as he was discovered, he was covered in children.

Zack yelled out, "Dog pile!" and the next thing Brandon knew, he was at the bottom of it. All the commotion brought Joanie out from the music room to settle down the children. When she saw Brandon in the middle of the kafuffle, her mouth dropped open in surprise. At once, her face became animated with delight. Brandon managed to free himself from the grasp of his captors and walked over to meet Joanie in the doorway.

"Look at you!" Joanie exclaimed, running her fingers lightly over his grizzly jaw.

"Yeah, I know," Brandon remarked, taking her hand in his. He feasted his eyes on the sight of her, consuming every detail of her eyes, her skin, her hair, her mouth. "Aren't you a sight for sore eyes?" His words involuntarily verbalized his thoughts, as time seemed to stand still between them. The sweetness of her smile conveyed her pleasure at being admired and appreciated by him. They could have stood there forever except for the fact that Jessie and Aaron were still tugging on their legs.

Joanie sent the children back to watch their movie and told them that she was going up to the kitchen with Brandon. They could play with Brandon when the movie was over. She glanced over to take note of where they were in the show and determined that she would get about forty-five minutes alone with Brandon before the troops ascended.

The young couple stole away to the refuge of the kitchen. Since Brandon had not eaten, Joanie fixed him a plate of leftovers and poured for them each a cup of tea. They sat down together at the big oak dining table and got caught up on the events of the past two days.

Normally, two days apart would not be so significant, but these two days had been filled with so much grace that there was much to share.

Chapter 45

The experience of commemorating Christ's triumphant entry into Jerusalem on Palm Sunday was awe-inspiring for Brandon. He poured out his heart as the church sang out, "Hosanna to the King!"

But as the Mass unfolded, with the reading of the Passion of the Lord, Brandon was moved to complete humility. He contemplated on how the first followers of Christ could laud Him as the Messiah and then later hand Him over to be crucified. These were the people who had walked with Him; they had seen Him and had heard Him while He was on earth. How was it that they could have betrayed Christ?

Brandon prayed for forgiveness for the times he had failed to bear witness to Christ since he had become a Christian. He realized that faith was a gift that could not be taken for granted. It needed to be cared for, guarded and protected, nurtured through prayer, through the Word, and through the Sacraments. How he longed for the Sacraments. *Just one more week.*

✝   ✝   ✝

Sundays had become a cherished day for Joanie and Brandon. Not only did it begin with the celebration of the Mass, but the rest of the day was spent together with family and friends in an atmosphere of fun and relaxation. It was the day of the Lord, the day set aside for worship and praise and restoration of the mind, body, and soul. The Collinses knew well how to enjoy this day and Brandon had come to a real appreciation for it.

This Sunday it was the men's turn to cook. The women folk were banned from the kitchen while the boys set into preparations for brunch. Brandon tended the bacon, and Isaac was on toast duty, while John prepared a culinary masterpiece of eggs, onions, peppers, mushrooms, and cheese. Aaron and Zack were in charge of setting the table and making the juice.

It was bantering and fun from the word go. Brandon enjoyed his role as big brother in the family. He loved the time he spent with the young Collins boys, and he admired the way John interacted with his sons. Having grown up without a father, Brandon was eager to learn all that he could from this man. Everyone needs a hero: John Collins was that and so much more for Brandon.

When brunch was finally prepared, Aaron had the honour of ringing the bell and gathering in the clan for mealtime. It was a wonderful spread, highly praised by all.

The Collins children were especially exuberant at brunch that day. The meal was filled with all kinds of jocularities, from Isaac doing disappearing tricks with his bacon, to a food fight between Zack and Aaron, to which John quickly put an end.

The air was filled with a sense of anticipation and excitement. It was one week to Easter. Lent was drawing to a close, and all the family was focussed on Brandon's big day.

The women, including Jessie, dug into clean-up quickly after brunch in order to free up the rest of the afternoon. The family had been invited to visit their cousins on an acreage out of town. They would be having a potluck supper. Judy whipped up a quick casserole, and at John's request Amie prepared her speciality, chocolate swirl cheesecake, for dessert. As a Lenten observance the family had given up sweets during the week; therefore, desserts on Sundays in Lent were especially prized.

As the boys began to disperse after brunch, Brandon caught John's attention. "Have you got any new projects on the go, John?"

John gave Brandon an expression that was not easily discernible and answered, "As a matter of fact, I do. I've been kind of waiting to show it to you, too, son. Come on."

John knew when Brandon wanted to talk to him in private; they had used this signal more than once. Family members did not even come to question the ritual anymore. The two men went out to the garage.

Brandon's demeanour was different this time. He appeared almost nervous. John secretly enjoyed watching Brandon shift about awkwardly for he knew what was on Brandon's mind, and he had prepared himself for what was about to happen.

Brandon began, carefully calculating his words, "John, I've been waiting for this moment for some time now. I have something important to ask you . . ."

His voice trailed off, distracted by John who had walked over to the far wall and was taking something down from an upper cupboard. The object was wrapped in a cloth. Brandon watched curiously as John brought it over to one of the side counters. Brandon stepped up to get a closer look.

John replied, with real sincerity, "I've been waiting for this moment for some time now, too, Brandon."

Brandon looked at the man before him, wondering if in fact John knew what he was about to ask him. "Sir?" Brandon asked, bewildered by John's manner.

"Go ahead. . . . I didn't mean to throw you off course. You were saying?" John prompted him.

Brandon regained his line of thought and continued with purpose. "Well, John, you know how I feel about Joanie. We've been courting for quite some time now. And like you pointed out, courtship is a time to discern direction in a relationship. Well, I've come to a decision."

With a look, John encouraged Brandon to go on.

He continued, "John, since my retreat at the monastery . . . I think I'm being called to the priesthood."

John's eyes nearly jumped out of his head. His face betrayed his obvious confusion, and his eyes implored Brandon for an explanation.

The smile that crept up at the corners of Brandon's mouth told John that Brandon had gotten him. Brandon had assessed his opponent in this game. He knew John had been having fun at his expense, and he had decided to make a quick manoeuvre.

John laughed and admitted, "I guess I had that coming to me. Go on!"

Brandon laughed with John and, with a new air of confidence, he proceeded, "Sorry about that John, but I couldn't resist! What I'm trying to do here—so awkwardly—is to seek your permission to ask Joanie to marry me." Brandon stood back and waited. . . . Some moments in life just seem longer than others.

John nodded his head and turned to the object lying on the counter before them. "You know I'm going to say yes, Brandon, but before I do, I want to give you something that I made for you."

He opened up the loosely wrapped cloth to reveal a beautifully crafted rosewood crucifix with a golden corpus affixed to it. He passed it to Brandon who took it into his strong hands and examined it carefully.

"I want you to hang this in your home in a prominent spot, so that each time you look up and see Jesus' outstretched arms on the cross, you'll be reminded that *that* is what love is all about.

"When you take for yourself a wife, Brandon, you are accepting the call to lay down your life for her. And believe me, over the years there will be many opportunities for you to do just that. It's the many little sacrifices each day that will call you to die to yourself for the sake of your loved ones."

John pointed down to the cross, indicating the sacrifice Jesus had made for His loved ones.

"I believe you're ready to do that. And it gives me great joy to grant you permission to ask Joanie to marry you. Of course . . . she always has the right to turn you down."

John winked at Brandon and patted him gently on the shoulder.

Brandon was speechless, gazing at the crucifix in his hands. His fingers moved gently over the details of the ornately carved wood, and finally they traced over the outstretched arms of the crucified Lord.

He turned over the cross, and there on the back John had inscribed: *Behold . . . the arms of love.*

Brandon's voice was reverent, husky with emotion, hanging in the air just above a whisper. "I'll do that for Joanie, sir . . . and with joy."

"I believe you will, Brandon," John returned, smiling proudly at the young man. "You've come a long way in a short time. And I guarantee you that the Lord will bring to completion the work He has begun in you. You'll find marriage filled with joys and sufferings, each one designed to lead you and your wife and your children to heaven. That's the goal, son. Keep your eyes fixed there, and you'll survive anything."

Brandon nodded thoughtfully. There was a time in his life when such a speech would have convinced Brandon of the futility of marriage. Now it inspired him on to nobly pursue the greatness of the marriage covenant. He longed with all his heart to give himself entirely to Joanie, and he was now one step closer.

"Thank you, John . . . for the crucifix," he lifted it up admiringly, "but mostly for all you've done to direct me on my path as a Christian. I never had a relationship with my own father. I consider you to be the dad I never had. It means a great deal to me that you made this for me. I'll remember what it means."

"Good," John said, with finality. "Now, I guess we should head back into the house before we arouse too much suspicion."

They started toward the door when John added, "Oh, by the way, Brandon, I wouldn't recommend trying out that priesthood thing on Joanie, it might not go over so well with her!"

Brandon acknowledged the sound advice with a nod and a chuckle. He thanked John for so graciously granting his permission, in spite of the jesting.

John led the way into the house, with Brandon following behind carrying the crucifix. When they got inside, Katie and Amie stopped what they were doing at the counter to go over and see what Brandon was holding. Soon several family members were gathered around to admire their father's handiwork.

John explained that it was a gift for Brandon's Baptism. He thought it would be a helpful reminder throughout the preparation of Holy Week.

Joanie stood back, proudly taking in the scene. Brandon caught her eye from across the room and winked at her in that certain way that always made her feel so cherished.

Chapter 46

Monday morning Brandon woke up with a powerful urge to call his father. He was not sure why he felt it so strongly, but he trusted the instinct and so complied.

He and his father got along fine now. They went out for dinner whenever James came to town. Each time Joanie could join them it was a real bonus, for James was especially fond of her and he greatly enjoyed her company.

Though Brandon had told his father about his initiation into the Church at Easter, he had never thought to invite his father to come to it. Somehow he figured his father would not really care for all that religious stuff. Now, prompted by the Holy Spirit, Brandon realized that he would have been remiss not to have included his father in this important event.

The phone rang two, three, four times. Finally, the answering machine picked up. Brandon left his father a message with the details of the time and place of his Baptism, expressing his hope that his father might be able to attend. He understood if it did not work out; it was no big deal. The fact was, Brandon thought to himself as he hung up the phone, he really did not count on his father showing up. But maybe it would make his old man feel good just to have been invited.

✝   ✝   ✝

Holy Week seemed to drag by: an obvious opportunity to practise the virtue of patience. Finally, Thursday arrived. Brandon slipped by the staff lounge at lunch hour that day. Joanie was out with Paul on a shoot.

Brandon joined Tessa as she was finishing her lunch at the big table. The friendly receptionist smiled at Brandon as he sat down with his coffee. He never ate at work.

Now that everyone knew that Brandon was a Christian, it was so much easier for them to enjoy a good visit together. In fact, other people at work often had questions that they would throw at Brandon, Joanie, or Tessa, opening up some very dynamic conversations.

"You've got an obvious glow about you, Brandon. I'd say that halo of yours has sure polished up nicely," Tessa teased him.

"Settle down," Brandon said in his steady, calm voice. "Don't you go picking on me now, or I won't invite you to come to my dunking!"

"Well, you'll have a hard time keeping me away from it, Brandon," she replied.

"Good," his voice lightened, and a smile beamed across his face. "And Karl will be there too, I hope."

"You bet. And Joanie's invited us over to her parents' place afterwards. So you're stuck with us." She put her hand on Brandon's arm and smiled at him, as one smiles at a dear friend. "I'm really happy for you, you know."

"Thanks, Tessa," he returned, patting her hand and nodding. "You've been a good friend." Then smiling warmly at her, he asked, "How've you been feeling lately?"

Tessa, now four months pregnant, glowed with maternal charm. "Fine, thanks. I'm so glad that first trimester is over. But even at that, I'd go through it all again just to be able to have a baby!"

"Well, you look wonderful in maternity clothes . . . it suits you!" Brandon could not look at Tessa without being moved by the beauty of the new life within her. *Someday that'll be Joanie with our baby.* That day could not come soon enough!

Just then, Taylor came over with his usual charm and broke into the conversation.

"Well, well. Rumour has it, Brandon, that you're going down officially this weekend," he mocked Brandon, giving him a shot in the shoulder.

Brandon moved with the punch and glanced up at Taylor. "You laugh now, but you'll be next, buddy. Just when you think you're completely safe—Bang! God'll show up when you least expect it."

"Nah, not this heathen. I don't think I'll ever have the pleasure of meeting God," Taylor returned, scoffing at Brandon's comment.

"Oh," Brandon went on, in an ominous tone, "you *will* get to meet Him someday, Taylor, that's for sure. Whether you stay with Him or not . . . well that's entirely up to you."

Taylor looked at Brandon, not quite sure if he had taken his meaning correctly.

Tessa joined in, "We all meet Him on judgment day, Taylor, whether you believe in Him or not. But don't worry about that," she added, in light humour, "He's got alternate arrangements for those who aren't interested in staying with Him." She patted Taylor on the shoulder, as she got up to leave.

"Ha! Ha!" Taylor returned, unamused in a friendly sort of way. Turning to Brandon, he added, "Well, hope you have a good one, buddy. As for me, I'll be partying hard on this four-day weekend. It's not too late for you to bail out, you know, if you'd rather join in on a really good time."

"Thanks, no, Taylor," Brandon replied. "I think I'll stick to my original plans."

"Okay, but don't ever say I didn't try to save you!" Taylor waved his hand at Brandon as he left the lounge, something of a farewell salute.

Brandon shook his head and chuckled. He liked Taylor.

✝   ✝   ✝

That evening, when Brandon got home from work, he changed the sheets on his bed. He took an extra pillow, sheet, and blanket and set them on the end table in the living room. His mom and Dan would be staying at his place for the weekend. Brandon would sleep on the couch; it was plenty comfortable.

He was so pleased that he could be sharing this weekend with his mother, not merely by her physical presence, but through her spiritual support. They were of a common faith now, and the very idea of it still gave Brandon reason for grateful pause.

✝   ✝   ✝

St. James' Church was not quite full when Caroline and Dan arrived. Brandon had waited in the welcoming area to greet them, but quickly excused himself to join the choir.

The Easter Triduum choir combined all the musicians and singers of the parish into one large group. Brandon had eagerly accepted the invitation to play guitar and sing. It was for him the icing on the cake, to be able to participate musically in this great event.

And while Brandon knew there would be many more celebrations of Easter over the course of his life, this Easter had the distinction of being the first.

Holy Thursday Mass, commemorating the Last Supper, set into motion the entire continuation of the Easter Triduum. It included Good Friday Service and the Easter Vigil, at which time the Resurrection would be celebrated.

Following Holy Thursday Mass, the Blessed Sacrament was processed through the church to the Altar of Repose for adoration until midnight. The Blessed Sacrament would then be taken away from the church. The door of the Tabernacle would remain wide open, empty of the Blessed Sacrament, as a reminder that the Lord had been taken away from His followers to be handed over for death. The Sacrificial Presence of the Eucharist would be gone on Good Friday, brought in only for the distribution of Holy Communion during the Good Friday service. No Mass would be celebrated that day in observance of the passion and death of Jesus.

As Holy Thursday Mass ended, Brandon was acutely aware that this would be the last Mass celebrated until the Easter Vigil. At that time he would stand in full communion with the Church and receive, for the first time, Jesus in the Holy Eucharist. His heart waited, poised in vigilant anticipation.

As the church cleared silently following the Mass, Joanie motioned for Brandon to meet with her in the gathering area. He put away his guitar and followed her out. Brandon's mother and Dan were waiting for the young couple. Joanie enthusiastically introduced Caroline and Dan to her parents.

Their visiting did not last long, as plans needed to be discussed for the rest of the evening. Joanie was trying to arrange travelling to accommodate those who wanted to spend time in adoration.

"Brandon, since Mom and Dad are going to take the little ones home right now for bed, I thought we could drive everyone else back to the house after adoration," she suggested.

"That's fine with me, but I don't have enough seat belts. Who's staying?" he inquired.

"Maggie, Amie, Katie, and Isaac, you and me," she counted out on her fingers, "that makes six."

"Why don't we keep the van then," he offered.

"How do you suggest we get home?" inquired John, interrupting the younger couple's deliberations.

"Well, you're welcome to take my Pathfinder," Brandon said as he reached into his pocket to get the keys.

"I don't know—" John began to protest.

"No, it's fine," Brandon stopped the objection. "Look, I can't give you my permission to date in it, but if you promise to restrict its use for courting, well then you can have it."

The look on Brandon's face and the tone of his voice left Caroline completely confused. "What are you talking about, Brandon?" she asked, looking around the group to see if anyone else was confused by this off-the-wall comment.

John laughed and nodded in agreement. "I'll keep that in mind, Brandon," he said, exchanging keys with the young man. John turned to Caroline and remarked, "Your son is just giving me back a bit of my own."

Caroline's face still denoted her confusion, but she did not pursue the topic.

By this time Judy had rounded up the littlest Collins children and was anxiously waiting to get a very whiny four-year-old home to bed. They said good-night and left.

Caroline and Dan had decided to stay and pray for awhile. For a Protestant, Dan had developed quite a love for the Blessed Sacrament. Time spent in adoration with his wife had become a routine event in his life now. He looked forward to it every week at their parish in Calgary. Jesus was truly present in the Blessed Sacrament; there was no doubt of that in his mind.

His prayer, as he knelt in adoration, was always the same. *Someday I'll receive You, Jesus, in the Bread of Life. Prepare my heart for that day.*

Brandon gave Dan and his mom a key to his apartment so they could go home to bed whenever they wanted. With plans all settled, the group made their way back into the church to pray.

The church was quiet and still; the lights were dimmed. They went and sat in a pew close up to the side altar which had been set up as the Altar of Repose. Adoration was not an unfamiliar mode of prayer for the Collins children. Their family made an effort to regularly spend time with the Lord in this way.

For Brandon, though, there was something new and wonderful in this night spent in adoration. He felt like the apostles, waiting for Jesus who had gone to pray in the Garden of Gethsemane—only Brandon had no trouble staying awake tonight. His heart was on fire, consumed by the love of Christ present in the Blessed Sacrament.

When Joanie touched Brandon on the shoulder to leave, he could not believe that over an hour had passed. He wanted to stay and pray, but he was responsible for getting these people home to bed. To his surprise, his mom and Dan had already left. Stepping out of the pew and getting down on both knees, he bowed reverently with one last, quick prayer, and left the church.

Everyone filed into the van and Brandon drove the family home. No one was very talkative. Among them there was a sense of awe and wonder as they entered into this holy liturgical season. The silence was profound. Brandon made a quick exchange of keys with John and headed home.

✟   ✟   ✟

The austerity and beauty of the Good Friday Service evoked tremendous passion within Brandon. He found himself so gripped with emotion through-out the service that he struggled to sing his parts in the choir.

When the time came for the veneration of the cross, Brandon's heart seemed to stand still. As he knelt to kiss the wood of the cross, he paused in awe at the love of Jesus. Through His blood poured out, Jesus had washed clean *all* of Brandon's sins.

Rather than returning to the choir, Brandon went to a pew and sat down, buried his face into his hands and wept for love of his Saviour. Joanie saw Brandon sitting there. Her heart went out to him, knowing how painful and beautiful the entire experience must have been.

She continued singing, praising Jesus for His abundant mercy and grace which flowed out to all of creation from the Cross. She pondered how the human heart can scarcely take in the meaning of God's mercy, that He would send His only Son to die for us.

✟   ✟   ✟

When the service ended, Brandon, his mother, and Dan went over to the Collinses for supper. It was a meagre meal, simple but sufficient. The visiting was delightful. Grandma and Grandpa Ledoux had joined the family that evening as well. It gave Brandon such satisfaction to see how well his mother and Dan fit in with the family.

Grandpa Ledoux seemed to take a particular interest in Brandon's mother throughout the visiting. He kept looking at her curiously. Finally, he asked, "Caroline, what was your maiden name?"

"Mahoney," she answered.

"Thomas and Annie Mahoney were your parents?" he inquired further.

"They were." Caroline's face became animated, and she looked at Grandpa with great interest now.

Grandpa laughed, glancing over at Grandma Ledoux. "As we sat here visiting, I just kept thinking I was seeing Annie." Turning back to Caroline, he stated, "You are so much like your mother. . . . I was certain you had to be their little Carrie."

Caroline started at the sound of that name. Only her father had ever called her that. It had been a lifetime since she had heard it used. All at once, her senses were inundated with the memory of her parents. "How did you know my mom and dad?" Her voice was full of wonder.

"I met your father riding the rails during the thirties. I hooked up with him in the Edmonton area. He found out I was a musician and dug up an accordion for me. He played guitar and had a buddy, Ted Sooter, who played fiddle. We formed a band and earned our keep travelling from town to town looking for gigs. Your father, Thomas Mahoney—God bless his soul—was a wonderful guitar player . . . and the voice he had on him. . . ." Grandpa's voice trailed off, lost in a memory of another time, another world.

Joanie looked over at Brandon, her eyes sparkling as she delighted in the fact that the paths of their families had crossed two generations earlier.

Grandma Ledoux smiled. "I kept looking at you Caroline, thinking I had met you before. I would never have put it together. The last time we saw your mother and father, you must have been about six years old. Your father was very proud of his daughters." She smiled, remembering.

"In fact," she went on, "I can still recall you and Judy playing together as little girls." She shook her head gently as her eyes revealed that she was bringing to mind a distant memory. Turning to Grandpa, she added, "Remember the time Caroline and Judy got stuck up in the hayloft with those baby kittens?"

"I sure do," Grandpa chuckled. "Pigtails and all!"

"Judy, being a few years older than Caroline, had taken her up to see the new litter of kittens," Grandma explained.

"And Carrie was afraid to climb back down," Grandpa interjected. "I can still picutre Annie climbing down that old wooden ladder with Carrie in her arms, because Carrie refused to come down with anyone else." His gentle eyes smiled warmly at Caroline.

"You know," said Caroline, "I vaguely remember that!"

"So do I," laughed Judy. It was such a distant memory. How remarkable it was for these two women to share it together.

Grandma Ledoux went on, addressing Caroline, "We were so saddened to get word of your parents' deaths. We were living out on the farm, and they were here in the city. We simply had lost contact with them. Life was busy in those years. Everyone was raising a family, working hard to make ends meet. . . ." Grandma sighed as she, too, was now lost somewhere in the world of yesteryear.

"But Brandon"—Grandpa cut in, distracted in his own thoughts—"looks nothing like a Mahoney!"

"No," Caroline agreed, "he favours his father for looks."

"And how!" Joanie exclaimed.

Caroline nodded. "It's almost eerie, isn't it?" she asked Joanie.

Joanie laughed and nodded. Brandon smiled and kept quiet.

"But," Caroline added, "he did inherit his grandfather's love for music."

"I should say," Grandpa concurred. Looking at Brandon, he added, "You do your grandfather proud, son!" Then, thoughtfully, he said to Caroline. "And all this time I marvelled at what a powerhouse of faith Brandon had become so quickly after his conversion. He's been moving us all with his strong convictions and determined will ever since he came into this family. Now I understand . . ." Grandpa looked over at Brandon, "with prayer warriors like Thomas and Annie Mahoney in heaven praying for you, it's little wonder. . . . You didn't stand a chance, son!"

"Thank God," Caroline said, smiling. It warmed her heart to hear such talk of her parents. Ever since her conversion, she had felt so much closer to them. She understood now the communion of saints. Those having died in Christ and living in the joy of the resurrection never cease to pray for the needs of those here on earth.

Caroline looked directly into Grandpa Ledoux's eyes. "I had lost my faith until Brandon and Joanie came along. And to think it was you and Daddy behind this whole set up!"

Everyone started laughing. It certainly was remarkable how Joanie and Brandon had come together in love and in faith. Considering their family histories now, it all seemed to make good sense.

The conversation moved on with Grandpa entertaining the family with stories of the band years. Caroline soaked up every word.

Joanie and Brandon sat back, holding hands, blessed by the love of their families. They had a proud heritage of hard-working, dedicated ancestors who had lived heroically their faith and had given everything to pass it on to their families. And tomorrow, Brandon would be joined fully into that family of faith through Baptism.

Reluctantly, Brandon and Joanie pulled themselves away from the visiting. They had a few solo parts to sing at the Easter Vigil and they needed to practise. Brandon was naturally nervous, as this was all so new to him. They excused themselves and went downstairs to the music room.

Brandon dug out the music from Joanie's choir bag and began setting things up. Joanie came over and slipped her arms around his waist and hugged him warmly.

Wrapping his strong arms around her, he asked, "What's that for?" It was not often that Joanie was so openly affectionate.

Joanie sighed deeply, closed her eyes, and whispered, "I'm just so happy, Brandon, to be sharing this Easter with you. I love you so much. And I think it's wonderful that our grandfathers were such good friends. Who'd have thought two generations later their families would still be doing music together?"

"I'm not sure that we weren't just a match made in heaven," he said with amusement.

"I'm convinced we were," Joanie stated emphatically.

Brandon smiled and squeezed tighter. It felt good to have Joanie in his arms again. The last few weeks had been so busy he had hardly spent time alone with her. They remained that way for only a short while, when a voice interrupted their embrace.

"Cut it out there, you two!" Joanie and Brandon looked up to see Maggie standing in the doorway, playfully shaking her head at them. She went across the music room, got her violin, and winked back at them over her shoulder, leaving the two young lovers laughing with amusement.

"I guess we should get on with this," Brandon observed and then he confessed, "I'm not sure that I can go through with it, Joanie. You saw me today. What if I don't make it?"

"You'll be perfect," Joanie assured him, with a kiss on the cheek. "You'll see. The Easter Vigil brings with it a whole different set of emotions from Good Friday. The mourning is over, and your heart will be so full of joy, you'll just have to sing!"

Her smile conveyed to Brandon the absolute confidence she had in what she was saying. He resigned himself to her good judgment, and they settled down to work on the music.

Chapter 47

Joanie was right. As the Easter Vigil approached, the emotions that were taking hold of Brandon's heart were unlike those of the previous day. He was almost intoxicated by the anticipation of the event.

Caroline and Dan had gone visiting with friends. They planned to meet up with Brandon at eight o'clock that night for the Easter Vigil.

With nothing to do, Brandon went over to offer help at the Collins house for the evening preparations. It was decided that the best help he could be was to take out the boys and Jessie and keep them occupied. Brandon did not mind the role of babysitter, since it gave him something to do to keep his mind off the clock. He packed up the children and took them bowling.

Isaac and Zack had bowled a few times before and were pretty good at it. This was the first time, though, for Aaron and Jessie. Brandon found the entire process quite entertaining. He had limited experience at trying to teach something to little children.

One cannot leave out any details when explaining something to a child, or so Brandon learned. When he told Aaron to pull back his arm and let the ball go, Brandon was not expecting for the boy to drop the ball behind his back. The heavy ball thudded down on Brandon's toe. It smarted, but left no permanent damage.

Then, with everything going smoothly after the eighth frame of the second game, Jessie whispered in Brandon's ear, "I've got to go potty, now!"

Brandon was not prepared for this new experience. In all the times he and Joanie had taken out the children, Joanie had always dealt with this situation. Where was that woman now, when he needed her the most?

He desperately looked around, wondering if there might be a kind woman nearby to help out. Jessie was shy and clung on to Brandon's neck. He realized he would have to take her himself. But should he take her into the girls' washroom or the boys'?

He made a quick decision when she clenched her teeth together and said, "Hurwy, Bwandon, I'm going to pee my pants."

He darted into the men's washroom, burying Jessie's face in his shoulder to hide her eyes. He stepped into a cubicle with the child and set her down.

She looked up at him and coached him on, "I need helwp with my button."

He undid her pants, set her on the potty, and turned around while she went pee. He said a quick prayer that she would know how to wipe herself, which she did. Then he helped her pull up her pants and button up. He flushed the toilet and quickly headed toward the door, with Jessie's head tucked down again.

"Bwandon," the child called out, her face smothered in his shirt. "I need to wash my hands!"

Hygiene was not a priority for him at the moment. Nevertheless, he did not want to upset the little tyke. He looked around, waited for a boy to finish his business, and then took her to the sink to wash their hands.

When he finally finished the whole ordeal, he breathed a sigh of relief and wondered to himself if he would ever survive fatherhood.

Brandon's confidence in future parenting was boosted after the bowling game when they got back to the Collins house. Jessie had insisted on cuddling with Brandon in the rocker if she had to have a sleep. He snuggled up the little cherub in a blanket and softly sang her a few of her favourite songs. He surmised that it was moments such as this that made the less pleasant jobs of parenting worthwhile.

Before half an hour had passed, Jessie was sound asleep. The late nights and early mornings of the busy weekend had caught up to her. Her mother had warned her that she would not go to the Easter Vigil that night if she did not take a nap.

Brandon carried the sleeping form of the four-year-old to her bedroom. He put Jessie on her bed and tucked the blanket around her. Gently, he kissed her forehead and gave her a blessing.

Brandon came back down to the kitchen. Judy looked up from her work, caught his eye, and thanked him.

He walked up to the gracious woman and said, "No, Judy, thank you!"

Judy smiled and kissed Brandon on the cheek in her motherly way.

Brandon had supper with the Collinses, but right after eating he went back home to get ready for Mass. He slipped back over at seven to pick up the older girls, as they were all involved in doing the music.

☦   ☦   ☦

As Brandon walked into the church that night, guitar in hand, he paused. Joanie turned to see what his hesitation was. Brandon pulled her back beside him. He pointed up to the main doorway and observed, "When I walk through those doors into the church tonight, it will be the last time that I do so as an unbaptized man."

Joanie smiled at him and pulled on his hand as she led him through the doors and into a new life where he would forevermore share fully in the Sacraments of the Church. They walked up the centre aisle together, sensing the awesomeness of the night.

The choir set up, tuned up, warmed up, and then . . . waited.

The minutes seemed like hours to Brandon. Mike came and sat beside Brandon. He pointed out that after the liturgy of the Word they would take their places with the other two candidates and sponsors in the front row. The seats behind were reserved for family.

When Brandon saw his mother and Dan arrive, he went out to meet them and directed them to the reserved seating. The Collins family arrived early enough to get a pew near the front so the children would be able to see. Mark and Justine arrived, and Brandon ushered them in to sit with Joanie's family. Brandon was just about to return to the choir when Joanie took him by the arm and turned him to face the back of the church.

His father had just walked in.

Brandon's heart skipped a beat. He never expected that his father would come. Joanie led Brandon back to greet his dad who was looking very much like a fish out of water.

Joanie's beautiful smile set James at ease. If not for this girl, he would never have set foot in a church. In all his years, he had never trusted a religious person. But Joanie was different to him. He had been forced to look beyond his stereotypic ideas because of his desire to get to know Brandon again. In the process, James had become captivated with Joanie's delightful personality. He could see why Brandon had fallen in love with her. He was proud of them both and earnestly wanted to be a part of their lives now.

James had received Brandon's message with much gratitude. He had hoped that Brandon might include him in this event, but he was not about to push himself back into Brandon's life. The invitation to come tonight meant more to him than he could ever communicate to his son.

His bright blue eyes shone back to greet Joanie, and he lifted the corner of his mouth in a smile that looked just like Brandon's. Brandon was a twenty-year-younger cloned version of this man. No wonder Joanie liked James so much. In spite of his sinful lifestyle and completely secular outlook on life, he had that irresistible Vaughn charm. How she prayed for him to find Jesus. Having seen what a wonderful Christian man Brandon had turned out to be, she had great hope for this lost soul before her.

"Welcome, James," she warmly greeted him.

"Joanie, you get more beautiful each time I see you," James returned.

Brandon stood there, awkward in his own feelings of gratitude and shock. "Dad," his voice was barely audible.

"Son." James' pride in Brandon echoed in the full resonance of his low voice.

"I'm so grateful you're here, Dad."

Joanie held Brandon's hand with both of hers and added, "We both are, James."

"I flew in from Toronto this afternoon, Brandon. I wouldn't have missed being here for anything, after I got your call on Monday."

James reached out his hand and placed it on Brandon's arm. The prodigal father's heart ached at the thought of all those lost years. He had missed out on so much. He would not miss out on anything else, if he could help it.

Brandon suffered a moment of panic, wondering if he should take his father to sit by his mother in the reserved seating or not. Just then he felt a hand on his shoulder. Brandon turned to see his mother who had come to greet James.

She smiled warmly and welcomed him with all the graciousness of a queen. Caroline led James up to the front pew and introduced him to Dan. Brandon was left standing there with Joanie.

Joanie asked when the last time was that his mother and father had seen each other. It had been almost seven years ago at Brandon's grade twelve graduation. "And," he added, "they did not say a word to each other the whole time."

✟ ✟ ✟

Finally, the lights were dimmed, and the commotion at the back of the church told them that the Easter Vigil was about to begin. First, there was the beautiful ceremony of the blessing of the fire. From this fire the Easter candle was lit and processed to the front of the darkened church. The light was then spread throughout as each person held a small white candle and waited for the flame to be passed on from one person to the next. From darkness to light, the entire church had become illuminated with the light of Christ.

The ceremony reminded Brandon of how the light of Christ had been brought to him through the bold evangelization of a young woman who so earnestly kept that flame burning brightly in her life. As he accepted the flame with his candle he said a prayer that he, too, would never be ashamed or afraid to pass that light on to others.

After the candles were all lit, Joanie took Brandon's hand and led him up to the front pulpit. Silence filled the church. Joanie began singing the Exsultet, that glorious song to magnify the holiness of this night, commemorating the resurrection of the Lord. The young couple sang out the verses in turn until they joined their voices together at the end in beautiful and simple harmony.

The walls and ceiling of the candle-lit church echoed in the richness of these two young voices. This song would be sung throughout the entire world in each Catholic Church as the Easter Vigil was celebrated universally that night. The connection to two thousand years of tradition, to all Christians throughout history, and indeed to all of humanity redeemed by Christ, was truly stirring to the soul.

The candles were blown out, and the congregation listened as the readings from Scripture recounted the story of Salvation History. The lights were kept off in the church during this time. Then, with the singing of the Gloria, the lights were turned on and the entire congregation sang out joyfully: "Glory to God in the highest!" There was a reading from the New Testament Epistles, followed by a praise-filled chorus of "Alleluia", as the choir led the congregation in the Gospel Acclamation. The Gospel of the resurrection was proclaimed by Fr. Steve. His preaching was especially inspiring that night. Brandon listened and prayed, hoping his father's heart would somehow be touched.

Finally, the time of the celebration of the Sacraments of Initiation and the Rite of Reception of the candidates into the Church had come. Since the other two candidates had been baptized in other Christian denominations as children, Brandon would be the only one baptized there that night. The other two would be received in a ceremony separate from Baptism. They would all be confirmed and receive Holy Communion for the first time.

The other two candidates would have the opportunity for Confession between their entry into the Church and receiving Communion. But, just as the holy and wise old monk had told Brandon, with the waters of Baptism all of his past sins would be washed away. He would be made a new creation in Christ.

The first part of the ceremony was the litany of the saints, petitioning the intercession of those who were now fully alive in the presence of the Lord in heaven. The blessing of the water followed this.

As each phase of the ceremony unfolded, Brandon could feel the whole world being pushed out of his mind and heart. He was entirely focussed on the precious gift which he was about to receive. He renounced sin and made his profession of faith, feeling the significance of each vow to which he gave the assent of "I do".

When Mike tapped him on the shoulder, he realized the time had come. The moment for which he had waited and prayed for so long was now upon him.

Mike directed him to the font in the sanctuary. Brandon leaned over as Fr. Steve raised up his hands, filled with the newly blessed holy water, and proclaimed, "Brandon James Augustine, I baptize you in the name of the Father, and of the Son, and of the Holy Spirit."

Brandon stood back up as the holy water trickled down around him. The smile that illuminated him was of pure elation. He reached up with both hands and wiped the water from his face and hair. He wanted to shout out praises, but his mouth was held mute by the stifling intensity of joy that had stolen over his spirit. Tears began to wash down his cheeks.

No one could look upon this young man and not see tnat ne had become a new creation in Christ. Brandon was given a white garment to put over his clothes, signifying his dignity in Christ.

When the time came for Confirmation, Fr. Steve laid his hands over Brandon and the other candidates and prayed for the gifts of the Holy Spirit to be poured out in their lives. In Brandon's turn, Fr. Steve anointed his forehead with the sweet smelling chrism and pronounced the words, "Brandon James Augustine, be sealed with the Gift of the Holy Spirit.'

As he met Fr. Steve's eyes, Brandon conveyed an expression of utmost gratitude for this holy servant of God. Through his life dedicated to the priesthood, Fr. Steve had now bestowed upon Brandon spiritual life in the Sacraments of Initiation.

Fr. Steve nodded, acknowledging Brandon's gracious appreciation. He humbly said, "Peace be with you."

Brandon replied, sincerely, "And also with you."

Then in an ancient gesture, rarely used anymore, Fr. Steve tapped Brandon's cheek, symbolizing the adult Christian's need to be able and willing to defend the faith. The two men smiled, knowing that Brandon was willing to suffer so much more than that for the sake of the Cross.

Feeling the weight of Mike's hand, still on his shoulder, Brandon stood up and turned to Mike and hugged his friend.

"Thank you," was all Brandon could utter. The two words seemed so inadequate to convey his appreciation for the support and friendship that Mike had given to Brandon over the past several months.

Fr. Steve invited the congregation to welcome the three new Catholics into their midst. As people began to clap, they soon rose to their feet. The sound was like thunder, as everyone was swept away by the power of the Holy Spirit moving among them.

Together, Brandon and Mike returned to their places in the choir for the continuation of the celebration of the Eucharist.

Throughout the Eucharistic prayers, Brandon's heart stayed focussed intently on the gift of the Holy Sacrifice of the Mass. He knew very well that this was the Banquet Feast of the Lamb. It was heaven touching earth, sustaining all of mankind, making present to all the Eternal Sacrifice of Christ.

As the time for Communion came, Brandon led Joanie by the hand and took his place at the front of the church with the other two candidates. Brandon remembered every Mass he had ever attended, watching his beloved receive Jesus. How he had longed for the day when he could participate fully with her at the banquet table of the Lord. It was almost hard to believe that the time had now come.

Brandon opened his mouth and received the Sacred Host on his tongue. He turned to the distributor of the Precious Blood, took the Chalice to his lips, and received the Blood of Christ, his Saviour, poured out for his salvation.

His passion for Jesus was all-consuming. Brandon was so completely aware that in his own humble flesh he had now received Jesus: Body, Blood, Soul and Divinity. Suddenly, the words of St. John's Gospel flooded his heart and mind.

He who eats my flesh and drinks my blood has eternal life, and I will raise him up at the last day. For my flesh is food indeed, and my blood is drink indeed.

Brandon took his place, kneeling in the pew beside Joanie. He did not open his eyes again for a long time. He did not want anything to distract this time of thanksgiving to Jesus for the awesome gift of the Holy Eucharist.

Brandon knew he would never be the same again. Everything had changed inside him. Spiritually, he was a new creation. He had been filled with so many graces through the Sacraments, how could he ever turn his heart from God again? He recognized, yes, that in his frail fidelity, he would stumble and maybe fall. But he prayed for the grace to never lose his faith in Jesus.

When most of the congregation had received Communion, Joanie gently placed her hand on Brandon's shoulder. It was time to return to the choir. He followed her over and, taking their places, they led the choir in the Communion meditation song. Brandon and Joanie sang the verses. The choir and the entire congregation joined in on the choruses of "Hallelujah". . . . It was a night for rejoicing.

It was just as Joanie had said to him: Brandon's heart was so full that he needed to sing out his praises to the Lord. The final blessing was followed by a rousing traditional Easter hymn. The church swelled with the sound of praise.

The people poured out of the church with great enthusiasm to meet for fellowship in the place of welcoming. Before joining family and friends, Brandon took Joanie by the hand, and together they knelt to make their prayer of thanksgiving following the Mass. Jesus was within him and Joanie was beside him. It just did not seem to Brandon that it could get much better than that.

☦   ☦   ☦

They returned to join the congregation, now mostly assembled in the welcoming area. Brandon became bombarded with the good wishes of family and friends.

He managed to catch up with Tessa and Karl who had found Joanie.

Tessa threw her arms around Brandon and exclaimed, "I'm so proud of you!" Tears flowed from her sparkling blue-grey eyes. Brandon clasped hands with Karl and thanked them for coming.

Mark and Justine made it over to them. Mark slapped Brandon on the back and mussed up his hair. "You did it, buddy! You did it!" Mark's enthusiasm was so warming to Brandon. "And who knows, maybe next year I'll be the one taking the plunge. It's good to see you going in first to test the waters!" Brandon grabbed his friend by the shoulder and pulled him in for a hug.

This newly-baptized Christian was on top of the world tonight. The abundance of graces which God had bestowed upon him were far too many to count. Brandon could not contain his joy. It was there for all to see.

Over Mark's shoulder Brandon caught Justine's eyes, filled with tears of joy. He pulled open his hold on Mark and drew Justine in. Kissing her on the cheek, he whispered a sincere thanks.

By this time Joanie was visiting with Brandon's parents and Dan. James was truly on his best behaviour, and Caroline was demonstrating such graciousness. Brandon was overwhelmed at the sight of them. Quickly introducing Mark and Justine to Tessa and Karl, Brandon excused himself from his friends and walked over to greet his parents.

His mother stepped forward to congratulate her son. She took him into her gentle arms and kissed him tenderly on the cheek. Then holding his face between her hands, she looked deeply into his eyes and uttered, "Praise be to Jesus! You keep that faith burning brightly, son."

Brandon nodded and kissed her back lovingly. He shook Dan's hand and thanked him for his support as well.

Brandon turned to his father. He began to thank his dad for coming but tears welled up in the son's eyes.

His father, not one to give in to sentiment, put his hands on Brandon's shoulders and stated, "I have never felt so proud in my entire life as I did tonight, son. I can't even say at which moment I was the proudest. The whole service, the whole night, everything about it . . ." his voice trailed off momentarily. Then, finding his husky voice again, he said, "Keep it up, son, and you might just make a Christian out of me yet!"

Brandon laughed, recognizing his father's sincerity mingled with jesting. Brandon hugged his dad. As he did, he realized that this was the first time he had hugged his father since he was eight years old. He held on, firmly. It was a moment he did not ever want to forget.

James was transported back to a time that was all-but-forgotten in his life. He remembered holding a small child in his arms: his son. How little his appreciation had been back then of the tremendous privilege of fatherhood.

James was a successful man in business: wealthy, handsome, and esteemed by his peers. He had every comfort, luxury, and pleasure that a man could desire. But it all amounted to nothing, compared to the warmth of his son's embrace. He would have given it all up now in a heartbeat to be able to go back and be again a father to Brandon.

As they stepped back from that embrace, the son's and father's eyes met. There was love.

Joanie stood to the side. She hooked her arm into Caroline's. Her young heart was bursting with joy.

Caroline was pleased. In spite of all the pain that James had caused her, she had experienced tonight a grace of forgiveness and of healing. Through her love for her son, she could now look at James with new eyes. She could love him again with a new heart, and she was able to pray for him: *Jesus, bless James to come to know You, someday, somehow.*

Judy and John finally made their way over to be introduced to Brandon's father. They extended to James the invitation to come and join in the festivities at their home. At first James objected, but John—a match of equal manly presence—would not accept "no" for an answer. James acquiesced and got directions to the Collins home.

In the midst of all the commotion, Brandon finally caught up with Fr. Steve. Reaching into his lapel pocket, Brandon handed the young priest an envelope.

"Fr. Steve, I could never thank you enough for the gift of your priesthood and for the friendship you've given me this past year. Thank you for bringing Jesus into my life so completely tonight!"

Fr. Steve's eyes communicated the joy that was so characteristic of the young pastor. He was a priest who knew how to shepherd his flock with tremendous love. "Brandon, there are few things in a priest's life that are as rewarding as witnessing an adult embrace the Lord the way you have. You have blessed me many times over. I thank you for that."

Judy caught sight of the two men together and seized the opportunity to get pictures. She motioned to John who had the camera, and she sent Joanie to find Mike. Soon there was a whole group of family and friends gathered again at the front of the church taking photos to commemorate this special occasion.

With the photo session over, everyone began preparing to leave. Brandon asked John if it would be all right for him to drive Joanie back to the house. He first had a stop to make at his apartment, but they would not be long behind. John agreed and the young couple headed out.

Brandon pointed up to the door as he and Joanie were crossing the threshold. He leaned over and said, "I'm walking out of here a baptized Christian." As Joanie smiled up at him he put his arm around her and pulled her close to his side, mindful that it was her love that had brought him here in the first place.

Chapter 48

"Everyone's going to be waiting for us back at Mom and Dad's," Joanie said, as Brandon parked outside the front doors of his condo.

"Let them wait," he returned in a confident tone, "I have something to get here first."

"Well, I'll just wait for you down here, Brandon," Joanie stated, subtly reminding Brandon of their agreement not to go alone to his place.

"No, you won't, dear." It was not his words nor how he said them, but the look in his eyes that sent a chill up Joanie's spine. "And don't worry," he smiled at her in his reassuring way, "I've already cleared this with your father!"

She could not figure him out, but Joanie knew Brandon was up to something. Her heart raced as he opened the vehicle door for her and led her into the building.

As they entered his apartment, the crucifix which Joanie's father had given to Brandon immediately caught her eye. She had not been over to Brandon's place since Brandon had received the gift. The beautiful work of art hung above the fireplace, boldly proclaiming Brandon's faith in Jesus Christ to all who entered.

Joanie walked over to it and touched the wood gently. Brandon had gone into his room and returned. He tapped his pocket to indicate that he had what he had come to get.

The sight of Joanie, standing beneath the cross, stirred Brandon's heart. She was wearing the red dress that he liked so much. The string of pearls around her neck reminded him that tonight he had joined her as a citizen of the Kingdom: that pearl of great price. Above her, the outstretched arms of the King claimed Joanie as His beloved sister. And those same, powerful arms welcomed Brandon to share in the inheritance of His Kingdom.

Brandon recalled John's counsel on sacrificial loving. Brandon knew he would follow the King wherever He led. Brandon would pick up his cross and carry it each and every day. He would lay down his life for his beloved, in imitation of the One who had called him to this moment.

Joanie smiled over at Brandon, but the look in his eyes left her breathless. Her voice faltered, just above a whisper. "Are we ready to go?"

Brandon shook his head and came to stand before her, under the crucifix. "I have something for you first."

The fullness of his low voice resounded in Joanie's ears. Time and space faded into a vague abstraction for Joanie as her heart raced on. She did not dare to speak.

Brandon took her hand in his. Her dark, penetrating eyes never lost his gaze, as he went down on bended knee and lifted her delicate hand up to meet his lips in a kiss.

Gently, the words came from his heart, "Today has been the happiest day of my life. But . . . my joy would be made complete if you would do me the honour of consenting to be my wife. So I'm asking you, Joan Catherine Collins, will you marry me?"

Joanie stood motionless. Her eyes were lost somewhere in his. She felt as though the touch of his warm lips on her hand was the only thing keeping her connected to reality. He waited patiently, never moving a muscle, never taking his eyes from her intense gaze.

All at once, a smile began to illuminate her face, shining brilliantly through the tears in her eyes. Bringing her hands to his face, she leaned down and touched her lips to his forehead in a gentle kiss. She breathed deeply the fragrance of the chrism with which he had been anointed. The rich fragrance evoked the sweet memory of Brandon's Baptism and Confirmation that evening.

Her hands gently held his face as slowly she went down on her knees to kneel with him. She was completely absorbed in his gaze, and her fingers lightly caressed his face. Finding her voice, she whispered, "I will, Brandon. I will marry you. . . . And then together, our joy will be complete!"

Tenderly, he gathered her into his arms of love.

They remained in that embrace, unaware of time. The sensations of the moment completely overpowered the momentum of time. The exquisite feeling of the soft material of her dress which loosely clung to her back, the soft hair which brushed up against his cheek, the delicate head which was nestled between his neck and shoulder, the movement of her body as she breathed in and out the fullness of life around her: all these sensations entreated his strong arms to hold on gently. He now possessed in those loving arms someone more precious to him than life itself.

Thank You, Father, for Your daughter. Pour out Your grace into our hearts that through our love we will give glory to Your Name.

A thought broke through his silent prayer of thanksgiving. He had forgotten something. Brandon sat back on his feet and reached into his pocket, revealing a small, blue, velvety box. He opened it for Joanie.

Inside, there was a delicately crafted diamond ring. The diamond in the middle of the setting was accentuated by a smaller diamond on either side. The ring was exquisitely beautiful in the simplicity of its design.

Joanie looked from the box to Brandon's eyes, but remained speechless. Her tears were flowing freely now, and Brandon affectionately wiped both her cheeks dry. She laughed timidly at his tenderness. Her heart would have exploded had she tried to say a word.

Brandon took the dainty ring out of the box and, bringing it to his lips, he kissed it before placing it on Joanie's finger. She could hardly bring her-self to look down for fear that she would discover that it was all a dream.

Brandon brought her hand to his lips and gently kissed it, keeping his eyes fixed in her gaze.

Finally, Joanie looked down at the ring. The precious gem sparkled back up at her. She only looked briefly, for what was truly precious in her eyes was the love that was pouring forth from Brandon. All she wanted, at that moment, was to bathe herself in that love.

Helping her up, Brandon and Joanie stood once again before each other. He lifted his hands to touch her soft, smooth face. "Joanie, I want you to know that I had always intended to kiss you for the first time after I proposed to you. But I'm not going to now." Cradling her face with both his hands, he looked deeply into her eyes. "I want to wait until we stand together at the altar. But I also want to be sure that you're okay with that." He waited for her response.

Turning her face into the palm of his hand, she kissed it tenderly and smiled. "Brandon," she said, looking back up at him, "I have always trusted your sense of timing in our relationship. I do want you to know that I desperately want to be kissed by you . . . but I'll wait until the time is right. . . . I love you so much."

His hands made their way to the back of her head, moving his fingers gently through her soft hair. Pulling her closer to him, he softly kissed her on the forehead and whispered, "I love you, too, Joanie. And I want you to know that I completely desire, not only to kiss you, but to have you as my wife. When the time is right, after we're married, I will never withhold my affection from you again."

Brandon drew Joanie's head to rest against his shoulder. She could feel the pounding of their hearts, one against the other. She wrapped her arms lovingly around his waist, thrilling at the feeling of being held in his strong but tender embrace. When her hands met, the feeling of the ring on her finger reminded her that she and Brandon were now engaged to be married.

The courtship was over and the betrothal had now begun.

Quietly, but with reluctance, Brandon interrupted their embrace. "I'd better get us over to that party, or your father will think that we've eloped!"

Joanie laughed at the very idea. She kissed Brandon softly on the cheek, took his hand, and followed him out the door.

So much had happened that night. It was all too beautiful for words. Brandon was now Catholic, they were engaged to be married . . . and he had almost kissed her for the first time.

As they drove to the Collinses, Brandon held Joanie's hand, loosely resting it on the gearshift. They did not speak. The silence was far too sweet. Joanie rested her head on Brandon's shoulder and silently prayed.

Thank You, Jesus, for bringing Brandon into my life. Let me love him with all the beauty of the love You intended between a man and a woman, a husband and a wife. May our life together give glory to Your most Holy Name.

Joanie fixed her eyes upon her hand. As the Pathfinder made its way through the city streets, the flashes of street lights coming through the windows played with the shimmering diamond. The sparkling gem boasted to the world of the love and commitment that existed between this newly betrothed couple.

✟ ✟ ✟

The party was well under way at the Collins home. Everyone was there and waiting for the guest of honour to arrive. Brandon held Joanie's hand as they walked through the crowd of people, keeping their secret hidden. She did not want anyone to see until her mother had.

Judy saw the young couple coming across the room and had a curious intuition about them. A mother knows.

Joanie and Brandon stopped before her and Brandon presented Joanie's hand for her mother to see. Judy clapped her hands with joy and reached out to take her daughter into her arms. By this time several people had caught on to the excitement which spread like wildfire throughout the room.

John, prepared for the occasion, brought out a large bottle of wine and with Isaac's assistance filled the glasses. At last he raised his cup and began:

"There are few greater honours for a father than to be able to announce to his family and friends the engagement of his beautiful and loving daughter to such a fine, young, Catholic Christian man. So I first toast God who has blessed us all to be here tonight."

The crowd called out, "To God!"

"Next," John went on, "I toast Jesus Christ for His life, His death, and His resurrection."

With enthusiasm, they all exclaimed, "To Jesus Christ!"

"Next I toast Brandon for the many gifts he has received tonight. You have inspired us all for some time, Brandon, to be better Christians. I can't imagine how powerfully the Lord will work through you now that you have full access to all the graces of the Sacraments. We toast you for the work the Lord has done and will continue to do in your life!"

Everyone cheered, "To Brandon!"

"And finally," John concluded, "I toast this young couple. Brandon and Joanie, you have virtuously grown in your love and commitment to each other. May God bless you as you enter into your time of betrothal."

The shout rang out, "To Brandon and Joanie!" The noise of cheering filled the stately old house. Joanie and Brandon stood at the centre of the celebration, their hearts soaring.

In the midst of all the festivities, Katie called out, "Aren't you going to kiss her, Brandon?"

Joanie blushed as Brandon put his arm around her waist and answered, "I'm sorry, but I'm waiting until she says 'I do' before I kiss her. But," he continued as the crowd began to react, "I cordially invite all of you to be there to witness it."

Everyone laughed and cheered on the young couple. Joanie was overwhelmed by all the excitement around her and within her. She clung on to Brandon, leaning against his tall frame for support.

✠   ✠   ✠

The night wore on and by two-thirty in the morning, people were finally finding their way home. Many of the small children had fallen asleep in corners all around the house. It took quite some time to sort it all out and make sure no one got left behind.

Brandon stayed to help clean up as much as possible. Finally, Judy patted his back and said, "The rest will wait 'til morning, son."

He leaned over, kissed her cheek, and hugged her warmly. "Thank you for everything, Judy," he uttered, softly. "I could never express my gratitude to you for all you have been for me."

She patted his back gently and said, "Oh, you have, Brandon, you already have."

He said good-night to the family, and Joanie walked him to the front porch. "I'm afraid I won't be able to sleep tonight," she confessed.

He laid his hand on her head and said, "I pray that you will . . . and that you'll have beautiful dreams, because I know I will."

He drew his hand down the side of her face until her jaw was nestled into the palm of his hand.

She turned her face into it and kissed it lovingly. "Good-night, sweetheart," she whispered.

✠   ✠   ✠

Brandon went home. His mother and Dan had left the Collinses hours earlier, so he was quiet entering the apartment. He lay on the couch in the darkness and smiled. The aroma of chrism filled the room, and he thought back to the events of the Easter Vigil.

He fixed his eyes on the dark outline of the crucifix high above him. Closing his eyes, he pictured Joanie as she had stood there before him that night. He could feel her as he had held her in his arms. His whole life had changed so drastically in one night. He would forevermore be a new man, living with a new purpose.

His thoughts became more and more disjointed until all at once he was asleep. His body surrendered to the total exhaustion which had slipped over him like a warm blanket. He did not move again until morning.

✠   ✠   ✠

Joanie struggled to keep awake. She so desperately wanted to relive in her mind the events of the evening. But the fatigue in her body pulled persistently at her thoughts until sleep won over. She slept so deeply that she was not even aware of having dreamt.

Everyone slept late the next morning. As soon as Joanie opened her eyes, she closed them again, wanting to transport her mind back to the night before. But as she felt the weight of the ring on her finger, she just had to roll over and look at it.

Amie was awake, lying in her bed across the room. "Joanie," she spoke out dreamily, "what does it feel like to be engaged?"

Joanie pictured Brandon and smiled. "Wonderful," she replied.

Amie propped herself up on her elbow and tilted her head sideways, taking in Joanie. "I hope that the man I marry will be as wonderful as Brandon."

"Oh, he will be, Amie," Joanie assured her, "because God has a perfect plan for you. Just trust Him to find for you your perfect match when the time is right."

Amie remained pensive for a moment and then added, "Well, I'm glad he found Brandon for you."

"Thanks, Amie," Joanie answered, looking straight at her sister. Amie was a wonderful girl, bright and beautiful. Her personality sparkled with a sincere and pure charity for everyone. She was as easy to read as a book. She could not tell a lie if her life depended on it. Her charm shone through her contagious smile. It was simply impossible not to be happy around Amie.

Joanie got out of bed and went over to sit by her sister. She held her hand out for her to look at the ring. Taking hold of Joanie's hand, Amie examined the ring carefully. As Joanie watched her younger sister, she said, "You know, you all will be my bridesmaids: Maggie, you, and Katie. And Jessie will be my flower girl."

Amie sat up and hugged Joanie tightly. "I love you Joanie. I'm gonna miss you when you move out."

"I'll be around, lots," Joanie assured her. "You won't get rid of me that easily!"

Laughing together, they got up for the day.

Chapter 49

It did not take long for news of the engagement to spread. Everyone at the station made a big deal over it when Joanie showed up for work on Tuesday. There were flowers from Mr. Lemay to congratulate the young couple and a bottle of wine that he warned them not to open at work.

Even Taylor was duly impressed. In spite of his rough edges, the charm and beauty of this young couple in love was not lost on him. He congratulated Brandon. "After all," as he put it, "if you had to get caught by somebody, Joanie's better than most."

✛   ✛   ✛

Plans for their wedding and preparation for marriage soon became the focus of attention for Joanie and Brandon. They had spoken with Fr. Steve and had set a date, deciding on the Labour Day weekend in September. It would give Joanie time to finish her written counterpoint exam in May and her vocal exam in June. They could then spend the summer attending to the many details of the wedding celebration.

Fr. Steve set them up with a married couple who taught Natural Family Planning. There would be no more marriage prep classes offered again until fall, so he agreed to meet with the couple monthly to help them prepare for marriage. He was not worried, for he knew Joanie and Brandon were entering into the Sacrament of Marriage with a far better understanding than that of most couples.

Joanie and Brandon had used their time of courtship well to lay a foundation for a relationship based on mutual trust and respect. They were of one mind and heart when it came to following the Church's teachings regarding marriage and family planning. They were disciplined and self-sacrificing. Their decision to get married had not become obscured by a sexual relationship that would have formed premature bonds and disordered dependencies. All these things were evidence of the love that was between them—a love that would stand the test of time.

The immediate details of planning a wedding were quickly sorted out: booking a hall and a caterer, arranging music for the wedding and dance, making invitations and choosing a photographer. It was a great deal of fun planning together, but the couple was very conscious of not allowing things to become too extravagant.

Neither Joanie nor Brandon wanted a showy wedding, but the size of the wedding party had to be made large enough to involve all of Joanie's sisters.

Brandon asked Mark to be his best man with Mike, Ben, and Isaac standing in the wedding party. Zack and Aaron were included as ring bearers and that way no one was left out.

Joanie and her mother picked out a simple but stylish pattern for bridesmaid dresses, and Joanie chose a pale blue colour in honour of the Blessed Virgin Mary. They decided to wait until Joanie had finished her exams before they would start sewing.

The mother and daughter cherished the time they spent together shopping for a bridal gown. It did not take long to find a wedding dress that was exactly Joanie's style.

It was simple, with a classic, elegant line. The fitted bodice was daintily accented by a scalloped neck, formed from embroidered floral patterns. The shoulders were smooth, opening up into full-length, satin, fitted sleeves, scalloped at the wrist with small pearls. It came to a dropped waistline from which hung a full length skirt with layers of light-weight, satiny fabric. There was no train. The fingertip-length veil started from a pearl-studded comb, with a blusher that came forward to cover the face.

✝   ✝   ✝

Mark and Justine were planning their wedding for mid-July, and so the two couples shared ideas and swapped notes. It was fun having something in common, but the best part was the great discussions they would have.

Mark had become quite a proponent for chastity and Natural Family Planning. Sometimes it even shocked him how much he had changed in so short a time. The two couples provided mutual support for each other: each understanding the challenges of chastity, yet both reaping the manifold blessings of the virtue.

Justine sparkled like a diamond whenever Mark shared his new convictions. The deepening of the love between the two of them was clearly evident in the expression of Mark's respect and admiration for his future bride. He treated Justine like a queen, and she in turn made him feel like a king.

Brandon and Joanie had been blessed with this from the beginning of their relationship. Still, it was encouraging for them to see how chastity could make new an old and tiresome relationship—breathing life into a love that had been dying.

✝   ✝   ✝

Spring is a long time in coming on the Canadian prairies. Just when one thinks it has arrived, winter shows up again and drops another blanket of snow. Finally, one day, when all hope seems to be gone, spring breaks through, triumphant. The warm breezes melt away all the evidence of winter and draw people outdoors. Spring rains clean up the dirty-looking streets and gradually bring back to life the barren trees as they bud forth their new array of greenery.

Joanie's studies and practice schedule had intensified to the point that she had to cut back on her commitments with *New Spring*. Work at the station became a challenge as she struggled not to be distracted by the stress of her upcoming exams. Time spent alone with Brandon had all but disappeared. Each night she went to bed exhausted.

It was a long haul, but finally, one stormy spring day in May, she wrote her grade four counterpoint exam. It was the last of the written components needed for her degree in singing, and she was relieved to be coming to the conclusion of this long, arduous process.

Brandon came to pick Joanie up at the school where the exams were being held. She sat down in the vehicle, mentally fatigued, but feeling quite confident all the same. To celebrate, Brandon took her to dinner, which Joanie cut short to get home to practise. She had three weeks until her voice exam, and she desperately guarded each opportunity that she had to prepare herself. Brandon took her home, and she excused herself to get to work.

Brandon hooked up with Isaac, and the two of them played guitar together, as they often did these days. Isaac was, in Brandon's estimation, a natural-born guitarist. He had that certain rhythmic feel for the instrument that cannot be taught. It was instinct. The fact that they both shared this innate gift was the basis for a strong bond between the two.

Isaac was thirteen now and looked up to Brandon as the hero that Brandon truly was in the young boy's life. The twenty-seven-year-old was an excellent role model, rock solid in his faith and dedicated in his pursuit of virtuous living.

But the admiration was mutual, for in turn Brandon admired Isaac's pure and undivided commitment to his faith. Brandon jealously wished that he had had Isaac's convictions when he had been thirteen. He knew that Isaac would not make the mistakes that he had made. The youth's path would be free of the many pitfalls with which secular living is beset.

Brandon, grateful for where he was now in his life, was determined to give that same solid foundation to his own children someday.

✝   ✝   ✝

The night before Joanie's singing exam, she asked Brandon to take her out. She did not want to think about the next day. She wanted to take her mind off her music.

"Distract me anyway you can," she told him, "within moral limits, that is," she qualified.

So Brandon told her to get all dressed up, and he took her to a very classy restaurant for wining, dining, and dancing. Joanie was not much of a drinker, but the dining and dancing part surely did appeal to her.

The Skyline was a beautiful restaurant, set at the top of a hotel in downtown Saskatoon. With windows on three sides, it boasted a spectacular view of the river and the landscape, which extended for miles beyond the city limits. As night descended upon the quiet city, the young lovers watched the street lights flicker on, one by one. Soon the river was shimmering in a luminous reflection on this perfect summer's night.

It was a blessed time alone together, treasured that much more because they had been denied this luxury over the past few months. They talked about wedding plans; they talked about marriage and children; they talked about building a home together. The evening grew old, far too soon.

Brandon warned Joanie at ten-thirty, "This is it, Joanie, the last dance. You've conned three extra dances out of me with your alluring charm, but I'm taking you home after this one."

She gave him a little pout that did not faze him at all. Resigning herself to her fate, she cuddled up closely and snuggled in for the last dance to the soft music. She could have gone on dancing forever in his strong arms. When she was alone with Brandon, all the outside world seemed to fade into nothingness: she had absolutely no worries.

She closed her eyes and breathed deeply, trying to draw in every sensation of the moment. When the dance finally ended, Brandon led her, reluctantly, off the dance floor and home. They did not talk much in the car. Joanie played with Brandon's hand on the gearshift.

He got out and walked her to the front porch, kissed her tenderly on the hand, and blessed her to have a peaceful sleep. As he began to walk away, she pulled him back by the arm and hugged him one last time. He kissed the top of her head and this time he opened the door to the house for her and directed her inside, saying, "You'll do fine. . . . I'll be here to pick you up at nine-thirty."

She daintily waved her fingers "good-bye" and went in the house to bed.

✟   ✟   ✟

Sleep did not come easily for Joanie, but it did come at last. The next day she was up bright and early, warming up her voice and doing some exercises to stretch out the tension in her body.

Amie, her accompanist, was running over the pieces at the piano. Joanie was very grateful that Amie was able to play for her. After years of performing together, they worked well as a team. Any singer knows the value of a good accompanist. Amie was just that: a confident and accomplished pianist who consistently rose to the occasion.

When Brandon arrived, the girls were ready to go. He drove them to the location for the exam and promised to stay and wait; he had a good book to read. Joanie registered herself and returned to sit down with Amie and Brandon for the long wait. They made small talk, and Brandon tried to distract both girls by reading passages from his book. Still, the time dragged on as though minutes had turned into hours.

At last, it was their turn to go in. Brandon kissed Joanie's hand and patted Amie on the back. He reached into his pocket, pulled out his rosary, and winked at the two girls as they followed the examiner into the studio.

The expression on Amie's face said it all when, an hour later, the two girls returned to the waiting area.

"She aced it!" Amie began, enthusiastically. "I've never heard Joanie sing so well!" Amie's eyes sparkled with pride for her big sister. She clung onto Joanie's arm and gave her a little shake. "Tell him, Joanie."

"It went well," Joanie asserted in a practical tone, "but I don't want to get my hopes up: examinations can be very unpredictable. But in any case, I'm done." A smile broke over her calm face, and she reached up and hugged Brandon. "I'm done. I can finally spend time with you again. I don't even care how it turns out now."

Brandon hugged her tightly and responded, "I'm glad you're done, too, dear. But I also believe Amie when she tells me you did well. I could hear you somewhat, from out here, and there is no one who could contest the strength and beauty of that voice of yours."

"Thank you," she said humbly. "Now, would you please take me and my most esteemed accompanist out for an ice cream?"

Brandon positioned himself between the two young ladies, extended his arms for them to hold, and escorted them out to the Pathfinder.

When they got home Joanie's mother had planned a big supper to celebrate the occasion. It was a warm spring day, the kind that says that summer is almost here. Joanie and Brandon enjoyed a wonderful evening of playing with the little ones in the park. The day rounded off nicely with a campfire and singsong, inaugurating campfire season "officially open" for the summer.

Joanie felt happy and free. With the constraints of long hours of practice and study behind her, she could now begin to focus on plans for their wedding.

Chapter 50

"It'll just be for two nights," Brandon assured Joanie. By the look in her eyes, he could tell she was warming up to the idea. Joanie did not answer; she was still thinking about it.

"No way!" Justine was not caving in on this one.

"Please, honey. Come on. It's our last shot at freedom!" Mark pleaded his cause.

Joanie laughed at the dramatic lengths to which these guys would go in order to get the girls' permission to leave for a three-day camping trip. "Oh, come on, Mark! Last shot at freedom? Are you getting married to Justine in three weeks, or going to prison?"

Seeing the amusement in Joanie's eyes, Mark began to laugh along with her.

"Bad choice of words there, buddy," Brandon nodded in agreement with Joanie.

With arms crossed in front of her, Justine kept her cool eyes fixed on Mark.

"Sorry, honey. I didn't mean it that way," he apologized to his future bride. "But all we're asking for is a short three-day camping trip—for old time's sake. Look, neither one of us is planning to have a bachelor party. This would be it."

"I promise to bring him back to you alive and well," Brandon assured Justine.

"Easy promise to make now, Brandon," Justine returned, "until Mark ends up as feed for fish at the bottom of the Churchill River System!"

Instead of laughing at her ridiculous assertion, Mark snuggled up to his beautiful fiancée, snuck his arm around her shoulder, and kissed her softly on the cheek. Justine stiffened at first, but as Mark persisted with his romantic overture, she began to relax.

Giggling softly, she pushed him away. "Cut it out, Mark! You're not going to get your way with me like that," she insisted.

"At least not for three more weeks," Brandon added.

Everyone started to laugh, and Justine gave Mark an affectionate smack on the arm.

"Please, Justine," Mark said looking at her with gently pleading eyes. "I wouldn't go if you didn't say yes."

Pressure of the subtle kind. Put it all on me! Justine went over the entire scenario in her mind and threw it back at them. "You guys show up here with the whole thing planned out. You've got maps; you've booked off time from work already—"

"Only on condition," Mark clarified for her. "We just wanted to be sure we could do it in the event you both said yes." Mark's eyes sparkled with that irresistible boyish charm that he possessed.

Justine gave a reluctant groan and then said, "Fine!"

"Yes!" the boys called out in unison.

Brandon caught himself, turned to Joanie and added, "I mean—that is, of course—if you give the okay, as well." He smiled at her, playfully entreating her with his eyes.

Joanie shook her head and laughed. "Yes. But just you remember," she warned, shaking her finger at him, "I need a groom here in two months as well. And preferably you! I'm not sure I could find a replacement on that short a notice."

Brandon grabbed her hand while she was still shaking it. He kissed it affectionately as he gathered her up into his arms and implored her, "Well, please don't start looking for a replacement until you're absolutely sure you'll need one."

✝   ✝   ✝

And so it was that the two young *coureurs de bois* planned their journey into the wilderness. With gear packed and canoe strapped to the top rack of Brandon's Pathfinder, they took in eight o'clock Mass Sunday morning and from there, headed north.

It was a tremendous feeling to be out on the road together again. They had never felt closer. Although they had always shared an intimate friendship with each other, they now had something between them that cemented that bond. They both had faith in Jesus Christ. They talked the whole five hours of the drive. They laughed over old times. They shared regrets over past failings. They disclosed their dreams for the future, and they exalted God for His tremendous mercy and grace in their lives.

The open fields of wheat, canola, flax, and barley created a patchwork quilt, covering the gentle contours of the sleeping land. The grid system of roads created seams across the fabric, stretching out as far as the eye could see. As they drove further north, though, the patchwork quilt began to appear tattered, torn apart by an increasing number of poplar groves and spruce trees.

Before long, Brandon and Mark had passed through the portal to the northern frontier. Pine trees lined the winding way, standing by the roadside like sentinels on guard, as deeper into the wilderness the young men pressed on. Here and there the guards had fallen off duty, leaving breaks in the forest walls, through which the young *voyageurs* caught glimpses of crystal, clear lakes: the hidden treasures of this formidable land.

Brandon opened his window as they drove along and breathed in the fresh northern air. It was a cloudy day and the air was crisp. "Hope you packed some warm clothes, Mark. It's still pretty cool at night up here," Brandon commented, looking out into the trees.

"No fear, mate," Mark replied. He was an experienced camper from years of northern excursions with his dad. Brandon had tagged along on many of those memorable camping trips.

Mark's father had taught them all about wilderness survival. Brandon was always grateful for the presence of Mr. Jacobs in his life. He knew that Mark's parents had concerns about the boys' relationship, with Brandon always getting Mark into trouble. But when camping with Mark's father, a respect for the authority of the voice of experience would stir Brandon into a docile obedience and an openness to learning. It was one of those things in adolescence that probably saved Mark and Brandon from total rebellion.

It was good to be back in the north. The boys had not gone camping together for two years now, but still the routines were second nature to them. They communicated in silence as they unloaded at the service station in Missinipe. They would launch off here, travel as far as they could get before nightfall, and set up camp. They had packed meat for supper that night, but after that it was catch fish or go hungry.

Brandon and Mark stood on the dock, taking in the vastness of the majestic scene. Shores of spruce trees, so thick that they appeared like well manicured lawns, lined the far side of the lake. Yet as the lake opened up to the northeast, there was a narrow passage where no separation between the sky and the water existed.

The brilliant blue body of water, a part of a chain of lakes which made up the Churchill River System, lay before them invitingly. It had the appearance of an old friend beckoning the boys to step down into their canoe, take up the challenge, and live the adventure that it promised.

Without breaking the silence, they got into the canoe and pushed off the dock. Like a well-oiled machine with synchronized motion, the powerful strokes of the two woodsmen pulled the canoe forward through the glassy surface. They could cover a fair distance in short time on a calm day like this. The cloud cover was gone, and the day had warmed up.

They paddled hard for an hour, neither one talking. It was enough to breathe in the air, to hear the purling sound—as the paddles broke the surface of the water with each stroke—to feel the canoe pushing through the crystal lake, and to fill their eyes with the pulchritude of creation: pure and undisturbed.

The late afternoon sun beat down on them. An occasional cloud brought a moment's reprieve from the intensity of the heat. They were both ready for the break when Brandon, who was at the bow, laid his paddle across the canoe and leaned on it.

The canoe pushed on through the water for another few minutes, gradually slowing until it floated along in the current. Brandon reached down and took a drink from his water bottle.

When Brandon turned around, Mark saluted his friend with his hat, as he lowered it down into the fresh water of the lake and then placed it back on his head of wavy brown hair. The coldness of the water dripping down his hot face in the heat of the June sun was pure refreshment.

Brandon removed his own hat and wiped the sweat off his brow with the backside of his hand. Smiling, he imitated his friend's action, soaking in the simple joys of nature.

The smile on their faces and the look in their eyes set the challenge between the two northern travellers. How long could they go without breaking the silence? Finally, Mark jerked his head forward, indicating for them to push on. The silence remained unbroken.

After another hour of hard paddling, Mark pointed off to the right with his paddle. There was a little cove with a small peninsula jutting off the far side of it.

"There's camp," Mark said, plainly.

Brandon nodded in agreement, smiling as he met Mark's intense green eyes. The silence had not really been broken, only slightly cracked. There was no need to put in a wedge and split it wide open . . . not just yet.

Mark resumed paddling and skilfully steered them in to an open spot along the rocky edge. They tied up the canoe and unloaded their gear, packing it up the slope to an open spot on the ground.

The location had obviously been a favoured campsite by other northern travellers. There was a crude campfire pit that had not been used in days, but recently enough not to have been overgrown. The grass was flattened out in one area, giving evidence of the tents that had provided shelter in this cozy little corner of paradise.

"Well, let's set up camp," Brandon began. "Tent over here where there's some shelter, in case the wind blows up tonight?"

"Sure," Mark agreed. They set to work and in no time they had the camp looking like a home. Mark gathered up some kindling and started a fire, while Brandon took the axe and chopped some more wood.

The late afternoon was turning into evening, and it did not take long before the boys were covering themselves in mosquito repellent. Therein lay the only set-back of any great northern adventure—pesky mosquitoes. Even as they slapped at mosquitoes and sprayed on the repellent, these two seasoned campers knew that the scourge of mosquitoes was a necessary evil of most northern experiences. There had been worse years, though, for the blood-sucking insects.

"Pass that can over here," Mark called out, holding up his hands to catch it.

Brandon tossed the can to his friend. "I will never understand, as long as I live," Brandon commented, while still wiping the spray around his face and neck, "why God created mosquitoes."

"To tempt new Christians to swear, I suppose," Mark returned, his face contorted in the effort to reach over his shoulder and spray his back.

The two friends laughed, exchanging that look of knowing.

Neither of them used foul language anymore. It was something understood between them. They were the only two members of a very specific support group for redeemed secular cads. Swearing and dirty jokes were like little doorways that opened up to the immoral mentality of their former lives.

Brandon had become very disciplined in this manner, directed through grace to this virtuous practice. He knew good Christians who infrequently used foul language. Even John and Judy Collins were known to have uttered the occasional foul word. But Brandon recognized, for himself, it was much like a recovering alcoholic who refuses a drink around those who can enjoy alcohol without ever getting drunk. Brandon, in his determination to abandon the impurity of his past life, had vowed to keep his mouth clean.

For out of the abundance of the heart the mouth speaks, he would remind himself, quoting from the Gospels.

Joanie admired and respected this self-discipline in her chivalrous knight. She was the fair and chaste maiden for whom he had abandoned all immodesty and impurity in order to become worthy of her love. It was as simple as that. He would have gladly laid down his life for her. This was nothing by comparison. And still, it was a training ground upon which sanctity was being forged in this man.

After Mark's conversion, he had followed Brandon's remarkable example. Since they had supported and encouraged each other in so many sins together in the past, the lifelong friends were a natural support and encouragement to each other along this Christian journey.

Mark had realized after his conversion that respect was of the essence in his new relationship with Justine. And respect was something that came through a disciplined decision. It was not enough to say he respected Justine. He had to live it.

How could Mark demonstrate respect to Justine while telling dirty jokes in her company or otherwise? How could he demonstrate respect for the Lord while using the Lord's name in vain—casual fillers in empty conversations? How could he demonstrate respect for his future bride while watching dirty movies or looking at pornography? How could he demonstrate respect for the future mother of his children while making lewd and crude references to human sexuality through vulgar explosions of the tongue?

No. Respect, chastity, love, and honour had to be put into practice by daily turning away his heart, his eyes, and his mouth from sin and the near occasions of sin. It was a decision lived out moment by moment. And it was all for the love of a woman who had brought him to the love of God. It was as simple as that, for this was a testing fire through which holiness was being forged in this man.

The two friends continued their camp duties without complaining and without swearing over those pesky mosquitoes.

They had decided to stay both nights at this spot, and from here they would paddle off and fish the next day. They noticed on their map of the river system that another hour downstream would lead them to some rapids. They would shoot them the next day and then portage back across a narrow passageway indicated on the map.

They set to work making supper. Brandon fried up the steaks and cut up some potatoes which he pan-fried with much seasoning and a generous amount of butter. They opened up a couple of beers and sat back to relax and enjoy the meal. The sun hung around for awhile, giving them time to finish eating at a leisurely pace. Mark complimented the chef. It was not only a satisfying meal because they were hungry, but because Brandon was a good cook. After supper Brandon took their left-over food supplies and dishes and secured it all in a cache, high up a tree, some fifty feet away from their camp, in case of bears. Mark cleaned up the campsite, then pulled out his harmonica.

The two friends went to the shoreline where they sat to watch the sunset. Mark, a skilled blues musician, serenaded the sun as it made its farewell salute to the day.

Clouds were blowing in from the west. Still, there was enough of a break near the north-western horizon to allow for the light to shine up from underneath. It extended out in an array of glorious colours, textured by the movement of the clouds. It was a Saskatchewan northern sunset, incomparable in value to the true outdoorsman.

The cloud cover that had blown in helped to keep the night from getting too cold, but the breeze was beginning to stir up into a wind by the water's edge. Knowing their camp was well protected, the boys climbed back up the slope and stoked up the fire which had burned down to a bed of coals. They got a good blaze burning and made themselves comfortable.

Mark stirred up stimulating conversation about the Catholic Church. He had been making a fair study of it for the past few months now and wanted to swap notes with Brandon.

Mark was a methodic student; he left no stone unturned in his pursuit of truth. He loved the challenge of pushing his mind to take in as many facts as he could cram into it. Academically, he was in love with the unlimited opportunity that the Catholic Church offered to study theologians and saints extending back two thousand years in history. Added to that, the five thousand years of Old Testament history made it all so alluring to the young scholar's mind.

Brandon could relate, having experienced the same insatiable appetite for learning when he had first become a Christian. He had toned down, though, to a steady-paced diet of good reading, listening to great speakers, and the occasional indulgence in just this type of conversation.

Night was approaching dawn when, finally, the young theologians decided to go to bed.

☦   ☦   ☦

The boys slept in as late at they could, resisting the brightness of the day until at last the sun broke through the trees that had been shading the tent. Once up, Brandon and Mark did not waste time. They checked their cache, which was still secure, filled their day pack with a good supply of gorp—a mixture of nuts, dried fruit, and chocolate chips which Mark had put together—and headed out.

They were at the rapids within the hour; the breeze had moved them along quickly. They took a break along the smooth shoreline, got out of their canoe and stretched their arms and legs.

With challenging rapids ahead, stretching out over a quarter of a mile, the boys decided to do a walk-through. As the young woodsmen scouted the path they would follow, they noticed a break in the rapids part way. This would make an ideal spot to pull off to shore. The rushing, white waters splashed and swirled, calling out the challenge as the boys discussed their plan.

As they walked back over the section which they had plotted out mentally, they decided they would put out markers to forewarn them of the larger boulders that lay in their path. There were tree stumps and branches extending over the edge of the shoreline that they could use for hanging their markers.

"Here, Mark," Brandon called out, pulling off his own T-shirt, "take off your shirt, and we'll hang it there, just ahead of that boulder. You're steering, so remember that's a hard starboard when we get to that point."

Mark tied his T-shirt over a dead branch at the spot Brandon had indicated. "We'll use your pink shirt to mark the hard port back there," Mark teased his friend, as he pointed to a stump near the water's edge.

"The shirt's not pink," Brandon defended his masculinity against the friendly attack. "It's salmon! Joanie picked it out for me because she likes the way it accentuates my tan!"

"I'm sure the bears and fish are impressed; nevertheless, we're calling it 'pink for port' today, Mr. G.Q.!"

Brandon flexed his muscles. "Eat your heart out, buddy!" He proceeded to attach the shirt to a stump.

After years of working out regularly, Brandon's muscular body was toned and taut. And although Mark was strong and in good shape, he appeared small next to Brandon.

"Yeah, yeah! Well, fortunately for me, Justine happens to like the lean and lithesome type. And I can still take you any day on the tennis courts!"

"Well, Mr. Lean and Lithe, just be sure you can hold your own back there in the stern. I'm counting on your superior *voyageur* instincts to make sure we don't crash. After all, I did promise Justine I'd bring her back a groom in one piece."

The two adventurers stood over the rapids for one last mental picture. They ran over the plan of attack, making sure they were both on the same wavelength, then headed back down to the canoe.

They stripped off their hats, shoes, and socks, leaving them with their gear on the shore. They were about to get really wet! Slipping on their life jackets, with a last drink from their water bottles, they stepped into the canoe and pushed off. White waters were calling.

With minds completely focussed on the task at hand, everything else was forgotten; all time slipped away. It was just them and the river, leading them on. They knew from experience that they had to work with the movement of the water in order to avoid being swallowed up by the force of its mighty current. Their arms pulled forcefully. The water splashed up against their bodies. Their wills were set with determination . . . and the entire experience was completely exhilarating.

Within ten minutes the boys had successfully navigated their canoe to the break in the rapids and over to the shoreline in the calm waters. Pulling their canoe up onto the shore, the two adventurers threw off their life jackets and lay back in the sand to dry off and catch their breath. After several minutes, having soaked in the glory of their victory, they portaged their canoe back to their gear, collecting their shirts along the way.

With the satisfaction of having met the challenge, they got back into their canoe and paddled out to a small cove to begin fishing. It was time to stop playing and to begin focussing on survival. They would be awfully hungry by suppertime if they did not catch any fish. Fortunately, after an hour Mark landed a huge pickerel.

"Well, I know what I'm eating for supper tonight, buddy!" Mark called out, as the fish flopped around in the canoe.

"Don't you count me out just yet," Brandon returned. "I won't be going hungry tonight!" Sure enough, within the hour Brandon had landed a pickerel that clearly rivalled Mark's catch.

They headed back to camp and filleted their fish down by the water's edge. When they were finished they both agreed that Brandon should be chief cook, while Mark chopped more firewood for the evening. They ate an early supper, savouring every bite of the fresh fish, sautéed with wine, cooked to perfection over the fire, and served with rice. Their tin cups were filled with wine as they sat back and enjoyed the excellent cuisine served in the splendour of nature.

Near ten o'clock they witnessed another spectacular northern sunset as they sat on the shore of their little peninsula. The clouds had cleared enough by nightfall that the boys were hoping to be able to enjoy northern lights and watch the stars. But with the days just having passed the summer solstice, the light never completely faded into darkness this far north. Only the brightest stars made a faint appearance that night. Mark challenged Brandon to pick out as many constellations as he could, but Mark was clearly the astronomer of the two.

The two stargazers lay back, pondering the vastness of the universe. In the past they had marvelled at all the wonders of creation, so clearly evident in the wilderness. This time, though, they marvelled not only at the wonders, but at Him who had created them in wisdom and in beauty.

When it got too cool to stay by the lake, they headed back to their camp for another late night of talking and joking around the fire. They both agreed that of all the camping trips they had made together, this had been the best. But it was not because of what they had experienced together up north this time; rather, it was because of what they had waiting for them back home!

✟   ✟   ✟

Brandon dropped off Mark at his apartment late Tuesday night, both enjoying that sense of satisfaction which comes from time spent in the sublimity of nature and in the company of a good friend. They were exhausted, but renewed physically and spiritually, all the same.

Arriving back at his own condo, Brandon checked his messages—seven of them. He skipped through each one disinterestedly, hoping only to hear Joanie's voice before he collapsed into bed. Finally, the last message on the machine was hers, left only an hour earlier.

"Welcome home, Brandon. I just wanted to leave you a message saying good-night to you before you went to bed. Hope you and Mark had a wonderful canoe trip. Justine and I had a great day together on Sunday. I missed you . . . my whole family missed you! I'll see you at work tomorrow. . . . I love you. Good-night."

He replayed the message a few times, until he had satisfied his ears with the sweet sound of her voice.

✟   ✟   ✟

Wednesday morning passed by with no sign of Brandon. Joanie had hoped she might meet up with him in the lounge at coffee time, but she realized that he must be trying to catch up on lost time at work. With disappointment, she returned to her cubicle where she found a note taped below her pictures of Jesus and Mary. It was from Brandon. He wanted to take her for lunch, and she was to meet him at his vehicle promptly at twelve.

She busily got back to her day file, doing her research, setting appointments for the afternoon, carefully avoiding lunch-hour engagements. When noon hour arrived, the young research-reporter wasted no time in getting out to the parking lot.

Brandon was waiting, leaning against his Pathfinder. The metallic silver-grey was a wonderful backdrop for the rugged adventurer. Joanie feasted her eyes on him as she walked across the parking lot. His arms were crossed, as was his right foot over his left. He was so handsome in his tan pants and steely-blue shirt, with sleeves rolled up in that Brandon way.

His blue eyes shone out from across the distance like the beacon from a lighthouse guiding her in. One of his eyebrows was raised in his usual calm yet intriguing way, and his mouth was held in a half-smile. She could feel him taking in her every movement as she approached. That used to make her feel self-conscious, but now it just made her feel loved and cherished.

Once close enough to him, he stood up straight, slipped his hands around her waist, and drew her near. "If there ever was a time I wanted to kiss you, now is it," he confessed, meeting her eyes with his own.

She smiled, placed her arms up around his neck, and hugged him tightly, whispering softly in his ear, "I missed you, too."

She leaned her head against his shoulder, and they held each other in a warm embrace, neither one of them caring whether or not they would have lunch. It was enough just to be together in each other's arms. Joanie loved the way she could hear Brandon's heart beating when he held her this way. His muscular body was strong, and she felt safe and secure, held close to his heart.

"You smell so good, I could eat you," she said.

"Oh, so you are hungry?" he returned.

They finally decided on picking up a drive-thru lunch and then heading out to a nearby park to eat.

After telling her all the details of the trip, Brandon said, "Mark and I have decided we'll be going again next summer for sure."

Joanie threw a disgruntled look at him, crossing her arms.

"That is, with you and Justine, of course," he finished his thought, smiling under raised eyebrows.

"Well, that sounds a bit more reasonable," Joanie scolded him. "You may not know it to look at me, but I'm quite the outdoorsman myself," she boasted.

"You're right," he agreed, "I wouldn't know that to look at you. But," he added, wincing away from her playful smack on the shoulder, "you've been known to surprise me before with hidden talents."

By this time they had finished their lunches. Brandon lay back in the grass and manoeuvred himself until at last his head rested on Joanie's lap.

She laughed at him as he closed his eyes contentedly and asked that she wake him up in time to get back to work. "You sure are spoiled," she remarked.

He just opened his eyes and gave her one of his irresistible smiles.

"Fine," she said, "you win!" She glanced at her watch and figured they had fifteen more minutes all to themselves. Softly she stroked her fingers through his hair.

"Times like this are far too few," he commented, keeping his eyes closed

"Someday, sweetheart . . . someday soon," she replied, wistfully.

Chapter 51

Summer seemed to have come in full force that year. By early July it was terribly hot with spells of thirty-five degrees Celsius for days on end. The nights never seemed to cool down entirely. Joanie would lie awake for hours with bouts of insomnia brought on by the intense heat and exaggerated by the preoccupation of her mind as she made plans in the middle of the night for upcoming events.

Brandon teased her that had she chosen an earlier wedding date, she would now be sleeping in his air conditioned apartment with him at night; although, he suggested, she might not be getting any more sleep under those circumstances than she was getting now.

Joanie just shook her head at his intimation and gave him a playful smack. The teasing and openness between them reflected their heightened anticipation of nuptial bliss. He grabbed her hand and kissed it tenderly, waggling his eyebrows at her, making them both laugh.

✞   ✞   ✞

One evening, during that heat wave, Joanie and Brandon were out playing tennis. It was a poor game. Played out by the heat of the day, Joanie was not putting her heart in it at all. They called it quits and headed off the court. Joanie walked over to her side, took a drink from her water bottle, and gathered up her things.

By the time she had looked back to where Brandon was on his side of the court, two young women were standing with him. Joanie instantly did not like something about the situation. As she walked over to where they were standing, she felt her stomach tying in knots.

Brandon had been gathering up his stuff when he turned around and found Kelsey and Trina standing right there behind him.

"Brandon Vaughn!" Kelsey exclaimed. "Well, I thought you had dropped off the face of the earth. You haven't returned a call in a year's time. I had all but given up on you. I would have, too, if you weren't such an alluring prospect." She smiled coyly, putting her hand up on his collar.

Brandon stepped back and removed her hand with his. His eyes were cool, but inside he was fighting back panic over the impending situation with Joanie.

"Kelsey," Brandon acknowledged her, "and Trina," he added, looking at her less aggressive companion, "I've been busy."

His mind searched for how to adequately deal with this situation. By this time Joanie was standing off to the side, behind the two strangers. Dressed in fashionable tennis outfits, these women were boldly beautiful.

Brandon moved around them and, putting his arm over Joanie's shoulder, he pulled her closer to him.

"This is Joanie Collins, my fiancée," he began.

"I know you," said Trina. A pleasant smile of recognition came over the pretty girl's face. "You're a reporter for CNB local news, aren't you?"

"I am," Joanie responded, gracefully. This girl was no threat, but there was a flame burning in the eyes of her friend that was terribly disconcerting to Joanie.

"Fiancée!" burst out Kelsey. "Wow! Brandon Vaughn getting hitched! Now there's a good one," she laughed. Turning to Joanie, the beautiful blonde continued her amusement. "Sorry, honey, but I just gotta know what it was you did to make Brandon take the plunge! Are you pregnant or something?"

Joanie was completely dumbfounded. She could not begin to find words to respond to this woman.

Brandon jumped in, "That's enough, Kelsey. Look, we gotta get going, we're late for something. Bye."

He led Joanie away with the sound of the bold girl's laughter ringing in their ears.

Brandon opened the vehicle door for Joanie, and she sat down, mutely. He got into the driver's seat and drove away as quickly as he could. After several blocks, he pulled off to the side of the road, stopped the engine, and looked over at Joanie. She was staring straight ahead, her face vacant of expression.

"Joanie," he began, "I'm sorry about that. I . . ." He was lost for words and really wished Joanie would say something.

"It's fine," she said, coolly, her voice revealing that it was not. "Let's get going." She indicated for him to drive on.

"No," he persisted, "it's *not* fine! What could be fine about it? Joanie, talk to me. I don't know what to say if you don't tell me what's going on in your mind."

She looked over at him. She was proud and collected, her eyes were cool. She motioned with her hands that it was over. She had no intention of talking about it. "Come on, Brandon, let's go. Don't worry about it."

Reluctantly, he started the vehicle. Never before had he experienced Joanie's cold shoulder. He was at a loss to deal with it, except to respect the fact that maybe she just needed time to process. The whole experience had been so unforeseen and awkward.

When he pulled up in front of her house, she thanked him, said a quick good-night, and hopped out. She was half-way up the walk before Brandon knew what was happening. She had never left so abruptly before.

He drove off, not even waiting for her to get inside the house. He was hurt by her coolness, even though he understood it.

✟   ✟   ✟

There it was: his past. Though Brandon had encountered women from his past since his conversion, he had always managed to deal with those situations on his own terms. The hard part this time was watching Joanie being slapped in the face with it.

He had promised always to guard her heart and protect her; yet, what had he done this time to protect her in the face of insult? Nothing. How had he tried to defend her honour? He hadn't. Had he made the effort to give witness to Christ by mentioning his conversion? Not at all. He had cowardly run away from the situation, hoping somehow that would make it go away. But it hadn't. He felt awful.

He went home and wrestled with his thoughts all night. Sleep completely evaded him.

✟   ✟   ✟

As soon as she got in, Joanie took a shower and said good-night. When her mother asked about her, she just indicated she was tired from too many nights of poor sleep. She went to bed and lay there, silent tears burning down her cheeks.

She was confused by her emotions. She reminded herself time and time again that she had forgiven Brandon long ago for his past. What did that mean if she could not deal with it when she had to face it?

Who were those girls? Had he slept with both of them, or just the brazen one, Kelsey? She shuddered inside. She did not want to know.

No details! Let it go. Forgive him. It was in the past. Love him for the man he is today.

But love had become an abstraction in the escalating turmoil which had besieged her heart.

Say it and maybe you'll feel it. . . . I love him. I love Brandon. I do. I really do. . . . But I hate his past! And I feel so empty inside right now, Jesus.

She tried to pray, but she could not. Her heart was in a grip, and she could not force the constricting hands to let go of it. She lay in bed crying silently, her chest heaving muted sobs under the burden.

Her sisters came in quietly to go to bed. Joanie just pretended to be asleep to avoid discussion. She lay in this confused state of limbo for a long time before sleep finally took over.

The next two days at work were torture. Joanie tried to be her normal self, and she was a fairly good actress. Still, she could not put on the role completely, and she found herself occasionally in the washroom, running cold water over her red-rimmed eyes. Fortunately, she carried some make-up in her purse. Her work was below her usual high standards, lacking the heart and conviction she normally brought to whatever she did. To her surprise, no one commented.

✟ ✟ ✟

Brandon never showed up in the staff lounge. He did not leave Joanie any notes at her cubicle. Their relationship was not going to be sorted out at work. He had far too much respect for Joanie to do that to her.

But the heart of the young man ached. All he could do was pray for Joanie, pray for healing.

He did not call her at home the next night. Was he being a coward or was he respecting her boundaries? The line was becoming blurry and he was not sure how to proceed. He called up Fr. Steve; it was time for spiritual direction.

✟ ✟ ✟

Fr. Steve was well acquainted with Brandon's past and his relationship with Joanie. He listened attentively as Brandon recounted the events that had brought him to the young pastor's rectory.

Fr. Steve, handsome, athletic, virile, and strong, was not oblivious to the pain caused by modern, secular living. He had felt the call to the priesthood following a dramatic conversion that had been set in motion by the breaking-off of an unseemly relationship in his early twenties.

As a young man he had hurt—and been hurt—by giving himself in a sexual relationship that had no parameters of commitment and responsibility. The old girlfriend had gone on to marry and later divorced. She had a six-year-old daughter from that broken marriage whom she was now raising by herself. Fr. Steve still prayed for her that she might find the way to Christ and be healed.

Fr. Steve, having been pulled out of the despair of brokenness and pain, had found Jesus. Through the prayers of a devout mother and father and the infinite mercy of God, he had been restored to grace.

He had discovered love: true love, sacrificial love, dying-to-self love, dying-on-the-cross love. And eight years later he stretched out his arms, prostrate on the floor, and was ordained into that sublime love of Jesus Christ.

Fr. Steve was a wonderful priest, a true shepherd, knowledgeable in the faith and steadfastly in union with Rome. He worked untiringly for the love of Jesus. He brought the Sacraments to the faithful with tremendous joy. When he celebrated Mass, he had that special gift of bringing all those present with him to Calvary. Of course this is the reality of every Mass, but Fr. Steve had a way of drawing people's awareness into that mystery. His reverence for Jesus in the Blessed Sacrament was real, and it was inspiring.

He was a humble man. It was that same brand of humility that Brandon wore—the kind that comes from knowing what a wretched sinner he had once been in his life. It was the kind of humility that recognized the undeserving mercy and grace which he had received and continued to receive each day. It was the kind of humility that allowed him to look at each person, beyond any sinful lifestyle, and say: "But for the grace of God, there go I!" It was the kind of humility that drew people to Christ—because it was real.

Fr. Steve listened to Brandon and then asked, "Do you love Joanie enough to let her go if she is not able to come to terms with your past, Brandon?"

Brandon paused. He was willing to lay down his life for Joanie, but what was Fr. Steve asking him? Had Joanie already come to talk to Fr. Steve? Was he preparing Brandon for the blow? Brandon searched his heart. Could he let Joanie walk out of his life now? Did he love her enough to let her go?

Tears filled his eyes. He was not able to articulate an answer because he was not able to pull his will that far away from his heart. *Love is a decision. It is not a feeling.* There are times when a man must make a decision, in love, that goes against the stirrings of the heart. Had it come to that for Brandon and Joanie?

A lone tear rolled down Brandon's cheek, his eyes were downcast. Fr. Steve waited. He was never rushed. He sat and waited. He prayed.

From somewhere deep within Brandon, by the power of his will—resolutely upright—he answered, "I guess I do."

It would kill Brandon to lose Joanie, his heart's desire. Yet if he had to do it, he would allow her to move on with her life so that she could find someone else.

Brandon could not even begin to imagine Joanie with another man. He cringed at the thought of Joanie kissing another man, when Brandon had longed so much for her lips. His heart ached at the thought of any other man thrilling at the touch of her hand, caressing her soft hair, enjoying the sweetness of her smile, feeling the warmth of her body next to his in her gentle embrace. Could Joanie's eyes ever look upon another man with the same kind of love she had shared with Brandon?

As Brandon submersed himself in his thoughts, he realized these were such simple acts of intimacy, treated by society as commonplace and casual. Yet Joanie had never shared any of these with any man but Brandon. She had saved her heart and her affection entirely for the man she would someday marry. It was humbling for Brandon to know that she had stored up all these treasures for him, undeserving as he was.

He pondered how it must be torture for Joanie to know that he had not saved any of these for her. He had shared complete physical intimacy with so many other women. What must it be like for Joanie to stand before another woman, knowing that woman had slept with the man to whom she would someday be married? What must it feel like for Joanie to have another woman looking at her future husband, with eyes that have seen only that which a wife should see? What must it do to her heart to know that these other women had memories of sexual affairs with the man who would someday be the father of her children?

The thought of it all was so utterly repulsive to Brandon now. He wished he could erase all of that history so that Joanie would be the only woman with whom he would ever share physical intimacy. He wanted so much to return to her the gift which she had reserved for him, of being his one and only in every way. It hurt so much now to know how his past had robbed that from both of them.

And the pain did not stop there with Joanie and himself. Brandon thought of all the other women he had hurt. He remembered an aborted baby, his own flesh and blood, murdered within a former girlfriend's womb. At the time he had felt no remorse, only relief. How many countless chemical abortions had taken place, through affairs with women who had been on the pill? How many broken hearts had he left behind? So many girls had given themselves to him completely, with him there to take, offering nothing but a night's pleasure in return.

Brandon knew he deserved to suffer the pain he was now experiencing. There are consequences to sin, and so many people are affected by sin. But Joanie did not deserve to suffer this pain. He wished he could free her from it.

Maybe the only way to free her from this pain was in releasing her from their relationship. Could Joanie really leave him now and move on? After all they had been through together, had it really come to this?

Fr. Steve was nodding his head thoughtfully, when Brandon looked up to meet the priest's compassionate eyes.

"Love is patient, Brandon," he said, softly. Fr. Steve could always quote scripture eloquently, his low, gentle voice never rushing a word. "Love is kind; love is not jealous or boastful; it is not arrogant or rude. Love does not insist on its own way; it is not irritable or resentful; it does not rejoice at wrong, but rejoices in the right. Love bears all things, believes all things, hopes all things, *endures all things*. Love never ends."

The words washed over Brandon, like rain coming down on a hot summer day. In his heart he tried to assess if his love for Joanie were equal to this standard. *Endure all things.* For Joanie's sake! Yes, he would endure whatever was to come.

"Brandon," Fr. Steve's steady voice called him back. "Love is patient. Give her time. This is a deep wound for both of you. You know, in our society human sexuality has been reduced to mere pleasure, and so many people have bought into that lie. It's killing our society, one soul at a time. Human sexuality is sacred and only belongs within the sanctuary of marriage. When it's reverenced as it should be—for the gift that it is from God—it's beautiful and holy. Look at the examples of the wonderful marriages around you, Brandon. God intended for sex to be the cement that bonds the love in a marriage and that's why he made it so pleasurable and wonderful.

"Satan has convinced so many people in our world that sex can be enjoyed outside of marriage and that there are no consequences. But look around at the sinfulness of people's lives, the pornography, the fear of disease, the pain, the hurt, the loneliness, the depression, the abandonment of children growing up without the security of a father in the home, the breakdown of the family, the millions of babies brutally murdered each year within their mother's womb. How can we ignore the consequences?

"Sin blinds us to truth. When you lived in darkness, Brandon, you were not able to see how your sins were hurting yourself and so many others. The reason you feel the pain of them so strongly now is because your eyes have been opened. Joanie has always had a well-formed conscience, tuned into truth. It's protected her from getting lost in the lies around her and has given her the strength to bring others to the light of truth. But it also makes the burden of your sinful past even heavier for her. She has never dealt with your past completely—she has never had to put a face on your sins. But she'll come around. I know she will. She's strong in her love for you and for the Lord."

Her mother had said the very same thing, Brandon thought, looking deeply, almost past Fr. Steve's dark eyes.

"It's unfortunate that she has to suffer because of your past," Fr. Steve continued, "but I know she will come to accept that suffering and turn it into an instrument of love for the Lord. God can transform all pain and suffering for His greater glory. Joanie knows this, and she lives it each day in little sacrifices, just as you have learned to do.

"By uniting our suffering to Christ's sacrifice on the cross, Satan is robbed of the power of sin. God can always make greater glory come out of our failings than any damage that Satan tries to achieve through our sinfulness. You and Joanie have a great opportunity before you to give glory to God.

"Don't worry about Joanie leaving you. She won't. I only asked if you were willing to let her go for your sake, not for hers. It's an important question to ask yourself. You have to examine the parameters of your own love for her. How selflessly can you live it out?

"It would have been no effort for you to have answered me had I asked you if you were willing to die for Joanie. Sometimes to live out love is even harder than to die for love. You are strong in your love for Joanie and in your love for the Lord. Be patient. God has lessons for you both to learn right now. . . . Be patient, and your love will be strengthened through this."

"What do I do? Do I try to call her or wait for her to talk to me?" Brandon wanted some practical direction here. *Tell me what to do, Father!*

"Wait for God to direct you, Brandon. Pray. You'll know what's right. . . Pray."

"That wasn't the answer I was looking for, Fr. Steve." Brandon's voice betrayed his disappointment in the young cleric.

"I know, Brandon, but it's the only one I can give you. I'll be praying for you and Joanie—you know that."

Brandon looked into the priest's eyes and saw into his heart. He was a true prayer warrior, fasting regularly and spending an hour or two each day before the Blessed Sacrament. Few people knew the intensity of Fr. Steve's prayer life, but Brandon did. They were close friends. In his humble way, Fr. Steve drew people to Christ. Prayer and fasting. It was as simple as that. Yet, truly it was the battlefield on which sanctity was being forged in this man.

Brandon asked Fr. Steve to hear his confession, which he did. The knowledge that his soul had been washed as clean again, as it had been on the day of his Baptism, was reassuring to Brandon. The grace of the Sacrament of Reconciliation was there to fortify him through this struggle. He left the rectory in peace and went over to the church to pray before the Blessed Sacrament.

Two hours later, Brandon walked into his apartment. He checked his messages. None were from Joanie. He showered, took his rosary, and went to bed. He fell asleep somewhere during the fourth sorrowful mystery—*The Carrying of the Cross.*

Chapter 52

The next night, Thursday, there was an early band rehearsal. The time had been moved up to accommodate a function that some of the members had to attend later that evening. It was the first time Joanie and Brandon had seen each other since the tennis match two nights before.

Joanie tried to be her normal self, but she was notably impatient throughout the practice. The rehearsal ended early, as planned. Joanie was about to refuse Brandon's offer for a ride home when the look on his face reminded her that she had an obligation to respond to him openly. But as they drove, she just could not bring herself to talk.

The only time the silence was broken between them was when Brandon asked if she would not mind stopping with him to get a few groceries. She walked in with him. He held her hand, but she took no pleasure in it, and he could sense that. Still he held onto her hand, because love is a decision, not a feeling.

They went up and down the aisles together in silence. Brandon pushed the cart and picked out what he needed. He tried to make some small talk about the food, but Joanie could not bring herself to respond. She was angry at herself for being so petty, but for some reason she was not able to rise above it.

They had just walked out of the store when a voice called out Brandon's name. It was the voice of a young woman. Joanie rolled her eyes and stopped beside Brandon who had turned to address the lady. There was a certain quality in the woman's voice which Joanie immediately recognized: sarcasm.

"Brandon Vaughn, aren't you a sight for sore eyes!" She made no notice of Joanie standing with him.

Brandon smiled politely and ran his hand nervously across his jaw and back around his neck. "Ashley Wilson," he acknowledged her.

The shapely, attractive woman, who was not as tall as Joanie, had a thick mane of blond curls and exquisite, green eyes. She was older than Joanie by a few years.

"Well, I'm surprised you remembered my name. You obviously have forgotten my phone number," she continued, with an incriminating tone. "Why do you have an answering machine if you never intend to return messages?"

By this time Ashley had acknowledged Joanie. Ashley stopped herself from going on, as she fixed her eyes upon Brandon's companion.

Brandon's discomfort with the situation was apparent. Joanie's cool demeanour, as she stood by his side, did not help.

Why, God, twice in a row? How much of this does Joanie have to take?

"Ashley," he began the introduction, "this is my fiancée, Joanie Collins."

Ashley almost choked over the word fiancée. Her reproachful eyes stared back at Brandon. "Since when are you the marrying type, Brandon? I thought you were strictly the love 'em and leave 'em type."

"Ashley," he began, desperately contrite, "I don't blame you for your bitterness toward me, and I deserved that comment, I'm sure, but over this past year things have changed. My life has changed and ... well, Joanie's been a big part of that."

He looked over at Joanie. She was holding her head and shoulders proudly now, though her eyes were still cool. It was obvious to him that she was making an effort to be supportive. He went on, "I'm a Christian now and I've changed my life."

"Christian?" Ashley blurted out the word. "Well, then this should really have an impact on you, now. . . . I left you messages that you never returned last August. I wanted to let you know that I was pregnant, and that I was planning to have an abortion. No prizes for guessing who the father was. Anyway, I guess I wanted to give you a chance to know before I went through with it. It just choked me that you didn't even have the decency to return any of my calls. I finally went ahead with the abortion, and I gave up trying to contact you. But . . ." There was a change in the tone of her voice; it became softer, sincere. "Well, when I saw you here tonight, I figured that you deserved to know the truth."

Joanie felt Brandon crumble under the blow. Listening to Ashley speak, Joanie realized that she had not been the only one hurt by Brandon's past. It was time to rise above her selfishness and self-pity. Joanie stepped into the conversation. "Ashley, that must have been terrible to go through alone." Her voice was sympathetic and heartfelt.

Ashley was sincerely moved by Joanie's uncontrived response. Ashley shrugged her shoulders, smiled meekly, and in a moment of candour she added, "Well, I've gone through a lot of changes over this past year, as well."

Brandon, finding his voice, said faintly but with real emotion, "Ashley, I am so sorry for so much of my past. I can't begin to tell you. But I want you to know that I am sorry that I used you and caused you so much suffering."

Ashley looked at Brandon. He was real. He had changed. She smiled at the young couple and, putting her hand on Brandon's shoulder, she replied, "It's done now. Thank you for the apology, but I guess I used you as much as you used me! I wish it could have turned out differently, but life goes on. Hey," she said, picking up her voice in real champion fashion, "good luck to you both. I hope everything turns out great for you!"

"Thank you, Ashley," Joanie replied. "And thank you for stopping us tonight. I'm sure Brandon's grateful for what you told him. I know I am." Joanie smiled, compassionately.

Brandon nodded and put his hand on Ashley's arm, saying, "I can't make it up to you for what happened, but I will pray for you that good will come out of it in your life. I hope everything goes well for you, too, Ashley. You deserve better."

With that Ashley headed into the store, while Brandon and Joanie continued out to his vehicle. They unloaded the groceries from the cart, got in, and drove off. Brandon reached over and held Joanie's hand. They were silent; there was a lot to absorb.

"Drop me off at Fr. Steve's, Brandon, please." Joanie's voice was soft, and she kept her eyes focussed straight ahead.

Brandon looked over at her and nodded. He did not press her to talk. He understood. As they drove, he kept her hand gently in his. While he could sense that Joanie was still distant from him, she did not take her hand away.

When they pulled up to the rectory, he softly kissed her hand before letting go. She looked at him through pained, tear-filled eyes, but she did not say a word.

Brandon said in his low, gentle tone, "I'll wait here to be sure Fr. Steve's in, then I'll head over to the church to pray." He always carried his church key because he liked to make frequent visits to the Blessed Sacrament. Fr. Steve had given him a key long ago for that reason.

She walked up to the door and waited a moment. The door opened, and she stepped inside the rectory. Brandon drove up the block to the church, parked, and went in to have a heart to heart with Jesus.

✞   ✞   ✞

When Joanie arrived at the rectory, Fr. Steve had been expecting her. He knew she was coming, in the way that deeply spiritual people sense, feel, or know things. He had cancelled another appointment an hour earlier on account of that spiritual intuition and then sat, waiting . . . praying.

It was eight-thirty when she arrived. Embarrassed for having come without calling, she asked if it would be all right for her to come in.

"Joanie, you are always welcome here," Fr. Steve greeted her warmly. He had a great deal of affection for Joanie, as he did for all of the Collins family. Her parents had welcomed him into their family when he was still a seminarian and had supported him greatly in his preparation for priesthood. He loved Joanie like a sister.

She was crying before she made it to the couch to sit down. Fr. Steve offered her tissue from a nearby box.

"Would you hear my confession, Fr. Steve?" she asked, meekly.

Fr. Steve listened to her confession. He offered very little advice at the time. For her penance, he told her to pray a decade of the rosary and offer it up for Ashley. She looked up at him and nodded obediently. He gave her absolution.

Joanie sat there on the couch. Normally after Confession she felt relieved, restored, renewed. Not this time. She awkwardly began to get up to leave. Fr. Steve put up his hand to stop her and invited her to sit down and talk.

"I wanted you to have the grace of the sacrament, Joanie, before we spent time in spiritual direction," he explained to her. "This is far too painful a cross for you to carry without support."

She smiled. Her tearful eyes met the deep, dark eyes of this holy priest, with relief. "Thank you, Fr. Steve."

"Listen, Joanie, you're hurt and confused over how to deal with Brandon's past. But as you told me, the biggest burden is that you failed in loving him unconditionally."

She nodded, breathing through heavy sighs.

"Well, that's behind you now," he reminded her of the absolution she had just received in the Sacrament of Confession. "Once a sin is forgiven, Joanie, it's gone. Don't relive it. Move on."

His gaze penetrated her soul.

Fr. Steve is a good shepherd, she reminded herself. She trusted him for that.

"Love is a choice, Joanie. Choose it and live it. When you fall short of that, get up and start again. Choose it and live it. Brandon loves you more than life itself. He can't undo his past, though he would if he could. It has to be harder on him than it is on you because of the love he has for you. He would never want for you to have to suffer for his sins. But it is a cross that you both must bear. Wouldn't it be easier to carry it together?"

Joanie nodded, thinking about Brandon waiting for her before the Blessed Sacrament.

"God is purifying you, Joanie, in your love, by giving you this opportunity to go beyond yourself. Every time you are tempted to indulge in self-pity over Brandon's past, choose to love. Every time you are tempted to judge the women from his past, choose to love. Every time you are tempted to hold his past against him, Joanie . . . choose to love."

The priest smiled at Joanie. He could sense she was beginning to discover that place of peace within her: that holy place within the soul where the Lord dwells in His people. Sin closes the door to that holy sanctuary within. Grace opens it again—grace that she had just received in the Sacrament of Reconciliation.

They talked for a while longer. Joanie felt consoled by Fr. Steve's gentle guidance. As she listened to the words of this humble servant of God, she found herself able to let go of the pain that had so gripped her heart and obscured her vision.

Getting up to leave, Joanie thanked Fr. Steve, hugged him as a sister hugs her big brother, and left.

It was twilight as she headed up the street to the church; the heat of the day had broken, and the evening was now warm and comfortable. The consolation of Jesus' loving presence was with her. She gently rolled over the beads of the rosary in her hands as she prayed for Ashley.

It felt good to pray again. Her heart was growing stronger with each Hail Mary. She finished her decade and walked on in the stillness of her heart. All the turmoil of the past two days had robbed her of that stillness.

As she continued in prayer, Brandon's image came to mind. The thought of living life without him suddenly gripped her heart. She stopped walking, frozen by the very idea of it. Joanie could no more live without Brandon than she could live without her own heart. He was her heart now.

Suddenly, the floodgates of her love opened wide. Tears flowed freely, but not tears of pain anymore. They were tears of release. Oh, how she loved Brandon!

She walked up to the church side door, where she knew he would hear her knock. When he opened the door, Joanie stepped inside and threw her arms around his neck and held on.

Brandon held the fragile, tender woman. He loved her with everything that was within him. Together they wept in each other's arms.

Finally, he led her by the hand to a pew and they sat down to talk.

"I'm sorry, Brandon, for all my selfishness over the past two days." She spoke through muted sobs.

"I understand it," he replied. He gently touched her soft hair as she leaned forward, still clutching the rosary in her hands.

"It was wrong of me to hold your past against you when I had already forgiven you for it so long ago. I guess I was willing to forgive as long as I didn't have to face it. That wasn't right. I needed to grapple with the full implications of it so that I could forgive you completely. I'm beginning to understand better about unconditional love."

"I never doubted your love for me, Joanie," Brandon assured her.

She looked over at him for a moment. There was so much love in his eyes. She reached out and took his hand in hers, sorry for the way she had rejected it over the past few days. Looking down at that strong yet gentle hand, she said, "I'm proud of how you dealt with the situation tonight with Ashley, Brandon. The respect you showed her was admirable. I guess that was what got me off my high horse and over to Confession. Up until then I was just nursing hurt and anger. Anger at you and at God. . . . I couldn't even pray. I felt so betrayed. It was stupid, I know. . . .

"But tonight, when I first saw this woman standing there, all I could think was, 'Has every woman in this city slept with you, but me?'" Letting go of him, she buried her face in her hands. "Just knowing that all of these other women have had a part of you that I've never had, made me feel so small and inadequate . . . and cheated."

She was crying now, and each sob stabbed into Brandon's heart. "Joanie, if I could undo those mistakes, I would. But I can't. My past is there, and it'll show up again, I'm sure. There'll probably be girls at Mark and Justine's wedding that I've slept with, friends of Justine. It's amazing that we've gone this long before it caught up to me, to us—"

Joanie interrupted him, suddenly distracted by a thought, "How often do you get phone calls from old girlfriends?"

Brandon shrugged his shoulders, "Once or twice a month still. It used to be more often."

"What do you do?"

"I ignore them," he confessed, "I never return them. I guess I'm too much of a coward. . . ." He didn't know what to say next.

Joanie turned toward him now and put her hand on his. "You're not a coward, Brandon. You stood and witnessed for Jesus, tonight. That took fortitude. . . . And look how it affected Ashley. I think she experienced some healing through it. I hope so. We should pray for her." Joanie paused, still thinking about things and then added, "I wonder how many other abortions there have been?"

"One for sure," he confessed. "My girlfriend in high school. . . . I was seventeen, she was sixteen. After her, I never dated a girl again on a steady basis. I figured I was safer and the girls were better off. I thought I couldn't hurt anyone that way." He shook his head, "Man, was I a selfish fool!"

Brandon kept shaking his head, his eyes had filled with tears. Joanie took him into her arms, and together they cried some more. They were healing tears.

Joanie knew that she would not give in to self-pity anymore. It was a sword which Satan had been using to lance into Brandon's heart. She would not inflict this pain on him again. His past, whenever it would come up, was a cross they would carry together.

Through his tears, he softly spoke. "Those women may have had a part of me physically, but, Joanie, *you* are the only woman in my life whom I have ever loved from the heart. I am so sorry that I can't offer you the gift of my virginity. You deserve to marry a virgin. But when we are married, and when we can finally come together as one flesh, it will truly be a first for me, in spite of my past. You, Joanie, will be the first and *only* woman that I will give myself to completely, without reservation . . . every part of me will be yours. That's what I long for. That's what I live for now."

Joanie held on to Brandon. The wound that had opened up two nights ago on a tennis court was now healed over, thanks to sacramental grace and a whole lot of actual grace. Love was a choice. And when it came to Brandon, it was an easy choice for Joanie to make.

Joanie pulled herself back from Brandon, smiled at him, and said, "I couldn't even imagine what my life would be like without you, Brandon. You are my heart now. And I cannot wait to give myself to you completely, without reservation. Every part of me will be yours, too."

She kissed him on the cheek and wiped away his tears.

Brandon reached into his pocket and took out his rosary. Taking Joanie's hand in his and kneeling to pray, he led them through the glorious mysteries.

✝   ✝   ✝

When Joanie got in that night, her mother was reading a book, waiting up for her daughter. "Come and sit with me, Joanie," Judy said, motioning for Joanie to snuggle up with her on the couch. "Is everything okay between you and Brandon?"

"It is now," Joanie replied, putting her head on her mother's shoulder and taking her mother's hand in hers.

"Can I ask about it? Maggie told me, after rehearsal tonight, that there was something wrong. She thought maybe we should talk."

Joanie shook her head and smiled at the thought of Maggie. *Sweet, perceptive Maggie, she notices everything but never tries to pry.*

Joanie began to tell her mother all that had happened following the tennis game two nights earlier. She communicated the roller-coaster ride of feelings she had experienced, the meeting with Ashley, Fr. Steve's spiritual direction, and how she and Brandon had reconciled in the church.

Her mother listened carefully, pondering the situation. Finally, she commented, "Isn't it wonderful how God places people in our lives—first at the tennis court, then Ashley, and of course, Fr. Steve. It was all directed toward something that you and Brandon had to work through together.

"I've often wondered when you would be confronted by Brandon's past. It's always amazed me that you could have remained sheltered from it for so long. I'm relieved that you have finally dealt with it, Joanie. I've been praying for this for a long time. God knew when the time would be right.

"You know, as life goes on, Brandon's past will be less and less an issue in your lives. It will always be there, which is good, because I think that's what keeps him so humble when he deals with people. I always laugh when I think of how he chose the name Augustine for his Confirmation. It was so appropriate for him.

"Everyday that man grows in holiness and virtue. He is such an inspiration to all of us. Your father and I could not have chosen a better husband for you. I thank Jesus for Brandon, everyday."

"So do I, Mom," Joanie said.

The mother and daughter stayed on the couch for a long time, talking and enjoying the time of grace that God had given them to share.

Chapter 53

"One Mississippi, two Mississippi, three Mississip—it's getting closer," Zack announced with a great deal of excitement.

Jessie shuddered at the roaring thunder and tucked her head into Brandon's shoulder. She was not really afraid as much as she was enjoying the game with Brandon.

The children were all excited as they gathered by the living room window and watched the display of lightning. Aaron and Zack were the weather forecasters, keeping the family updated as to the progress of the storm.

One of the greatest delights in summer, to which the Collins children always looked forward, was a thunder and lightning storm. All day long John had been pointing to the clouds on the horizon, saying something was brewing. Indeed there was. By four in the afternoon the skies had darkened, and the heavens opened up, pouring down rain for four hours.

Brandon found it amusing to experience life through the eyes of these children: they took so much delight in such simple things.

☦   ☦   ☦

It was an especially busy week for Brandon and Joanie, with much to do to help Justine and Mark with wedding preparations. Friday night arrived before they knew it, with rehearsal, hall decorating, and a party to follow at Justine's parents' house.

Brandon was the best man, and Justine had asked Joanie to be her bridesmaid. It was a small wedding party. Justine's older sister, Kathleen, was matron of honour, and Joanie was next in line, matched with Mark's younger brother, Tim, who was twenty-one. It was fun for Joanie and Brandon to be involved together in this event.

Driving home that night, following the rehearsal party, Brandon asked Joanie, "Is everything okay?"

"Sure. Why do you ask?" She was startled by the question.

"I told you there would be women here at this wedding from my past.... I was just worried that maybe that'll make you feel uncomfortable," he explained.

"Brandon, I'm okay. I'm glad you told me. But I want you to enjoy yourself for Mark's and Justine's sake. It is so good to be a part of this wedding. I don't want to spoil it for anyone by being selfish and sulky," she replied.

"Well, I'll do my best to avoid any awkward situations," he promised. "Of course, if I've got you in my arms all night, dancing, no one can bother us," he said, taking her hand and kissing it tenderly.

"Regardless," she assured him, "I'll be fine. You don't have to apologize to me anymore for your past, Brandon. I know where I stand with you. Let's just decide to approach each situation that presents itself to us as an opportunity for evangelizing and to pray for healing for those women."

"Fair enough," he responded. Brandon got out and walked Joanie to the door to say good-night.

✝   ✝   ✝

Joanie spent all day Saturday at Justine's helping with last minute details and getting ready for the wedding. It was such a pleasant day, a real time of bonding. By two o'clock they were all ready to go. The ceremony was not until three, but Justine was determined not to be late for her wedding.

Her father drove them to the church, arriving by ten to three, and they waited at the back until Fr. Steve indicated that it was time. Pastor Kline had come to assist in the ceremony and was at the back of the church to greet the bridal party. The signal came, everyone took their places, and the music began.

Joanie thrilled at the sight of Brandon, standing at the end of the aisle in his tuxedo. *Just two more months.*

As he gazed at her, stunningly attractive in her forest-green bridesmaid gown, his eyes told her he was thinking the same thing. She took Tim's arm, and he led her to her place. She and Kathleen stood attentively, watching as Justine walked down the aisle on her father's arm. She was breathtakingly beautiful.

Justine always carried herself with such style and grace that it was beyond the imagination how she could be even more radiant today, but she was. It was a touching moment when Mark shook Justine's father's hand and kissed her mother. He then took Justine on his arm to the front, where they stood before Fr. Steve and Pastor Kline.

It was a joyous ceremony, filled with laughter and tears. Brandon kept looking over at Joanie as if he were counting down time until they stood before the altar and professed their vows.

Mark and Justine communicated a deep, mutual love and respect as they exchanged their vows. Everyone present could sense that this young couple had found what it would take to stand the test of time. It was an honour to be a witness to their union.

The busy schedule of the day kept everyone on their toes. There was hardly a chance to think. Brandon was a perfect chauffeur, taking the bridal party around town, from the church to the photo studio and from the studio to the reception. It was a great deal of fun, with horns blaring up and down the streets of Saskatoon, saluting the bridal car—a typical scene for a Saturday in July.

The dinner and the reception were delightful. The highlight for Joanie was listening to Brandon as he toasted the groom. He was a good public speaker, with his voice so clear and full. His physical presence commanded the attention of everyone present, and he spoke honestly, from the heart.

"I have decided for two very good reasons not to tell any stories about Mark's past here tonight. The first reason is that in less than two months' time Mark will be toasting me at my own wedding and well, what goes around comes around. And the truth is, he probably has more dirt on me than I've got on him, since I was the one usually getting us into trouble.

"The second reason is that a few months back Mark made some pretty important changes in his outlook on life. Thanks to the faith and love of a very beautiful woman, Mark made the decision to become a Christian. Since that time, nothing has been the same for Mark and Justine. In fact, it was their mutual faith that brought them here today. It's a blessing for us all to be witnesses to the union of this remarkable couple, equipped with all the graces of the sacrament, ready to set out on the adventure of a lifetime together. We thank you both for that honour.

"I know a lot of people here maybe have not had a chance to witness what Christ has done in Mark's life. Just start talking to him for a few minutes and you'll soon figure out there's something different. He's got a smile on his face that won't wash off, and he mentions Jesus just about every other sentence.

"Mark, it's been so good to have been a part of your life. You were, for me, the brother I never had. You've been a friend through thick and through thin. We were perfect heathens together, and thanks be to God that phase in our lives has ended, and we now walk together as Christian brothers. I salute you, buddy, for all you've been in my life. And I toast you, for all that is to come. The Lord has done some amazing things through you, so far, and I know He will continue to bless your life with Justine. So without further ado, I raise my glass to you, Mark Jacobs. To the groom!"

Everyone stood according to tradition and toasted Mark along with Brandon. Joanie was beaming, and when she caught Justine's eye, she could see that Justine was beaming as well.

With the ceremonies and rituals all over, it was time to relax and enjoy the dance. What a wonderful wedding dance it was. Mark and Justine had a Christian DJ who played great Christian music as well as old time waltzes, polkas, and butterflies. It was a family dance, with all the dynamics that go along with that.

Joanie's family had all been invited which meant Brandon and Joanie did not get too many dances alone without Jessie in between them. There were other young boys there with whom Isaac, Zack, and Aaron made off to go and play. Maggie, Amie, and Katie, to Brandon's amusement, attracted a steady stream of young men to the dance floor.

Toward the end of the evening, Joanie and Brandon finally got their chance alone together. Jessie had fallen asleep in a corner.

Brandon led Joanie onto the dance floor and swept her into his strong arms and held on. He could not take his eyes off her: she was so exquisitely beautiful to him. She just smiled back, soaking up all the attention he lavished upon her.

Joanie realized that it is so hard not to feel like a queen when the man you love keeps placing you on the throne of his heart.

Chapter 54

Summer was a wonderful time in the Collins household. John was a teacher, and he had all that time off to spend with his family. They did not have a lot of money for travelling, but what they lacked in travels they made up through all sorts of creative ways to amuse themselves on a low budget. Family get-togethers, football, baseball, and soccer games, swimming at the pools, and the occasional camping trip made the season fun and full for everyone.

John undertook all kinds of projects in his shop over the summer, and the children learned a great deal working alongside him. Judy spent most of her time out in their yard tending her vegetable and flower gardens. Hospitality was the trademark of this family who opened their doors to a steady stream of company. Evenings inevitably ended up with campfires and singsongs outside or with very lively card games and such inside.

✝   ✝   ✝

Family life, though, has its moments. Each day there are many opportunities for reconciliation when the choices people make fall short of the call. . . .

✝   ✝   ✝

One morning John got up, miserable from the moment he had stepped out of bed. His morning offering had been half-hearted, but he was satisfied in having fulfilled his routine devotion.

He came down into the kitchen. The place was a pigsty. Dishes had been left out from the night before, stacked underneath breakfast messes that had not yet been cleaned up. And crumbs—everywhere there were crumbs—on the floor, on the counters, on the chair upon which he sat after getting his coffee.

He picked up the newspaper and began to read.

Judy came in from outside. She had been up early, enjoying working in her flower beds before the heat of the day forced her back indoors.

"Good morning, handsome," she cheerfully greeted John, stopping to give him a kiss on her way by.

He made some sort of grunting noise and received her kiss with obvious annoyance.

Now Judy had a choice. She could grab her husband and kiss him passionately, playfully entreating him back to a friendly demeanour. Or she could be hurt by his coolness and carry on about her business, resentfully. She chose the latter.

In fact, she began to stew over how irritable her husband had been the past few days. There were his little negative ways of correcting the children, his pessimistic overtones to every conversation, his lack of interest in what everyone else was doing. In one smooth stroke, Judy had painted her husband with a very dark colour in her mind.

She began to tackle the mess in the kitchen. Where were her children? *How can anybody, in good conscience, make a mess and walk out, leaving it for someone else to clean up? That someone else is always me. Mom, the slave. Mom, the doormat.*

John's irritability grew with each dish that got slammed into the dishwasher or banged around in the sink. Now he had a choice. He could get up and offer his wife some help, making the most out of a messy situation. He could be playful and enjoy her company on this beautiful, sunny morning and maybe go out for a walk together when they were done. Or he could snap at her for making so much noise and interrupting his peace and quiet. He chose the latter.

"You're gonna break something over there. Cool it, would ya?"

Judy had a choice at that moment, but the blood rushing to her brain, making her see red, prevented her from recognizing that choice. She reacted in full-blooded heat. "If you can do better, John, then get up off your lazy ass and do something to help!" With that, she stormed out of the kitchen and up the stairs.

Once a stone is tossed into a pond, the ripples are very hard to stop. Only a stronger tide can wash them away. In the Collins house that day, the tide of love was being held back by an unseen force.

As Judy stomped up the stairs, she ran into Katie—literally. Katie's art pencils, paper, and paint went flying everywhere.

"Paint on the carpet, Katie! What are you doing, walking around with paints?" The volume of Judy's voice was cranked on high.

Katie shrank back from her mother's anger and quickly began picking up her things. Now Katie had a choice. She could recognize that her mother was having a bad day and try to not aggravate her, bearing the wrong done to her with patience. Or she could take a defensive stance and point out that her mother was the one at fault in this situation. Katie chose the latter.

"I didn't do this—you did!" the sixteen-year-old griped as she gathered up her things. "And besides, it's dry paint. I can vacuum it up."

"You can, and you will," her mother persisted, ignoring her opportunity to apologize and help her daughter clean up the mess which she had caused. It had been all John's fault, anyway. "And if I ever hear you speak to me in that tone of voice again, young lady, I'll tan your pretty little hide!"

Judy stormed into her bedroom and slammed the door.

Katie's shoulders shook with the bang and she rolled her bright blue eyes at her mother's temper tantrum. Grumbling to herself, she did the vacuuming. In fact, she vacuumed the entire staircase, not out of love, but because it needed it, and she was afraid that had she not, her mother would have tied into her even more. Katie returned to the place where she had left her art supplies only to discover that they were gone.

"Jessie!" she yelled out—knowing, beyond the shadow of a doubt, what had happened to her things.

Jessie came running around the corner all smiles, dressed up in a swimsuit and rubber boots, carrying an umbrella.

Children can be so weird! Katie thought to herself.

"Where are my paints and paper and stuff?" the older sister dived in with her accusation.

"I don't know," Jessie shrugged, as she began to walk off.

Katie could have left it at that, but she was in a foul mood by now and alluring choices were presenting themselves to her.

"You look so stupid, Jessie. Why do you walk around in those silly outfits all the time?"

Jessie turned and looked at her big sister. Little children are less aware of choices. They simply react to things. The tone of voice, the unkind words, the look of disdain coming from Katie, stripped the four-year-old of all her pleasure and amusement.

"Well, you're a stupid, ugly girl! And I hate you, Katie!" Jessie threw out her words with as much venom as a four-year-old can muster from within. She threw her umbrella at Katie and ran off to her bedroom, crying.

Katie ducked away from the flying umbrella, left it lying on the floor, and walked off, looking for her missing art supplies.

"What was that all about?" her father demanded, as Katie entered the kitchen. He did not look up from his paper.

"I'm looking for my art supplies. Someone took them while I was vacuuming. I bet it was Aaron," she thought out loud.

Beginning to head out of the kitchen, her father stopped her. "Whoa! Get back here! Dishes! In fact," he growled, his jaw set firm and the furrow in between his eyes etched deeply, "Isaac! Zack! Get down here—now!" His voice bellowed throughout the old two-storey.

The boys came running because when Dad used that tone of voice, that's what they did!

"Get this pigsty cleaned up, *now!* What kind of slobs are you all, that you don't even notice the mess? I'll be back in a little bit, and I'd better find it spotless in here, or there will be hell to pay! Katie, stop sulking! Now get to work!" With that, the back door slammed, and John headed to his workshop for some time alone.

When a growling bear lumbers off into his cave, who would dare to follow?

"Okay, boys," Katie took charge, "sweep the floor and start putting away the food. I'll do the dishes."

"Who made *you* boss?" Isaac was quick to jump into the pond with everyone else that day. Those ripples were very enticing.

"I'm the oldest one here, so do what you're told." Katie huffed around, a real martyr for the cause.

Now Isaac had a choice. He could dive in and help, be obedient to his father, get the mess cleaned up without a fuss, and then get back to his things. Or he could tear a strip off of Katie. He chose the latter.

"You think you're so good! You're just a vain, stupid teenager who spends all her time in front of the mirror. Too bad you're so ugly!"

His words were well aimed. He knew where to hit.

Katie crumbled under the blow. Tears pouring out, she chased Isaac and Zack out of the kitchen. "Get out of here. I'd rather do it myself than to spend another minute with you! Get lost!" She threw a plastic cup across the room at Isaac, catching him on the back of his shoulder as he ran out, laughing, with Zack close on his heels.

Through sobs and tears, Katie cleaned the kitchen. *First Mom, then Jessie, then Dad, now Isaac. Everyone hates me!* Self-pity was very successfully swallowing up all of Katie's energy. Cleaning was a slow process, each task taking more strength from her than she had to give. Finally, the job was done. Katie walked up to her room, lay down on her bed, and cried some more.

Everyone had gone to their corners, consumed in their own selfishness. The ripples were less perceptible now, but they were still there, hidden in the hearts of everyone who had jumped into the pond that morning.

The day went on. Whenever two people passed each other in a hall or in a room, nothing was said. There was no apparent sign of the anger—its job was done. What were left behind were resentment and self-pity, veiled forms of pride.

✣   ✣   ✣

Aaron had not been around during the explosive fights that morning; he had kept to himself when he heard all the yelling. At six years of age, this blond-haired, brown-eyed prince had a maturity at times that was beyond his years.

He had been in their bedroom when Jessie came running in, crying after her encounter with Katie. Now Aaron had a choice. He could ask Jessie what was wrong and try to console her. Or he could get upset with her for having knocked over the Lego farm which he had been building all morning. Aaron chose the former.

"Why are you crying, Jessie?" The older, caring brother left his scattered farm behind and went to his sister's side. He lovingly put his little hand on Jessie's shoulder.

When a young child shows pity to another, it is truly sublime. The innocence and simple faith of such children is often the most likely channel of grace in a home. This was the case for the Collins family that day.

"Katie yelled at me and told me I was stupid," Jessie whimpered.

"She's having a bad day. Mommy yelled at her. And I heard Mommy and Daddy yelling at each other earlier in the kitchen. Everyone's angry. Why don't we go out to the fort and play? We can pretend it's a church and pray for everyone to be nice again."

Jessie perked up. The two little prayer warriors gathered up some things to take with them and headed outside, carefully sneaking out the back door so as to avoid getting yelled at along the way.

✞   ✞   ✞

It was summertime; the older kids were all capable of fending for themselves for lunch, and so they did. Judy made sure the little ones got fed and then she left them to their own business.

Aaron and Jessie spent most of the day playing church in the fort which stood up above the sandbox. Aaron was the priest and Jessie was the nun. Together they prayed before the Blessed Sacrament in a small tabernacle that Aaron had fashioned with Lego. Then they went about the yard healing the sick, feeding the poor, and preaching the Good News. Catholic children play Catholic games.

Judy paid little attention to Aaron and Jessie. She kept busy with her gardening, steeped in her own bitterness. At one point, though, she looked up from her flower bed and began listening to Aaron, the young priest. He had a scarf over his neck like a stole and a little pocket Bible in his hands. He was preaching to Jessie who wore a pillowcase over her head like the veil of a nun.

"When you are nice to people and forgive them, you make Jesus happy. When you are mean to people and hurt them, you make the devil happy. So go and spread the Good News to all the people."

With that, Jessie jumped up from the stool she had been sitting on, and the two ran off to spread the Good News in another corner of the yard. Judy observed the two children repeat the scene a few times before they disappeared back into the fort.

Judy was impressed with what solid preaching came from the six-year-old priest. Although it had been a simple message, it was just what she needed to hear. *From the mouths of babes,* she mused.

✝ ✝ ✝

Sitting down in the grass, Judy took her hat off and wiped her brow. It was a perfect summer day. There was a light breeze dancing through the yard. Wiping the dirt from her hands, Judy got up and walked over to the garage.

John did not look up from his work as his wife approached. She hesitated a moment. Now Judy had a choice. She could ask John to forgive her for all her unkind words and uncharitable thoughts. Or she could lecture him for his grumpiness over the past few days. Judy chose the former.

She slipped her hands around her husband's waist from behind. She could feel his muscles tighten at first, irritated by her intrusion. She leaned her head on his strong back and hugged him warmly. The tension in his muscles began to let go.

Softly, Judy whispered, "I'm sorry, John, for saying you have a lazy ass."

He began to laugh. Putting down his tools, he turned around and took his wife into his strong arms. "I'm sorry I didn't get off my lazy ass and help you out in the first place."

They laughed and held on.

"I love you," Judy murmured, her head tucked in comfortably between John's neck and shoulder.

He kissed her hair and answered, "I love you, too."

Judy looked up to meet John's gaze. The few wrinkles around the soft blue eyes made his smile even warmer. He was still the most handsome man she knew. She gently stroked his temples, noticing the grey. It was a distinguished look. Everything about him was so familiar to her, so alluring, so right. She was at home in his arms.

John beheld his wife. The loveliness of her dark-brown eyes never faded, it just drew him in ever deeper. Time had not eroded the attraction he had for this woman, it had only intensified it. Her beauty etched itself more profoundly in his heart with each passing day. This was the one and only woman with whom he desired to grow old.

Now John had a choice. He could remain captivated by the loveliness of his wife. Or he could get back to his work. John chose the former.

He leaned down, drawing his wife's face up to his own, and kissed her tenderly. This was exactly what Judy needed. She received his warm lips lovingly, ardently full of desire for her husband.

She wrapped her arms around his neck, pulled her body in closer, and returned her husband's kisses affectionately, lovingly, passionately. There was no opportunity for love lost between these experienced lovers. There was no hurry to pull themselves apart.

The tide of love poured down upon them, released through the power of forgiveness. They abandoned themselves to that tide. The ripples of selfishness washed away from their hearts. They gave themselves to each other freely. The grace of that sacrament, which they had entered into twenty-four years earlier, still remained powerfully efficacious.

Judy rested her head against her husband's stalwart frame. Time went unmeasured, as she lost herself in his embrace.

"You know what I like about you, Judy?" His voice was low and tender.

"What's that, John?" She did not lift her head from his shoulder.

"As passionate as you are when you get angry, you're even more passionate when we make up. It's almost worth fighting over." He laughed, thinking about her fiery personality. She was a woman of passion!

Judy laughed with him.

John breathed heavily and then whispered, "I'm sorry I've been so miserable these past few days. I know I've been pretty hard to live with."

"Really? I hadn't noticed," Judy murmured, through a smile.

John chuckled and squeezed tighter.

"I didn't expect it to be this hard," he said, pensively.

"Joanie?" Judy knew her husband's heart well.

"Joanie, Maggie, Amie. They're all getting ready to move on with life. They grew up too fast, Judy. When did it happen?" His voice faded.

Her husband was a sentimental fool at times, which was precisely what Judy loved about him.

"Time slipped away on us, John," she mused. "But those girls sure turned out beautifully, didn't they?"

"Wow!" John's eyes looked straight ahead, but he was seeing his three oldest daughters: beautiful, strong, young women. He was so proud. The tear running down his cheek said so.

Judy kept her eyes closed and held on to her husband.

With a sense of resolution, John stepped away from his wife, took her hand in his, and led her into the house. Judy followed behind her husband, knowing what he was about to do. She knew her husband's mind well.

John asked Aaron and Jessie to come into the house with them. When he got inside he called down the troops. It took a few minutes, but soon everyone was present and accounted for.

"I would like to apologize to each one of you for my behaviour earlier today. I should not have yelled at you or at your mother. I'm sorry for having been so miserable." John made eye contact with each of his five children standing before him as he made his apology.

"I'm sorry, too," Judy joined in. "Especially to you, Katie. Did you ever find your art supplies?"

"Yes, Mom. They were on the bookshelf in the living room," the sixteen-year-old replied.

"I put them there," Aaron piped up. "I saw them on the stairs and thought you had forgotten to put them away."

John, Judy, and Katie exchanged a smile that communicated their appreciation for this saintly child in their midst.

"Anyway," Katie went on, "I forgive you both, Mom and Dad." She walked over and gave them each a kiss on the cheek. Then she turned to her brothers and apologized, who in turn apologized to her for their rudeness. Katie and Jessie made up as well, with a big hug.

Now that the pebble had been thrown into the pond, the ripples of contrition and forgiveness were going out. Everyone stepped into the pond because those ripples can be so enticing. The water was refreshing, indeed.

With all the mishaps of the morning sorted out, John suggested they pack up the family and head out for the remainder of the day. Blackstrap Lake was not quite a half-hour drive from town. They could pack a supper and have a barbecue out there. The beach and park would be quiet mid-week.

John even suggested that the kids call some of their cousins to come along. After all, what was the point of driving a fifteen-seater van if you couldn't fill it sometimes?

Judy called Joanie at work and asked if she and Brandon wanted to bring out Maggie and Amie after work and join them for supper. Judy knew John would appreciate having his daughters around him.

The plans were all made, and the family set out. Brandon brought out two guitars, one for himself, one for Isaac. The day came to a close with a singsong and campfire.

John and Judy held hands and soaked up the love with which they were surrounded. John leaned over and whispered in his wife's ear, "How would you like to pick up where we left off in the garage this afternoon?"

Judy smiled, but did not answer. She kept her eyes focussed on the fire before her.

"What do you say, when we get home tonight, that we rendezvous in the second room on the left side of the hallway upstairs?" he persisted, affectionately.

Judy smiled, but she still did not answer. Instead, she turned and kissed her husband. It was a lingering kiss, her soft hand holding his face.

A few of the younger children groaned and rolled their eyes. Joanie smiled over at Brandon as he played the guitar.

He winked back at his fiancée. *Soon, sweetheart. So soon, I can almost taste it!*

Chapter 55

The lazy days of summer seemed to crawl by. Joanie had never been so anxious for summer to end. Still, in the midst of her anticipation there existed a nostalgic melancholy. She was particularly attentive to her sisters and brothers, taking every opportunity to enjoy doing things together. Though Jessie was terribly excited about the wedding, she also seemed to have a real sadness about the impending changes in their home. Each night she would crawl into bed with Joanie.

Brandon and Joanie took many walks together in the warm evenings. Brandon would inevitably lead them back to the spot where they had first professed their love. That was their spot. They would sit on a rock and talk, sharing dreams and making plans for their future. It was a blessed time.

The love between them had a life and energy of its own. Every touch of the hand, every small embrace, stirred the deep longing within them to be one. Yet there was a tremendous strength, which came from their practice of self-discipline, that prevented them from pushing the boundaries of their relationship.

One evening, as Joanie leaned her head on Brandon's shoulder, she confessed, "Brandon, I'm really nervous."

"About what?" he asked.

He glanced down at her face, and the expression she bore said it all.

"Oh? That!" he verbalized his comprehension. "So am I."

"You?" Shock echoed in her voice. "Why would you be nervous?"

He looked at her, almost wounded by her response.

She realized the implication of her question, but was not quite sure how to take it back. "I'm sorry, Brandon, that wasn't very sensitive."

He took both of her hands in his own, and stepping around to face her, he said, "Apart from my faith in Jesus, there is nothing more important to me than loving you. I have never wanted anything in my life as much as I have wanted to be with you as husband and wife. Why is it so hard to believe that that would make me nervous? I mean, here you are, my perfect, spotless bride. I'm almost afraid to touch you."

"Brandon," she corrected him, "I am *not* perfect."

"You are for me . . . and that's what counts." He swept back the loose curls that framed her face, his hand lightly caressing her soft skin. "And you have kept yourself so pure and chaste. I wish I could offer you that same gift, but all I have to offer you is my contrite heart . . . and I know that you will not spurn that."

She smiled at his scriptural reference and placed her hand softly on his cheek. She had a distant gaze as she looked into his eyes, as if she were looking at his soul. "I want you so much, Brandon, sometimes it's all I can think about. I have a really hard time concentrating on things these days."

He laughed and pulled her into his arms, gently pressing her head against his shoulder. His fingers moved through her loose, long hair. With a sigh, he whispered, "I wish I could kiss you right now."

"You could kiss me right now," she replied.

Stepping back to take her into his gaze, he questioned her with his eyes.

"But the only reason you hold that privilege with me," she explained, with a twinkle in her eye, "is because I can trust, so completely, that you won't."

Brandon shook his head with a laugh. "You know, ever since I met you and became a Christian, my life has become so full of paradoxes."

"Any regrets?" she asked.

"No regrets," he assured her, pulling her close again for a hug.

"I love you, Brandon," she whispered softly, enjoying the feeling of being held close to his heart. "As nervous as I am at times, I can hardly wait to be your wife."

Brandon kissed the top of her head and smiled at her sweet innocence. "You know that reminds me," he said, "are you certain you don't want me to book a hotel room for our wedding night?"

With her arms wrapped around him, she squeezed tightly. "I've already told you, Brandon, I don't want to spend our wedding night in some hotel room. After all this time, all I want is for you to take me home. I don't care if we ever leave your—our—apartment again."

"Well, that might get a little awkward with our jobs, you know. We only booked off three weeks. And it would be a shame to let those plane tickets that my dad bought for us, go to waste."

"Plane tickets . . . to where?" Joanie asked, looking up at him with her winsome gaze.

"Uh-uh," Brandon responded, shaking a scolding finger at her, affectionately. "That's for me to know and for you to find out!"

"Why don't you tell me?" she entreated him, sweetly.

"Do you really want me to spoil your surprise?" he asked her, knowing the answer to the question.

"No," she replied, honestly. Joanie sighed, resting her head against him once more and then commented, "Your father's been awfully generous with us."

"Dad's got money, he can afford to be generous," Brandon stated. He chuckled at the thought of his father. "He just wants so much to be a part of our lives."

"He's a very important part of our lives, Brandon. I love your father a lot," Joanie said, smiling warmly at the thought of James Vaughn.

"Well, he sure loves you," Brandon acknowledged. "You've won him over completely with all your charm. It really would not surprise me at all if he becomes a Christian."

"That's what we've been praying for, dear," Joanie reminded him. "And if he does, he'll have a wonderful role model in his son." Joanie pulled herself back again and smiled up at Brandon. He was such a dedicated and loving Christian man. Her heart ached with longing to be his wife.

Brandon could feel the longing in her gaze. "I love you, Joanie," he said, softly.

"I know," she said, "but don't ever stop telling me!" She smiled and snuggled up closely again to her devoted lover. "Two more weeks," she said dreamily. "It seems like forever."

✠   ✠   ✠

That night in bed, Judy was restlessly tossing and turning. Finally, John could not take it anymore. "Okay, you've got my attention. What's on your mind?"

"Oh, I'm sorry, John, did I wake you?" Judy asked, sweetly.

"No, I was dreaming that you were tossing and turning and then *I* woke *you* up. This is really *my* dream, and we're both still asleep."

She laughed and cuddled up to him. He lifted his arm to allow her to curl up closely, and he gently caressed her hair with his fingers. "What's up?"

"Do you realize that we only have two more weeks with all of our children living safely and soundly under our roof? Every night when I go to bed I just keep wishing that time would stand still."

John laughed and replied, "Well, I doubt that Joanie and Brandon are feeling that way."

She laughed in spite of herself. "No, I don't suppose they are."

"Do you remember," he asked her, "how anxious we were to start out on married life together?"

"Uh-hum. And I also remember how un-anxious my mother was. I guess the more things change, the more they stay the same."

"You know," he added, "it is nice that we don't need to wait anymore." He followed up his intimation with some playful caresses. Judy returned his affection, in kind.

After twenty-four years of marriage, the flame of love still burned brightly between this couple. It was a fruitful love, for in their openness they had brought forth eight children. It was a selfless love, for in their loving service they had raised up godly offspring. It was a faithful love, for in their fidelity they had laid down a firm foundation on which their children stood.

The flame of that love had been passed on to each of their children. Now they, in turn, were going out into the world and bringing Christ to others. So it was that the fire of love which had made John and Judy one in Jesus Christ, was the very same fire of love that burned in Joanie's and Brandon's hearts.

Love is a consuming flame. It reaches out and ignites other hearts. Those hearts, in turn, are also consumed by the flame. And so it has been that, throughout the centuries, Christianity has spread from one home to another—one heart at a time.

This is the power of the Sacrament of Marriage.

Chapter 56

Joanie woke up with a smile to greet the dawn. It was early, and the house was just beginning to murmur with the sounds of people coming to life. The morning light streamed in through the window, bringing with it all the hopes of this special day.

The rehearsal had gone smoothly the night before. Joanie was not sure why, but she had not felt nervous about the ceremony at all. There had been so much fun and excitement in the air. The last advice Fr. Steve had offered them was to relax and go with the flow. Joanie and Brandon were quite capable of that.

Fr. Steve happily stayed back after the rehearsal to hear Joanie's and Brandon's confessions. Their souls washed clean again, the young couple was ready to enter into that glorious sacrament which awaited them at the altar the next day.

The rehearsal party had been a wonderful time, but had left everyone quite exhausted. Joanie laughed to herself, remembering how her mother had kicked Brandon out of the house just before midnight. "After all," she had told her future son-in-law, "tradition is tradition."

Joanie did not remember what time she had fallen asleep. She and her sisters had lain awake half the night talking. None of them wanted to let go of their last night together. So it was that sleep had to overcome them, each in their turn. Joanie was the last of them to succumb.

Now she was the first to pull herself from its grasp. Hugging her pillow, she rolled out of bed and knelt on the floor to make her morning offering. The simple words of the prayer seemed to have new meaning this morning, for as she offered up her day to Jesus, she realized she was offering up the rest of her life.

Today she would cross an important threshold: a threshold that would take her from living as one, alone in Christ, to living as one in Christ with Brandon. She remained there for a while, meditating on the newness of life which this day offered to her. She was profoundly aware of God's blessings and grace.

She slipped downstairs to find her mom in the kitchen. She was glad to be able to have these few minutes alone with her. They did not say much. There was no need. The significance of the day was upon them and they silently blessed each other with the love that was between them.

Joanie hopped into the shower and began the long process of preparation for the wedding. It seemed that time was flying past at record speed, and she could hardly keep up to it.

✟   ✟   ✟

With loving care, Judy did up each of the satin-covered buttons on Joanie's wedding gown. Her sisters stood by and watched as Judy laid the string of pearls around her daughter's neck. It was all any of them could do to keep from crying. Joanie was absolutely radiant.

"Okay," Katie said, seriously assessing the situation. "Something old, well that's your gloves from Grandma. Something new, that's your pearls from Brandon. Something borrowed—something borrowed? What did you borrow?" Panic was rising in her voice.

"This," her mother spoke up as she handed Joanie her rosary. It was a dainty, pearl-beaded rosary, which had been given to Judy when she was just a child from her grandparents. "You can carry it in your bouquet."

Joanie smiled and nodded.

"Okay," Katie continued with purpose. "Something blue . . . and that's your garter."

Joanie playfully pulled up her gown to reveal the dainty article around her slim leg. The girls gave a squeal of delight, watching the show Joanie put on for them.

Judy reproved her daughter, saying, "I hope you don't do that tonight at the dance!"

"Oh, Mother, be serious!" Joanie exclaimed. "You know me better than that."

Her mother laughed and shook her head. "I'm going down to make sure your father's ready with the camera for some pictures. You girls come down in order when I call. You first, Jessie."

Judy tapped Jessie's little nose and smiled warmly at the little girl who looked like an absolute angel in her flower girl dress.

One by one, the five sisters paraded down the stairwell. Isaac stood at the bottom, videotaping, and John snapped pictures on the camera.

Each girl looked stunning in her formal attire, but as Joanie stepped down to greet her father, his heart stood still. This was it. His little girl was getting married. He choked back the tears and tried to stay focussed.

She was too beautiful to describe. It was not the gown or the hairdo or even the elegant string of pearls around her neck that made her so radiant. It was the light of love that was illuminating her entire being. And it was absolutely transfiguring.

Her mother handed her the bouquet of red roses, which Brandon had insisted upon for his bride. In it, Judy had carefully attached the rosary.

As Joanie felt the beads under her fingers, she knew she was carrying with her that day the faith and love of generations of devoted Christians.

She and Brandon were now beginning their own story, passing that faith on to future generations—a faith founded on the saving grace of Jesus Christ. The final chapter of their story would be told someday, when at the end of this road they would both arrive home at last in heaven. She reached up to touch her pearl necklace and thanked God that He had chosen Brandon to be the man with whom she would make this journey.

✝   ✝   ✝

They arrived at the church in plenty of time and waited in the car, as guests were still arriving at the last minute. Finally, John gave the signal and the bridal party emerged from the vehicle. They entered the back of the church, and Joanie could feel the buzz of excitement that came from the guests within.

Fr. Steve was there to greet them. He gave Joanie a warm hug and whispered in her ear, "I don't ever remember seeing so radiant a bride. God bless you, Joanie!"

She hugged him back tightly; she did so love this servant of God. He returned to the front of the church for the ceremony to begin.

Before going to take her place, Judy tucked a tissue into Joanie's hand, like only a mother would do. Joanie laughed, which saved her from her tears for the time being.

All at once, the music was playing and Jessie was making her way up the aisle, just in front of Katie. Joanie took her father's arm and waited.

When Amie was near the front, Maggie turned one last time to look at Joanie before she headed up. Joanie smiled back at her dear sister, communicating all the love that she felt in her heart.

There was a gentle tug on her arm, and the bride looked up at her dad. That was a mistake; she could not look into his eyes, not yet. This was such a sacred moment between father and daughter. She squeezed his arm tightly, and with a gracefulness that was so characteristic of her, she walked up the aisle on her daddy's arm.

Watching his bride approach, Brandon's heart was full of thanksgiving. That God had saved him from his sins was an incomprehensible grace. But that He would have shown so much love to Brandon to have given him Joanie for a bride—was truly beyond mercy. He prayed that his heart would never grow dull to the gift he was receiving at this moment in his life.

Brandon could not begin to take in all of the beauty of Joanie—his one and only, his spotless bride. She had never been more radiant to him; still, as each moment passed her beauty became even more resplendent. He felt so undeserving of this graceful woman as he watched her come closer, step by step. Yet as he caught a glimpse of her eyes, sparkling at him through the soft veil she wore over her face, he was assured of her love. He was at home in that love and completely at peace in her presence. There were no cold feet for this groom; he was standing exactly where he wanted to be. And he knew full well that this indeed was holy ground.

Joanie kept her eyes fixed on Brandon, standing in his black tuxedo, waiting at the front of the church for her. He was so handsome. His bright blue eyes lit the way, drawing Joanie closer, one step after the other, into his love. She could not hear or feel anything around her—just the pounding of her heart as she approached her groom. He was everything for which she had ever prayed in a husband. Joanie thanked God for having shown such favour upon her that she and Brandon would now stand before Him and be joined together as husband and wife, in Jesus' name.

Brandon stepped forward to meet his bride. He took her father's out-stretched hand and thanked him sincerely. In a gesture of complete grati-tude, he turned to Judy and kissed her on the cheek, whispering, "Thank you!" Joanie reached out to her parents and hugged them both, lovingly.

Joanie then took her place alongside her groom, and Brandon led his bride to the front of the church. There they stood before Fr. Steve, before the community of faith, and before God.

✟   ✟   ✟

The wedding Mass proceeded with incredible joy. Fr. Steve gave a beautiful homily, based on Ephesians five, verses twenty-one to thirty-three: Marriage signifies the love of Christ for the Church, His bride. The union of Brandon and Joanie would now be a sacrament, bearing witness to the world of Jesus' love for the Church. This was the means by which they would both grow in holiness as they would sanctify each other day by day in the covenant of mar-riage. And in witnessing the holiness of their love, others would be drawn to faith in Jesus Christ.

Fr. Steve reminded Brandon that it would be in his willingness to serve Joanie that he would most reflect the love of Christ. Brandon was being called to lay down his life for Joanie, just as Christ sacrificed Himself for His bride to make her holy. Joanie was being called to be submissive to her husband and recognize the authority which God had given to Brandon, as her husband. Brandon was to be the head of their home, just as Joanie was to be the heart. As they lived in this mystery, they would give glory to God in their lives, and God would certainly bless them abundantly with His grace.

Fr. Steve extolled the beauty of the love that everyone had witnessed between Brandon and Joanie in their relationship, and he blessed them to continue to grow in that selfless love. As he spoke, the entire congregation was drawn into the love of this young couple. It was certainly true that their relationship had already given beautiful testimony to Jesus Christ: His saving grace, His healing power, His abiding faithfulness, His patient and steadfast love. By the time Joanie and Brandon finally stood to profess their vows, there was a real sense of anticipation throughout the entire church. Everyone waited attentively.

Joanie felt as though she had entered into eternity, and the sound of Brandon's voice, as he tenderly made his vows to her, was the only thing that kept her connected to the present moment. As she professed her vows, her voice wavered under the strain of emotion. She breathed slowly and continued as clearly as she could. Her eyes shone through the tears and sparkled up at Brandon through her veil.

Brandon brought the blessed ring to his lips and kissed it, breathing all of his love into it. As he began to place the ring on Joanie's delicate finger, her hand trembled. He softly caressed the top of her hand in a soothing and calming way. She felt safe and secure in his touch. Gradually the trembling subsided, and she was able in her turn to take his ring, kiss it, and place it on Brandon's finger. She fixed her eyes on his strong hands as she gently guided the ring to its place. When she looked back up to meet his gaze, his eyes were now filled with tears, as well. She could not hold back her own.

Fr. Steve spoke out, "If you two don't stop it, *I'll* be crying next." Everyone laughed, for indeed there were very few dry eyes in the church by this point in time.

Their mothers took Joanie's and Brandon's baptismal candles, lit them from the flame of the Easter Candle, and passed them on to their children. It was from this flame that the bride and groom lit their wedding candle. They then blew out the individual candles, symbolizing that the two had now become one in Christ.

Fr. Steve introduced the couple to the congregation, "It is now my great honour to present to you Mr. and Mrs. Brandon and Joanie Vaughn."

The congregation clapped enthusiastically. Then Fr. Steve motioned for silence and went on. "I understand Brandon and Joanie have been waiting for a long time for this, and I don't want to make them wait any longer. So, Brandon, I now invite you to kiss your bride."

A hush fell over the church. People were sitting on the edge of their seats. Brandon slowly lifted the veil from Joanie's face. She was the most beautiful and precious woman in the world to him. He could not begin to contain in his heart all of the love he felt for his bride, and he could not hold back all of the desire he had for her.

Bringing his hands gently around to cradle her face within them, he drew his face down toward hers. Joanie closed her eyes so as not to let any other sense rob her of the thrill of the moment, as his warm and gentle lips pressed against her own. There was tenderness; there was commitment; there was self-giving; and above all, there was love: patient and enduring love.

She had waited her whole life for this. Now here she stood with her husband, savouring the love that flowed between them as their lips opened to receive the gift of each other. Bound together in the covenant of marriage, they were finally one, through the mystery of this holy and beautiful sacrament. The entire world shut off for them as they held each other in that loving embrace.

Brandon tasted the sweetness of Joanie's lips. The sublimity of that first kiss was beyond compare. His lips delicately caressed hers, drawing forth and returning the very breath of their love. As Brandon stood back tall again, he tuned in to the cheering and clapping all around them.

Joanie could not help herself. She reached up and pulled Brandon back down for another kiss. The congregation roared with laughter. There was something so beautiful, so pure, and so wholesome in the love between this couple. The guests, who were there as witnesses, could not hold back all of the emotions that this tender love evoked as they broke into spontaneous applause.

Following this part of the ceremony, two microphones were brought to Joanie and Brandon. The musicians began to play and Brandon took Joanie's hand in his as they sang in perfect harmony, *Flesh of My Flesh,* that beautiful wedding song.

It was most appropriate, for music had been such an important part of their relationship all along. Their voices rang throughout the church with clear resonance. It was a treasured gift that Brandon and Joanie shared with each other and with which they blessed the entire congregation that day.

After Communion, they knelt and prayed together. Brandon could not find words in his heart to thank his Heavenly Father for the gift of this precious daughter who had been given to him to be his wife. How could any groom sit next to his bride and not be moved by the responsibility entrusted to him: to love her, to protect her, to provide for her, and ultimately to lead her to their heavenly home? It was awesome.

It was only in leaning on Jesus that Brandon knew, in all certainty, that he would be able to fulfill his duties. He opened his heart to all the graces of the Sacrament of Marriage and prayed for the gifts of wisdom and holiness.

Joanie was moved to humility, kneeling before God at the side of her husband. Gratitude filled her heart. She prayed for the gift of love, desiring that she would be for Brandon a tender, caring, and nurturing wife and mother in their home. She prayed for all the graces they would need to grow together in purity and holiness all the days of their life.

Joanie slipped her hand into Brandon's hand as they prayed. He held on tightly. They were one, at last.

After Communion, Joanie's sisters went over to the choir, and there they sang *Ave Maria*. As they did, Joanie and Brandon took a rose and placed it before the statue of Mary. Together they prayed silently, consecrating their marriage to the Immaculate Heart of Mary, that through her intercession she would help them to grow in holiness and draw them ever closer to her Son. The sound of her sisters' voices filled Joanie's heart with peace. She smiled up at Brandon. Taking her hand, he led her back to their seats at the front where they joined their hearts with the prayer that was being sung on their behalf.

After the signing of the register, Fr. Steve allowed the newlyweds to kiss again. "As if I could stop them . . . now that they've started!" he added, playfully.

Brandon took Joanie again into his arms and tenderly kissed her. There was no mistaking the distinctive beauty of this couple's love for each other. And the amazing thing was that this special quality did not come from some specific gift or charism that was theirs alone. What existed between Joanie and Brandon was the outgrowth of the choices they had made: to reserve their physical affection, to practise self-discipline, and to die to self for the sake of the other. These were the stepping stones along the path which they had chosen to follow to prepare themselves entirely for marriage.

There was no holding them back now. The energy released between them was like that of an erupting volcano. No one near them could escape the heat of their love. It was inspiring to all. It somehow drew every person there into the awareness of the sacredness of marriage. In the vision that this young couple presented to the world, everyone could see how beautiful the love of a man and a woman was intended to be, in God's most gracious design.

Chapter 57

The rest of the day unfolded as a wedding day will, with all of the busyness of photos, bridal lines, receptions, and speeches. Joanie and Brandon were swept up in the whirlwind of activity.

The reception was held in a large hall, elegantly decorated under the direction of Justine; it reflected her classy touch. James Vaughn had insisted on picking up the bill for the caterers, and with three hundred people in attendance at the wedding that was no small contribution.

Mike and Ben were the MCs for the reception. They informed all the guests, as the bridal party arrived, that Joanie had insisted that there be no restrictions placed on the tinkling of the glasses. "Apparently she enjoyed her first kiss so much that she really doesn't want to have to stop," Mike reported.

"That's right, Mike," Ben concurred. "In fact, Joanie has already told me that if the guests don't tinkle their glasses enough for her liking, she's gonna start tinkling her own!"

From that point on, the evening was filled with the sweet music of crystal wine glasses. Joanie and Brandon did not mind at all. What newlyweds wouldn't rather kiss than eat anyway?

Mike and Ben continued a program throughout the wedding reception. They were natural entertainers, keeping the atmosphere light and full of fun as they told jokes, sang songs, and acted out their idea of what Joanie and Brandon would be doing on their fiftieth anniversary.

Ben put on a white curly wig, trifocals, and threw a shawl over his shoulders to play the part of Joanie. Mike put a half-bald wig on his head, grabbed a cane and a pipe, and played the part of Brandon. Together they sat in a couple of rocking chairs.

Rocking away, the elderly Mike began to talk in a creaky old voice. "After fifty years of married life with you, Joanie, I only have one concern."

"What's that?" Ben answered, putting on an impressive imitation of an old woman's voice.

"This letter I found in your drawer the other day." Mike produced an envelope and handed it to Ben.

"What're you doing going through my drawers, you old kook?" Ben snapped, snatching the letter out of Mike's hand.

"Looking for that letter," Mike returned.

"Well, what about it?" Ben asked.

"Who's it from?" Mike inquired.

"You! You crazy old fool! You wrote it to me before we got married," Ben replied, backhanding Mike on the shoulder.

"I never did!" Mike protested. "Just read that garbage."

Ben opened the letter and began to read: "My dearest Joanie, soon we will be wed. I cannot wait to be your husband when I can finally indulge myself with your sweet kisses and tender embraces. Your long, dark, curly hair . . . your fiery, deep brown eyes . . . your young and slender figure . . . all entreat me to want your love. I promise to be faithful and true to you, my dark-haired, dark-eyed beauty, for as long as we both shall live. Eternally yours, Brandon."

"See, that's what I mean," Mike insisted. "It may have my name on it, but I never wrote that slop!"

"Give me a break—are you trying to tell me that I married the wrong man?" Ben asked, with his hands on his hips.

"You must have, because that is not my letter," Mike said, with finality, taking a puff on his pipe.

"Well then, do you suppose it's too late for me to go back and find this mystery lover?" Ben asked, with a glimmer in his eyes.

"I'm afraid so, dear. The man who wrote that letter would never recognize you now. See what I mean," Mike went on, pointing to the letter with the crook of his cane. "Long, dark, curly hair . . . well your hair is short and white now. Fiery, deep dark eyes . . . well, I don't know how anyone could tell if they're fiery or dark anymore behind those trifocals you wear. And young, slender figure . . . now listen honey, don't get me wrong, you look great for having had ten kids and all, but that body of yours ain't young and slender anymore!"

"So what do you suggest I do then, Brandon?" Ben inquired of his old companion.

"Look, throw away that trashy letter and keep this one," Mike said, handing Ben a new envelope.

"What's this?" Ben asked, as he opened it up to read: "My darling Joanie, as we prepare for marriage I sit here and dream about indulging myself with your sweet kisses and tender embraces for a lifetime. I can hardly wait until your hair turns white, and you wear it in a becoming, elderly style. I long to gaze into your eyes through trifocals that could never serve to dim the fire that burns there. I thrill at the thought of seeing you after you have borne for us many children. I promise to be true to you, my one and only, for as long as we both shall live. Eternally yours, Brandon."

Ben took off his trifocals and threw an absolutely hilarious look at Mike who just sat there rocking and nodding.

"Now tell me, honestly, what kind of crazy old fool would write a letter like this? Only an old kook would ever think of handing over this kind of sentimental hogwash to the woman he was about to marry!" Ben folded up the letter, shaking his head incredulously.

"Look, woman!" Mike sat up, pointing his pipe to the letter. "I'm the crazy old fool who wrote that letter. And I'm the old kook who would have given that to you fifty years ago . . . if I had only realized then how much more beautiful you would be by the time we had been married fifty years! So there!" With a grunt he added, "Happy anniversary, honey!"

"Brandon," Ben sat shaking his finger at the old-timer rocking beside him, "you always were a romantic old fool . . . which is why I married you fifty years ago, and which is why I'd do it all over again today! Happy anniversary, dear!"

There were very few guests at the wedding who did not recognize which couple had inspired such a production. As the audience applauded, Brandon left the head table and went over to Grandma and Grandpa Ledoux. "Let's get a couple of experts like you to show us youngsters how to do it right!" he insisted.

As the glasses began tickling around the hall, Grandpa stood up and took Grandma into his arms for a long and beautiful kiss. When they were done, he called out, shaking his finger in the air, "It takes fifty-three years to get that good at kissing . . . and an awful lot of practice."

The hall filled with laughter as the guests cheered on this couple who was so dear to all of their hearts.

"Grandma and Grandpa Ledoux," Ben announced into the microphone, "have nine children still living, three in heaven, fifty-eight grandchildren, and eleven great-grandchildren so far—but Brandon and Joanie are going to get to work on that right away to try to make it an even dozen!" Everyone laughed as Brandon waggled his eyebrows at Joanie.

Ben continued, "Brandon and Joanie, it seems that the path of marital bliss has been well paved for you two young lovers. May you always enjoy the love and grace of the Sacrament of Marriage, the way Grandma and Grandpa have taught us all so well!"

As people applauded Ben's statement, the tinkling began again. Brandon stood up with Joanie and dipped her back for a long, lingering kiss.

Grandpa Ledoux called out from his seat, "You'd better kiss her like that while you're young, Brandon, 'cause they don't dip so well after fifty years!"

The reception continued with Joanie's siblings entertaining the crowd with a song they had written for Joanie and Brandon. They welcomed Brandon to the family and Jessie presented him with a certificate, officially recognizing him as their big brother. Maggie, Amie, and Katie toasted the bride, and Mark toasted the groom. It was a fun evening, made memorable by the love and affection of those gathered to honour the young couple.

Brandon and Joanie delighted in the company of every person present. How can one possibly convey the gratitude that comes from experiencing all of the love and support of family and friends? With Joanie standing by his side, confidently and clearly, Brandon made his address.

"There are so many people to thank here, please forgive me if I leave somebody out." He began by thanking the guests, the caterers, the musicians and, the bridal party. He thanked Mike and Ben for being such good MCs, and Grandma and Grandpa Ledoux for being such wonderful role models. He then continued.

"Fr. Steve, I want to thank you for the gift of your priesthood. That you bring Jesus to us each time you celebrate Mass would be enough to thank you for. But you have also blessed our community with solid preaching, which charitably and uncompromisingly proclaims the truth. You shepherd your flock faithfully. You inspire us by your example. You have been for me a mentor, a friend, and a light for my journey. I thank you.

"It gives me tremendous satisfaction to share this day with my mother, Caroline, and her husband, Dan. Mom, we've been through a great deal together in life, but now that we have both become Christians, I assure you, the best is yet to come!

"And to my father, James Vaughn, I can't tell you how your presence in my life has blessed me over this past year. I look forward to years of sharing our life and happiness with you. Thank you for all of your support and love.

"To Joanie's family, how can I begin to thank you all for having taken me in? You've taught me so much about what it means to be a Christian man. You've been for me a model of family that I will always strive to recreate in our new home. In a world that makes every effort to destroy the family, you shine forth as a light for everyone to see what God has called families to be. You have inspired me and given me hope, not only for our family's future, but for the future of mankind.

"Our Holy Father, Pope John Paul II, speaks about the springtime of faith in the Church. When I walked into your home and into the entire parish life at St. James' Church, I felt that springtime. It's real, and it's happening, and it's breathing new life into the Church . . . and it's transforming all of creation.

"To Judy and John, above all, thank you for bringing Joanie into this world. Thank you for raising her up to be the bright and beautiful Christian woman that she is. Indeed, it was through her bold and shining example that I first saw the light of Christ. . . . I'll never forget that moment in my life. It was that same light of faith that brought me to the fullness of Christianity, through my Baptism and new life in the Catholic Church. I know I could not have been blessed with a more perfect and beautiful bride than the one whom you so lovingly presented to me today. Thank you.

"To Joanie, thank you for loving Jesus so much that, even when I was a sinner, you were willing to lay down your life for Him and show me the way! Thank you for loving me so much that you have laid down your life for me today, so that we might have a new life together in Christ."

With that, Brandon leaned forward and tenderly kissed his bride.

✠   ✠   ✠

There was a break after the reception while the dance was being set up. Finally, the DJ announced that the bridal party was coming in. Brandon escorted Joanie to the dance floor where they danced to a beautiful Christian love song.

Brandon fixed Joanie in his gaze: his perfect, beautiful bride. He sang to her the words of the song as he effortlessly guided her around the floor. Joanie never took her eyes from his. She wished the moment would go on forever. Softly, she sang back to him the tender words of love.

For two dances they remained lost in each other's arms. But by the third dance Jessie, who could not be held back any longer, joined them . . . and so began the wedding dance.

It was a wonderful evening of celebration with family and friends. Paul Petros, who had played the role of cameraman all day, did not miss a moment of the joy. He had watched this relationship grow, from Brandon's brash and hedonistic attraction to Joanie her first day at work, through Brandon's struggle with abandoning his old life and his conversion to faith in Jesus Christ. Paul had seen revealed, through the time of Joanie's courtship with Brandon, how dynamically her love for the Lord, for life, and for Brandon animated everything she did.

Though Paul had only ever been a Christian by name, he had been moved by Brandon and Joanie's witness to consider the deeper meaning of faith in his own life. His wife, Camille, having attended Joanie and Brandon's wedding and reception, was beginning to understand why Paul was so enthusiastic about the friendship he had come to share with Joanie and Brandon at work. Camille delighted in watching Paul's eagerness to capture on film every detail of the celebration of this remarkable couple's wedding.

As the dance carried on into the night, Joanie was particularly grateful for the opportunity to dance with her father and brothers, her grandpa,

Brandon's father, Mark, Mike, Ben, and Paul. These men were of such significance in her life. She wanted to share with them the joy that was hers today.

Joanie danced with all of the many children present at their wedding. She was one of those brides who by her loving nature attracted children to her. They banded around her, all wanting to tap into the energy and joy that was radiating from her in every way.

Brandon, too, had a steady entourage of children, for he had become a real child-magnet in the time that he had known the Collins family. He did manage, though, to pull himself away in order to dance with his mother, Judy, Grandma Ledoux, Justine, Camille, and Tessa.

It had only been one year earlier when Brandon had danced with Tessa at her own wedding. Now, with their four-week-old baby girl there, Tessa and Karl's marriage was a clear reminder to Brandon and Joanie of the miracle of life that happens when a man and a woman become one. It was a miracle to which this newlywed couple was completely open . . . and hoped with great anticipation to experience.

Brandon also made sure to get in a dance with each of Joanie's sisters, thanking them personally for their love and support. He was truly blessed to be the big brother in this amazing family. It was an honour that he did not take lightly.

By midnight, the DJ announced that the bride and groom were leaving. The guests gathered around to form a circle and then sang a song of blessing for the newlyweds. A song was played, giving everyone the opportunity to dance around the couple, closing in and pulling back out from them. The children had the most fun, especially Aaron and Zack who made every effort to crash Brandon each time.

Finally, Brandon and Joanie left the hall and went out to their vehicle. The Pathfinder had on it a sign which read: *Just Married!* It had been decorated in that familiar style of paper flowers, with tin cans streaming from the back bumper. Brandon opened the door and carefully helped Joanie pull in all of her gown.

Chapter 58

"Welcome home, Mrs. Vaughn!" Brandon said, looking over at his bride as he pulled up into their parking stall at their condo.

His eyes danced with affection and anticipation. She sat and waited for him to open the door for her. Taking the hand which he so gallantly offered, she stepped out of the vehicle, like a queen returning with her king to their very humble palace.

She began to take a step, and Brandon raised his hand to stop her, saying, "No . . . my bride does not walk up those stairs."

He placed the set of keys between his teeth and reaching down, he swept her up into his strong arms. Making sure they had gathered in all of her gown, he began up the walk to the apartment building. Joanie laughed as Brandon struggled to open the door, but he refused to put her down.

Once inside, he carried her up the three flights of stairs. She clung snugly around his neck. She loved the feeling of safety and security that she experienced being held in his loving arms.

When they reached the apartment door, Brandon skilfully manoeuvred himself to get it opened, without letting go of his bride. Once unlatched, he pushed the door open with his foot and paused to catch his breath.

"We're finally home, Church-Girl," he said with a twinkle in his eyes.

"Wherever I am with you, will be home for me . . . Church-Boy!" Joanie replied, her eyes now dancing with anticipation.

Turning her gaze momentarily toward the apartment, Joanie noticed the crucifix on the wall above the fireplace. The open arms of Jesus on the cross beckoned them to come in and to share in the new life which they now had—a life of dying to self and of living for each other, in Christ.

Joanie drew her left hand across Brandon's cheek, and pulling his face to hers, she kissed him. Their lips met with fire and passion. They abandoned themselves to the passion of their love. They poured out into each other all of their love and affection, all of their months of waiting and anticipation, all of their hidden hopes and dreams, as their breath mingled between them, and their lips drew deeply from the wellspring of their love.

Their lips were still burning with the flame of their love as Brandon stepped forward and crossed the threshold of their new home and their new life. He held Joanie securely in his arms of love. Using his foot, and without turning back, Brandon closed the door behind them.

കൗ

For this reason a man shall leave
his father and mother
and be joined to his wife,
and the two shall become one.
So they are no longer two but one.
What therefore God has joined together,
let no man put asunder.
(Matthew 19:5-6)

കൗ

Special Thanks . . .

I gratefully acknowledge all the support and help of the many people who shared my vision for this book and who encouraged, directed, and prayed for me along the road from author to publisher. A special thanks to all our friends at Our Lady of Lourdes Parish and from the Catholic Home-Schooling Community in Saskatoon. Your families shine forth as beacons of hope in our world. Thank you for giving me a model of Catholic Christian community and for demonstrating that the Catholic culture is alive and well, as we live in the new springtime of faith of which Pope John Paul II has spoken.

Thank you to those who read my manuscript:

Joseph Couture (your insights and enthusiastic support were absolutely invaluable to me—from one writer to the other), April Mireau and Kelly Redl (here's to long talks, nachos, and sleepovers that will someday yet happen), Peter Couture, David Couture, Stacey Redl, and Bridget Martin: thank you all for your enthusiastic feedback which helped to keep me focussed on the value of the ministry which this book offers to young people like you!

Hannah Marcoux, it was your enthusiasm for this book that finally carried me over the finish line!

Kathy Katrick and Val Fuller, who read an early manuscript and were able to share my vision with enthusiasm, even at that infant stage of writing, thanks for the encouragement to continue. Kathy, your spirit of evangelizing inspires me in so many ways. Val, I thank you and your family for the many prayers.

Andréa Ledding, I appreciated your insights, discerning eye as a proof-reader and most of all, your sense of humour and enthusiastic support! Thanks!

Jeanne Manson (you have inspired me my whole life by your example of love and charity—you are so very dear to my heart!), Kristin Mann, Janice Mann, Janet Couture, Eva Marcoux, Val Marcoux (you are such a gift in my life!), Denise Schreiner: thank you all for taking the time to read my manuscript, providing input, and being so very encouraging.

Claude & Annette Mireau, if only you knew how much inspiration I drew from your friendship, mentoring, and the model of your lives dedicated to Christ, in order to write! Thank you for giving the right words of encouragement when I needed it the most and for babysitting for me so that I could devote time to writing. Claude, I sincerely appreciate how you took time from your busy job to assist me as a proof-reader!

To my brothers and sisters:
Mary, Gerald, Louise, James, Edward, & Albert:

Thanks for the wonderful memories of having grown up in a great Catholic family with you! It is a tremendous gift in life to still be close to each of you and to share a faith that binds us all together in Christ. Praise God!

Mary Couture, you dedicate your life each day to sharing Christ with others through your generous love. Thank you for the gift of music you shared with me as I was growing up and with which you bless my children now. And thanks for the great photo for the cover!

Gerry & Janet Couture, you have inspired me for years by your dedication to faith and family. Your family's enthusiasm for this work lifted me up so many times when I wasn't sure if I could do it.

Louise & Bernie Smyth, you have been a wonderful example of dedicated Christian parents for me! Louise, thank you for inspiring me my whole life with the example of your life! Your input and enthusiasm were greatly appreciated. Thank you for the excellent write-up you did for the back-cover!

James & Elizabeth Couture, the example of your family life was a great source of inspiration for me. Thank you for your support, encouragement, helpful advice, and practical assistance (babysitting for me) throughout this project!

Ed & Jackie Couture, your dedication to family and faith is very inspiring. Thank you for the many times you helped out with my children so that I could dedicate time to this project. Thanks, Jackie, for the feedback you gave me early on in my writing—you directed my efforts and helped me to get my feet off the ground as a writer.

Albert Couture, thank you for letting us use your nice, new, black car! But mostly, thanks for always being there to help out in so many ways! You are an awesome brother!

Special acknowledgment goes to:

Eva Marcoux, you are a shining example of Christian charity and generous love to all who know you. You have blessed me so many times over, and I thank God each day for having you for my mother-in-law. Thank you for your help and support with this book.

Mark & Léa Mallett, thank you for taking time to provide me with important feedback, helpful advice, and believing in this work. You are pioneering new territories in music ministry for the Catholic Church. Mark, your music is amazing—thanks for the theme song *Arms of Love*! You have been anointed as a herald of the Good News and your music cuts straight to the heart. I pray for God to continue to bless the good work you are doing in His Name.

Janelle Reinhart, thank you so much for reading and promoting my novel. Your cover write-up was wonderful! Your music is an absolute gift to the world, strengthened by the depth and devotion that comes from your Catholic faith. I know that you will continue to do great things in His Name through your awesome ministry.

Shawna Kunz, you did a beautiful job on the cover for this novel. It was a real blessing to work with such a dedicated Christian woman, who shared with me the vision for this book. God bless you!

Gary and MaryEllen Redl, thank you for so often opening your home to my children, allowing me opportunities to work without interruptions. Your generous love inspires me, and your support for this work encouraged me when I was not sure if I could do it.

Dave and Terrie Kostur, thank you for saying "Go for it!" with such gusto! Your friendship blesses our lives daily.

André and Carolyn Leblanc, thank you for your advice, helpful direction, office space when I needed it, and believing in this ministry.

Myles and Loren MacLennan, thank you for believing in the value of this ministry and being there for us with your friendship, encouragement, and support. Your friendship, Loren, is a gift I truly cherish!

Brittany Robinson, thank you for taking time to answer my many questions about journalism and research-reporting. Blessings!

Ron Ecker, thank you for sharing with me your expertise in typography and layout design. Your assistance was invaluable!

David Carter, thank you for the assistance in setting up a website.

Louis and Val O'Reilly, and Pierre and Laura O'Reilly, we appreciate your support of this ministry, your help, your guidance, and your friendship.

Kevin and Fran Butek, thank you for all your support! Your friendship has been one of the greatest gifts that has come to us through this ministry. Blessings on your family!

Michael and Colleen Arsenault, thank you for all you have done to promote *Arms of Love* and its message of purity and truth. It has been a real blessing to work with you.

Fr. Alex MacLellan, thank you for taking time to pen such a beautifully written foreword for this novel. May you be richly blessed, as you bless our Church daily through the gift of your priesthood.

To my chief editors, I owe the biggest debt of gratitude:

Lil Schroeder, how could I begin to express my gratitude to you for sharing your time and expertise as chief editor for my novel? Your input was awesome, your discerning eye was an invaluable resource for me, and your sensitivity to my writing style was most appreciated. I learned so much from you. It was most encouraging to receive your enthusiasm along with your professional advice. You are a wonderful, generous woman, and I appreciate you very much.

Gay Couture, you have shared my successes and failures and have supported me my whole life in good times and in bad. You have been for me unconditional love from the first moments of my life, and I am so blessed to have you for my mom! Thank you for the time you dedicated to help edit my novel and to do the painting for the front cover. The whole-hearted support you have for this work means more to me than I can express!

My husband, Jim, you were my first and last editor and greatest inspiration! You saw me through this project and gave me timely advice, criticism, support, and most of all, unconditional love—especially on those days when I was not so receptive to your timely advice, criticism, and support! If it had not been for you, this book would never have come together for me. I thank God each day for the gift of the wonderful husband that you are and for your dedication to God and our family! You truly are the love of my life—the only one with whom I want to grow old!

Special Dedication:

I pay special honour to the memory of two of the biggest heroes in my life: my dad, Gerry Couture, and my father-in-law, Vernon Marcoux. These men demonstrated throughout their lives the dedication and devotion to their faith and their families that is so needed in our world today. I thank God each day for blessing me to have been formed and nurtured in their love!

From the bottom of my heart:

Thank you, again, to my husband and to our beautiful children, Hannah, Rebekah, Mikaelah, Jacinta, Matthew, Gemma (born just twelve days after *Arms of Love* first came to print), Benjamin and Jacob (two more blessings in our family since this all began!). You were so patient and generous with me as I dedicated many hours to this project. May the graces from all those many sacrifices that you made, for the sake of this ministry, bear fruit in the lives of those who read this book. Your love, prayers, and support sustained me through the hard times. You have been—and will always be—my greatest inspiration for writing! You have all given me so many beautiful examples of sacrificial love, and I could not imagine a day of my life without you!

To Jesus Christ, may all glory and honour be Yours
for having shown the world what it means to love
when You stretched out Your
Arms of Love on the cross
for each of us!

About the Author

The Marcoux family January 2007
Back Row: Carmen holding Gemma, Matthew, James holding Benjamin
Front Row: Mikaelah, Rebekah holding Jacob, Jacinta, Hannah

Carmen Marcoux

. . . is a prairie girl, born and raised in Saskatoon, the sixth child from a family of seven. She received her B.Ed. from the University of Saskatchewan. Carmen and her husband, Jim, now have eight children, whom they home-school. They are actively involved in their parish community at Our Lady of Lourdes, in Saskatoon, where Carmen has a particular interest in youth and music ministries.

The inspiration to write came from a desire to promote the idea of courtship and to encourage families and young people to embrace the virtue of chastity by putting courtship into practice in their lives. Putting a fresh new look on what many people deem an old-fashioned idea was the motivation for writing this novel. It is Carmen's hope to be able to continue writing fiction that inspires readers to explore the truth and beauty of the teachings of the Catholic Church.

Fiction is a wonderful means to evangelize. There are all too many examples of lifestyles that go against Gospel values and the Church's teachings. There is a need to have heroes in our lives, fictional and real, who model what it means to be fully Christian in this day and age. Many people are out there trying to live according to God's laws. They are as real as you, and they are transforming our society—one heart at a time.

"The task which awaits you—the new evangelization—demands that you present, with fresh enthusiasm and new methods, the eternal and unchanging content of the heritage of the Christian faith." Pope John Paul II
(Commissioning Families, Neo-Catechumenal Way. 1991.)

Since *Arms of Love* first came to print in 2002 Carmen has begun speaking at rallies and conferences promoting

Purity, Chastity & Courtship

Carmen (November 2002)

"The most beautiful thing I have experienced, since beginning this ministry, is seeing the enthusiasm with which young people are embracing the message of purity. It is an honour to be a 'herald of hope' in our world. I thank God for having blessed me with this opportunity to proclaim His Good News to a world that is dying to hear it. ~ *Carmen Marcoux (April 2004)* ~

Carmen is available for a limited number of speaking engagements each year.

To book Carmen to come speak at an event or to purchase copies of her talks, call 1-800-705-7396.

Also available is Carmen's brochure *"Twenty Tips for Christian Courtship".*

Have Carmen's novels, Arms of Love and Surrender, made a difference in your life?

We are a family of ten. We have dedicated our livelihood to working towards building a Civilization of Love through Catholic fiction. Through this work thousands of lives have been touched and changed: young and old, men and women alike! In order to continue bringing this much-needed message of purity, faith, hope, and love to our world we need your support, both in prayer and financially.

If *Arms of Love* or *Surrender* have made a difference in your life, please consider making a donation to help this ministry continue. We can not do it alone! This is a full-time ministry; however, we do not have charitable status and thus are not able to provide you with a tax receipt. We pray that God will bless you abundantly for your generosity!

To make a donation

Please visit our website **www.courtshipnow.com** Or call us at **1-800-705-7396.**

Or send it to us by mail to: **One Way Publishing House Site 500 Box 17 RR5 Saskatoon, SK. S7K 3J8 CANADA**

Arms of Love ~ the CD single

. . . is a beautiful tribute to a couple's desire to honour each other by remaining pure before marriage. Fitting as a wedding song!

Love is all a man is really wanting,
Much more than the physical kind.
Longing for a lover to love him deep inside,
Hoping she can bring him back to life.

You are the one I've always wanted
Oh, I didn't know—I didn't want to see
That true love pays the price
of giving selflessly
I thank the Lord that you gave it to me . . .

Based on the novel!

In your arms of love, I am healed.
In your arms so sweet,
you have the power to set me free.
When I closed my soul
Oh, you opened up my heart
And you took me in your arms of love.

How I long for you to kiss me.
Oh, I long for you to hold me every night.
I will wait for you,
Oh, will you wait for me?
Until we're one, I'm content to be . . .

In your arms of love, I am healed.
In your arms so sweet,
you have the power to set me free.
When I closed my soul,
Oh, you opened up my heart
And you took me in your arms of love.

We change the world one heart at a time.
And I'm so thankful
that you started with mine.

Hear the song performed by Catholic Recording Artist Mark Mallett and his wife ~ Lea.

In your arms of love, I am healed.
In your arms so sweet,
you have the power to set me free.
When I closed my soul,
Oh, you opened up my heart
And you took me in your arms of love.
Oh, you took me in your arms of love.

Check out their other many great resources for Catholics, including their Rosary CD, Divine Mercy CD, contemporary Christian song CDs, and special tribute to our beloved John Paul II.

www.markmallett.com

20 Tips
for Christian Courtship

by Carmen Marcoux
(author of Catholic Novels,
Arms of Love and Surrender)

ROMANCE: HANDLE WITH CARE

Have you ever thought of your life as a love-story just waiting to be written? What will that story be like? Who will you include in your story? Will it be the kind of story you will want to share with your children someday, or one that leaves you filed with regrets?

Most young people will say that they are hoping to someday get married. Yet finding lasting love in the life-long commitment of marriage is something that many young people fear they will never find. With divorce rates at over 50% in our culture, is it really still possible to beat the odds?

Jeremiah says this:

"For I know the plans I have for you, says the Lord, plans for welfare and not for evil, to give you a future and a hope."

(Jeremiah 29:11)

Do you trust God is capable of delivering on this promise?

I believe it is possible to beat the odds. If God is calling you to marriage, He is ready and willing to supply you with all the graces and virtues you will need to make it work! But we are not likely to get there by playing all the defective "dating games" that the world presents to us in the name of romance. I heard a wise man once say, "If you want to have that one-in-a-million kind of love in your life, you have to be willing to be a one-in-a-million kind of person!" Are you ready to beet that challenge? Is it worth it to you to be able to write the kind of love-story that God has in store for you?

It is my hope that the brochure, 20 Tips for Christian Courtship, will help to inspire young men and women to holy romance when that time in life comes, according to God's call. It is an invitation for you to consider making courtship your game-plan to live out purity in your life, to discover holy, God-glorifying romance, and to pave your way to lasting love in marriage.

BULK DISCOUNTS AVAILABLE

To order copies of this brochure, please visit:
www.courtshipnow.com
or call **1-800-705-7396**

The New Evangelization

The task which awaits you—the new evangelization—demands that you present, with fresh enthusiasm and new methods, the eternal and unchanging content of the heritage of the Christian faith.

Pope John Paul II
(Commissioning Families, Neo-Catechumenal Way. 1991.)

One Way Publishing House is dedicated to bringing you exciting new literature that you can use to evangelize.
Keep watching for more titles as we build this ministry.

The Purpose Driven Catholic
by Ken Yasinski, founder of **Face to Face Ministries** in Canada, will be released in **2007** by **One Way Publishing House.**

Through his ministry, Ken has touched the lives of thousands of youth and adults alike. His gift of sharing the truths of our Catholic faith with clarity and charity resounds throughout **The Purpose Driven Catholic,** communicating the same passion and convictions that motivate and inspire his audiences when he speaks.

To find out more about Ken's ministry work visit
www.facetofaceretreats.com

The Purpose Driven Catholic challenges all readers to holiness and to embrace God's purpose for their lives.

To order copies of this book, please visit:
www.courtshipnow.com
or call **1-800-705-7396**

Evangelizing . . .

"I agree with you that fiction is a great way to evangelize. . . . I could not put the book down and wept many tears. God can work powerfully through you to bring the truth to young people. I applaud you for your work and shall pray for the success of your ministry."

Tom Roach, 71 years old

"Not only is it beautifully written, with characters who become like friends, but it proclaims the truth of chastity and the glory of man and woman, with a boldness which is necessary amidst the false voices of this secular world."

Susan Cammack, 44 years old

"You would not believe the impact your book had on me and the way I see my life now. For the first time in my life, when I pray, I feel a response and I can see the Holy Spirit working in my life—and I credit the change to your book. I think you have an amazing gift, and I will pray that you are able to continue touching and changing people's lives through this book. It is fantastic!"

Heather Shepherd, 18 years old

"It has changed my out-look on life and faith completely! I think your book is amazing and I found that I could not put it down for one second! For me finding a book that is that good is very hard. Your book has inspired me and it helped me know that seeing is not believing, believing is seeing! It also showed me that there is hope in finding love and that people can change! Your book is the best I have ever read. Thank you!"

Lauren Johnston, 12 years old

Through your story I not only learned more about relationships, but also about my faith. It was so much easier for me to understand our Catholic Church than any other book I had ever read that focused on the Church. I am so blessed that you were inspired to write a story where I felt God was speaking directly to me.

Rebecca Thomas, 20 years old

Life-changing . . .

"It has changed me so much, it's unbelievable. Nothing has ever had that big of an impact on me. You brought Christ into my life and that's the biggest gift you could give someone".

Asja Duffy, 15 years old

"I don't think I will ever read a better book. It was so gripping that it felt like a movie to me. It has all the elements of a great novel: a terrific story line, true-to-life characters, and a tremendous lesson to be learned by all. Courtship is truly the best path to take before marriage. I really hope that as many people as possible will have a chance to read this book. If so, many lives would be changed. I know that it certainly has changed my life!"

Daniel Zimmer, 14 years old

"*Arms of Love* is the most amazing book I've read by far. I have read many books that made me think lots, but this particular one changed me. Before I started reading the book I felt like I really wanted and "needed" to have a boyfriend, but after completing *Arms of Love*, I know that for the time being Jesus is the only man I want and need in my life. I have always promised myself and others that I was going to save myself 'til marriage, and I thought I could do it, but after reading this book I know I can do it."

Niki Guadet, 18 years old

"I absolutely loved the book and was inspired to give up dating and all of the heartache that goes along with it. I am going to wait for my future husband to ask my father if he could court me, and it's ok if that doesn't happen for a while. God knows when the right time will be. Your book totally changed my life for the better."

Christine Lautsch, 18 years old

"It was the most inspirational novel I have ever read. I really felt God talking to me through it in many ways, answering questions I didn't even know I had."

Michelle Kehler, 16 years old

Inspiring . . .

"I am refreshed and inspired by the whole story."

Kevin Bentler, 33 years old

"God has inspired, gifted and challenged me with your book, *Arms of Love*. I've already read it around four times, and I continually go back to it for a reference. Even though it is fiction it has so much truth to it, and that gives me hope to wait for something better than what only this world has to offer me. "

Jennifer Bourdon, 19 years old

"It has been a channel of God's grace for me in that He used it to show me the bare truth about forgiveness, letting go of the past, and starting anew. God used your book to supply hope to me where despair was gaining a foothold. I loved this book so much and I greatly anticipate another one."

Mark Hagman, 24 years old

"I found the character Joanie to be absolutely inspirational. Her constant devotion to our Lord and her resolve to guard her heart had reminded me of my need to love the Lord above all and to trust in Him, that He will provide a man who can love me the way I deserve to be loved."

Lisa Resendes, 26 years old

"It was by far the most amazing and inspirational book I've ever read! Even though these two amazing characters aren't real I still look up to them as role models. In reading this book I decided that courtship is definitely the way to go."

Catherine Burnham, 15 years old

"I find it has given a new springtime to my vocation as a wife and mother."

Paula Compeau, mother of eight

We would love to hear from you at
One Way Publishing House!
Please send your feedback to Carmen at
readerfeedback@courtshipnow.com